ABOUT T

Steven Smith lives in Suffolk
This is his second novel.

www.stevensmithauthor.com

BY STEVEN SMITH:

THE TREE OF LIFE
The Map of the Known World
The Ordeal of Fire
The Last Days

This Sacred Isle

www.stevensmithauthor.com

STEVEN SMITH

THE ORDEAL OF FIRE

monster field press

First published by Lulu.com in 2010
This edition published by monster field press in 2016

ISBN-13: 978-1537035826
ISBN-10: 1537035827

A CIP catalogue record for this book is available from the British Library.

All the characters in this book are fictitious, and any resemblance to actual persons, living or dead, is purely coincidental.

Set in Garamond

For Lucy

- SYNPOSIS -

Prester John rules the Known World with an iron grip; his fanatical *Redeemers* stalk the land, crushing all resistance. Adults are branded on their forehead with the *Null*, which removes their free will and brings them under the control of the Redeemers.

Elowen Aubyn, a fourteen-year-old girl, lives in an Orphanage in the little town of Trecadok. Bullied and lonely, she yearns for freedom and excitement. Her life is changed by an encounter with a stranger named **Tom Hickathrift**. Hickathrift declares that he is an agent of the *Illuminati*, a forbidden sect that has sworn to overthrow Prester John. He asks Elowen to travel with him to the Illuminati's hidden sanctuary in the northern land of Prevennis. Frightened and confused, Elowen refuses to run away but is left with no option when **Vortigern**, seeking Hickathrift's aid, arrives in Trecadok. Vortigern possesses a map, which reveals long-lost secrets that could threaten the rule of Prester John. However, he is closely pursued by Redeemers. They attack the town and murder both Vortigern and Hickathrift. Before he dies, Hickathrift entrusts Elowen with the map and begs her to seek the sanctuary of the Illuminati.

Reluctantly accompanied by **Diggory Bulhorn**, the head-boy of the orphanage, Elowen embarks on a dangerous journey, hunted relentlessly by the Redeemers. Along the way she is befriended by **Bucca**, one of the ancient *Eldar* folk and a wolf named **Ulfur**; Bucca teaches Elowen more about the *Earthsoul*, the energy that sustains all life, and she begins to learn how to control its power.

Needing to cross the ocean to reach Prevennis, Elowen and her companions find passage with the smuggler **Black Francis**, himself a fugitive from the slave-trading *Sea Beggars*. Before they set sail in his ship, the *Husker Du*, they are attacked by a Redeemer; although they escape, Elowen is badly wounded by the Redeemer's poisoned blade.

Meanwhile, in Prevennis, the teenage **Prince Asbjorn**, known as Bo, spends most of his time exploring the half-drowned lower chambers of the royal palace. The king's second son, he is all but ignored by his mother and the rest of the court. Being albino, he is considered weak and far inferior to his older brother and heir to the throne, **Crown Prince Haakon**. Their father, **King Olaf**, has long defied Prester John by refusing to allow his people to be branded with the Null, and by protecting the *Barbegs*, who are Eldar inhabitants of Prevennis.

But there is treachery afoot. Haakon desires the throne so, with the aid of his doting mother and **Lord Lucien**, Prester John's most deadly servant, betrays and murders King Olaf. Bo refuses to pay homage to his brother so is sentenced to death. Yet, with the aid of **Bjorgolf**, Chief of the Barbegs, Asbjorn escapes from the palace and soon encounters Elowen and her companions. At the invitation of Bjorgolf, they all make for the Gladsheim, the mountain refuge of the

2

Barbegs. Fleeing through the Hlithvid forest they escape the chasing Redeemers and reach the safety of the Gladsheim.

However, this respite is short-lived. Determined to find the map that Elowen carries, Lord Lucien leads his army to the Gladsheim. Bjorgolf tries to persuade the tribe to stay and defend their home but he is opposed by **Draug**, who wants to depose Bjorgolf and become chief himself. Bjorgolf persuades the tribe to follow him and a bitter and humiliated Draug chooses exile, vowing revenge.

As battle approaches, Black Francis leaves the Gladsheim, much to Elowen's disappointment. Although hopelessly outnumbered, the Barbegs have one slim chance of deliverance: on the border of the Gladsheim lies the Myrkvid, a forest trapped in a curse of a permanent winter. Elowen breaks the curse by summoning **Ekseri**, the guardian of the Myrkvid. Gathering the creatures of the forest about him, Ekseri marches to fight alongside the Barbegs.

Bjorgolf appoints Asbjorn to lead the defence of the Gladsheim. With only a few hundred Barbeg warriors they hold off the enemy long enough for Ekseri and his host to join the battle. Yet they cannot turn the tide of battle and are driven back with heavy losses. However, with defeat seemingly inevitable, Black Francis and his crew unexpectedly return and bombard the enemy with the guns of the *Husker Du*. This surprise attack gives Elowen and her companions the chance to regroup and attack anew; the enemy's strength wanes and the battle is won. Lord Lucien comes face to face with Elowen and upon learning that she is the daughter of an Adept, mysteriously spares her life before fleeing the battlefield.

During the battle, Asbjorn faces Haakon in combat and slays his brother. Although fearing that he lacks the strength to be a true leader, Asbjorn realises that he cannot ignore the suffering of his people and vows to claim the throne and rid Prevennis of the followers of Prester John.

With the battle over and Lord Lucien gone, Elowen is free to complete her journey and, accompanied by Diggory, sets off for the sanctuary. En route they are attacked by Draug, who blames Elowen for his exile; Diggory fights him off, though he reluctantly spares the Barbeg's life. They reach the sanctuary, and safely pass the map into the care of the Illuminati.

PART ONE

CHAPTER ONE

The Stone Giant

C louds rolled down the mountains like foam-flecked ocean waves. They swept across the forest, bringing rain and smothering the sun.

Wet, cold and tired, Elowen sprinted through the forest, her damp feet squelching with every step. As she tried to dart between two redwood trees, she tripped on a protruding root and fell to her knees. She pulled herself up and leant against a tree-trunk. 'We've lost it *again*.'

'I told you this was a big mistake,' said Diggory as he caught up with her, panting heavily, his normally spiky ginger hair flattened by the rain. Their friendship, forged during many hardships, had strengthened in the sanctuary, but Diggory remained argumentative to his core. 'I must be mad to go along with your plan. Hyllebaer is going to string us both up when she finds out we are in the Old Forest.'

'She won't find out,' said Elowen. In defiance of sanctuary rules, they had crossed the Kaldr River and delved into the Fornskogr, the Old Forest. Elowen knew they risked serious punishment: the Old Forest was out of bounds to all. She tried to reassure Diggory. 'We'll be back at the sanctuary before nightfall. No one will notice we were gone.'

Diggory wiped his dripping nose. 'I'm glad you're so confident. I don't see why we have to risk our lives trying to find this damn unicorn.'

'I want to see it with my own eyes,' said Elowen. They had been close, so close. Glimpses of a swishing white tail, a flowing mane and, so Elowen thought, a spiral horn.

Diggory remained unconvinced and after each sighting huffed, 'It's just your imagination.'

Elowen refused to be discouraged. Rumours of the unicorn had swept through the sanctuary ever since Hagenback, the curator of the menagerie, claimed to have spotted the creature on the fringes of the Old Forest and few doubted his word. The very thought of seeing the unicorn fired Elowen's imagination; it represented mystery, intrigue and danger.

Four months had passed since she had left Trecadok, four months that had turned her life upside down. She had once been a lonely orphan girl, trapped, caged. She had known nothing but the town's grey walls. Like countless others across the Known World, certain truths had dominated her life. The authority of God. The unquestioned rule of Prester John. And the Holy Null, forged in Cold Iron and the instrument through which Prester John protected his subjects.

All that had changed. She had seen marvels and miracles. She had endured horrors and witnessed the cruelty of those loyal to Prester John. When she had first arrived at the sanctuary it appeared the answer to all her dreams and she had never imagined wanting to go or be anywhere else. She had longed for peace, quiet and safety, but now she had all those she found that something was still missing. She wondered if the mountains that encircled the sanctuary were now the borders of her world, borders she was never again destined to cross. The journey to the sanctuary had been perilous and gruelling, but it had given her a taste of excitement and adventure; she craved more, a craving that made her restless.

'The rain has almost stopped, let's keep going,' she said, urging Diggory forward.

'We should be getting back,' said Diggory. 'It's getting darker and I don't want to be out here at night. And what's more, hunting a unicorn without weapons is madness.'

Elowen left the shelter of the tree. 'We aren't *hunting* it. We don't need weapons because we don't want to hurt it.'

'It's the unicorn hurting us that concerns me,' said Diggory, plodding after her.

A path slippery with moss meandered around the redwoods and cut through banks of drooping fern. Summer was dying, but the forest still hummed with life. Fruiting bodies of fungi grew fat and greasy in the dank air. A pine hawk moth, lured from its resting place by the growing darkness, fluttered above a clump of sweet-smelling honeysuckle. Startled by the hissing of a wild cat, a pine marten scurried up the nearest tree.

Elowen searched for signs of the unicorn such as tracks, trails or scratches on tree trunks, but saw nothing. She shivered and not from the cold. Many dark rumours circulated about the Old Forest, rumours of dangerous creatures and ancient powers. Some scholars told ghoulish, lurid tales of ghosts. Elowen did not know the truth of those tales, but as she walked beneath the towering redwoods, older and taller than those that supported the sanctuary, she found it easy to believe malevolent beings lurked close by.

'Why do we always end up in such miserable places?' said Diggory.

'It could be worse,' said Elowen, tiring of his complaining. She held in a harsher response as she reminded herself that, once again, Diggory was loyally by her side in a dangerous place. He could be annoying and moody, but he never let her down. Trying to be more conciliatory, she said, 'We'll soon be done.'

'I hope so. At least we don't have that mangy wolf padding behind us any more.'

Elowen smiled. Diggory had not been fond of Ulfur and had barely concealed his glee when the wolf decided to remain in the Myrkvid forest rather than travel to the sanctuary. For her part, Elowen missed Ulfur. Their bond had been especially close, as it was through the wolf that she had discovered her ability to communicate directly with animals, to understand their calls, cries and thoughts as clearly as human speech. Since arriving at the sanctuary, she had learnt that the ability to understand animal speech was called *Linking*. But to Elowen's disappointment, the Illuminati considered *Linking* a minor skill, a trick and one that had little, if any, value in the struggle against Prester John. In Elowen's view, the battle of the Gladsheim, where the forest beasts helped defeat the enemy, proved the opposite, but she was just a scholar and no one listened to her opinions.

Elowen and Diggory reached a fast-flowing stream, a tributary of the Kaldr, spanned by a bridge formed of slabs of granite supported on five stone piers. They edged across slowly. Diggory was in too foul a mood to talk, so as she walked, Elowen reflected on the time she had spent at the sanctuary, weeks of study along with the other children, learning under the strict tutelage of Hyllebaer the Wise, one of the Adepts.

Elowen had discovered that there were many different kinds of people from many different lands in the sanctuary. The displaced, the rebellious, radicals, heretics, freethinkers. Some were Adepts; most were not. But all had fled to the sanctuary to escape the tyranny of Prester John.

When a child in the sanctuary turned fifteen, the age of Choosing as it was known, they began training as an apprentice Adept, yeoman warder, experimental philosopher, scribe, artisan or steward. For Elowen, that day fast approached, a fact that weighed heavily on her mind. She expected and hoped to become an Adept, just as her mother had been. She worked hard, grappling with disciplines new to her such as geometry, zoology, logic and anatomy. Compared to other scholars, Elowen felt slow and uneducated. However, Rubens, one of the two Masters of the sanctuary, had taken the time to give her private lessons. Why Rubens had chosen her for such a privilege, she knew not, but it enabled her at least to keep pace with her fellow scholars. She saw much less of Grunewald, the other Master, and for that, she was thankful. She found the old man frightening and he never missed an opportunity to criticise her.

It rained again, thumping down in thick blobs and bringing Elowen back to the present. The rain seemed personal,

11

as though it attacked her with a will of its own. With Diggory close behind, she trudged on, drenched to the skin. For the first time since their search for the unicorn had started, Elowen's confidence in finding their quarry waned. She tried to steel her resolve. She touched the limestone pendant tied around her neck. It had once belonged to her mother, and Elowen possessed nothing she treasured more. She had never met her mother, but somehow through the pendant she drew strength and courage.

Shortly they came through a gap in the trees and out into a wide clearing marked by a lone rowan and formations of granite rocks, widely scattered as though they had fallen from the sky. A tingle played down Elowen's spine.

Diggory scratched his head. 'What's this place?'

'I think it's the Odjur, the heart of the Old Forest,' said Elowen.

'Why don't we rest here for a moment? We've been walking for hours.'

Before Elowen could reply, another voice answered, 'No, children, this is not a safe place to rest.'

Hyllebaer the Wise emerged from the trees. She was dressed in a tatty black gown and supported herself with a twisted elder branch. Her sparkling eyes were shiny black beads in a face as brown and wrinkled as dried leaves. Elowen gasped in alarm. They were in trouble now.

'What are you doing here?' said Diggory, his mouth running away with him.

'Trying to find that foolish girl,' she said in a throaty voice, pointing at Elowen. Hyllebaer struggled to remember names and always resorting to calling Elowen 'girl' or 'child'. 'You know full well that entering the Fornskogr is forbidden. I am disappointed in you. What do you have to say?'

Elowen blushed and looked down at her feet. 'I'm sorry I disobeyed you. I just wanted to see the unicorn.'

'And you thought you could best accomplish that by running into the Fornskogr with this half-wit?'

Diggory tried to protest but Hyllebaer lifted her hand and he wisely kept his mouth shut. She continued, 'I am furious with both of you. You have caused a great deal of concern. Master Rubens instructed the yeomen warders to search for you.'

Elowen tried to explain. 'I thought—'

'Enough,' said Hyllebaer. 'We must return to the sanctuary. Say nothing more until we have passed safely through the Odjur.'

'*Safely?*' said Diggory, seizing on the worrying word. 'What do you—'

Hyllebaer's withering glare halted any further questions.

The rain eased to a drizzle but dark clouds hastened the onset of evening. Elowen and Diggory followed Hyllebaer in silence, their heads bowed. She led them round the rocks, keeping close to the edge of the clearing. She kept turning around, silently urging them to hurry but a low growl halted her. The shrubs ahead rustled and a creature burst out into the open. It had the head and body of a horse but with cloven hooves and a long, sharp, spiral horn growing from the middle of its forehead. The unicorn.

It made an angry snorting noise and faced them with its ears flat back and tail swishing.

13

Diggory cried out in alarm. Hyllebaer grabbed his arm. 'Be silent, boy. And don't move.'

Elowen kept her eyes on the unicorn. Trembling with excitement, she took a couple of steps forward but still kept her distance.

'Let me deal with this,' said Hyllebaer, trying to hold Elowen back.

Elowen wriggled free of her grip. 'I know what I'm doing.'

'Reckless girl,' said Hyllebaer but she allowed Elowen to walk forward.

'I'm here,' said Elowen to the unicorn. 'You're safe. I'm your friend.'

To Elowen's relief, the unicorn relaxed; it lifted its head high and its ears flickered. Elowen winked at Hyllebaer, feeling more than a little pleased with herself. The *Linking* worked. The unicorn grunted and words came to her.

Not safe. Danger is close.

'I won't hurt you,' said Elowen.

The unicorn approached her. Elowen found its musky smell somehow familiar, comforting, like a fragment of a memory. She allowed the unicorn to sniff her palm, and patted it along the neck and withers.

Forest not safe.

An unearthly noise whipped across the Odjur, a noise so piercing that even the unicorn flinched. Thin cracks ripped across the trembling ground. Elowen's Linking with the unicorn broke; the creature bounded back among the trees and disappeared.

'What's that noise?' Elowen heard Diggory ask.

Hyllebaer grimaced. 'Do not move.'

The ground shook again. Elowen heard a grinding sound, like a millstone turning. The rocks moved as though picked up by invisible hands. They rolled together and formed shapes: two arms, two legs, a torso and a head. In seconds, a towering figure rose above them all. A stone giant, one of the dreaded karnamen, with two hollows for eyes, a slight protrusion for a nose and a gaping hole for a mouth.

'I must deal with this alone,' said Hyllebaer to Elowen and Diggory. 'Go back to the sanctuary.'

'We can't leave you here,' said Elowen.

Hyllebaer pushed Elowen away. 'You do not have the skills to help me.'

Diggory tried to pull Elowen towards the trees. 'Come on, she's right.'

Elowen refused to budge. She watched as the karnaman loomed over Hyllebaer, who reached out a hand towards it; the golden threads of the Earthsoul coiled around the Adept and she cried aloud, 'Be still, old one.'

The golden threads surrounded the karnaman; motionless, it stared at Hyllebaer.

'Return to the earth, old one,' said Hyllebaer.

The golden threads around the stone giant broke and scattered. Like a man swatting away a fly, the karnaman swept its left hand towards Hyllebaer and the impact threw her back several feet.

The stone giant stood over Hyllebaer and lifted its left leg to crush her. Out of instinct and desperation, Elowen picked up a small rock and threw it at the karnaman. It struck the giant on the left leg and bounced off harmlessly, but the karnaman stepped back and stared at Elowen. Wanting to distract it further so that Hyllebaer could escape, Elowen waved her arms and yelled, 'OVER HERE, LOOK AT ME!'

The karnaman flexed its arms and strode towards her. Diggory sneaked behind the creature and dragged Hyllebaer into the cover of the trees. Elowen focused on the stone giant, trying to block out everything else. The golden threads throbbed all around her. She tried to control them but the karnaman was too fast; he jabbed his fist and knocked her over. Badly winded and dizzy, Elowen struggled to her feet. Her left arm ached and she tasted blood on her lips.

The karnaman pulled its arm back, ready to strike another blow, a harder blow. Elowen heard footsteps. A man shouted. Rubens, the Master of the sanctuary, ran into the clearing, bear-like in a red fur-lined coat, his face partially hidden by a hood. The stone giant took a long step backward. Rubens lowered his hood to reveal his thick, oily hair and bearded face. He held out both hands towards the karnaman and spoke words Elowen did not understand, but the power of his voice pulsed through her and her skin goose-bumped.

The karnaman broke apart—its limbs became once again lifeless stones resting on the soft, spongy soil.

Elowen sank to her knees, nursing her injured arm. Rubens knelt beside her. 'You are hurt, child. Let me see.'

Despite his kindness and attention to her, Elowen always found Rubens intimidating and felt awkward around him. Reluctantly, she held out her arm.

'Ah, I do not think it is broken, only bruised. The cut in your forehead is shallow, nothing to worry about. You were brave, Elowen, but fortunate not to be seriously wounded.'

Elowen did not feel fortunate but, remembering the karnaman's strength, she realised Rubens was probably right. 'How did you find us?'

He flashed a toothy smile. 'I was told of your rash journey into the Old Forest and was keen to make sure you were safe. I was almost too late. But talk can wait, first we must see to Hyllebaer.'

They found her beneath the trees that circled the Odjur, with Diggory hovering around her like an anxious mother hen. She had regained consciousness and as soon as she saw Elowen she said, 'You are alive, girl. I feared—'

Rubens placed his palm on her forehead. 'Save your strength, my friend. Danger has passed.'

'Master? The karnaman attacked, I never thought it—'

'Hush now, it was not your fault,' said Rubens.

Hyllebaer closed her eyes and rested her head back down on the ground.

Four other men emerged from the trees. They wore leather jerkins, simple linen trousers and a single white flower in their cloth caps, and each carried a short, one-handed sword. They were yeomen warders, the closest the Illuminati had to soldiers. Rubens greeted them warmly. He had taken on responsibility for their training and deployment; the crackle of musket-fire rippled through the forest every evening as they practised their drills. The yeomen warders showed great loyalty to the Master.

Rubens instructed the warders to carry Hyllebaer back to

the sanctuary, and ordered Diggory to go with them. The boy looked reluctant but was clearly too frightened to disobey another order.

'Hyllebaer won't die, will she?' said Elowen.

Rubens smiled and shook his head. 'Our best physicians will care for her. Do not worry, child. There are few stronger souls than Hyllebaer.'

'Why did the karnaman attack us?'

'I do not know,' said Rubens. 'But this is not the time to discuss such matters. Let us go back before this night brings forth any further terrors.'

*

By the time Elowen and Rubens had returned to the sanctuary the waxing moon was painting the spider web of platforms, rope bridges and wooden buildings in silver light. Hundreds of tiny lanterns shone among the trees; a starry canopy beneath the sky. Grunewald, the other Master, was waiting for them. He leant upon his walking stick, as still as a watching hawk. He was not alone. An Orok accompanied him, short, stocky and bow-legged. He looked sombre in a long, black coat-like garment with an overlap in front, fastened at the close by five buttons. His weather-beaten, swarthy face was broad and flat, with high-set cheekbones and a small nose. The tops and sides of his head were shaved, leaving only a short forelock in front and long, braided hair behind. A red scar ran diagonally across his face.

Elowen had seen Oroks in the sanctuary from time to

18

time. They kept themselves to themselves, arriving unheralded and slipping away on mysterious errands. She struggled to get used to seeing them as flesh and blood beings. Throughout her childhood, Elowen had believed that the Oroks were a cruel race, deniers of the Saviour and enemies of God, more like monsters than people. She remembered countless sermons proclaiming that the Oroks were the foul offspring of two terrible, demon-like giants. From their pulpits, priests raged that the Oroks knew no laws or decency, that they buried their prisoners alive and devoured raw flesh. Elowen recalled tales of pious armies loyal to Prester John defending the Mother Church against hordes of bloodthirsty heathen Oroks. She had learnt that such stories were distortions of the truth, but the Orok now in front of her still made her uneasy. Elowen looked away to avoid meeting his piercing gaze.

Rubens and Grunewald greeted each other with a perfunctory nod; they seldom attempted to conceal their mutual loathing. The hostility between the two Masters formed a fault-line through the Illuminati and their arguments during assemblies had grown increasingly fierce. If one Master raised a proposal, the other was sure to oppose it. Grunewald commanded the most respect among the Adepts but Rubens was popular with the stewards and the artisans, and the yeomen warders followed him without question. Elowen often reflected on what Albruna, Chief of the Barbegs, had once told her: *two masters rule the Illuminati and no tribe can have two Chieftains for long. One day, trouble shall come of it.*

'Master Grunewald, so you have come to meet us,' said

19

Rubens in a mocking tone. 'I am honoured that you found the time to leave your precious aviaries.'

The sanctuary maintained extensive aviaries and the ravens were Grunewald's pride and joy. He spent hours tending them and it was often joked that he resembled the birds; when out of his hearing, some called him the 'old raven'.

'Word reached me of your ordeal and I saw Hyllebaer taken to the House of Healing,' said Grunewald to Elowen in his dry, scratchy voice, ignoring Rubens. 'You know the rule forbidding anyone to enter the Fornskogr, a rule you flagrantly disregarded. Your foolish actions placed lives at risk.'

Elowen blushed and stuttered an apology.

'The girl did not act from malice and no real harm has been done,' said Rubens. 'I do not believe that Hyllebaer is badly injured.'

'It was by luck only that disaster was averted,' said Grunewald. 'I wonder what could have roused the karnaman. Despite their strength they are slow to anger.'

'I am sure the creature's attack was unprovoked,' said Rubens, stumbling over his words a little. 'They are far more dangerous than you are willing to admit. We should drive them from the Old Forest. We have the power to do so.'

'Yes, but it does not mean we have the right to use it,' said Grunewald. 'The duty of the Illuminati decrees that we strive to protect all living beings, and that includes the karnamen.'

'The world has changed,' said Rubens. 'The duty you refer to is no protection against Prester John.'

'Perhaps not, but it prevents us from becoming like him,'

said Grunewald. 'You know as well as I do what has happened to Adepts who have forgotten that.'

The Masters glared at each other like two men preparing for a duel before Grunewald said, 'The hour is late, I will leave before words are spoken that we all regret. Elowen, I trust you shall be a little less headstrong in future.'

Elowen nodded penitently.

'Good,' said Grunewald. 'And remember—there is an assembly at dawn tomorrow.'

Elowen nodded again. She had forgotten all about the assembly. The thought of spending dull hours in the dusty Chapter House lowered her spirits further.

Grunewald limped off into the darkness, followed by the silent Orok. When they had gone, Rubens said to Elowen, 'I am sorry you were caught in the crossfire of that exchange, especially after everything you have been through tonight.'

Elowen dismissed his apology with a shrug. Rubens managed to adjust the volume and timbre of his voice to suit different situations. At times his voice became strident, domineering; other times it had a musical quality, like a lullaby. 'Are you quite sure you won't go to the Infirmary?'

'I'm fine,' said Elowen, anxious to get away.

'Very well, I shall see you soon and perhaps our next meeting will be less dramatic,' said Rubens with a short laugh. He pulled his hood back over his head and sauntered away, his heavy footsteps clanking on the wooden panels.

Elowen returned to her dwelling, one of the many tree houses built like giant birds'-nests around the redwood trunks. Branches and thick layers of leaves formed the roof

21

of her dwelling and its walls were constructed from wooden beams. Inside, it was cramped and sparsely furnished, with a motley collection of blankets for a bed, and some bowls and mugs for eating and drinking. Books, all cheaply printed copies, were scattered across the floor: Nezo's *Logic*, *Physics and Ethics*, *Bestiary of the Known World* by Rottlisea, *Elements of Geometry* by Duclei, and Al-Avecenni's *Mathematics*. A few drying clothes hung from a droopy line. Her travelling clothes formed an untidy heap in one corner: a fur coat, trousers, boots, mittens and sealskin socks, all worn, frayed and patchy from many hard miles battling through rain, dust, snow and ice.

Although rickety and messy, she cherished her home; she had got used to the creaking and, at times alarming, swaying during windy days. She enjoyed the chance to be alone with her thoughts.

A small note had been pinned on the door of her dwelling. Elowen pulled it off and held it up to the moonlight to read. She recognised the spidery handwriting of her friend Lárwita.

New invention. You must see it.

Curiosity flickered within her; Lárwita was strange but never dull; if he said he had something worth seeing he meant it. Elowen decided to visit him after the next day's assembly.

Tired and aching, she snuggled under her blankets, listening to the restless groaning of the timbers and branches. Every time she closed her eyes, she saw the mighty karnaman, its stone fists ready to crush her. She was relieved that Rubens had arrived in time to save them, and angry with herself. She had thought she was being so clever searching for the unicorn. Deep down, she had wanted to show how strong and clever she was, but all she had managed to do was make a fool of herself, and endanger and hurt others.

Elowen tried to think of more comforting things and, as they often did, her thoughts switched to absent friends, to Ulfur, Black Francis and Bo. She liked to imagine what they were doing. She imagined Ulfur padding through the forest, returning to his pack. Black Francis and Bo she saw on board the *Husker Du* as it cut through the waves. She missed them all and longed to tell them everything that had happened to her since she had arrived at the sanctuary. Such thoughts soothed her and Elowen found her eyelids too heavy to keep open. The gentle wave of sleep washed over her.

*

Sinuous columns of smoke rose from the city of Gorefayne. Flames illuminated the low greasy clouds, casting an orange glow. The moon and stars were lost; years had passed since the inhabitants of Gorefayne had seen them.

From his vantage point in the high tower of the Zeerord castle, Lord Lucien looked down at the open mines and pits, the chimneys vomiting smoke, the blackened churches and decrepit hovels. Like an outstretched skeletal arm, a bridge reached across the copper-coloured river that divided the city. The view reminded Lucien of the doom paintings of hell hanging in the Ulsacro palace: images of fiery suffering and torture. Whatever hell had to offer, Lucien

23

doubted it could be any worse than the horrors of Gorefayne.

Nevertheless, as the only known source of Cold Iron, the city was the beating heart of the Holy Empire. Endless caravans of slaves poured into Gorefayne to work the mines, slaves drawn from every corner of the Empire. From his throne in the Ulsacro, Prester John ruled vast swathes of land and countless people. But without the Cold Iron mined in wretched, tortured Gorefayne, his dominion could not endure.

The Zeerord was not a castle of great lineage. Built during the Long War to protect the priceless mines, it was a formidable slab of granite: cold, angular, menacing. The castle housed no renowned paintings, tapestries or sculptures. Lord Lucien's chamber had little furniture, just a heavy oak table, a single chair, a candle. The only personal item he had was the mirror he always carried with him when he travelled, the special mirror that allowed him to receive Prester John's orders when he was far away from the Ulsacro. Lucien preferred to live simply. He wanted no distractions. The unexpected defeat at the battle of Gladsheim still plagued him—it unlocked a door within his mind, unleashing memories he had long subdued.

The boy's cheeks are wet with tears. Naked, he shivers in the damp cold of the dungeon. The irons gnaw remorselessly at his ankles and wrists, twisting and tearing skin. He hears footsteps. He hears laughter. They are coming. Urine dribbles down his legs, forming a warm pool around his feet. They are coming. The door opens.

Lucien stepped away from the window, hoping movement would dislodge the memories.

Punches and kicks rain down on him, a barrage of pain. A priest chants. Words shouted. Words screamed. FALSE PROPHET. BLASPHEMER.

Lucien punched the wall; pain shot through his arm and made his body shudder.

The torturers leave the boy curled up in a ball on the cold stone floor. His body throbs with pain. Hatred infects his blood. He wants them to suffer as he suffers.

Lucien kicked the chair, sending it spinning across the chamber to break against the far wall.

The face of the girl. She repeats the same words, the same impossible words. I am the daughter of an Adept.

Lucien ripped off his mask and massaged the broken skin of his face. The daughter of an Adept. He thought he knew which Adept too, although the possibility troubled him.

Flowing black hair. Her laugh. Her battle cries. The unicorn charging across the battlefield.

That face. More than a dozen years had passed since he had last beheld it; a face echoed in the girl's, or did his mind play tricks on him, filling in details that were not truly there? No, he was certain. It was the child. He had never expected to see her again. He whispered to himself, 'I must find her. Above all else, I must find her.'

There was a heavy knock on the door and a voice announced, 'Lord Lucien, I have brought the prisoner.'

The present veiled the past. Lucien put his mask back on and uncurled his aching hand.

The door opened and a Redeemer stepped inside the room. His creased white robes wrapped around his body, and he wheezed and gasped, as though each breath was a struggle. He dragged behind him a short, hooded figure, no taller than a child.

Lucien gestured for the Redeemer to leave. The hooded figure waited in silence but trembled.

'So you sought an audience with me,' said Lucien, pacing around the prisoner. 'Few of your kind have the courage or audacity to make such a request.'

A crackling, high-pitched voice said, 'I am grateful to you, Lord Lucien. And you will not be disappointed, for I have information that will be of great value to you.'

'If you disappoint me I will show no mercy.'

The prisoner hesitated; the force of Lucien's words had achieved the required effect. 'I shall not fail you.'

'I hope so, for I am still confused as to what drives you to betray your tribe.'

'*They* betrayed *me*. It is no longer my tribe. They forced me into exile. And the girl, she conspired against me. I want her to suffer too. I want vengeance.'

Lord Lucien stopped pacing and faced the prisoner. 'I am told that you know of a path over the Jorkull Mountains, a path that leads to the sanctuary of the Illuminati.'

'I found it and can lead you there. It was a path made long ago by Barbeg trackers. But I warn you that it climbs high into the mountains and is very cruel.'

'The Brotherhood can endure any hardship. You are sure that this path leads to the sanctuary?'

The prisoner nodded swiftly.

'And you are certain that Elowen Aubyn is there?'

'Yes, I am sure of that.'

'Then, it seems as though you will be of some use to me,'

said Lucien. He removed the hood from the prisoner's head to reveal the dark eyes and white, spiky beard of a Barbeg. 'Truly you are far from your home. Tell me your name.'

The Barbeg bowed his head. 'I am Draug.'

CHAPTER TWO

The Chapter of Light

Morning brought an unwelcome reminder of the approach of winter: a chill, gusting, damp-smelling wind that hurried bruise-coloured rain clouds across the sky.

Elowen picked her way along the rope bridges that linked the wooden buildings of the sanctuary. She dreaded the assembly. They were dry, long-winded occasions full of boring speeches. Elowen wanted to spend her day reading in the Hall of Learning or helping Jacob the Elder in the Physick Garden, but attendance at the assembly was compulsory for scholars and, after her misadventures of the previous night, she did not want to further antagonise Grunewald.

Elowen followed the stream of people meandering towards the Chapter House: Adepts, scholars, experimental philosophers, scribes, artisans and stewards. She strolled past the refectory, the misericord, the kitchens and the infirmary; as she passed the latter she thought guiltily about Hyllebaer and hoped that she was recovering.

Weighed down by a lack of enthusiasm, Elowen slowed as she approached the Chapter House. Octagonal in shape, eight trees supported it. Once inside, Elowen came into the murky, square-shaped chamber, facing steeply rising rows of benches. As usual, the seats chosen by those in attendance reflected the divisions within the Illuminati. On the left-hand side of the chamber sat most of the Adepts, supporters of Grunewald. The artisans, scribes and stewards, almost all loyal to Rubens, congregated to the right. The scholars clung awkwardly to the neutral space in the middle. Two ornate chairs stood on the chamber floor, both facing the benches.

The chamber was stuffy and hot, with all the windows closed. The stodgy air churned with the odour of sweaty bodies, musty clothes and unwashed feet. Flies buzzed around the chamber and thick dust coated every surface.

The story of Elowen's encounter with the unicorn and the karnaman was clearly already well known. The scholars sniggered among themselves as she entered the chamber. One said, 'Where's your unicorn horn, Elowen?'

This caused fits of laughter among the scholars. Blushing, Elowen spotted Diggory, who was sitting on the lowest bench. He shuffled up to allow room for her to sit down beside him and scowled at the other scholars. He said to Elowen, 'Ignore them, they're idiots.'

'It doesn't matter,' she said, hiding her embarrassment.

'You're right. Anyway, you look better than you did last night.'

'I'm sore but I'll live. Have you heard anything about Hyllebaer?'

'I spoke to Bruyn on the way here. He works at the infirmary. He said that Hyllebaer has a couple of broken bones but she'll be fine.'

29

Elowen sighed with relief. 'She's made of strong stuff.'

'Aye, though I fancy we might not be in her good books for a while.'

'Are we ever in her good books?'

Diggory shook his head. 'Probably not, but I think that Grunewald is even angrier with us. I think we should keep well out of his way too.'

Elowen looked behind. The Orok who had accompanied Grunewald the previous evening was sitting two rows back. He caught Elowen's stare and smiled. Elowen blushed and turned away, a shiver tickling her spine. Rubens and Grunewald entered the chamber. Rubens strode in first, chest puffed out, head held high. Grunewald hobbled in behind him.

The buzz of conversation faded to a silence broken only by an occasional cough or sneeze. Rubens sat in one of the chairs on the chamber floor, straightening and adjusting his clothes as he did so. He sported a gold chain collar set with precious stones: the symbol of his office.

Dressed plainly and supported by his walking stick, Grunewald remained standing and addressed the assembly. His aged and scratchy voice reached every part of the chamber. 'The power and dominance of Prester John is growing. Reports have reached me of his armies massing in the south. It is said that the Mother Church is dispatching more soldiers and missionary ships west across the Ocean of Perpetual Gloom, seeking the New World, seeking fresh lands to conquer and people to enslave.'

Worried whispers flowed around the chamber and Grunewald held up a hand to signal for silence. 'We must be strong and we must be vigilant. We have been safe here for many years but we can ill-afford complacency. Only yesterday, two of our order ventured into the Old Forest, risking both their lives and the lives of others by their foolish actions.'

Diggory sank low in his seat. Elowen blushed; she didn't know where to look. The eyes of the whole assembly bored down on her. She heard whispers and giggles from other scholars. She sensed Grunewald enjoyed humiliating her and she hated him for that. She felt powerless; she could say nothing to defend herself. She hoped Rubens would intervene and speak in her defence but he remained silent, content to pick at his fingernails.

'We cannot indulge such follies,' continued Grunewald. 'However, there are more important matters to consider. An opportunity has arisen to strike a blow against Prester John, a blow from which he may not recover.'

'That is a bold claim,' came a voice from one of back rows. A steward named Uttukku stood. He had a florid face and long, lank hair. Elowen knew that he was a close friend of Rubens. 'I trust that the Master will share all he knows of this *opportunity*.'

Grunewald glared at Uttukku. 'My friend, I can say little at this time. But know that I propose a quest, one of unparalleled importance. When you finally know all, you will understand why secrecy is vital.'

'What need is there for such secrecy, surely we can all be trusted?' said Uttukku. There were muttered agreements from many, especially on the right-hand side of the chamber. 'There are no enemies here.'

31

'I did not call anyone in this room an enemy,' said Grunewald. 'In the weeks to come I shall be in a position to tell you all the exact details of my plan. Until then, I ask for you to trust me.'

'It is not a question of trust,' said Naboth, the keeper of the vineyard and another who was loyal to Rubens. 'I question your authority to make decisions without the assembly's agreement.'

'That is not my intention,' said Grunewald. 'If the will of the assembly is against me, if it does not trust my judgement, I shall not proceed with my plan.'

'Does Rubens not have a voice in this?' said Uttukku.

Rubens stroked his gold chain collar and paused for several seconds before answering, 'I have discussed the matter with Grunewald and he knows my feelings.'

Elowen found it a strange response, neither supporting Grunewald, nor openly defying him.

'Do I have your trust?' said Grunewald to the assembly. 'Let all those who oppose me in this raise their hands.'

Predictably, many on the right-hand side of the assembly raised their hands, but they were still in the minority.

'This assembly has spoken and I am gratified by your support,' said Grunewald, clearly satisfied he faced no stronger opposition. He pulled out a piece of paper from his pocket. 'I have a list of names, names of those I have selected to become part of the Chapter of Light, the company that shall undertake the quest. Those chosen must meet me at the scriptorium at dusk today and I suspend all their normal duties forthwith. They must say nothing of the quest to anyone outside the Chapter, however trusted.'

'I wouldn't want to be part of that Chapter of Light,' said Diggory to Elowen and she nodded her agreement. She knew Grunewald was bound to choose only experienced, powerful Adepts to aid him and so it proved. The list he read out included the names she expected such as Cathbad, Amairgin, Sadko the Minstrel, Briccriu, Gula the Wise and Marya Morvena.

Grunewald said, 'There is one more name. The last member of the Chapter of Light is Elowen Aubyn.'

*

Even as Elowen trudged out of the Chapter House, she had still not recovered from the shock. Why had Grunewald selected *her* for the Chapter of Light? Surely it was a mistake? She was only a scholar. What could she offer that the other Adepts could not? And she had lessons to attend. She did not want to fall behind the other scholars, especially in subjects she struggled with such as arithmetic and geometry. She wanted to speak to Rubens, feeling sure that he would clear up the mess, but he had stormed out of the chamber as soon as the assembly had finished.

'Trust you to get involved in this,' said Diggory as they stepped outside.

'I knew nothing about it,' she said, stung by his comment.

'If that's the case, why did Grunewald pick you and not some other Adept?'

'How should I know?' said Elowen. The quest frightened her and she wanted to take her mind off it. She remembered the note she had found the previous night. 'I'm going to see Lárwita now. Do you want to come along too? He says he has a new invention.'

Diggory rolled his eyes. 'He *always* has a new invention. I haven't seen one that works yet but I'll come to see what he's up to now. I could do with a laugh.'

Lárwita lived and worked in the Hall of Invention, a cone-shaped building constructed around the very tallest tree in the forest. The wooden door was closed so Elowen knocked twice and waited. She read the motto inscribed above the doorframe: *Knowledge is our weapon.* The elemental philosophers were a vital part of the struggle against Prester John, although Elowen had little understanding of their secretive work. A muffled voice from behind the door called out, 'What is the purpose?'

Elowen, familiar with the password question, said, 'The search for light.'

Someone turned the handle but the door remained closed. Swearing came from inside, so Elowen gave the door a hard shove with her shoulder and it creaked open.

A tall, skinny boy with scruffy blond hair greeted them. A pair of lenses set in a metal frame, an instrument he called his spectacles, rested on his nose and ears, and gave him an expression of permanent surprise. He clutched a small leather-bound book that Elowen had never seen him without. As he seldom ventured outside, his skin remained pale; his work absorbed him completely.

Lárwita smiled as Elowen and Diggory stepped inside but as usual struggled to make eye contact. He kicked the door shut and cursed in his dull, flat, Volkgardic accent, 'Damn thing. It keeps getting jammed.'

Elowen tried not to smile. She often pondered how someone as intelligent as Lárwita could struggle with the simplest actions. He inhabited a world of his own, often not responding to the people and things around him. He moved awkwardly, as though uncomfortable in his own body. Elowen occasionally saw him wandering into the refectory for food, his shirt unbuttoned, his hair uncombed, his mind still back in the workshop. Although nominally a scholar, Lárwita's precocious ability meant that he spent more time in the Hall of Invention working with the experimental philosophers than in classes: his tutors could teach him little about physics, geometry and arithmetic. He lived a largely solitary life, burrowed away in the workshop, designing, building, tinkering. Elowen liked him. He was a gentle soul, absorbed by his passions. He never boasted. He was himself at all times. His conversations often wandered into places that Elowen could not follow, but that intrigued her more. Despite his knowledge and ability, most people treated him as an oddity, a source of amusement. Some scholars, and a few experimental philosophers, called him 'Loopy Lárwita'. It saddened Elowen to see him ignored, mocked, side-lined. She knew what that felt like.

'I didn't see you in the Chapter House,' said Diggory. The two boys had become friends, despite Diggory's relentless, though not ill-natured, teasing.

'I forgot about the assembly,' said Lárwita, playing with his wispy hair. He glanced shyly at Elowen. 'Are you...well? I heard about the karnaman—'

'I'm fine,' said Elowen, keen to change the subject. 'What is it you wanted to show me?'

'Come this way,' he said, his head bowed. 'No one else is in the workshop.'

Elowen and Diggory followed Lárwita, who walked with his arms swinging and a lop-sided gait. The workshop rose to a conical ceiling. Tables, books, tools and drawings filled every conceivable space. Elowen admired various astronomical instruments: a brass astrolabe, a refracting telescope, a ship-shaped sundial and an armillary sphere.

'This place is a mess,' said Diggory.

Lárwita pointed to a mass of folded silk. 'This is what I've been working on. It's nearly ready. I just need to test it. What do you think?'

Elowen frowned. 'What is it?'

Lárwita chewed his fingernails. 'It's a balloon, a device for flying.'

'A device for *flying*?' said Diggory. Even Elowen had to bite her lip to suppress a giggle.

Failing to notice their amusement, Lárwita continued his explanation. 'It's very simple. Hot air fills the silk balloon, and then it lifts off the ground.'

Diggory folded his arms and shook his head. 'I've never heard such nonsense. Birds fly. People don't.'

Lárwita moved the silk to reveal a wicker basket. 'This is where the passengers stand while the balloon is flying. I got the idea from some ancient drawings I found in the Hall of Learning. The Pankas tribes in the New World used balloons to make symbols and giant drawings of birds and animals on the plains of Caypacha. The symbols were so large that they must have been drawn with the intention of being seen from above.'

'But... *flying*?' said Elowen. 'Does it work?'

Lárwita scratched the back of his neck. 'Ah, yes, I think it will; I'm *sure* it will. The experimental philosophers don't agree but—'

'I reckon it'll work,' said Elowen, bewildered by his creation but wanting to sound supportive. It had the desired effect and a faint grin formed on Lárwita's lips. Encouraged, he showed Elowen the sandbags, which he said he planned to use as ballast. He spoke faster and faster, his words tumbling on top of each other, and some of his sentences tailed off incomprehensibly. He opened his book and showed them a host of diagrams; Elowen did not understand much of what he was talking about but she found his enthusiasm, his sheer love of discovery, fascinating.

'I think it's ready to fly,' he said, his hands flapping. 'I'm going to move it to a meadow south of the sanctuary and from there I should be able to test it safely.'

'Safely?' said Elowen. 'Are you sure it'll be safe?'

Lárwita smiled his shy, lop-sided smile. 'I believe so. I'd like you both to help me with the first flight.'

Diggory puffed his cheeks. 'You must be joking. I'm not breaking my neck in that thing.'

'I'm not sure how much help I could be,' said Elowen.

'Please come, none of the experimental philosophers want to help me. They think I'm mad.'

'They might be right,' said Diggory.

Elowen felt guilty. The balloon was important to Lárwita. She was about to reluctantly offer some help when she heard someone knocking heavily on the door. Along with Diggory, she followed Lárwita. He started to ask for the password but was cut off mid-sentence by a gruff, 'Just open the door, boy.'

He yanked the door open. Rubens stood there, with his arms folded in front of his puffed-out chest. He was still wearing his gold chain collar. 'I thought I might find you here, Elowen.'

'Is everything all right?' she said, unnerved by his sudden appearance.

'I need to speak to you,' he said. 'Boys, leave us.'

'We can wait for Elowen here,' said Diggory.

Rubens narrowed his eyes and tilted his head back and to the side. 'No, boy, you are not needed.'

'Don't worry, Diggory,' said Elowen, not wanting her friend to get into trouble. 'I'll see you later.'

Diggory sloped off, grumbling; Lárwita followed a step behind him.

Elowen felt Rubens's hand on her back and he steered her back into the workshop. There he strolled around, examining the instruments and objects. He pointed at the balloon. 'These experimental philosophers have vivid imaginations.'

'I think they're very clever,' said Elowen.

'Oh yes, very clever, no doubting that,' said Rubens, sounding far from sincere. He folded his arms again and stared at Elowen. 'I am profoundly concerned about you. What Grunewald said at the assembly came as a shock to me so I can scarcely imagine how you feel.'

'I don't want to be part of whatever it is that Grunewald is planning,' said Elowen.

'My dear child, if it was within my power to change it then I would, without hesitation.'

38

'But can't you persuade him to choose someone else?'

'Quite impossible. Grunewald's mind is made up.'

'I don't understand why he picked *me.*'

Rubens held up his hands. 'I cannot give you any answers. This quest, whatever it is, belongs to Grunewald.'

'Don't you know what his plan is? But you're a Master too!'

Rubens shook his head. 'You are a clever girl but there is much about the Illuminati you do not understand. Grunewald does not confide in me. He has his own plans, his own little plots. Yes, he might speak grandly of defeating Prester John but I fear what lurks behind the veil of his fine words. I must warn you, Elowen, I am afraid that Grunewald is trying to seize total power in the sanctuary and I do not know to what lengths he is prepared to go.'

'Can he do that?'

'The Creed of the Illuminati forbids there being just one Master, a law designed to protect us from tyranny, a law Grunewald seems determined to break.'

'But what *am* I to do?' said Elowen.

'You know that I am fond of you and that I always have your best interests at heart. I might sleep better if you kept me informed of Grunewald's plans. I need you to be my eyes and ears.'

Elowen hesitated. 'But Grunewald said those chosen for the Chapter of Light cannot talk to anyone else about the quest.'

'Indeed he did and I have not the smallest doubt that you will adhere to that rule faithfully. However, has Grunewald demanded secrecy for the good of the Illuminati, or does he desire to protect his own schemes and plots? I fear that he seeks to exploit your potential for his own ends. Do not allow yourself to be used by him, do not allow yourself to be his tool.'

Elowen certainly did not want that but she still had doubts. 'I don't want to betray his trust.'

'Your first loyalty is always to the Illuminati,' said Rubens. 'And on my word, if you carry out this favour for me it shall remain a secret, our secret. Will you promise to do this for me?'

'Very well, I promise,' said Elowen. 'I'll do as you ask.'

'A wise decision. Say nothing to Grunewald, of course. He feels...threatened by our friendship. Only he, your friend Diggory and I know that you are the daughter of an Adept. You have been wise to keep quiet about your mother, just as we agreed.'

'It's not fair,' said Elowen. 'I'm not ashamed of her.'

Rubens gave her such a hard look that Elowen lowered her head to evade his penetrating glare. His voice changed, and with his gentle tones blunted, his words bludgeoned her. 'There are many good reasons for you to keep quiet on the subject, reasons that, in time, you will learn about and understand.'

'I want to know more about her, that's all.'

'And one day you shall,' he said, his voice regaining its soothing, silky tone. 'However, you must realise that being in the Chapter of Light places you in danger. I dare not be any more specific than that. Heed my words. There are malevolent forces at work within the sanctuary. Be cautious. Be vigilant. Trust no one but me. And do not forget your promise. For the good of the Illuminati, and all that we have achieved here, I need to know what Grunewald is planning. '

*

The scriptorium was a small room adjacent to the Hall of Learning. Scribes normally worked there, translating documents or writing out manuscripts by hand. Elowen nervously stepped into a rectangular room lined with two rows of desks; each desk had an inkwell and a supply of penknives, quills and parchment rolls. The room reeked of ink and vellum.

The red light of dusk poured through four circular windows and exposed symbols on the wall: globes, stars, crescent moons and a lidded eye. Grunewald stood behind a low table cluttered with scrolls and piles of books. The scarred, bow-legged Orok lurked in the corner, almost hidden by shadow. Elowen's chest tightened with nerves. As she looked around the scriptorium, she realised everyone else had already arrived, so she sat at the desk at the back of the left-hand row. The chair creaked and the others stared at her. She feared everyone was thinking the same thought: *why is she part of this? She is just a child.*

Grunewald glowered at Elowen. 'Now that we are *all* here, we can begin. You have all felt the power of the Earthsoul, you have all *used* its power. Only through the Earthsoul's power can we defeat Prester John. He knows and fears this. Most of all he fears the place where the Earthsoul is the strongest. The Tree of Life.'

The Tree of Life. It sounded familiar to Elowen, like the echo of a dream.

'It is said that this tree is the very wellspring of all life,' continued Grunewald. 'Without it the Earthsoul will fade. However, it is believed that the tree has not bloomed for many ages, sickened by man's desecration of the earth, by the infection of Cold Iron. If the tree were to bloom again then the Earthsoul would be replenished, and the power, the pestilence of Cold Iron would be broken, thus extinguishing the source of Prester John's power. And that is why he wishes to destroy it.'

'Destroy the tree? Can he do that?' said Marya Morvena, a female Adept with black hair that flowed down to her waist.

'Certainly, but first he has to find it,' said Grunewald with a knowing smile. 'And that is where we have the advantage.'

'So you know where the tree is?' said Amairgin, a druid from the green, wind-swept islands west of Helagan. He was dressed in a harlequin cloak, with a stiff horn-like hat. His sunken eyes, thin lips and distant expression gave him the appearance of a marble statue rather than a living, breathing person.

'Not yet, but we are close to finding the tree,' said Grunewald. With difficulty, he bent down and picked something up from the table. He held it aloft for everyone to see. With a shiver of excitement, Elowen recognised it: the Map of the Known World.

'The Tree of Life will never be found on a map, not even this one,' said Grunewald. 'But this map can set us upon the path to finding it. This is the first step.'

'But why is the Tree of Life not shown on the map?' said

Amairgin, a question that had occurred to Elowen but one she had been too shy to voice.

'The location must remain a secret,' said Grunewald. He hobbled up and down between the two lines of desks. 'If it were found and destroyed then the Earthsoul would die. The consequences would be catastrophic for all living things. With no Earthsoul to counteract the evil of Cold Iron, there would be no defence against Prester John. The Tree of Life has been protected and with good reason.'

'Is it the Illuminati who protect it?' said Elowen, unable to hold in questions any longer.

'No, of course not,' said Grunewald irritably, making Elowen regret opening her mouth. 'That responsibility fell to beings of far greater knowledge and power, the Elementals, for there is one for each of the four elements: earth, fire, air and water. It is said that the Elementals concealed the secret to the Tree of Life's location within four objects of immense power known as the Mysteries. Each Mystery forms a step on the trail to finding the tree. Once we have found earth, it shall lead to fire, then fire to air, then air to water, and then finally, water to the Tree of Life.'

'Master Grunewald, you are mistaken,' said Sadko the Minstrel, his flowing robes rustling as he stood. 'The legend of the Four Mysteries is a tale told by bards and storytellers. It has no basis in truth.'

Grunewald thumped his walking stick onto the floor. 'After long years of study I am convinced the Mysteries are real. Some, their foolish hearts full of pride, have sought the Mysteries before but never with success. They lacked this map and that is where they failed and we shall succeed. We

43

shall find the tree and nurture it to bloom, thus crushing the malignancy of Cold Iron. This is not simply our best hope of defeating Prester John; I believe it is our only hope.'

Grunewald held up the map again, though it was too far away from Elowen for her to see any detail. 'On the right-hand side of the map there is the symbol of the tree, beneath it is the ancient Manus symbol for the number one. Both symbols are drawn against the Orok city of Erdene, at the centre of which stands the temple of Bai Ulgan. It is my belief that the first Mystery, the Mystery of Earth, is held in Bai Ulgan, guarded by the earth Elemental. That is where our journey must take us.'

Journey. Elowen went cold at the mention of the word. What did Grunewald mean?

'Please, come closer,' said the Master. They formed a circle around the front table although Elowen lingered towards the back of the group and had to stand on tiptoe to see. The Orok stood close to Grunewald, and Elowen was careful to keep away from him.

His joints cracking, the Master reached for the pile of books on the table and picked up the third volume from the top. Richly bound in leather, the book released a whiff of dust and stale paper when Grunewald opened it. He rested the open book on the table for all to see and pointed to a drawing on the left-hand page. It showed a castle-like building, with thick encircling walls, box-shaped towers and sharp-tipped buttresses.

'That is the temple of Bai Ulgan,' said Grunewald. 'It is a wonder of the Orok lands, with walls made not of stone but of sun-baked mud-bricks. My heart skips with joy at the

44

thought I may see it with my own eyes. Within the temple is a labyrinth, believed to be the resting place of the first Mystery.'

'But Bai Ulgan is in Gondwana, the Orok lands—it would take an army to reach the temple,' said Sadko the Minstrel. 'I have heard tales of the steppes to chill the heart. It is said to be a land occupied by men with the head of a dog, and by creatures with neither neck nor head, but with a face set in the middle of their chests.'

Elowen shivered at Sadko's descriptions.

'Those are the tall tales of merchants and travellers and you should ignore them,' said Grunewald. 'Although I admit that the journey may be perilous, I still prefer this company to an army, for our chief hope is in stealth and secrecy. You have all been selected as the best able to deal with the demands of this quest. I shall not lie to you though. It is likely that some, if not all, of us will not survive this quest. If you do not want to be a part of this, I respect your wishes. So, if any of you wish to withdraw now, please raise your hands.'

Not one of the Adepts flinched; they accepted their duty with grim fortitude. Elowen, though, acted impulsively. Her hand shot up.

Grunewald threw her a poisonous look. 'Very well, you are all dismissed. Return here at dawn. Elowen, wait behind please.'

The others filed out, muttering among themselves. By their angry expressions, Elowen guessed that they were talking about her. She tried to convince herself that she didn't care; at least she was no longer part of the quest.

45

When everyone else had gone, Grunewald said, 'Elowen, you cannot withdraw from the Chapter of Light.'

Outraged, it took Elowen a moment to find her voice. 'But you said if I didn't want to—'

'No, I said that any of the others could withdraw. You are too important.'

'What...what do you mean?' she stammered. 'Why do you think I'm important?'

'Because you are the child of an Adept.'

'Why does that matter?'

He drew a deep breath. 'Female Adepts are barren. Whether it is some effect of their ability to control the Earthsoul, or a cruel trick of nature, I know not. Whatever the truth, children are almost never born to Adept mothers. You should not exist, child, you are an anomaly.'

'But there must be others,' said Elowen, her head spinning and terrified by the very thought of travelling to the harsh lands of the east. 'Why do I have to go?'

'Elowen, there are no *others*,' said Grunewald angrily. 'Believe me, if there were I would be inclined to choose them ahead of you, especially after your antics last night. You cannot be so careless and irresponsible. You have a duty, a great duty, upon you.'

'I didn't ask for it,' said Elowen, her hatred of Grunewald growing all the time. 'I don't want to be treated differently.'

'But you are different, Elowen,' he said. He closed his eyes, and after a pause added, 'I did not want to say this in front of the others, but it has long been prophesised that only a child of an Adept can complete the quest of the Four Mysteries and nurture the Tree of Life into bloom.'

46

Elowen tried to make sense of what he was telling her. 'But how...how could I do such a thing?'

'I do not know for certain, but to discover the answer you must travel into the Orok lands.'

CHAPTER THREE

The Grand Master

Grunewald decreed that the Chapter of Light should set forth for Bai Ulgan within three weeks, which left precious little time to prepare. The Chapter met every day in the scriptorium. Elowen's responsibilities were few and, despite Grunewald's talk of her *importance*, she sensed that she would be little more than baggage during the long journey, a journey she dreaded. Bewildered by everything she had heard about being the child of an Adept, and troubled by the hints and warnings Rubens had given her, she became suspicious of Grunewald's motives and feared he was playing some kind of cruel game.

She hated the Chapter meetings. Most of the others ignored her, especially the Orok, although with the exception of Grunewald, he spoke to no one else either; Elowen never learnt the Orok's name, not that she wanted to get to know him. But more than once he had peered at her, a strange expression on his face, as though he was examining her, judging her. She sensed sinister intentions in his dark, narrow eyes.

The hours Elowen spent preparing for the journey to Bai Ulgan meant she never saw Diggory and Lárwita, and she missed them. She loathed hiding anything from her friends but had no choice. The quest's true purpose had to remain a secret.

Rubens visited her after every Chapter meeting. He listened carefully to her descriptions of Grunewald's plans. He said little and often seemed distracted, lost in thought. The only time that he reacted was when Elowen mentioned Grunewald's intention to leave within three weeks.

'*Three* weeks?' he had said. 'That is much sooner than I had expected. That is a problem.'

'Why?' Elowen had said.

He had smiled and patted her on the head as though she was a well-behaved puppy. 'Do not concern yourself, dear child. You have done well.'

She fretted on what Grunewald had told her about being the child of an Adept. She tried to press Rubens on the subject but he dismissed her concerns. 'They are old folk tales. Ignore his bluster. But as I said, speak about this to no one else, for others share his views and it may cause…difficulties.'

Elowen was hardly reassured but Rubens refused to speak further about it.

She was beginning to feel overwhelmed by the prospect of the journey to come. So when on the fifth day of the Chapter meetings, Grunewald called an early halt to the session to attend to his aviaries, Elowen was relieved. Her first thought was to find Diggory and Lárwita but she discovered the former was in lessons and the latter was, as usual, busy in the Hall of Invention. She fancied stretching her legs so she decided to climb down a rope ladder and go for a stroll along the Sandwalk, a path that threaded south through the forest for a mile before swinging east and back round to the sanctuary.

It was late afternoon; golden light filtered through the forest canopy. Elowen found the Sandwalk much narrower than she had remembered. She collected several scratches on her hands and legs as she pushed through entanglements of bracken and bramble.

As the path widened, Elowen realised she was close to the Estates, a broad clearing in the forest used for growing vegetables, fruit, herbs and medicinal plants. As well as two walled gardens, there were beehives, sheltered orchards of pears and apples, a nuttery glowing with autumnal colours, and small strip-fields bursting with parsnips, carrots, winter radishes and cabbages.

Being on ground level, the Estates were not considered as safe as the rest of the sanctuary, and so were patrolled by yeomen warders. Elowen wanted to keep well away from *them*, so continued to follow the Sandwalk. It coiled around the smaller of the two walled gardens, the Poison Garden, which was contained within moss-stained stone walls and surrounded by untamed bushes with branches like gnarled hands. Elowen peered through the rusty gate and spotted Old Attalus, the keeper of the Poison Garden. He was bald, with a beak nose, bagged eyes and a narrow chin. He worked alone; the Poison Garden was his domain and he allowed no one else to help him with his secretive work. What he grew there, and for what purpose, Elowen could scarcely guess but she had heard many rumours of deadly plants and fungi. Old Attalus stopped his work and stared at her, his face carved into a haughty sneer. Blushing, Elowen hastened away.

The path sloped down to the walled Physick Garden. The brick wall was fourteen feet high and two topiaries flanked the gate, large yews clipped skilfully to resemble giants. One giant held a club in his hands while the other, smaller than the first, cowered in fear.

'Elowen, my dear! I'm pleased to see you.'

The Physick Garden gate swung open and Jacob the Elder, the chief gardener, bounded through. He had a long, thin face with a sharp nose, drooping grey moustache and narrow beard. His clothes were plain and functional: a cap, a scruffy shirt, linen trousers gathered at the knees, and an apron with a single pocket. A little terrier with a sandy, shaggy coat trotted alongside him.

Elowen liked Jacob and often came to the Physick Garden to help him sow seeds, weed and dig. She enjoyed the exercise, the fresh air, the jokes that Jacob told. It was a release from the sanctuary's stuffy atmosphere.

'Taking a walk in the forest, eh?' said Jacob. The terrier sniffed around Elowen's feet, yapping excitedly and wagging its little tail. 'A lot has changed in the garden since you last visited. I'd love to show you.'

'Yes, I'd like that,' said Elowen, as she knelt and scratched the terrier behind the ears.

'I'm glad to hear it,' he said, wiping his muddy hands on his apron. 'I see less of you these days but I guess you're busy now, what with being part of Grunewald's secret quest, or whatever it is that the old raven is planning. And from what I hear, you're quite the favourite of Rubens.'

'I don't know about favourite, I—'

'Come, lass,' he said, laughing and gesturing for Elowen to follow him into the garden. As he opened the gate for her, Jacob the Elder pointed at the topiaries. 'I swear the smaller one looks more like Old Attalus every day.'

'I doubt he'd thank you for the comparison.'

'I don't care a hoot what he thinks. He wastes all his time cultivating venomous vegetables when he could be growing something useful.'

As Elowen glanced again at the topiaries, she discerned a resemblance and doubted it was a coincidence. The two gardeners harboured a long-standing feud. Elowen did not know the source of their antipathy but both men enjoyed the bickering.

They strolled along the axial path that divided the garden, followed at every step by the little terrier. Jacob the Elder proudly showed her raised beds full of mint, parsley and valerian. There were tall forcing-pots for rhubarb, and soft-fruit bushes in warm positions close to the heat-trapping walls. Elowen savoured the garden's varied scents, even the earthy odour of the steaming compost heap. Several artisans worked in the garden, digging, weeding and pruning. Jacob the Elder spoke to each in turn, praising, encouraging and laughing.

As they walked on, Jacob coloured their conversation with jokes and, more than once, burst into song. Elowen found herself laughing, and some of her earlier melancholy lifted.

'You've been busy,' she said as they completed their tour of the garden and returned to the gate.

'There are many hungry mouths to feed in the sanctuary,

and ailments to cure,' said Jacob the Elder. He pulled out a small sharp knife from his apron pocket and used it to pick out dirt from beneath his fingernails. 'Most Illuminati forget or ignore us gardeners, but without food in their bellies, or remedies for their illnesses, their precious books are meaningless. Gardeners are more important than philosophers and warriors, never forget that.'

His last sentence was one of Jacob the Elder's favourite sayings and it made Elowen smile. 'I won't.'

'There are a lot of clever folk in this sanctuary, Elowen, folk of great wisdom and learning. Nevertheless, don't let any of them tell you how to think or act. Know your own mind. Don't allow others to use you, for sometimes fair words and fair countenance hide a dark purpose.'

Elowen knew that Jacob the Elder was speaking in general terms, he always enriched his speech with proverbs and aphorisms, but she sensed a warning in his words, and a meaning that perhaps she alone applied and the gardener did not intend. The undercurrents of conflict between Rubens and Grunewald were as clear and entrenched as those between Jacob the Elder and Old Attalus. Elowen glanced up at the two fighting giants and fancied she saw not the feuding gardeners, but the two Masters struggling for supremacy.

'Plants are my life and in truth the greater affairs of the Illuminati concern me little,' continued Jacob the Elder, tucking the knife back into his apron pocket. 'But my eyes do peer up from the soil from time to time. There are changes afoot. I sense it everywhere. Do you not feel it too?'

Elowen shrugged, not sure.

'We live in strange times, and who knows what the future may bring and which seeds will grow and which seeds will be lost in the soil?' he said. He gave Elowen a firm but playful slap on her back. 'Well, I won't keep you any longer. I suppose you have better things to do than waste time with an old gardener.'

'It's definitely not wasted time,' said Elowen.

He flashed a smile. 'You're a good lass and it always cheers me up to see you. Promise you'll come down more often to see me?'

'Yes, I promise,' said Elowen, feeling guilty as she knew, with the impending journey to Bai Ulgan, it was a promise she was bound to break.

'That's good. For reasons I cannot guess, you appear to shoulder many burdens. I do not ask you to tell me your business. Know only that I am your friend, and that a listening ear can ease many troubles.'

With that, he winked and, whistling merrily, walked back into the walled garden, the little terrier following closely behind. Elowen looked up at the two topiaries, feeling small under their shadows.

*

Mist enveloped the sanctuary; its clammy hands groped every tree and smothered every sound. Elowen shivered and ran a hand through her damp hair. She yawned widely without covering her mouth, certain that no one was around to see her.

It was Sunday morning and Rubens had called another assembly although he had given no clue as to his purpose. Other than his visits to her dwelling, Elowen had seen little of him.

With more and more artisans recruited as yeomen warders, vital repairs in the sanctuary often went undone. Roofs leaked. Doors swelled and stuck. Some of the bridges became loose and creaky, and vibrated worryingly as people walked across them, so Elowen picked her steps carefully. She reached the Crossroads, where the sanctuary's longest and widest walkways met. Several people passed her, all making their way to the assembly. Elowen stopped and peered down through the gaps in the wooden planks that formed the walkway; the ground far below had disappeared, lost in the mist. Even the mountains that surrounded the Vale of Bletsung were invisible.

'There you are.'

The familiar voice made Elowen smile. She turned to see Diggory; Lárwita accompanied him.

'It's good to see you, at *last*,' said Diggory.

'I'm sorry,' said Elowen. 'I haven't been ignoring you both. It's—'

'You can't talk about it, we know,' interrupted Diggory. 'I hope this Chapter of Light nonsense is over soon.'

Elowen didn't blame Diggory for being resentful. If the roles were reversed, she would feel the same. She ached to tell them she was leaving soon for Bai Ulgan, but knew it was forbidden to do so.

As they walked towards the Chapter House, Lárwita provided a welcome change of subject by declaring, 'I've been making some refinements to my balloon.'

'I hope it's an improvement on your first attempt,' said Diggory. 'It barely got a foot off the ground.'

Lárwita nodded. 'It'll work soon, I'm sure of it.'

By the time they reached the Chapter House, Grunewald had already taken his seat but there was no sign of Rubens, which puzzled Elowen as he had called the assembly. Elowen and her two friends took their usual position on the lowest bench, alongside the other scholars. Elowen was surprised to see Hyllebaer sitting there, bruised and bandaged but as formidable a presence as ever. She gave Elowen a hard look. 'I hear that you have been spending time in exalted company, girl.'

'You mean the Chapter of Light? I'm not important—'

'Well, let us hope you show more wisdom than you did in the Old Forest the other night, eh?'

'Yes, I'm sorry you were hurt,' said Elowen, fidgeting in her seat. 'It was my fault.'

'Indeed it was,' said Hyllebaer. 'But while you were unspeakably rash and foolish, I am told you were also brave and risked your life to protect me. I think, perhaps, there is still hope for you yet.'

Elowen smiled, knowing that was as much of a compliment as she was ever going to get from Hyllebaer.

The chamber doors opened and two dozen yeomen warders marched in, all with swords drawn. They formed a line in front of the benches, while four of them stood around the still-seated Grunewald, the tips of their blades held towards him.

'What is the meaning of this outrage?' said Grunewald. 'Yeomen warders, lower your weapons at once.'

'They follow my commands, Grunewald, not yours.'

Rubens strode into the chamber, his gold chain collar gleaming. The assembly became a disharmonious symphony of angry shouts and nervous whispers. Elowen's heart pounded. What was happening? Was it a trick?

Rubens held up a hand to demand silence. 'I have summoned this assembly for the gravest of purposes. My heart has never been as heavy or troubled as it is on this day. I can no longer ignore the treachery and scheming of Grunewald. He must answer for his actions.'

'Whatever it is I am supposed to have done, I am not answerable to you,' said Grunewald, aggressive and defiant despite the armed men surrounding him.

'But you are answerable to this assembly,' said Rubens, gesturing to the benches. He paced up and down like a stage actor and stroked his chain collar as he spoke. 'I have discovered the true purpose behind the Chapter of Light. You may have wondered why Grunewald was so eager to hide his plans from you. Of course, he claimed secrecy was essential, that he could not risk his plans being compromised. But his request for secrecy concealed nefarious intentions. He does not seek the power to defeat Prester John; he seeks only power for himself and the greatest prize of all: eternal life.'

There were gasps from all around the chamber.

'Eternal life?' said Grunewald. 'Have you taken leave of your senses completely?'

'The Chapter of Light is founded in deceit. It is fortunate that one member is still loyal to the ideals of the Illuminati. Elowen Aubyn, please stand.'

Elowen's whole body froze. All eyes turned on her. What was Rubens doing? She stood, her legs shaking uncontrollably. She was caught between anger and shame: anger at Rubens ignoring his promise and putting her through this ordeal, and shame at betraying Grunewald, whose wrathful expression was so strong Elowen had to look away.

'This poor girl came to me for help, worried and frightened as she was by Grunewald's behaviour,' said Rubens.

Elowen tried to cut in. 'That's not—'

Rubens spoke over her. 'Child, pray tell all present of the quest Grunewald has devised. I wish to hear the truth, not his honey-coated lies.'

In a cracked voice, Elowen reluctantly spoke of the quest to Bai Ulgan, finding every word painful.

When she had finished, Rubens said, 'Thank you, Elowen. Most enlightening. However, you have left out the most important part, for modesty's sake, I'm sure. You have not told us why you were chosen for this quest.'

Elowen's cheeks flushed. Not knowing what to do with her hands, she put them first in her pockets and then pulled them out again. Feeling queasy and light-headed, she mumbled, 'Because I'm the daughter of an Adept.'

Gasps of astonishment hissed through the chamber, followed by a volley of shouts.

'IT CANNOT BE TRUE!'

'LIES!'

'BLASPHEMY!'

Grunewald sat with his head in his hands. Elowen stood bewildered and afraid. She glanced at Diggory. He frowned and gave a look of anger, even disgust. He turned away.

58

Rubens appealed for calm. 'My friends, I know you are all shocked but it is the truth. We have standing before us a miracle.'

'Please, Rubens,' said Grunewald. 'Do not do this. She is too young.'

'Be silent, we have endured enough of your deceit,' said Rubens. He faced Elowen. 'Child, you trust me, don't you?'

'Yes...I mean—'

'Good. And I know you are frightened of Grunewald.'

Elowen felt as though she was standing outside of her body, unable to express anything. Rubens loomed over her, as though he had grown in size. An illusion surely, her mind scrambled by fear and stress, but an illusion that confused and confounded her. 'Well, I—'

His voice was so soft now, so gentle. 'Don't be ashamed to admit it.'

'A little perhaps, but—'

'I can see the fear in your eyes. Grunewald has kept you in ignorance, child. It is to my eternal shame that I did not protest more and for that, Elowen, I beg your forgiveness. Grunewald blinded me too. I saw goodness and decency in his heart when it was only filled with corruption and deceit. You deserve to know the truth, Elowen.'

She looked at Rubens, her heart pounding. He took a theatrical step backwards, looking around at the assembly. 'Elowen is the miracle we have been waiting for. A child born of an Adept. *A messenger.*'

The Master's words sparked a memory in Elowen, a memory of words that Tom Hickathrift had spoken about the Saviour many months before. *The messenger of a higher*

59

power he was. A being to restore the balance of the Earthsoul, to bring peace to men's hearts. Rubens was saying that she was a messenger too. Elowen's legs buckled. Surely it could not be true?

'It is said only one is born every generation,' continued Rubens. 'The Saviour was born of an Adept; he was a messenger, the very first messenger, the greatest messenger, many believe. Others followed, some great, some less so. Some heralded as prophets, miracle-makers, visionaries. Others were lost, their latent power undiscovered, ignored or punished. Such would be your fate, Elowen, if it were left to Grunewald. Skilfully he mixes lies with the truth. Yes, the Tree of Life is said to be the source of the Earthsoul, and no doubt Prester John wishes to destroy it. But there is something Grunewald has not mentioned, namely that the fruit of the tree confers immortality to anyone who consumes it. That is what he truly seeks. He is an old man, and like many alchemist and mystics before him, he wishes to prolong his life. For that aim, he is prepared to waste the lives of our most powerful Adepts and a child, and not just any child, the child of an Adept.'

'This is preposterous, I seek only the destruction of Prester John,' said Grunewald. 'Any talk of *immortality* is mere conjecture, there is no proof. Even if proof existed, immortality is of no consequence to me. And yes, I knew of Elowen's significance but I sought to protect her, not to use her, not to manipulate her. I refuse to endure these delusional fantasies for a moment longer. I ask the assembly to remove Rubens from the office of Master, an office for which he is patently unfit and has tried to exploit.'

60

His words sparked an explosion of shouting and finger pointing. The anger boiling within the chamber infected the flies inside; they tapped furiously against the windows as though desperate to escape.

Peace only came when Rubens stretched out his arms and called for quiet. 'Now we see the snake's fangs. Grunewald desires total dominion over the Illuminati. I cannot allow that to happen. Grunewald is betraying everything that we seek to build and protect. And he has not acted alone.'

Rubens signalled to the yeomen warders and they advanced into the crowd. They pulled the Orok and all the other members of the Chapter of Light except Elowen, to their feet, and forced them, at sword point, down to the chamber floor and made them stand in a closely guarded circle. Amairgin and Sadko the Minstrel argued furiously with the warders but received only shoves and punches in response. With her eyes closed, Marya Morvena made the sign of the blessing and muttered a prayer.

'Treachery must be punished,' said Rubens. 'Are there any among you who oppose Grunewald and his traitors being sent into exile?'

Fear crackled through the assembly. No one dared to raise his or her hand. Elowen's heart was hammering.

'Then I judge that the assembly has spoken with one voice and it has spoken wisely,' said Rubens. To the yeomen warders he said, 'Ensure that Grunewald and his followers, especially that Orok, are driven from the sanctuary and from the Vale of Bletsung. See to it that they take nothing with them. I do not wish for them to plunder the treasures of the sanctuary for their own ends.'

The Adepts condemned by Rubens were hustled out of the chamber, but the Orok remained, standing defiantly by Grunewald. The old Master stared at Elowen, his rheumy eyes sad, a deflated expression on his face, an expression of disappointment. 'Child, you have been deceived, but not by me.'

A yeomen warder grabbed Grunewald by the arm and tried to pull him up from the chair. The Master angrily flung off his grip; a sword flashed and Grunewald fell.

'NO!' said the Orok. He struck down the yeoman warder with a single punch.

Grunewald lay on the floor. An expanding pool of blood emerged from his body. Elowen pushed through the yeomen warders and knelt beside Grunewald. With tears tumbling down her cheeks, she grasped his cold, crinkly hands. 'I'm sorry, this is my fault.'

Grunewald opened his eyes enough for them to become slits of reflected light. 'Bai Ulgan, child. You must go to Bai Ulgan.'

'Don't try to talk,' said Elowen.

He opened his eyes a little more, straining and grimacing at the effort. 'Don't trust Rubens. Bai Ulgan, child. Bai Ulgan. Promise me you will go there.'

'I promise,' said Elowen.

'You are nothing like your mother, remember that,' said Grunewald. His voice faded, like the wind calming after a violent storm, his last words unintelligible. His chest stopped moving.

Rubens grabbed Elowen's shoulders and pulled her upright. He dragged her away from Grunewald and forced her to sit down on the benches. Her cheeks flushed with guilt and anger.

'Warders, lower your weapons,' said Rubens. 'This has gone too far. Get the Orok out of here.'

The warders obeyed his command. The Orok scowled at Rubens and said in a deep voice, 'You have Grunewald's blood on your hands. You are responsible for his murder.'

'Keep your tongue behind your teeth, Orok,' said Rubens. 'Grunewald's pride and foolishness caused his death. If he had gone peacefully then bloodshed would have been avoided. Pray do not make the same mistake.'

The Orok spat on the floor and stormed out of the hall.

'Clear away the body,' said Rubens. As the yeomen warders did so, Rubens faced the assembly again. 'It is time for change. The death of Grunewald is unfortunate but we must move forward. We Illuminati have failed to keep pace with the terrible dangers that afflict the world. I promise to change this.'

Naboth, one of Rubens's closest followers, stood and said, 'For too long we have been burdened with two Masters, and it has led to instability and weakness. I propose that we bestow the title of *Grand Master* upon Rubens. Only in his guardianship can we be safe.'

'You humble me, Naboth,' said Rubens with a bow and a self-satisfied grin. 'But I could only accept such an honour with the full support of the assembly. If any object to this, pray speak now.'

As Elowen had expected, there was no response. Fear of the yeomen warders silenced any dissent.

Rubens bowed again. 'I shall never forget this moment,

nor cease in my efforts to serve you with honour and dignity.'

As his supporters cheered, Elowen saw clearly that Rubens had used her; he had played her like a puppet to help him achieve what he desired: sole mastery of the sanctuary. She remembered the words of Grunewald. *Don't trust Rubens*. She hated herself for her weakness and stupidity. She was a fool.

Rubens dismissed the assembly, and many Illuminati traipsed away, heads bowed, silent, wary, frightened. Elowen recognised the disappointment on their faces; this was not what they had expected the sanctuary to become, this was not how they imagined their lives as Illuminati. Some glanced suspiciously at Elowen; she looked away to avoid their stares.

In contrast, those loyal to Rubens were in boisterous mood, laughing and singing. The Grand Master approached Elowen. 'You did well, child. You demonstrated your loyalty.'

'You lied to me,' she said.

He clicked his tongue. 'There is much you do not understand.'

'Stop saying that, I understand enough. You tricked me. You used me.'

'I have no time to listen to your petulant outbursts,' he said. 'Go with Werner—he will take you to the Master's Room.'

She turned. A yeoman warder waited beside her, grim-faced, unsmiling. Elowen said, 'Why do I have to go the Master's Room?'

'Because I *instructed* you to,' said Rubens. 'I will be there soon.'

Elowen followed Werner outside. Fluffy clouds with grey underbellies raced across the blue sky, forced along by the cool keen wind. Werner strode ahead, and Elowen had to run to keep up with him. When they reached the Hall of Learning, the yeoman warder pulled a large key from his belt and unlocked the door.

'Why is it locked?' said Elowen.

'By order of the Grand Master,' said Warner, as he pushed the door open.

Elowen stepped inside and Werner slammed the door behind her. She walked through the empty, silent Hall of Learning and up to the door of the Master's Room. She was surprised to find that it had been left ajar. She nudged it fully open, stepped inside and waited. With the shutters flung open, the dark chamber she had visited before was transformed. Light washed the room and revealed symbols on the wall: an hourglass, scales of justice and various geometric shapes. Blazing stars and humanised moons decorated the ceiling. Most striking of all was a bronze mask of an ancient god fastened to the wall behind the wooden dais. Crowned by vine and ivy, it resembled Rubens, with its dark eyes, thick hair and curly beard.

'How are you feeling?'

The voice of Rubens boomed beneath the low ceiling. Elowen jumped. The Grand Master stood in the doorway. She had not heard him come in. Seeing him again made her skin crawl. 'Is it all true, what you said about me being a messenger?'

'I never lie to you, Elowen.'

Elowen harrumphed. 'You never seem to tell me the full truth either.'

'Sometimes it is better not to know the full truth; sometimes the truth is too much to bear. You are a messenger, Elowen. And it is my duty, my honour, to protect you.'

Messenger. A spasm of shock rippled Elowen's body.

She thought about the Saviour. A flood of memories, fragments of images, prayers, hymns and songs came to her. She remembered tales of his *deeds of power*: healing the sick, calming storms and raising the dead. If she truly was a messenger, could she do such things? The memory of the altarpiece in Trecadok church jolted into her consciousness. It showed the Saviour before his execution, beside the hanging tree. She had stared at it countless times during sermons. She recalled every detail. The Saviour, his hands pressed together in prayer, his body as white as marble, his nut-brown, shoulder-length hair, his neatly forked beard, his soft, sad, doleful eyes. She blinked and saw herself standing there instead of the Saviour, beside that grotesque knotted tree, beneath those saucer-shaped clouds. The dove hovered above her head. The angels and disciples wept over *her* impending execution.

She shook her head, smashing the image. 'I don't believe you. I'm not a messenger. I can't be. It was hard enough to believe that my mother was an Adept, although I know in my heart that she was. But this…a messenger—'

'I am telling you the truth, Elowen,' said Rubens. The Grand Master smiled and put his hands on her shoulders. 'This is all so much for you to comprehend. And you are troubled by what happened at the assembly. Grunewald's death shocked us all. As much as it was right to expose his plots and deceptions, I did not desire his slaying.'

'It is convenient for you he is dead though.'

His lips curled. 'Grunewald's death was tragic but it must not deflect us from our true purpose. I have plans, Elowen, great plans. At the assembly you showed me true loyalty and I shall not forget it, nor fail to reward it.'

'I am not loyal to you,' said Elowen, unable to bottle her anger any longer.

'You are upset. I understand that, but what I did, I did for the good of the Illuminati.'

'But—'

He removed his hands from her shoulders. 'That is *enough*. Do not act like a child.'

Elowen's cheeks glowed with anger. She wanted to yell at him but it was hopeless. He was the Grand Master; he was in control.

Rubens walked over to the table that stood upon the dais and beckoned Elowen to follow him. He moved a pile of books and unfolded a parchment: it was the Map of the Known World. He ran his fingers over the map and looked at it wistfully. 'For all his lies, Grunewald was wise enough to understand the importance of the Four Mysteries. Think about it, Elowen. The Tree of Life. The source of immortality. It is within our grasp.'

Elowen frowned. 'But you said in the assembly—'

'Ah, I said what was necessary to defeat Grunewald,' he said. 'We *must* seize this chance. Together we can reveal the secrets of the Tree of Life and unlock its power.'

'Together?'

'Yes, for although I disbanded the Chapter of Light, I still intend to send a company to Bai Ulgan,' he said, rubbing his hands together. 'But I refuse to send the acolytes of Grunewald. Only those loyal to me will be given the honour. And you, Elowen, of course you will be included. I can help you to fulfil your potential, a potential denied by Grunewald. Immense power could be yours, if you let me guide you. And if we find the Tree of Life, think what it will mean: everlasting life.'

'I thought defeating Prester John was all that mattered?'

Rubens sighed and, with his hand on the small of her back, steered her over to the door, which opened to a tiny room, musty, smelling of old books and stale tobacco, and bare except for a bed and an empty shelf. A window looked out upon the forest canopy.

Rubens clapped his hands together. 'This was Grunewald's room. Until we embark on the journey, this will be your home.'

'My home? What about my dwelling?'

'It is being cleared as we speak. This is where you live now.'

'But why am I being moved? I'm happy—'

'You must understand the importance of ensuring your safety. What I am doing now should have been done when you first arrived here; only the perfidy of Grunewald prevented it. Now they know you are a messenger, others will be suspicious of you, even jealous. Here I can easily protect you. My yeomen warders guard the Hall of Learning day and night.'

'What danger could I be in?'

'Vigilance must be our watchword,' he said. He toyed with a key as he spoke. 'You will be safe here until we leave.'

'Why I am being treated like a prisoner? That's not fair.'

'It is for your own protection.'

Elowen panicked. 'What about my friends? Diggory and Lárwita will wonder where—'

'Elowen, you are no longer a child,' interrupted Rubens. He stood in front of the door, blocking her exit. 'Such friends are not worthy of you and will only hold you back. You must realise how special you are, and the great responsibility that rests upon you. Such responsibility requires sacrifice.'

A throbbing rage took hold of Elowen. She had been locked away before and she refused to let it happen again. She tried to barge her way past Rubens but he pushed her back; she stumbled and only just managed to avoid falling over.

'You must learn to obey me, girl,' he said.

His manner and tone reminded Elowen of the cruelty of Cornelius Cronack, the wicked bully who controlled the Trecadok orphanage. That thought made her angrier. She threw herself again at Rubens but this time he slapped her hard across the face. Elowen fell back onto the bed, more in shock than pain. Rubens licked his lips and rubbed his hands together. 'That was your fault, you should show me more respect. You may be a messenger but do not forget that I control you.'

With that, Rubens left and locked the door behind him.

CHAPTER FOUR

Across the Mountains

L ooking through the small solitary window, Elowen watched the sun climb above the mountains. The evening's rain left the glass sprinkled with hundreds of water droplets that now glistened like stars. The window opened only a few inches but if by some miracle Elowen wriggled her body out, she knew she would plunge onto the forest floor far below.

For three days the room had been her prison, the freedom of the sanctuary now a memory. She speculated what Diggory and Lárwita thought of her disappearance; she hoped they were not angry with her. She remembered the look on Diggory's face when he had learnt she was a messenger. Confused. Shocked. Hurt. The look of someone who believed he had been deceived.

Her only human contact was with Rubens. He acted friendly; he smiled and made jokes but Elowen dismissed his empty gestures. His web of flattery and kind-sounding words had snared her. It was so clear now, so obvious. She hated Rubens for exploiting her, but hated herself more for being stupid and naïve enough to be tricked by him.

Above all, she blamed herself for Grunewald's death. She

had helped set in motion the events that had led to his killing. She toyed with the pendant around her neck, her mother's pendant. Grunewald's last words came back to her again: *you are nothing like your mother, remember that.* As painful as it was to acknowledge, Elowen knew that Grunewald was right. She was certain that her mother would not have been duped so easily.

Messenger. The word dogged her every thought. What did it mean? Was she different, and if so, how? Should she feel different, look different? Elowen interpreted every feeling, every sensation, every ache and pain, as signs of some mysterious change, of unyielding steps to becoming something *other.* She looked down at her hands; they were still her hands. The same rough skin on her knuckles, the same hangnails she often snagged, the same lines across her palms. She caught her ghostly reflection in the glass. The same face, rounder and healthier-looking than it had been before she had arrived at the sanctuary. The same tumble of white-streaked hair. From the outside she was unchanged, but was there something else, unseen, deep within her, that was growing, changing her atom by atom?

Elowen flinched as someone unlocked the door. It opened and Rubens was there, smiling as usual.

'Are you well, child?' he said.

Elowen shrugged in response and turned away, pretending to stare out of the window.

'I have brought you gifts,' he said. 'You will find them most useful when we cross the mountains, the first leg of our journey.'

The *journey.* It was all he talked about. It was his obsession.

71

Elowen knew he longed to find the Tree of Life, not to defeat Prester John but for the promise of immortality, the prize he had accused Grunewald of seeking. He seemed willing to do anything, sacrifice anyone, to achieve his aim.

He dropped a sack onto her bed. Elowen watched from the corner of her eye as he pulled out a hooded coat of fur, double-layered trousers, leather mittens and sealskin boots.

'I want nothing from you,' said Elowen.

'These are clothes made by the Metsamaa tribes and they are much better than those rags you arrived in,' he said referring to the clothes given to her by Black Francis.

She bristled at the comment. Her travelling clothes may have been scruffy but she treasured them as a memory of a friend's kindness to her, and they were as comfortable as her own skin. 'Take these away. I don't need them.'

'Your old clothes were filthy and they have been burnt.'

Elowen spun around. Words burst out of her mouth. 'YOU BURNT THEM? THEY WERE MINE!'

'I see you are in no mood to show gratitude for my gifts,' said Rubens, unmoved by her anger. He stuffed the clothes back in the sack and left it on her bed. 'Perhaps in the days to come you will learn to show more appreciation for my generosity.'

He slammed the door behind him and locked it again.

Elowen wanted to scream to release the rage within her but no sound came out. She looked out onto the forest; the trees looked grey, left as still as statues by the lack of wind. She saw no birds. The sun was lost behind a phalanx of sickly yellow clouds.

Her stomach gurgled; she was ravenously hungry. Rubens

72

brought her regular meals but, out of defiance, she usually refused to eat them. Now her stomach ached and a vile, acidic taste formed in her mouth. Her leg hurt, the echo of the injury inflicted by a Redeemer many months before. The wound had long since healed to leave only a small white scar where the blade had pierced her flesh, but the pain often returned, a burning sensation that reached down into her bones.

A tapping sound distracted her. A robin perched on the window sill. It tapped its beak against the glass. Elowen tried *Linking* with the bird. Words came into her mind.

Danger. They are coming. Get out!

Elowen nudged the window ajar but the robin remained on the sill and did not try to fly away.

Danger.

Elowen's heart pounded, gripped by a terror she did not understand. The pain in her leg worsened. A thick mist swallowed the forest, turning the trees into vague, spectral shapes. There was no wind, no birdsong, no animal calls. Something was wrong.

Get out! Get out!

The bird flew off, its alarm calls fading as it rose out of sight. Muffled cries and a burning smell carried on the still air. She stared hopelessly at the locked door. She called out but no one came. She had to get out; every sense, every intuition compelled her to escape but she hesitated. Rubens would be furious if she tried to break out of the room. She touched her mother's pendant, her fingertips tingling at the contact with the limestone curves and edges. Fear flowed through her and somehow she knew that if she stayed she would be in terrible danger. She took a step back and then hurled herself at the door. It shook violently but remained on its hinges. Her shoulder ached with the blow but she tried again: this time there was a CRACK and the door lurched forward, its hinges broken.

Elowen stood still, paralyzed by fear. She felt pressure around her ribcage, like an ever-tightening band. The sack of clothes left by Rubens still lay on her bed. She pulled out the hooded coat and put it on. With her leg still throbbing, she limped into the Master's Room. The fireplace was cold and there was no sign of Rubens. The cries from outside grew louder and louder. Muskets fired. Something was wrong, terribly wrong.

She tiptoed into the Hall of Learning and found it deserted. She edged towards the main door. As she reached for the handle, the door swung open and she had to step back to avoid being struck.

Uriah, the steward of the sanctuary, stumbled into the room. Dirt and leaves smeared his gown, and his small hat sat askew. Wide-eyed with terror, he grabbed hold of Elowen and shook her. 'Where is the Grand Master?'

'I…I don't know,' she said. 'He's not here.'

'I must find him, only he can save us,' said Uriah, speaking so swiftly that Elowen found it difficult to understand him. 'They are here. They have discovered us at last.'

'Who?'

'The enemy,' said Uriah, tears tumbling down his cheek. 'The Redeemers are here.'

Elowen went cold, her arms and legs tingling. Now she understood why her old wound hurt again.

'They have discovered us at last,' repeated Uriah, shaking his head. 'You should hide, child.'

With that, he pushed Elowen away and fled back outside. Elowen hesitated. If she went outside she risked encountering the Redeemers, but if she waited they would surely find her. She remembered Diggory and Lárwita. They were in danger too and that made up her mind. She had to find them.

She edged the door open and stepped outside. Smoke billowed around the trees, and flames licked many dwellings and walkways. A flock of ravens swept into the air, released, Elowen guessed, from the aviaries. The ravens circled the sanctuary. They cried out a barrage of hard, noisy calls before scattering in a dozen different directions.

Footsteps. For a heart-stopping moment Elowen thought the Redeemers had caught her, but to her relief it was two yeomen warders, both with smoke-blackened faces and armed with muskets. One said, 'You are safer inside, child. The Redeemers are everywhere.'

As if to prove his words, a tall figure in white robes emerged from the smoke. In his right hand he carried a long bloodstained sword. The warders fired. The musket balls tore small holes in the Redeemer's robes. He jolted but made no sound, and still advanced.

'In the name of the Saviour,' said one of the warders. They scrambled to reload their muskets but were too slow. With two sweeps of his sword, the Redeemer cut them down.

Elowen screamed and stumbled backwards, the platform railing pressed hard into her back. She glanced down at the dizzying fall below. She was trapped. The Redeemer pointed his sword towards her and hissed, 'You are the child Lord Lucien seeks. Surrender and come with me.'

'She will do no such thing.'

The voice surprised both Elowen and the Redeemer. Hyllebaer strode towards them. The golden threads weaved around her elder branch. Elowen's heart leapt when she realised that Diggory and Lárwita lurked behind Hyllebaer, both grim-faced and terrified.

The Redeemer held his sword high, ready to strike but Hyllebaer swirled her branch, sending the golden threads into a frenzy of movement and incandescent colour; a pulse of blinding light threw the Redeemer backwards and over the railing.

The golden threads vanished. Hyllebaer fell to her knees and the branch dropped from her trembling hands. Elowen ran to her side. The Adept struggled for breath and her whole body shook. She gasped, 'I am far too old for this nonsense.'

'You saved me…how did you know I was here?'

'I suspected Rubens was keeping you somewhere secure,' said Hyllebaer between heavy wheezes. 'When the attack began these two rogues persuaded me to find you.'

Despite her fear, Elowen glowed with happiness—her friends had not forgotten about her. Diggory began to say something but Hyllebaer cut him off. 'Redeemers are swarming across the sanctuary and I have not the strength to fight them all. Boys, help me stand.'

Elowen protested. 'But you are hurt, you cannot—'

'Don't tell me what I can or cannot do,' said Hyllebaer.

She picked up her branch. 'We must get down into the forest. There is a rope ladder close by.'

'But will we be any safer down there?' said Elowen.

Hyllebaer nodded towards Lárwita. 'This young man has a plan.'

'What about Rubens?' said Elowen.

'Don't waste an ounce of strength worrying about *him*,' said Hyllebaer.

With the boys' help, Hyllebaer managed to stand and they struggled on towards the ladder. Screams of pain and terror echoed. Many trees were on fire and the air reeked of burning wood. Elowen feared an attack from the Redeemers at any moment. They passed bloated corpses of men and women. Elowen thought she was going to vomit and she heard Lárwita and Diggory retching.

'Keep moving!' said Hyllebaer.

They reached a lower-level platform from which a rope ladder led down to the forest floor.

'You children go first, I will only slow you,' said Hyllebaer.

'Can you manage it?' said Elowen.

'Girl, I have been climbing these ladders for more years than I care to remember and I have not fallen once.'

Lárwita's legs shook. 'I'll go down first. It makes sense as I'm the most likely to fall.'

Elowen was about to argue when a sudden chill took her and she felt her scar twinge. A thick cloud of clammy mist swirled around them. Four silhouettes slowly took shape, turning from writhing shadows into tangible forms. Redeemers.

77

Hyllebaer stood in front of the children, holding the elder branch with both hands. 'Elowen, I can hold them off long enough for you and your friends to escape.'

'They'll kill you,' said Elowen.

'Not before I kill them,' said Hyllebaer. The Adept turned the branch around in her hands; the air grew hot and shimmered like liquid. Elowen remembered Lord Hereward in the Old Tower back in Trecadok; she remembered his sacrifice…

'No, Hyllebaer,' said Elowen as the Redeemers advanced, their swords drawn. 'Don't do this!'

'It is too late,' said Hyllebaer. 'Go—save yourself!'

The Adept's voice carried such power that Elowen dared not defy her, so she scrambled down the ladder, gripping tightly onto the rope rungs. The two boys were already making their way down and she soon caught up. Diggory swore at Lárwita to go faster. Down and down Elowen went; she was getting closer to the bottom, almost there…

An explosion rocked the ladder. Shards of wood fizzed around and the air was sucked from her lungs. Her fingers loosened on the ladder, her foot missed the rung…

She landed on her back. Winded, shaken and queasy, she stood. She was relieved to find that Lárwita and Diggory had both reached the bottom too. Diggory cursed and swore as he brushed himself down, while Lárwita was as white as snow and looked as though he was going to be sick. His spectacles sat askew and he mumbled to himself as he adjusted them. Chunks of scorched wood and branches littered the forest floor, and the sanctuary above was lost in smoke and mist.

Diggory wiped blood from his lips. 'We ought to get going. They'll be after us.'

'What about Hyllebaer?' said Elowen. 'We can't leave her.'

'She's dead, we can't help her,' said Diggory. 'Hopefully she has taken the Redeemers with her.'

Lárwita gnawed his fingernails. 'Even if those Redeemers are destroyed, there are many more around.'

'Where are we going?' said Elowen, her mind still swirling from shock at the loss of Hyllebaer. 'We can't outrun the Redeemers.'

'This way,' said Lárwita. He scrambled away, heading southwards along the Sandwalk, and Elowen and Diggory followed him.

From the high canopy of the forest, lost in the mist and the web of interweaved branches, came the sound of ravens and crows squabbling. Elowen and her friends kept a quick pace. They knew the enemy was not far away.

The Sandwalk took them close to the Estates. The strip fields of crops were burning, the beehives toppled and smashed. Smoke billowed from the Physick Garden. Jacob the Elder's precious topiaries were ablaze. Smouldering bodies were scattered around the wall of the garden.

Elowen stopped, tears stinging her eyes. 'It's like the end of the world.'

'We have to keep going,' said Diggory, pulling at her arm.

'What about Jacob the Elder? He might still be alive.'

'Even if he is, there's nothing we can do to help him and there might be more Redeemers down there. If we get caught now, Hyllebaer's sacrifice was for nothing.'

Elowen knew he was right. She wiped her eyes and carried

on. To her surprise, Lárwita sprinted far ahead, energised by a surge of fear or excitement. He disappeared. Elowen and Diggory struggled after him. They soon came to a wide clearing. Rhododendrons and azaleas grew between the tree-trunks, and noisy ravens circled above them. Elowen gasped; in the clearing, a large silk balloon, like a bulging bloated bubble, rose from a wicker basket to which it was attached by thick cord. Just above the basket hung a grill containing a smoky fire, fuelled by oil-soaked pine cones. A series of ropes tethered the basket to the ground. It took Elowen a few seconds to realise that it was the flying device that Lárwita had shown her in the Hall of Invention—she understood what his plan was.

Lárwita was already stoking up the fire. He worked with an energy and vigour that, considering his spindly frame, amazed Elowen. As she got within earshot she said, 'You want us to fly away?'

He didn't look up from his work. 'Of course, it's our best chance of escape. It was fortunate that I was planning a test flight this morning. It's almost ready. I hope it can carry the weight of all three of us.'

Elowen turned to Diggory. 'Surely you don't think that this is a good idea?'

'I don't see that we have any choice. I'd rather take my chance with this thing than wait for the Redeemers.'

The balloon, filling fast with hot air, bobbed and swayed, causing the basket to strain at its tethers as though impatient to be released. Lárwita drew a knife from his belt and began cutting the ropes. 'Hurry, get into the basket. It's nearly time to take off.'

Elowen hesitated but Diggory nudged her forward. The ravens were still flying above them shouting out their hard call of 'crronk, crronk'. Ghostly horns sounded—distant but growing ever closer.

Elowen clambered into the basket, helped by Diggory who managed the feat with even less grace, toppling in head first. She felt the heat of the fire above her head and the smell of smoke filled her nostrils. Some instinct made her turn and her eyes fell upon her deepest fear. Out of the forest strode Lord Lucien, flanked by several Redeemers. Running behind him in an effort to keep up was a much smaller figure. Elowen squinted. It was Draug, the treacherous Barbeg that had tried to murder her.

Everything slowed. Sounds merged into a faint hum. Lord Lucien filled Elowen's world. He devoured her, consumed her. She shrank, while he seemed as tall as a giant. Since their last meeting, he had haunted her dreams, becoming no longer flesh and blood, but a wraith, a phantom. But he was real, very real. And he had found her.

'There's only one rope left to cut,' said Lárwita, bringing Elowen back to her senses. He jumped into the basket and reached out to hold the knife against the tether.

Lord Lucien and the Redeemers ran towards them. They were only yards away and closing with every second.

'DO IT! CUT THE ROPE!' yelled Diggory, trembling with fear.

Lárwita sliced through the rope: the basket lurched and left the ground. A Redeemer dived at full stretch to reach the basket but it lifted out of his grasp.

The balloon climbed swiftly. Elowen screamed. Diggory

grabbed her arms, too terrified to speak. Only Lárwita remained calm. He whispered, 'It's working, it's actually working.'

Strong wind currents buffeted them as they rose. Elowen feared that the basket was going to tip them out at any moment, but they soon stopped climbing and settled on a steady course. The silence was absolute. It grew bitterly cold, the warmth of the smoky fire lost to them. Elowen's ears ached and the tips of her fingers turned numb.

They climbed clear of the forest. Elowen braved a peek over the edge of the basket. The forest canopy below them was like a carpet of green, with Lord Lucien and the Redeemers only tiny dots in the clearing. Pillars of smoke rose from between the trees; the sanctuary was still burning.

'I don't think that even Lord Lucien can catch us up here,' said Elowen.

'I thought you'd be able to fly yourself, what with you being a *messenger*,' said Diggory.

'Don't be stupid,' she said. 'It's probably all drivel. Rubens lied about so many things.'

'Grunewald was convinced.'

'What do you want *me* to do about it?'

Diggory shrugged. 'Nothing I suppose. Just all seems odd, that's all. It's hard to think of you as some kind of prophet or angel.'

'Don't think of me that way then, I haven't changed. Treat me the same as you always do.'

'I'll try. I did wonder when I'd see you again though. I thought you had disappeared on some adventure. I didn't know Rubens was holding you captive.'

'It was horrible being locked away in that room.'

'It wasn't much fun outside either. Rubens declared a curfew and imposed all sorts of rules. No one dared complain; we were all too scared of the yeomen warders. The Redeemers may have destroyed the sanctuary, but I think that Rubens had already ruined it.'

They approached the mountains, which circled the Vale of Bletsung like a crown. The wind carried them towards a V-shaped gap between two lower peaks.

'Are we going through that gap?' said Elowen, pointing ahead.

'Yes, we won't be able to fly high enough to go over the mountains,' he said. Buffeted by swirling winds, the balloon lost altitude and drifted away from the gap, straight towards a mountain.

'CHANGE COURSE!' shouted Diggory, pointing ahead.

Lárwita stoked the fire. 'I'm trying. To manoeuvre horizontally I have to catch a different wind current. I think that'll work.'

'YOU *THINK*?' said Elowen and Diggory in unison.

'Well, I've never flown this before,' said Lárwita. He threw out the sandbags he had brought as ballast.

Slowly, painfully slowly, the balloon gained height, though it swayed, drawing closer to razor-sharp outcrops of rock. Elowen leaned the other way, willing the balloon to change direction.

Diggory covered his eyes and yelled, 'WE'RE NOT GO-ING TO MAKE IT!'

Elowen clenched her whole body, barely daring to breathe. As they climbed, the wind speed increased, and they floated away from the mountain and towards the gap. With a few feet to spare, the balloon squeezed through.

'We've done it,' said Lárwita, sucking his fingertips. 'The mountains are behind us now, we've escaped.'

'All thanks to you,' said Elowen, giggling with relief.

Lárwita smiled again and blushed.

Diggory exhaled and ran a hand through his red hair. He looked at Lárwita and said, 'You're mad and I don't know how you did this, but it's a miracle.'

They flew free of the ring of mountains. The sky was rich blue and dotted with fluffy clouds, the sun weak but proud. Elowen wondered how pleasant it would be to float upwards, to drift into the welcoming clouds, all as soft as pillows.

Wind carried the balloon east and far below them the landscape changed, the foothills surrendering to moors coloured purple by heather.

As they flew, Lárwita scribbled notes into his little leatherbound book, mouthing the words as he wrote them down.

'What are you writing about?' said Diggory, his teeth chattering.

'I note all of my ideas, thoughts and observations.'

'Why?' said Diggory.

'I want to make sure I don't forget anything. I tried to share my ideas with the experimental philosophers but they ignored me. They never took me seriously. They said my ideas were moonshine.'

Diggory grinned and Elowen thought he was about to make a sarcastic comment but the balloon jolted and they lost altitude. Lárwita tried to stoke up the smoking embers but it had little effect. 'The fire is almost out. We won't stay up for very much longer.'

'You mean we are going down?' said Elowen. The ground already looked much closer.

'Yes, now that the air inside the balloon is cooling we'll lose height,' said Lárwita. 'It might be a rough landing.'

Diggory put his hands together and muttered a prayer they had often recited in the Orphanage. 'O merciful Saviour, hear my woes…'

The wind pummelled them as they dropped, violently swinging the basket from side to side like a pendulum. They hit the ground. The balloon dragged them along and was only brought to rest when it snagged against a wind-twisted tree. The abrupt halt tipped the basket over and all three children fell out, landing on a cushion of springy heather. Elowen landed headfirst and the blow left her dizzy. She rubbed her head and when her vision stabilised, she saw Lárwita and Diggory pulling themselves to their feet. Diggory kicked the basket and grumbled to Lárwita, 'I think you need to work on the landing.'

Lárwita nodded silently, his forehead creased with thought. He adjusted his spectacles and examined the wreckage of the balloon.

Elowen tried to take in their surroundings. The heather-bound moors stretched for miles, broken only by ridges of sandstone. Hills lined the eastern horizon. To the west rose the Jorkull Mountains, their peaks now shrouded in mist.

'Where are we?' said Diggory.

'A few miles east of the mountains so this must be Halgaver,' said Lárwita. 'These are wild and dangerous lands, where cutthroats and bandits roam the countryside. We have to be careful.'

'As long as we are far away from Lord Lucien then I'll be happy,' said Diggory. 'How did he find the sanctuary?'

'Draug,' said Elowen, remembering how the Barbeg had lurked behind Lord Lucien.

Diggory's face flushed with anger. He paced around. 'I should've rung Draug's neck when I had the chance. He must have known a path through the mountains. And he knows about the tunnel between the Barbeg caves and the sanctuary. He'll lead Lord Lucien and the Redeemers to the Gladsheim. The Barbegs won't stand a chance.'

Elowen had not considered that. The Barbegs were now in terrible danger and there was no way to warn them. If Lord Lucien found his way into the Gladsheim, the Barbegs were doomed. A mad idea briefly crossed her mind: to go back to the Gladsheim. But she dismissed it as soon as it took shape. It was too far away and even if they got there, it would surely be too late. It was hopeless.

'Well, where are we to go now?' said Diggory, still unable to keep still. 'I don't think Lárwita's invention will fly again.'

Elowen looked at Lárwita, hoping he might have some answers but he stared at her blankly and pulled out his little book again. He talked to himself as he wrote.

'We can hardly go back,' said Elowen.

'Agreed but where else can we go?' said Diggory.

'What about the Altheart forest?' said Lárwita, without looking up from scribbling in his book.

Diggory shook his head vigorously. 'The Khiltoi live there and they're wild, dangerous savages.'

'The Khiltoi are not savages,' said Lárwita, closing his book. 'They're a noble and ancient tribe, and enemies of Prester John.'

'Aye, but why would they help us?' said Diggory.

Lárwita wiped his nose on his sleeve and shrugged. 'My mother died when I was a child, so I was raised by one of the village *spae-wives*, a seeress who foretold people's futures. She visited the Khiltoi once, long before I was born. She used to tell me stories about them. She said the Khiltoi were a wise and tender-hearted race, and not monsters as the Mother Church preached. Once they were friendly with men, at least they were until Prester John, the *Moljnir* as she called him, came to power.'

'It was a shame that your seeress didn't use her powers to foresee us falling out from the sky in that flying device of yours,' said Diggory.

'That's not how it works,' said Lárwita.

'Well, whatever stories you were told, I'm still not going into the Altheart, and that's flat,' said Diggory.

Fretful at the prospect of plunging into the Altheart, Elowen mulled over another possibility, a possibility that enticed and terrified her in equal measure, a possibility heavy with memories of a promise made to a dying man. She took a deep breath. 'Grunewald believed that finding the Tree of Life was the only way to defeat Prester John. I think we should go to Bai Ulgan.'

Diggory rolled his eyes. 'I for one am not wandering into the Orok lands. We got the map to the sanctuary. We did our bit—if the Illuminati failed that's sad but not our problem.'

'Everything that has happened is our problem,' said Elowen. 'I don't want to live in a world ruled by Prester John and if we can do anything to stop him, I'll do it. I promised Grunewald that I'd go to Bai Ulgan, and I don't intend to break that promise.'

'I think Elowen is right,' said Lárwita, wiping his spectacles with his fingers. 'We cannot go back. We don't know if any Illuminati survived. And while Prester John endures, we'll never be safe. We must do everything we can to defeat him. It's the logical decision.'

Diggory flung his hands up in the air. 'Very well, I'll trust your judgement. The temple of Bai Ulgan—God help us.'

'What about the balloon?' said Lárwita.

'We can hardly take it with us,' said Diggory.

'That's not what I meant,' said Lárwita, wiping his nose. 'If we leave the wreckage here then it will provide a clear sign for anyone to follow. We should try to hide it, bury it perhaps.'

'There's no time for that,' said Diggory. 'We can't wait out here on the moors. We don't have any food, water or shelter. Besides, I've a horrible feeling we've not seen the last of Lord Lucien. I don't want to wait around for him to find us.'

Lárwita bit his lip and did not argue any further.

'Do you know the way, Elowen?' said Diggory.

Elowen remembered Grunewald's plan for the journey to Bai Ulgan. The direction, at least, was clear. She said, 'We head east.'

*

Lord Lucien watched the balloon until it became a dot in the sky, smaller than the formations of noisy ravens that performed acrobatics on the wind. His chest tightened with anger and frustration. The child had escaped him again.

Draug squelched the muddy ground with his foot. 'That girl is a witch. It pains me that she lives still.'

'Your pain is of no concern to me,' said Lord Lucien. His attention was diverted as Redeemers dragged two bloodied men towards him and threw them at his feet. One of the men was tall, with oily black hair and a mud-matted beard. He kept his eyes lowered and he shook with fear. The other prisoner's sharp nose was broken and dripped blood onto his drooping grey moustache. He wore a shabby shirt, linen trousers and a dirty apron. Bruises, nicks and cuts covered his hands; he might have been afraid but he stared at Lord Lucien with proud and defiant eyes.

'These are the only survivors, my Lord,' said one of the Redeemers. 'The bearded man we found hiding in a tree. The other fought savagely and it took three of our brothers to subdue him.'

Lord Lucien sensed the men's fear and enjoyed it. He remembered being a prisoner, cast at the feet of his torturers, pleading for mercy. He wanted these men, all men, to endure the torment he once suffered. 'We do not need prisoners. Hang them both.'

His words had the effect he desired. The moustached man remained silent but his companion cried out, 'Spare me, I beg you. Show mercy.'

'Mercy must be earned. I offer to pardon your sins, and all

I ask for in return is your aid in finding the girl called Elowen Aubyn. Is she known to you?'

The bearded man flinched at the sound of her name. 'Yes, I know her well.'

Lord Lucien smiled his hidden smile. 'And who are you?'

The bearded man shook his head and said nothing.

'Silence only tightens the noose around your neck,' said Lord Lucien, sensing that the man was close to breaking.

The man gulped and licked his dry lips. 'I am Rubens, Grand Master of the Sanctuary.'

Lucien hesitated, a pause that allowed him to hide his surprise at the man's answer. 'That is a bold claim. Why should I believe you?'

'If you do not believe me, believe this,' said the bearded man. He reached inside his coat and pulled out a chain collar made of gold and enamel and set with precious jewels. He passed it to Lord Lucien with the words, 'This is the symbol of my office. Not that it matters now.'

'Rubens of Wapentake, the Mother Church's great foe,' said Lucien with no small satisfaction. It was a name that had mocked Prester John from countless heretical and seditious pamphlets. Lord Lucien dropped the chain collar into the mud. 'You have this day witnessed the true power of Prester John. Surely you see that the Illuminati are defeated?'

Rubens nodded.

'So you are willing to help me?'

Rubens nodded again.

'Good. Elowen Aubyn has escaped the sanctuary. Can you guess where she plans to go?'

Rubens shrugged. 'We had plans but—'

'Hold your tongue, Rubens, you've done enough damage,' said the moustached man. A Redeemer struck him on the back of the head and he pitched forward, his face in the mud.

'Defiance will hasten your death,' said Lucien to the man. He looked at Rubens, who was trembling more violently than before. 'Tell me of the plans you mentioned.'

Rubens ran his hand through his hair. 'We had planned a quest to discover the Four Mysteries. We sought the Tree of Life. It was to begin in Bai Ulgan, where I believe the first Mystery is hidden.'

His answer alarmed Lord Lucien and his mind worked over possibilities, troubling possibilities. He fought to control his voice. 'And you believe that the child will try to complete the quest? It is a perilous journey. The wilds of Gondwana are harsh and dangerous.'

'She is stronger than you know,' said the moustached man, wiping blood from his face.

'Be silent, Jacob,' said Rubens. Then to Lord Lucien he said, 'The child is wilful and headstrong. If she decides to seek Bai Ulgan then yes, perhaps she is foolhardy enough to try.'

Lord Lucien considered that for a moment. 'She escaped with two others, two boys. You know of them?'

'She had two close friends,' said Rubens. 'Both are weak and can give her no protection.'

'Both are weak and yet they escaped when so many of your precious Adepts died,' said Lord Lucien.

'Perhaps they were lucky,' said Rubens.

91

'The manner of their escape had little to do with luck. What do you know of the flying vessel they escaped in?'

He frowned. '*Flying* vessel? Lárwita has a mind full of strange inventions but I am surprised that one of them came to anything.'

Lucien had seen enough men begging for their lives to know the signs of lying. Rubens was a coward, but he was telling the truth. Lord Lucien said, 'You have been a great help, for which you deserve the blessing of God and Prester John. But there is more I must ask of you. It is well known that the Illuminati placed agents and acolytes across many lands. I believe that you know where they can be found. I believe that you will tell me all that you know.'

'I shall tell you everything, if you promise to spare my life,' said Rubens.

'You have my word.'

'Rubens, you cannot do this,' said Jacob the Elder. 'Think of everything we have fought for, everything we have struggled against. If you betray us now there will be no hope left.'

'There is no hope left,' said Rubens. 'And besides, I do not need counsel or approval from a *gardener*. These are matters beyond your meagre understanding.'

'I know enough,' said Jacob the Elder. 'I know you are betraying the Illuminati.'

'Hold your tongue,' said Draug, his impatience bubbling over at last.

'Your actions blacken the name of the Barbeg tribe,' said Jacob the Elder.

'That is a name soon to be forgotten,' said Draug with a

bitter laugh. 'Now that the sanctuary is destroyed I shall guide Lord Lucien to the Forbindelse tunnel that leads to the Gladsheim. When the Redeemers are finished here, it will be the Barbegs' turn to suffer.'

'No, that won't happen,' said Jacob the Elder. Evading the grasping hands of the Redeemers, he sprung at the Barbeg. Draug staggered backwards, holding his throat. Lord Lucien thought at first that the Barbeg had been punched, but blood gushed over and between Draug's fingers. Jacob the Elder clutched a small knife in his hand.

The Redeemers drew their swords and attacked Jacob the Elder but he made one last lunge, thrusting his knife into Rubens's chest. The Master grunted once and fell dead. Before Jacob the Elder moved again, the Redeemers drove their swords through him.

Lord Lucien looked down at the corpses and clenched his fists in frustration. With the Barbeg lost, so was the location of the secret tunnel leading to the Gladsheim. His victory had been tainted. The Barbegs would escape the punishment he had planned for them but their time would come; he would have his revenge one day. More serious was the loss of Rubens. The Illuminati agents scattered across the lands remained hidden for now. Lucien hoped that with the sanctuary destroyed they were leaderless and without direction, and posed no real threat to Prester John's plans. That still left the girl; he had to find the girl.

He looked up at the sky again. The balloon had vanished. The formations of ravens had scattered. The sky was silent. Lord Lucien said to the Redeemers, 'Burn the sanctuary, and do not leave one building standing. And then make preparations to cross back over the mountains. This time, we march east.'

*

Elowen and her companions abandoned the balloon and trudged on in single file, tired, wary and frightened. Lárwita turned around twice, staring mournfully at the wreckage of his creation. Elowen sensed his disappointment at having to leave all his hard work behind.

Their conversations were short and muted. Elowen worried that now they knew she was a messenger, Diggory and Lárwita would treat her differently. She found herself mulling over their every comment, judging every expression, every glance, every hand movement, searching for signs of suspicion or mistrust. Although neither of her friends said or did anything unfriendly or spiteful, Elowen could not ward off the fear that somehow she would be rejected, ostracized. She did not want to be alone.

The grim Halgaver offered the three travellers little cheer and, as though to match their mood, the weather turned against them. Giant dense clouds, like mountains in the sky, loomed overhead and threatened rain. The ceaseless, stampeding wind cried with songs and lamentations it had learnt in the days of the world's dawning.

Elowen and her friends were famished, so when they came across bilberry and crowberry bushes they ate greedily and filled their pockets with berries.

Diggory screwed up his face as he ate. 'Not as sweet as the berries in the Vale of Bletsung.'

'They'll have to do until we find some more food,' said Elowen, wincing at the bitter taste.

'There will be precious little to eat in these parts,' said Lárwita. 'Unless either of you can hunt.'

Elowen laughed, thinking that he was joking. However, one look at Lárwita's impassive face confirmed that he was, as usual, being serious.

'I can't hunt and neither can she,' said Diggory, gesturing to Elowen. 'Anyway, it's not like we have any guns, bows or spears. You can't hunt with your bare hands.'

'Then we'll be very hungry,' said Lárwita.

As the sun sank, the rain threatened by the menacing clouds appeared, steady at first, before turning into a squally downpour. Elowen and her friends plodded on, heads down, helpless against the rain that permeated every gap in their clothing. Elowen and Diggory kept a steady pace but Lárwita, far less used to walking in the wild, lolloped wearily and he slipped and tripped over several times.

'We're going to have to find somewhere to stop for the night,' said Diggory to Elowen. 'Lárwita can't keep going for much longer, and neither can I.'

'I'm tired too,' said Elowen. 'But this land is far too open, we need to find somewhere out of sight first.'

The gently undulating landscape offered little cover. As night fell, they had to make do with sheltering beneath a rocky outcrop. Mercifully protected from the rain, they huddled together for warmth and the exhausted Lárwita fell asleep. Elowen and Diggory talked quietly.

'I thought we'd live in the sanctuary forever,' said Diggory. 'I'd grown used to feeling safe.'

Elowen blew on her hands. 'I suppose I thought the same. I can't believe it's all gone. Do you think any Illuminati survived?'

'I doubt it,' said Diggory. 'If it hadn't been for Hyllebaer I think we'd be dead too. You know I used to think she was such a pain, I never thought she'd sacrifice herself for us like that.'

Elowen drew a sharp intake of breath; she didn't want to talk about Hyllebaer, it was too painful, too soon. Instead, she picked out some berries from her pocket, gave some to Diggory and ate a few herself; despite their unpleasant taste, they blunted the worst edge of her hunger.

'If we weren't safe at the sanctuary,' continued Diggory, his mouth full, 'I can't think of anywhere that'll be safe now. And I'm sure Lord Lucien was searching for *you*.'

Elowen had been thinking much the same. She tried not to dwell on it. 'I often think about Black Francis and Bo. If only they were here—'

'They can't help us now,' said Diggory. 'We're on our own.'

They set off again at first light. It had stopped raining and the early morning fog soon burned away, revealing the line of hills Elowen had spotted on their landing. The path through the hills followed a winding gorge; cliffs towered above them, eroded into terraces by wind and water. Ash trees and ivy colonised the cliffs, their roots driving into the rock to form wide splits and deep gouges.

Elowen and her friends walked cautiously. A peregrine falcon swooped over them with quick, stiff wing-beats and short glides. It circled about the cliffs and then closed its wings and plunged headlong down onto its unseen victim. Strange clouds ghosted across the sky; plump and pink-tinged, their dark bodies sprinkled with vivid bright patches, as though fires raged within them. A wind laced with a coaly smell hurried through the gorge. A sense of watchfulness grew within Elowen, as though eyes unseen tracked their every step.

'We've been to some grim places before but this...' Diggory ran out of words before adding in a whisper to Elowen, 'Are you sure this is the right way?'

The sound of rocks tumbling down from the cliffs silenced her answer.

They all stopped and scanned around. There was no movement other than the swaying trees, no sounds other than the moaning wind.

'A bird,' said Diggory. 'It must have been a bird.'

'No boy, not a bird.'

All three of them jumped. Two men emerged from behind a rock; both carried muskets. They were Nulled and their ragged clothes reeked of sweat and tobacco. One of the men was much taller and skinnier than the other. The smaller man was bearded, with a mouth hooked into a permanent grin, revealing rows of rotten teeth; his right-hand lacked a thumb.

'I think we've found some more cattle,' said the taller man to his companion, an evil glint in his eye.

'Aye,' said the other, dribbling onto his beard as he spoke. He pointed the musket at Elowen.

'Leave us alone,' said Elowen.

Both men sniggered. The taller one said, 'You'd be wise to

keep your mouth shut, little girl. My name is Naglfar, and this is Strolch. You're all coming with us. Old Glum will be very pleased to see you.'

- CHAPTER FIVE -

Old Glum

Naglfar tied the children's hands with rough, frayed rope while Strolch kept his musket trained on them. Naglfar pulled the rope so tightly that Elowen cried out in agony.

Naglfar grinned. 'Don't fret, child. You'll soon get used to pain. Now get moving.'

With muskets prodded into their backs, Elowen and her friends walked forward.

'Who are they?' said Diggory to Elowen and Lárwita. 'And where do you think they're taking us? Do you think they're working for Lord Lucien?'

'No, they are bandits,' said Lárwita.

'Bandits?' said Diggory, fear making his voice rise above a whisper.

'Be quiet, boy, or you'll lose your tongue for good,' said Naglfar.

Elowen and her friends did not take that as an idle threat so remained silent. They reached a stream that cut across the gorge and led to an opening in the cliff side.

'Into the cave,' said Naglfar.

When Elowen's eyes adjusted to the darkness of the cave,

she saw they stood on the shore of a wide pool of still water. A faint orange glow lingered over the far side of the pool. Two small, flat-bottomed boats had been left at the water's edge. They were oval, with the outer layer of each boat made from animal skin, and with a wooden paddle inside.

'Get in the coracle,' said Naglfar to Lárwita and Diggory, untying the ropes around their wrists and pointing to one of the boats. 'The girl comes with me.'

Strolch nudged the boys into the coracle and forced them to sit down. He pushed the little boat out and, with surprising nimbleness, climbed in. He paddled; the gentle swish of his strokes echoed.

'It's your turn, girl,' said Naglfar. Once she had stepped into the other coracle, the bandit pushed it into the water and climbed in. Elowen tried to shift her weight but rocked the boat so much it nearly tipped over.

'Sit still if you know what's good for you,' said the bandit as he paddled. 'This pool is deep and the water cold. Fall in there and I won't come after you. So, what's your name, girl?'

Elowen ignored him.

'Not much of a talker, are you?' he said, scratching himself like a flea-bitten dog.

As they crossed the pool, the orange glow ahead became brighter until Elowen saw Diggory and Lárwita standing on the far shore, guarded by the other bandit.

When Elowen got out of the coracle, Naglfar said, 'Now it's time for you to meet Old Glum.'

The bandits forced Elowen and her friends into a narrow

passage, the ceiling of which was so low they had to crouch to avoid hitting their heads. Eventually the passage opened into a cavern with walls of pale limestone and brownish red conglomerate, all streaked with dried bat droppings. Mineral-rich stalagmites, all coloured black, green, orange and white, rose up from the cave floor like spikes. Phosphorescent fungi ringed the edges of the cavern and glowed faintly with an eerie blue corpse-light. The stench of urine and rotting food lingered in the smoky air. To block out the smell, Elowen tried to breathe through her mouth.

A circle of figures sat around a pit fire: men as scruffy as scarecrows, women with wild hair and painted faces. They spoke with loud, sharp voices punctuated with coarse laughter. The bandits pushed Elowen and her friends towards the gathering.

'Look what we found wandering around outside, Old Glum,' said Naglfar.

The laughter and talking stopped and one of the men stood. He had straggly white hair and his nails reached out like a hawk's talons. He limped towards Elowen and sniffed her with his cold, dripping nose pressed against her cheek. He rubbed his blind, milk-coloured eyes. Licking his lips, he reached his hands towards her. Elowen flinched as he stroked her face with his nails.

'Ah, this one is young,' he said, his breath like the hot blast of a fire. His voice sounded like stone rubbing against stone. He picked at the scabby skin around his Null and added, 'Young is good. Young means we'll fetch a fine price at market.'

'What do you mean *price*?' said Elowen.

Old Glum dug his nails into her cheeks until they almost drew blood. Elowen gasped in surprise and pain.

'You are just cattle and cattle don't speak,' said Old Glum, his blind eyes wide.

The bandits chortled among themselves. Elowen rubbed her cheek. Beside her, Diggory and Lárwita trembled, their faces pallid.

'Naglfar, take the cattle to their pens,' said Old Glum. 'And send word to the Society. Tell them they can collect, if they pay of course.'

'What about the crone?' said Naglfar.

'Fear not, the chains will hold her,' said Old Glum with a dismissive wave of his hands.

Naglfar tied a damp blindfold around Elowen's head; it stuck to her skin like a leech. He grabbed her arm and dragged her along. She had the sense of going in one direction, then another and then another, as though they were following a maze. She jammed her foot in a hole and tripped, scraping her hands and arms on rough edges of rock as she fell. She yelled out in pain but was yanked to her feet and pushed forward again.

When Elowen was finally pulled to a halt and the blindfold ripped away, she found herself in a small cave. A single torch provided the only light and a foul reek made her retch. Water dripped down onto her head. Loose stones and bones littered the slippery floor. Lárwita and Diggory stood beside her, shivering with fear.

'Enjoy your lodgings, children,' said Naglfar as, to Elowen's surprise, he untied the rope around their hands. 'Don't try to escape. There are no bars and no guards, but this cave is deep beneath the earth. You are trapped down here, my young friends.'

With that, he left them. When the sound of the bandit's heavy footsteps had faded, Diggory said, 'How are we going to get out of this? We would've been better off taking our chances with the Redeemers.'

'Don't be stupid,' said Elowen. 'If the Redeemers had us we'd already be dead.'

'We don't know the intentions of these bandits yet,' said Lárwita.

'I think we can be fairly sure they're not trying to *help* us,' said Diggory.

'We're in enough trouble as it is without arguing among ourselves,' said Elowen. 'Let's concentrate on getting out of this place.'

'There is no escape from here, child.'

They all jumped. The croaky voice came from a dark corner of the cave. It belonged to an old woman with a nose that bent down and a chin that curved up. She had tangled, greasy hair and a patchy white beard. Sharp brown nails tipped her fingers and her eyes were half-hidden beneath thick bushy brows. Rusted shackles chained to the floor clasped her arms and legs.

Lárwita backed away and whimpered. 'I think she's Baba Yaga, the witch of the woods, the child-eater.'

The old woman laughed so hard that the shackles holding her arms and legs rattled like a demented musical instrument. 'Even in the deepest cave this tale follows me. Yes, I am Baba Yaga. But you are in no danger from me. Your accents are strange. Are you from foreign lands?'

103

Elowen nodded but did not feel comfortable telling her more than that.

Baba Yaga eyed her suspiciously. 'You are a strange one, girl, very strange. A *Volkhvy* I deem.'

Elowen said, 'I don't know what you—'

'So you wish to escape, yes? How, may I ask?'

Elowen put her hands on her hips. 'We'll think of something.'

Baba Yaga shook her head. 'The wretch that brought you here may have the wit of a beetle but in one thing he spoke the truth: we are deep down here and outside this cave there is only darkness, unless you know the way, which of course none of you do.'

'We'll find a way,' said Elowen. 'We've been in worse situations than this and survived.'

Baba Yaga smiled strangely. 'One wrong turn in the tunnels outside this cave and you will find yourself plunging down into a bottomless chasm. There is no need for gates or bars here.'

'Then why are you in chains?' said Diggory, pointing an accusing finger at her.

Baba Yaga laughed again. 'I am in chains because I know the way out. I offer you a bargain. If you release me, I will lead you to safety and can help you to reach wherever it is you are trying to get to.'

'This is a trick, Elowen,' said Lárwita.

'Lárwita is right,' said Diggory. 'If we let her go we're as good as dead.'

Elowen hesitated. Baba Yaga *did* look terrifying, but there was something else about her, something beyond her terrifying appearance, something intriguing. The words of Jacob the Elder came back to her: *sometimes fair words and fair countenance hide a dark purpose.* She wondered if the opposite was true too. Baba Yaga was perilous, Elowen sensed that, but perilous in the same way as the sea, or the bitter north wind. A force of nature rather than a sinister being. And she was not lying, of that Elowen was certain. 'No, she won't hurt us. She's our only chance of getting out of here. We must release her.'

The boys looked alarmed but Lárwita shrugged. 'I still think it's a mistake but I'll help you. Those shackles are rusty. They'll break if we strike them with one of the rocks on the ground.'

They did as he suggested and after repeated blows, the shackles smashed, showering the cave floor with rust. Baba Yaga shook off the broken shackles and sprung to her feet so swiftly that Elowen and her companions retreated in alarm.

'Free at last,' said Baba Yaga. She stretched her arms and legs, and a malevolent smile formed on her lips. 'Now that I am free I find that I am hungry. And three children, abandoned in a cave, far from help—'

'She'll kill us all,' said Lárwita. 'I warned you.'

Diggory stood in front of Elowen, his fists raised. 'You take one step towards us and you'll be sorry, witch.'

Baba Yaga threw her head back in laughter. 'Forgive my jest. The ignorant tell many stories—pay them no heed. Yes, those who cross me have reason to fear me, but I do not *eat children*. I am not a monster. I am of the forest and the forest is of me. And it is to the forest that I must return.

105

I stand in your debt, girl. You made the decision to free me. That debt I shall not fail to repay.'

Diggory gave Baba Yaga a sideways glance. 'We're not free yet though. We're still stuck in this damn cave.'

Baba Yaga pulled the torch from the wall. The flames writhed around her head and for a second she resembled a demon, wild and terrible, bathed in the sparkling light of fire. 'I promised to show you the way out and I always keep my word. Those who imprisoned me are about to learn the true cost of their actions. Follow me.'

*

Baba Yaga scuttled through the tunnels with the speed and dexterity of a spider. Elowen walked closely behind her; Diggory and Lárwita kept their distance.

'Can I ask you a question?' said Elowen.

'You just have, child,' said Baba Yaga without turning. 'Be wary of questions—you may not be ready for the answers. Wisdom ripens with age and cannot be hurried.'

'I see,' said Elowen, confused by Baba Yaga's response. 'Who is Old Glum and how did he capture you?'

'That is two questions, girl, but you find me in good humour so I will answer you,' said Baba Yaga. 'Old Glum is a slave trader. His cutthroats snare unwary travellers and sell them to the Society, which is always hungry for slaves. Such would have been your fate, had you not been blessed with the great fortune of meeting me.'

'What is the Society?' said Elowen.

'The Society for the Propagation of Pious Labour,' said

Lárwita, joining in the conversation. 'They're the slave traders of the Mother Church, sanctioned by Prester John. They collect slaves for the pits and mines of Gorefayne.'

'You speak the truth, boy,' said Baba Yaga. 'As to how I was caught in the net of Old Glum…well, it is no mystery. I have few dealings with the folk of the forest villages but on occasions I share with them my wisdom and my skill in the lore of animals, plants and healing. It happened that after curing a woodman's daughter of a fearsome fever, I was rewarded with a jug of strong ale. Alas, after a rare moment of overindulgence I fell asleep in the garden of my little hut. Some of Old Glum's followers were passing through the forest and fell upon me.'

As Baba Yaga spoke, Elowen caught a glimpse of a lonely life full of bitterness and anger. Elowen pitied her. She had been so frightened of Baba Yaga when they first met; she guessed that was how everyone reacted when they saw her.

The tunnel reached a level stretch, with walls smoothed by underground rivers long run dry. Evil-smelling vapours rose from barely perceptible cracks in the tunnel floor. Baba Yaga stopped and crouched down. Footsteps. A hacking cough. Into the flickering light came the shape of a man: it was Naglfar.

He stopped as soon as he saw Baba Yaga. 'How the hell—'

Baba Yaga jumped upon him. In a single motion, she broke his neck. His bones cracked like dry sticks snapping. The bandit fell limply.

Elowen had seen dead bodies before but the sudden violence of Naglfar's death left her sick and faint. Lárwita stood with his mouth wide open in shock. Diggory was stony faced, as though trying to block out what he had witnessed.

Baba Yaga knelt over the corpse like a cat toying with a mouse. She glanced up at Elowen and saw the look of disgust on her face. 'Believe me, I take no pleasure in killing.'

Elowen and her friends followed Baba Yaga until they emerged into the malodorous, fungi-ringed cavern where they had first met Old Glum, and there he sat again, surrounded by the other bandits. The smoky fire hissed and crackled. The stalagmites glistened like the teeth of a monstrous mouth.

When the bandits saw Elowen and her companions they sprang to their feet and grabbed muskets and swords. Baba Yaga pushed the three children behind her.

'So, Baba Yaga, you have escaped your cage,' said Old Glum, spitting out the last word, his blind eyes still trained on the ground. 'A shame, you might have fetched a good price at market. It is a waste but now you must die.'

Old Glum's followers cackled at his words but Baba Yaga did not retreat. 'There is no need for bloodshed here. I ask that you stand aside and let us go. It would be most unwise and dangerous to refuse.'

Old Glum laughed. 'You are in no position to threaten us.'

'So be it,' said Baba Yaga, shaking her head. She said to Elowen and the boys, 'Lie on the ground, and cover your ears.'

They obeyed but even with her ears covered, Elowen still heard the mocking words of Old Glum. 'You're a cruel one, witch, dragging these children out to share your fate, for they'll die with you.'

'No,' said Baba Yaga. 'It is not we that shall die this day.'

Baba Yaga raised her hands and the air around her shimmered; golden threads formed in wide circles, like ripples on water. The threads reached an incandescence that hurt Elowen's eyes before they disappeared. The fire died and darkness filled the cavern; the blue light of the fungi vanished. Muskets fired and lead balls whizzed through the air. Screams of pain and fear swallowed all other sounds. Elowen pushed her hands tightly against her ears, hoping to block out the screams but it was no good. Diggory quailed and pressed against her. The fire exploded back into life with a rush of flame and smoke, and light returned to the cavern. The bodies of the bandits lay contorted, broken. Only Baba Yaga remained standing. Blood dripped from her fingers like crimson rain. She was breathing heavily and the age lines on her face had deepened.

Elowen regarded Baba Yaga in horror. 'What…what have you done?'

'They refused to let us go. I did what was necessary.'

Old Glum was still alive. Baba Yaga pulled him to his feet.

'You're spawn of the devil,' he said, struggling to get free of the grip Baba Yaga had on his arm. 'I should've cut your throat when I had the chance.'

'Yes, that would have been wise,' said Baba Yaga. 'But it is too late now.'

'Are you going to kill me?'

'That is what you deserve. Instead, I shall leave you here alone. Then you will know the despair of imprisonment, a

109

despair you have inflicted upon countless others. That is my mercy.'

The impact of Baba Yaga's words was immediate and Old Glum moaned, 'This isn't mercy. I'll die of hunger and thirst. Kill me now, I beg you.'

Baba Yaga released her grip on him and he fell down onto his knees. She turned to Elowen and the boys. 'Get up now. We must go.'

They left Old Glum on the ground, crying and groaning. Baba Yaga led them back to the dark pool. She knelt and washed her bloodstained hands in the water. They managed to use the coracles to cross the pool. Elowen feared they would tip over but, more by luck than skill, they reached the far side. Once across, Baba Yaga smashed the coracles to put them beyond use and left the shattered pieces of wood and animal skin to float on the water.

As they emerged from the mouth of the cave, Elowen enjoyed the feeling of cool, fresh air on her face again. It was dawn, crisp and cold with the sun faint in the hazy sky. Mist rose from the stream that fed the cave pool. Frost gilded the grass. After long hours in the dark cave, Elowen squinted in the bright light and the frigid air made her lungs ache. She remembered that she was hungry, ravenously hungry, and thirsty too. She drank from the stream, scooping up handfuls of icy water with both hands. Lárwita and Diggory did likewise.

Looking tired and drained, Baba Yaga stood with her arms outstretched and eyes closed, chanting.

'What's she doing?' said Diggory, as he stood and wiped his mouth.

110

'I have no idea,' said Elowen.

'I don't think we should trust her,' said Lárwita, removing his spectacles for a moment and rubbing the bridge of his nose. 'You saw what she did to those people in the cave.'

Diggory grunted agreement.

'She saved our lives,' said Elowen. She was not sure why she was defending Baba Yaga but it seemed just. 'We'd never have escaped Old Glum without her.'

Diggory was about to say something when the sound of a horse's hooves silenced him. A single horseman approached them at a slow trot. He wore a padded, quilted jacket strengthened with strips of metal. A soldier ran behind him, dressed in a long red coat, a fur-trimmed hat and black boots, and with a bandolier full of ammunition slung across his chest. His weapons were fierce: a long crescent-shaped axe, a matchlock pistol and a sabre.

'My name is Nemal Chelovek, lieutenant of the Society,' said the horseman as he pulled his steed to a halt and dismounted. More heavily armed soldiers appeared and formed a line behind Chelovek. 'I did not fully believe Old Glum's message but now I see with my own eyes that it is true. Baba Yaga has been captured.'

Baba Yaga stretched out her arms. 'Captured you say? Do you see any chains?'

Chelovek hesitated, unnerved by Baba Yaga's confidence. He looked around. 'Where is Old Glum? And where are his men?'

'Where is Old Glum?' repeated Baba Yaga. She pointed back into the cave. 'Go in there and you will find him and what remains of his band of cutthroats.'

111

Chelovek's eyes narrowed and he rubbed the Null in his forehead. 'Cursed witch. The Society knows how to deal with your kind. Seize them!'

The soldiers advanced. Diggory and Lárwita cried out in fear. More soldiers had sneaked across from the other side of the little stream. They grabbed the two boys.

'Run, child,' Baba Yaga ordered Elowen, as the soldiers approached. 'Run and I shall follow you.'

Elowen protested. 'But—'

'Just run,' said Baba Yaga and she pushed her away. Elowen ran across the stream. The soldiers dragged Diggory and Lárwita away. The boys kicked and punched their captors in vain. Elowen stopped. She wanted to try to help her friends but the voice of Baba Yaga overpowered all other sounds.

'RUN, CHILD!'

Elowen heard Diggory and Lárwita calling out her name. But with tears burning her eyes, she obeyed Baba Yaga's command and ran. A clammy, choking fog rose from the ground, as though the earth beneath her feet steamed. Blinded by the fog, she stopped running. She dared not speak. Baba Yaga emerged from the fog. She seemed older somehow, with veins showing beneath her grey, almost translucent skin.

'We must hurry,' said Baba Yaga. 'This fog is of my own making but it will not endure for long.'

Elowen's heart raced with panic. 'What about Diggory and Lárwita? We have to go back and rescue them.'

'No,' said Baba Yaga. 'It is far too dangerous.'

'But you can help them, you're strong—'

112

'My strength is drained and I am too weary. There are some battles you cannot win.'

'We can't abandon them,' said Elowen as tears spilled down her cheeks. 'They're my friends.'

'Then they will understand,' said Baba Yaga. 'If you go back for your friends you will be captured. Do not make that mistake. You will not help them by being killed. Indeed, you will not survive for long in these lands without my help. I offered you a bargain in the caves and I still stand in your debt. I do not believe that coincidence led you to me. I have seen many troubling signs and portents of late. There are strange winds, strange lights in the sky and whispers from ancestors long forgotten. The world is changing. I sense you are part of this mystery. My home is not far, less than a day's march. Will you join me?'

Still thinking of Lárwita and Diggory, Elowen hesitated. To abandon her friends was a cowardly betrayal but she could not help them now. She wiped hot tears from her eyes and whispered, 'Very well, I'll come with you.'

CHAPTER SIX

The Hut of Baba Yaga

Elowen followed Baba Yaga through the winding gorge. The fog dispersed to leave a bright morning cooled by a lively wind. Baba Yaga leapt from rock to rock in a zigzag course and urged Elowen to do the same. 'If we are being pursued, it will prove hard for any trackers to follow our route if we don't leave footprints. These rocks betray less trace of our steps.'

'Do you think we are being *pursued*?' said Elowen.

Baba Yaga did not reply.

By midday, they came to the end of the gorge and went along a track that branched southwards towards the edges of a forest. Elowen was feeling tired and her gut ached with hunger; worse was the knowledge that her every step took her further away from Lárwita and Diggory. She asked Baba Yaga, 'Can't we rest for a little while?'

'No, not here. This is the most northerly tip of the Altheart. My hut is not far, we shall be safer there. You do not want to be wandering around this part of the forest when night falls. There are restless spirits here.'

Baba Yaga did not elaborate on those dark warnings as they passed into the forest. They walked among young sil-

114

ver birches with slender warty branches and bright yellow leaves that glowed in the clean sunshine. Elowen brushed a hand against the trunk of a birch, enjoying the touch of smooth bark. The ground beneath Elowen's feet was soft with moss and leaf-mould. Chaffinches and pipits busied themselves by skipping from branch to branch and tree to tree. A wolf howled, distant and mournful. It sparked a memory of Ulfur, and not for the first time she wished that the wolf was padding alongside her.

As they trekked on, the forest changed: the silver birches were older, their bark fissured with rugged cracks. Dead trees stood stripped of leaves and with bracket fungus clinging to their trunks; mouldering, insect-ridden, long-fallen trunks lay partially swallowed by the moist earth. Witches' brooms, dense growths of tangled twigs, hung in the branches like ghostly bird's-nests. Saplings of oak and beech pushed their way through the leaf-mould, like eager children jostling their elders. Three statues, all green with moss, lurked amid the trees. They portrayed deities long silent and forgotten. Two statues had large gouges ripped out of them: signs of violent, deliberate action. The third was intact and it represented a female figure with a plain, geometric face framed by multiple necklaces. The figure's hands rested on her protruding belly.

'We are close now to my hut, very close,' said Baba Yaga.

The trees thinned and, through the gaps between the trunks, Elowen spied a windowless hut, built upon supports made from tree stumps cut at the height of eight feet. The stumps, with their wide-spreading roots, reminded Elowen of chicken legs. A thatched roof, pyramid-shaped with a

115

chimney peeking out from its apex, perched on the hut like an ill-fitting hat. Around the hut ran a fence constructed from intertwined animal bones, interrupted only by a small gate, also made from bones.

'Welcome to my home,' said Baba Yaga, a smile creasing her face. She beckoned Elowen towards the hut and opened the gate. The entrance to the hut was through a trapdoor on its base, reached by a rickety ladder. Baba Yaga went first, scuttling up the ladder. Gingerly, Elowen followed.

The hut consisted of one large room. A wooden-framed loom stood at one end of the room and various items were strewn upon the floor, such as straw corn dollies, feathers, balls of string, pebbles, leaves and branches. Ancient leather-bound books stood on a shelf that bowed under their weight. Above the cold fireplace hung a tapestry showing symbols of the moon's three phases: waxing, full and waning. A birch broom stood in the far corner of the hut and positioned against it were a clay wine amphora and a wooden staff, more like a weapon than a walking stick. A single table stood next to the trapdoor opening and upon it lay a jug of water, two empty ale tankards and a small wicker basket, as well as several plates sprinkled thinly with nuts and rotten fruit.

'It is good to be home,' said Baba Yaga. 'And my friend is here waiting for me.'

A black cat lay asleep on the floor. As Elowen and Baba Yaga climbed into the room it woke up. It was thin, with its backbone, hips and shoulders prominent, and one of its eyes was silver-blue and blind. With a tenderness that surprised Elowen, Baba Yaga stroked the cat and whispered

116

soothing words. It gazed at Elowen with a sneaky, intelligent expression before yawning and curling up to sleep again.

Baba Yaga lit the fire, filling the room with welcome light and warmth. She picked up the jug and wicker basket from the table. 'I must leave you for a short time. I shall return soon with fresh water and food. Please, rest now and warm yourself by the fire.'

Baba Yaga disappeared through the trapdoor. Elowen sat cross-legged on the floor. She found the hut comforting, as though she belonged there. She ran her fingers against the birch planks that formed the walls; she could sense a little of the life that Baba Yaga lived. Elowen tasted the loneliness of long weeks, long months, without company. Days passing in empty units of time; the sun rose and set, the moon waxed and waned, and neither made comment on her life.

But it did not have to be so. Elowen discerned the warmth within Baba Yaga, deeply hidden though it was, like a candle locked inside a grim dungeon, left with barely enough air to stop it from dying. Elowen heard the taunts, felt the pain of stones thrown against skin, and the punches and the kicks. And she tasted the loneliness, the despair, which slowly fermented into anger and a bitter hatred of other people.

The trapdoor opened and Baba Yaga clambered back into the room. Foraged food filled her wicker basket and water splashed over the jug's brim. The cat peered up with interest.

'In autumn the forest provides a bountiful harvest,' said

117

Baba Yaga as she held up the basket for Elowen to see the food inside: sloes, wild cherries, sweet chestnuts, puffball mushrooms and honey fungus.

Baba Yaga prepared a meal and they drank the cold water, which flowed down Elowen's throat sweeter than any wine. A little strength returned to her body as she ate but her sense of comfort only increased her feelings of guilt. She had abandoned Diggory and Lárwita; they would not be eating, they would not be somewhere warm.

'Worry is written all over your face,' said Baba Yaga. 'You are thinking of your friends.'

Elowen nodded. The cat got up, stretched and rubbed around her legs.

'You made the correct choice,' said Baba Yaga. 'If you had gone back then you too would have been captured.'

'It still feels as though I betrayed them,' said Elowen. The very idea of her being a messenger seemed like mockery. She was not worthy of it. Her first real test and she had failed. She rubbed the pendant that hung around her neck. Her mother would not have run away, she would not have abandoned her friends. Elowen was sure of that and the thought made her more ashamed of her actions. *You are nothing like your mother, remember that.*

'Harden your heart. What is done cannot be undone.'

'But what will become of them?' said Elowen, as the cat snuggled down on her lap.

Baba Yaga wiped her fingers on her chest and yawned, signposting her boredom with the conversation. 'I expect they will be taken to the slave market at Rynokgorod.'

'The *slave* market?'

Baba Yaga shuffled closed to the fire. 'Yes, these are cruel times. Your friends are far beyond my aid.'

'But you're strong and powerful, if you—'

'They are lost,' said Baba Yaga, her voice rising to a shout. She took a deep breath and softened her tone. 'That is painful for you to accept, but your friends are gone and you will not see them again.'

'I don't believe that,' said Elowen.

'Then you are deluding yourself,' said Baba Yaga jabbing a finger towards Elowen to reinforce her point. 'That is a weakness. Your kind cannot afford to be weak.'

'What do you mean, *your kind*?'

Baba Yaga grinned, revealing her blackened teeth. 'From the moment I first saw you I knew you were a *Volkhvy*, an Adept as you say in the Common Tongue. Do you have the skill of *Linking*?'

Elowen nodded.

'It is as I thought. Rare such a skill is, especially in these troubled times. Many beasts and birds now resist Linking, being too suspicious, too frightened of humans. But a powerful effect on the Earthsoul you have, very powerful. And you could be more powerful still, with my guidance.'

'Your guidance?'

Baba Yaga nodded. 'You know of the Earthsoul, but you do not yet know how to wield its power, how to make it follow your commands. You may have moments when you are at one with the Earthsoul but they are fleeting only. I shall show you how to control the Earthsoul, so that the *zolotyye niti*, the threads of gold, dance to your song. Much you could learn from me.'

119

'I've had tutors before,' said Elowen, remembering the malign influence of Rubens. The cat grew tired of Elowen and returned to its previous position to sleep.

'But not like me,' said Baba Yaga. 'Eldar blood flows through my veins. Stay with me, live here and I shall teach you all that I know.'

'Why do you want to help me?' said Elowen.

Baba Yaga stood, grunting with the effort. 'The only question that matters is, do you accept my offer?'

Despite her misgivings, Elowen was too intrigued to refuse.

*

Elowen's training began the next day. When Baba Yaga roused her at dawn, Elowen felt as though a hundred hours sleep would not be enough to cure her tiredness. After a hastily eaten breakfast of nuts and berries, Baba Yaga ushered Elowen down the trapdoor. Once outside, the icy air took Elowen's breath away and she rubbed her arms to keep warm. The sun remained a weak glow, colouring the sky in watery crimson light. The trees that circled Baba Yaga's hut were alive with squawking birds.

'It is time to begin, child,' said Baba Yaga, her movements sprightly and fresh. She crouched down in a patch of bare soil and with her fingers drew a wide circle around her. She marked out four quarter-marks, like the directional points on a compass.

'What are you doing?' said Elowen, stifling a yawn.

'Helping you to take the first step,' said Baba Yaga. She

120

stepped out of the circle. 'You must learn to open yourself to the world around you, only then can you feel the Earth-soul with every inch of your being and only then can you guide its power. Your five senses are invaluable but they alone are not enough to comprehend the complexity of this world. Come, stand inside the circle, and do as I say.'

Still shivering from the cold and feeling a little foolish, Elowen stepped inside the circle.

'Settle your body,' said Baba Yaga, her voice softer than before. 'Feel the weight of your feet on the ground, take a deep breath and feel the air flow into your body.'

Elowen did so and a lightness came to her arms and legs.

'Close your eyes and imagine you are standing on the edge of a still pond,' continued Baba Yaga. 'Look at the surface of the pond. Now, imagine a small stone dropping into the water. As the ripples run out from where the stone dropped, follow them with your eyes.'

Elowen saw the pond and the sparkling ripples. Baba Ya-ga's voice was distant, like a voice heard in a dream. 'Follow the ripples, *smell* them. Reach out with your hearing, listen to the ripples as they slide across the surface.'

As Elowen did so, the ripples responded to her thoughts, her senses. Only once had she experienced anything similar: on the battlefield of the Gladsheim.

'Sense the pond becoming calm again,' commanded the voice of Baba Yaga. 'Watch as it vanishes, and feel your feet back on the ground. Feel the trees around you. Open your eyes.'

Elowen was back in the forest, standing in the circle beside the hut. Faint golden threads flowed around the trees.

121

Baba Yaga nodded. 'Only when you open your senses and focus your body and mind will the Earthsoul reveal its secrets to you. To do this you must learn to train yourself to be stronger. It is my duty to instruct you.'

'You want me to train like a warrior?' said Elowen.

'Being a warrior is not the same as being a *Volkhvy*. I will teach you how to survive, how to hone your senses and reactions, how to harden yourself. I am old but my body is strong and you must be strong too. You can find power through the Earthsoul but if you are not strong you will not long endure.'

'I'm strong,' said Elowen. 'I've survived more dangers than you know.'

'We shall see,' said Baba Yaga and she chuckled to herself in a manner that irritated Elowen. She scratched her wispy beard, and from the ground picked up a small birch twig. She held it up to Elowen. 'I have a little test for you, child. In a moment I will drop this and you must try to catch it with two fingers.'

'Why?'

A shadow of anger passed over Baba Yaga's face. 'Ask no questions—do as I instruct.'

Elowen realised arguing with Baba Yaga was pointless, so she readied herself to catch the twig, tensing her muscles and focusing her concentration. She did not want to fail and give Baba Yaga another opportunity to criticize her.

As soon as Baba Yaga dropped the twig, Elowen reached for it; she touched it but it slipped through her fingers and fell. To Elowen's annoyance, Baba Yaga laughed. 'There, you were far too slow.'

'Try it again,' said Elowen, her embarrassment turning to anger. 'I'll catch it next time.'

'Perhaps you will, perhaps you won't. That is not the point. A *Volkhvy* in true control of her body would not need a second chance.'

Elowen picked up the twig. 'You try it if you're so clever.'

'Very well. But first break the twig in two.'

'But that'll make it impossible.'

'Do as I tell you, child.'

Elowen did so, snapping the twig to be left with a piece measuring barely an inch.

'Good, now go ahead,' said Baba Yaga. To Elowen's surprise, she closed her eyes. Elowen paused for a moment and took half a step back: her anger with Baba Yaga mounted and she wanted to make the task as difficult for her as possible. Elowen lowered her hand, giving Baba Yaga less time to react, and dropped the twig.

With a movement so quick Elowen barely saw it, Baba Yaga snatched the twig with two fingers. Elowen said, 'How did you do that?'

Baba Yaga opened her eyes. 'That is what I shall show you, child.'

In the days that followed, Baba Yaga forced Elowen to endure a rigorous routine. Every day began with a modest breakfast and a series of physical tests: stretching, bending and twisting, and fighting with wooden staffs. At first Elowen found these tests a chore and her muscles ached after each session, but when a few days had passed, and she had grown used to the effort, she discovered an agility and strength she never knew she possessed.

Once each day's physical tests were completed, and morning was turning into afternoon, Baba Yaga led her into the forest. Elowen learnt how to move without attracting attention: moving past obstacles rather than over them to avoid silhouetting herself, using background noise like the wind and rain to cover the sound of her steps, and how to stay in the deepest part of the shadows to conceal herself. Baba Yaga taught her to listen and look around slowly to detect signs of hostile movement, and how to mask her smell by the use of aromatic herbs.

Baba Yaga showed Elowen how to sense the weather's changing moods by the smell and direction of the wind, or by the shifting shape and colours of clouds. She taught her about the sounds and calls of animals and beasts. Elowen watched spiders spinning webs to understand how they were shaped; she watched squirrels burying nuts for their winter store. Baba Yaga allowed Elowen little chance to rest. Her constant refrain was, 'Work harder! Practise and practise again, only that way will you learn!'

The training heightened her *Linking* ability, increasing her awareness of the forest being alive, of having different moods and rhythms. She felt the movements in the world around her as though they were connected to her own body. At night, her dreams were more vivid than any she had experienced before, and even during the waking hours, fleeting visions came to her: wide skies, distant mountains and hills; salty air, the taste of dust on her lips. She said nothing of these visions to Baba Yaga but they happened every day, and each time a little more intense.

Baba Yaga continued to test Elowen by asking her to

catch the twig again. Seven days after her first attempt, she succeeded.

'See, I caught it,' said Elowen, holding the twig up with two fingers as proof of her achievement.

However, Baba Yaga gave no praise. 'It is a start, but I shall only be satisfied when you can catch it blindfolded.'

'Blindfolded?' said Elowen. 'But that's impossible.'

'Difficult I grant you, but impossible?' said Baba Yaga, her eyebrows raised in a quizzical expression. 'Were my eyes not closed when I caught the twig? Did you not witness that?'

Elowen conceded that she had.

'Well in that case you still have much more to learn. But already I see a new strength in you, do you not agree?'

'I *am* starting to feel different. My senses are sharper, I have more energy. The stretching and bending helps.'

Baba Yaga laughed. 'Stretching and bending! I can only imagine how upset the ancient Eldar shamans would be to hear their disciplines described thus. Many centuries ago, the Eldar perfected these practices, practices driven and shaped by the Earthsoul. In their turn, the Adepts adopted them too, greatly improving their strength and understanding of the Earthsoul. Of course, the practices I share with you are but the smallest fragment of the main teachings, but what you learn from me will be enough.'

*

The days passed swiftly. Days crammed with intense training. Elowen's body ached and her mind felt stretched by so

125

many new ideas. As she awoke one morning, ready to embark on another bout of strenuous exercises, she realised it had been ten days since she had arrived at Baba Yaga's hut. Ten days. As they often did, her thoughts returned to Diggory and Lárwita. Where were they now? Were they still alive?

'What is troubling you, child?' said Baba Yaga as she led Elowen out into the garden, traipsing over grass turned white by the frost.

'Nothing, I'm fine,' said Elowen. Baba Yaga had made her feelings on the fate of Diggory and Lárwita very clear and Elowen was reluctant to raise the subject again.

Baba Yaga confronted her with another test. She pulled out a filthy blindfold from her pocket and wrapped it around Elowen's head. An uncomfortable memory of the caves of Old Glum flashed to Elowen, but she controlled it and pushed it to the back of her mind.

'It is time for you to see further,' said Baba Yaga.

'But what can I see with a blindfold on?' said Elowen.

'You have other senses. Remember the pond. Remember the ripples. You saw them with your eyes closed. Use what I have taught you. The Earthsoul can reveal many things.'

Elowen tried. She concentrated on settling her body, feeling the gentle caress of the golden threads of the Earthsoul around her. A mouse scuttled through the grass; a bird nibbled a birch seed. And despite the blindfold, she found she could see, not normal sight but a vision, murky at first, as though hidden by smoke, but slowly clearing. The world around her vanished, replaced by other sounds, smells and sights: a city of ugly wooden buildings, dusty shacks and

126

market stalls, all watched over by a citadel and a cathedral of many golden domes.

The vision drew her to a market square. Part of it was ring-fenced by ropes. Soldiers prowled outside the ropes; from their red coats, fur-trimmed hats, black boots and long crescent-shaped axes, Elowen recognised them as soldiers of the Society. Contained within the ropes were dozens of prisoners. She scanned the sad, lonely, frightened faces. Then, she saw Lárwita and Diggory. Their clothes had been reduced to torn rags. Mud stuck to their hair and their faces were black with bruises and dried blood.

Like the light of a candle extinguished by a sudden draught, the vision dispersed. Elowen ripped off the blindfold. She was still standing in the forest. Baba Yaga stood opposite, her face impassive, her eyes hard.

'I saw Lárwita and Diggory,' said Elowen, struggling to catch her breath. She described in detail what she had seen.

'I believe your vision showed you the city of Rynokgorod. I saw it once, many years ago.'

'It was too real for a dream. Lárwita and Diggory are in terrible danger.'

Baba Yaga folded her arms and exhaled slowly, her breath steaming. 'You knew that already.'

'But it's different now. I've seen them with my own eyes. We must do something. We have to save them.'

'Save them?' said Baba Yaga. 'That is nonsense. We cannot help them.'

'I don't believe that,' said Elowen. She dropped the blindfold. 'I'm going to Rynokgorod, whether you help me or not.'

Baba Yaga brought her hands together. 'Child, if you leave now you are making a terrible mistake. You may be a Volkhvy but you still have much to learn and if you find your friends you will not be able to help them.'

'You could come with me,' said Elowen, hoping very much that she would.

'This is my home and this is where I belong,' said Baba Yaga, folding her arms in front of her chest. 'The rest of the world is cruel and I want no part of it.'

'But what about the bargain? You promised to help me.'

'That I have done and I would continue to do so. But if you choose to leave, you must go alone.'

Elowen absorbed the implications of Baba Yaga's words. Alone. Fear rolled her stomach over. Could she survive alone? Could she save her friends? She did not know. But she was certain she had to try, even if she risked her own life to do so.

CHAPTER SEVEN

Pilgrimage

E lowen did not delay her departure. She returned to the hut straight away and gathered her few belongings. Baba Yaga followed her and, after gesturing towards the table, said, 'Take food for your journey.'

'Thank you,' said Elowen, trying to avoid her wounded gaze. She filled her pockets with handfuls of nuts, mushrooms and berries. Elowen was convinced she had made the right choice, but guilt at leaving Baba Yaga alone nagged her; it seemed ungrateful, callous. Elowen opened her mouth to say something but failed to find any words strong enough to express how she felt.

'You might as well take these as I have no use for them,' said Baba Yaga as she passed Elowen a few silver coins. 'To reach Rynokgorod, you must head north-east from here. Avoid any village you see. The forest-dwellers are suspicious of strangers. Once you are clear of the forest you will find a road leading east to the city.'

Baba Yaga picked up the wooden staff that rested in the corner of the hut. She also grabbed a scallop shell that lay on the table. She pushed them both into Elowen's hands. 'Travel in the guise of a pilgrim. If you encounter trouble, the staff may prove useful as a weapon too. Many pilgrims travel to Rynokgorod and if you travel as one of them you will arouse less suspicion.'

'Why do pilgrims go to Rynokgorod?'

Baba Yaga's expression soured. 'It is said the bones of a saint rest in the cathedral. Even in these dangerous times pilgrims travel from many lands to seek healing and good fortune. Walking miles to see dried bones seems like madness to me. Anyway, fix the shell to your coat, all the pilgrims wear them.'

Elowen studied the staff and the scallop shell. 'Where did you get these?'

Baba Yaga pretended not to hear the question and only answered when Elowen repeated it. 'A pilgrim passed this way once and left them here.'

'What happened to the pilgrim?'

Baba Yaga shrugged and said no more on the subject. Elowen sensed there was a story to be told but perhaps not a pleasant one. Baba Yaga took a step forward, her twisted nose only inches from Elowen's face, and said, 'Rynokgorod is a dangerous place. Its ruler is Bishop Serapion. He is a great ally of the Society and he has grown wealthy on gullible pilgrims and the slave trade. He is feared and with good reason. Do you understand?'

Elowen nodded.

Baba Yaga pointed to Elowen's forehead. 'You do not have the pustoj, the Null as you call it in the Common Tongue—this makes you vulnerable. You must try to cover your forehead with your hair. Do not attract attention. I only wish you would stay for longer. There is much more I need to teach you. I do not believe you are ready for what you are undertaking.'

'I'll be careful,' said Elowen.

'I hope so, child,' said Baba Yaga. 'Now, be gone. I have work to do.'

With that, Baba Yaga sat at the loom, although Elowen thought she was just pretending to work.

Elowen hesitated. She could not abandon Lárwita and Diggory but she was sad to leave Baba Yaga, who had saved her life and been so kind to her. She wanted to thank her and to apologise for leaving her alone again, but as she opened the trapdoor all that came out was, 'Farewell.'

*

The restless wind had scattered the broken remnants of the balloon: the silk canvas clung to the tree, rippling and billowing; pieces of the wicker basket were strewn across the mossy ground.

A line of tethered horses nibbled the wiry grass. Behind them stood a wagon with large, iron wheels. The sides of the wagon were decorated with embossed metal, and bronze figurines perched along the rim of the roof like mischievous imps.

Lord Lucien picked up a singed, oil-soaked pine cone. All around him Redeemers scoured the ground for tracks and footprints.

'They were here, and not many days ago, my lord,' said a Redeemer. 'From the tracks on the ground it appears they went east.'

131

'East,' repeated Lucien, letting the pine cone fall from his hand. He recalled what Rubens had told him about the girl; perhaps she was trying to get to Bai Ulgan.

A voice came from behind. 'Lord Lucien, there is a message.'

Another Redeemer bowed in front of him. 'My Lord, it is…the mirror.'

The mirror. It amused Lord Lucien to see how the Redeemers were afraid of the mirror, that instrument of Prester John's genius. Without another word, Lucien strode towards the wagon. He swung the double-doors at the back of the wagon fully open, stepped inside and slammed them shut behind him.

The inside of the wagon was dark, the only light being the mirror's faint glow, which revealed a bed and an untidy tower of books. Curled spikes of Cold Iron framed the mirror. Lord Lucien hesitated, aware of the pain to come. He knelt and placed his hands on either side of the mirror. He closed his eyes and tensed his body. The mirror crackled like a small fire and the surface glowed and shimmered. The spikes clamped down on his hands, into his skin, as cold as icicles. He struggled to breathe, his body paralysed by pain, his head aching. He concentrated. He channelled his thoughts in one direction: he fought the pain; he overcame the pain. 'I have come, my master.'

Gradually, like ripples dispersing on a pond, the mirror's surface calmed and a shape appeared: the face of Prester John.

'Many days have passed since last we spoke,' said the Patriarch of the Mother Church.

'Hard have been my labours,' said Lord Lucien.

'And your mission has been fulfilled?'

'The sanctuary is destroyed.'

Prester John closed his eyes and smiled. 'I knew you would not fail me. Truly, you are blessed in the eyes of God. You have won a momentous victory.'

'I hope so, my master.'

'But I sense you are not wholly satisfied with this triumph?' said Prester John, his eyes open again and a frown twisting his creased face.

Lord Lucien was reluctant to mention Elowen, but he found it hard to conceal his feelings from his master. 'I did not find the child.'

The spikes dug in a little deeper. Prester John's eyes narrowed. 'I would not concern yourself with her. Great trials await us all. I have issued the Edict.'

Lord Lucien took a deep breath, hoping to swallow any sign of trepidation in his voice. 'That is sooner than I expected.'

'There is no reason to delay, for it is but a beginning. The final stroke against the enemies of God and the Mother Church shall follow swiftly after. I have assembled the Grand Army. It will march after the winter snows have melted. It is imperative you return to the Ulsacro, to take charge of my army and prepare it for the campaign to come.'

'I am humbled by your trust in me,' said Lord Lucien. 'But before I return south I have much to attend to here.'

'I do not understand. You said the sanctuary has been destroyed.'

'And so it has, but I fear that some Illuminati escaped the attack. I aim to prevent them spreading their sedition any further. The risk they pose must be eliminated.'

Prester John blinked once. 'I do not wish to delay the execution of my plans. The trap has been set.'

'I shall return soon, I swear it,' said Lord Lucien.

The Cold Iron spikes released their grip, causing stabs of pain as they withdrew from his hands. The mirror's glow faded. Darkness rushed in to fill the spaces left by the retreating light. Lord Lucien meditated on what had happened. Events were accelerating faster than he had anticipated. He knew that Prester John considered the search for Elowen a distraction, and he knew he risked his master's anger by persisting in his attempts to find the girl. But for all his loyalty to Prester John, Lucien knew he could not abandon the search for Elowen. Nothing was more important to him.

It was almost dusk by the time he stepped outside the wagon. Four Redeemers greeted him, their white robes wet and splattered with mud. A man knelt in front of them. He had blind, milky eyes. Dirt and blood matted his hair. His filthy clothes were soaked through. He trembled violently and wept like a scolded child.

'We followed the tracks of the escaped Illuminati to a gorge yonder,' said one of the Redeemers, gesturing towards the east. 'From a large cave we heard weeping. We explored further and found this wretch. His name is Old Glum. He claims to have encountered the child we seek.'

Lord Lucien grabbed the man by the throat and pulled him to his feet.

'Don't hurt me,' said Old Glum. 'I'm a loyal servant of Prester John.'

'You have a chance to prove your loyalty. Tell me all that you know of the girl.'

'I curse her with every ounce of my being. When she escaped, the girl unleashed the witch Baba Yaga, the witch that slew all of my followers.'

Intrigued, Lord Lucien released his grip on the man's throat. 'You had the girl in captivity? Why?'

Old Glum dropped to his knees and rubbed the back of his neck. 'I've been honoured with the task of providing labour for the Society.'

'So, you trade in slaves,' said Lucien, starting to understand the man's coyness. 'And the girl was alone when you captured her?'

'No, there were two others, both boys I think.'

'You are sure of this?'

The man pointed to his blind eyes. 'As sure as I can be.'

'And who is this Baba Yaga?'

Old Glum's face flushed at the mention of the name. 'She's a witch that has long haunted the northern edge of the Altheart. She has terrible powers. I'd summoned the Society to collect the prisoners and take them to the slave market at Rynokgorod. But before they arrived Baba Yaga overwhelmed my followers. She murdered them all in cold blood and fled with the children.'

'And you were spared?'

The man wiped spittle from his mouth. 'The witch left me to die. With all my heart, I thank Prester John that godly men came to my rescue.'

135

Lord Lucien smiled his secret smile. The fool believed he was safe. 'Where do you imagine the witch and children went after their escape?'

Old Glum shrugged. 'I know not. It may be that Baba Yaga plans to return to the Altheart forest. If that were so, I doubt the children live still. Few return who visit the hut of Baba Yaga.'

Lord Lucien placed a hand on the top of Old Glum's head, a gesture of blessing. 'Thank you, you have proven a most faithful servant of Prester John.'

The man smiled a little. 'Please, I beg of you. Give me water and a little food. I've suffered so much. I've told you all I know. Is that not to be rewarded?'

'Indeed it is,' said Lucien. 'I grant you release from your suffering.'

Lord Lucien killed Old Glum with a single blow to his neck. He watched as the man fell. Lucien addressed the Redeemers. 'Bury this man and prepare the horses. We ride hard and without delay. I must find Baba Yaga.'

*

A light rain fell, dampening the leaf mould beneath Elowen's feet and filling the air with a rich, tangy scent. She found the percussive pit-patter of the raindrops calming, like tiny drumbeats encouraging her forward.

Throughout the forest, there were signs of the approach of winter: the birch trees dropped their triangular tooth-edged leaves; waxwings stripped a bilberry shrub of fruit; a male red deer bounded along, its antlers cast and its coat turning grey-brown. Soon the snows would come; the cold wind sucked in from the east carried that promise. All in the forest knew it; all in the forest expected it. The forest did not wait for winter with trepidation, unlike men as they watch for threatening clouds or mark off the signs of bad weather. The animals, plants and birds did not curse the coming of winter; they absorbed it into the rhythms of their lives.

As Elowen walked, she kept thinking about Baba Yaga's words to her as they had parted: *I do not believe you are ready for what you are undertaking.* Elowen was irritated by Baba Yaga's lack of faith in her. She grumbled to herself, 'I'll show her. I'm not afraid. I'm a messenger.'

By late afternoon, the sun was sinking fast, throwing blinding shards of light through the trees. The wind cooled. Elowen reached a point where the woods, which to that point had been largely flat and dry, became undulating and she had to pick her way down a steep slope, gripping onto tree trunks to avoid slipping over. After traipsing through large patches of boggy, sunken ground, Elowen discovered a clear path, narrow but well worn. She had been walking along the path for a few hundred yards when she spied a village, which was formed of a handful of huts and cruck houses. Chickens pecked at the ground, pens held pigs and goats. People worked or milled around, laughing, talking. The air was rich with smells of wood smoke, damp straw and cooking meat.

There was something enticing about the little village, a normality and peace Elowen found appealing. Perhaps the villagers would welcome her and give her food and shelter.

But she remembered the warning that Baba Yaga had given her: *avoid any village you see. The forest-dwellers are suspicious of strangers.*

Elowen knew that Baba Yaga was right. It was too risky. Besides, she had to reach Diggory and Lárwita as quickly as possible. So, she skirted around the village. To avoid being seen, she kept to the shadows, and used the sound of occasional gusts of wind to conceal the noises she made. Elowen felt a pang of loneliness as she slipped back into the cover of the trees and left the village behind.

By dusk, she had reached the north-eastern edge of the forest. As the trees thinned out, Elowen found herself at the top of an escarpment that looked out over a grassy plain. In the distance, perhaps five miles away, Elowen could make out a dusty ribbon she surmised was the road Baba Yaga had told her about. With the escarpment to descend first, she knew she could not reach the road before dark, so she decided to find somewhere sheltered to spend the night. She walked back a little way into the forest, and stumbled upon a weather-gnawed statue that rested against a fallen tree trunk, half-buried by windblown leaves. Elowen collected up the leaves and made a carpet of sorts on the ground so that it would not be too cold when she sat. She considered trying to make a fire but feared doing so might attract unwelcome attention. She munched on the nuts and berries Baba Yaga had provided, but she dared not eat too much as she had no idea where she would get more food in the days to come.

The night passed slowly and Elowen did no more than snatch a few moments of sleep. Each time she drifted to sleep, a creaking tree or an animal shriek startled her. The cold probed her clothes, exposing places where its icy fingers could get through. Miserable, tired and lonely, she tried to think of more pleasant things: soft beds, crackling fire, freshly baked bread and the comforting feel of a good book. However, the chasm between those comforts and reality only deepened her gloom. But for her friends' sake, she could not give up.

As the first light of dawn cracked the black sky, Elowen descended the escarpment, using a gouge that slashed down the rock face like an open wound. The mossy rocks were slippery but Elowen managed to scramble down.

Once at the foot of the escarpment, Elowen stopped to look ahead. After so many days enclosed by trees, she found it strange to be in a place so open and exposed. Small pools of red-stained water lay all around. Stunted shore pines and the trunks of long-dead trees stood on more raised parts of ground, like petrified markers of a sunken road. The spongy ground rippled beneath her, so Elowen used her staff to prod and find a dry passage to the road, which was little more than a dusty track, elevated from the low-lying plains that flanked it. The road was empty in both directions. She walked east. Other than the wind's mournful call, the only sounds Elowen heard were her footsteps crunching and the clicking of her staff as it struck the ground. Swollen clouds rolled around in the sky, red as though they had been coloured by drops of blood. To Elowen they looked unnatural, the imaginings of an artist's paintbrush rather than true inhabitants of the sky. A bitter smell drifted on the wind.

Something in the road ahead moved. From a distance, it resembled a large creature with multiple heads and limbs, but as Elowen blinked and looked again, the creature pulled itself apart and she realised that it was a group of people. Her first instinct was to hide but some of the people had already turned and were pointing at her.

Elowen decided that the best course of action was to act the role that Baba Yaga had given to her, the role of a pilgrim. She walked towards the people, keeping her pace even and unhurried. She tried to control her breathing; she tried not to appear worried or afraid.

The group were dressed in broad-rimmed hats and russet-coloured gowns drawn in above the waist with a belt. On their hats and clothes they had fastened scallop shells and pewter badges. They were all pilgrims, and they were all Nulled.

The pilgrims had been resting but as Elowen cautiously approached, they all stood and beckoned her to come closer. One, a rotund man whose eyes were almost hidden by his fleshy cheeks, spoke to Elowen but in a language she did not understand. He tried again in a crude attempt at the Common Tongue. 'Pilgrim?'

Elowen nodded, hoping her cheeks would not flush as they normally did when she lied.

'Rynokgorod?' he said.

Elowen nodded again.

'Good, good. Travel with us,' said the man, gesturing towards his companions, four other men and three women. 'Safer with us. Many bandits around.'

The pilgrims gave Elowen some cheese and bread, washed

down with a couple of swigs of wine. When they walked on, Elowen filed in behind them, feeling conscious of her deception. The pilgrims were flagging and they walked slowly. Elowen supposed that they had already travelled hundreds of miles. Despite their tiredness, they remained in good spirits; they told jokes and sang hymns of which Elowen recognised the tunes if not the words. She was glad that they did not speak the Common Tongue well; the less she had to talk to them, the fewer lies she had to tell. However, she loitered at the back of the group, keen to conceal that she was not Nulled. If they realised the truth Elowen knew their friendly smiles could turn into aggression.

The road wound through an unchanging landscape. A few other travellers passed the group: merchants in gaudy carriages, farmers with horse-drawn carts full of vegetables and a post rider hastening west. Much to Elowen's relief, none gave the pilgrims more than a cursory glance. However, she found the pace at which her companions moved frustrating. She needed to get to Diggory and Lárwita as soon as possible, but she dared not leave the group; they were her unwitting protectors.

Later, another group of pilgrims passed them going in the opposite direction. They were richly dressed and travelled on horseback. Despite the gracious nods and words they exchanged with Elowen's group, she sensed resentment and disapproval among her companions. It was clear they considered pilgrimage something to be endured as a hardship and the comfort of clean clothes and a fine horse to ride upon did not qualify.

Elowen smelt Rynokgorod before she saw it, a rancid,

sewer stink, and as the road coiled, she got her first glimpse of the city. As she had seen in her vision, the cathedral dominated the city. It gave the impression of having been carved from a single slab of stone save for its five golden cupolas. Elowen also beheld the golden pyramidal canopy roof of the citadel, the residence of Bishop Serapion. The other buildings huddled around the base of the cathedral as though for solace and protection. A wall encircled Rynokgorod, rising and falling like a wave as it followed the land's contours. Black clouds framed in silver light loomed menacingly above the city.

The pilgrims fell to their knees and recited prayers, their joy and relief at having reached their destination clear. Elowen felt a knot of fear in her stomach but she managed to greet the enthusiasm of her companions with a smile. She could not allow her true feelings to show.

Elowen judged that it was just before noon when they approached the city gates, which were open but watched over by several guards. A lofty tower stood above the gates, adorned by a bas-relief of a double-headed eagle. Elowen's throat went dry and it took all of her self-control not to turn and run away. She levelled her breathing and relaxed her muscles, taking control of her body just as Baba Yaga had taught her. The pilgrims strode happily towards the gates and Elowen kept pace with them. The guards grinned and muttered among themselves but to Elowen's relief they waved the pilgrims through without any questions.

The gate opened onto a broad street paved with wooden planks and flanked by steep-roofed timber buildings. Elowen slipped away from the pilgrims and into a whirlwind of noise and colour. Noble women draped in long, woollen coats and fur hats strolled without clear purpose, followed by gaggles of harassed servants. Bands of troubadours and minstrels played lively songs with harps, bagpipes and fiddles, hoping for coins from generous passers-by. Groups of wide-eyed pilgrims gasped and pointed at the sights around them.

A horse and rider forced a way through the crowds, sparking a melee of pushing, shoving and shouted curses. From the shops and workshops along the street came the ring of a blacksmith's hammer, the cries of shopkeepers, the whiff of baking bread and curing meat. Above all, the stench of body odour, of mud and horse dung lingered in the air.

Elowen found the noise and movement dizzying, as though she was swimming in a sea of faces: faces old and young, faces weathered and wrinkled, faces wise and cunning, faces cruel. Then she glimpsed a face that made her blood run cold; a face broad, flat and marked by a deep red, diagonal scar. It was the Orok that had accompanied Grunewald to the fateful council, the same Orok that had so unnerved Elowen. She blinked and the face was gone. She scanned the crowd but there was no sign of the Orok. She convinced herself she must have imagined it, that the chaos of the city had somehow tricked her tired eyes.

Someone grabbed her arm—a toothless old man, a peddler, holding up a handful of pewter badges and trinkets. She wriggled free of his grip and shook her head. He moved away to harass a group of weary and footsore pilgrims.

Elowen realised she had no clear idea of where Diggory

and Lárwita were. She tried to remember the vision she had experienced back in the woods; she recalled that her friends had stood in the market square so she allowed the crowd to sweep her deeper into the arms of Rynokgorod.

As she walked, she looked up at the cathedral's golden, onion-shaped cupolas; rising far above the rickety wooden buildings that lined the street, they gleamed like suns. Admiring the cupolas she was lost in thought when someone poked her in the back. Thinking it was another peddler, Elowen ignored them. Then, someone grasped her arm and turned her round. She faced a tall man with a thick beard that for a moment reminded her of Black Francis, but there was no warmth in his eyes. He pushed her off the main street and down into a narrow alley that ran between two wooden buildings.

The man put his oily hand over her mouth. 'I'm Grigori. If you struggle or make a noise it'll prove ill for you.'

Elowen became aware of two other men in the alleyway. Grigori released his grip on her. She was terrified but had no intention of submitting so easily. She clenched her staff and backed against the wall. 'If you come a step closer I'll strike you.'

One of the men tried to grab her, but Elowen parried his grasping hands with her staff and jabbed one end into his chest so forcefully he fell backwards.

The man swore at her and scrambled to his feet, rubbing his chest. Elowen readied herself for the next attack but Grigori pulled out a pistol and said, 'You've courage, child, but your staff cannot protect you. Drop it at your feet. I won't hesitate to fire.'

Elowen realised she had no choice. She let the staff drop. Grigori nodded to the two other men. They pinned her against the wall.

'Who are you?' said Elowen, defiant in her fear and anger. 'Who do you work for? Is it Lord Lucien?

'Lord Lucien? Now that's a name that has no right to rest on the lips of one so young,' said Grigori. He placed a hand on her forehead and he swept aside her fringe. 'So, it's as I thought. She does not wear the pustoj. This is the girl we were told to seek, I'm sure of it.'

Before Elowen could speak again, Grigori forced a hood over her head.

PART TWO

CHAPTER EIGHT

Outlaws

'They should be here by now.'

Bo nodded but said nothing, reluctant to share his fears. He lay on his stomach, gently tapping the hilt of his sword and peering down onto the wide, rutted road below. He shivered in the long shadows of the pine trees and ground his teeth as he waited.

'They should have been here by dawn. That is what the villagers said. I heard them with my own ears, Your Majesty.'

The whispered voice belonged to Fruma. He had proven a faithful friend and captain but Bo winced, as he always did, at the sound of the title *Majesty* and he could never persuade Fruma to stop using it. It had been bad enough when he referred to him as *Highness*, but at some point Fruma convinced himself that Bo was the king and should be addressed as such.

Many weeks had passed since Fruma had come to Bo at the Gladsheim. Fruma pricked Bo's conscience. In his heart, Bo would have preferred to remain with the Barbegs in their mountain refuge, or to have travelled with the strange, fascinating girl Elowen to the hidden sanctuary of the Illuminati. But Fruma reminded him of his duty, the obligations attached to his birthright. Bo was a prince of Prevennis. He was the rightful king, the only surviving child of his murdered father. His mother, born in Salvinia and not Prevennis, had no right of succession, but that had not prevented her from seizing the throne after her eldest son's death. Fruma's words on their first meeting stayed with him, echoed in his mind. *Do not abandon us, Your Highness. Your people need you.* Bo remembered feeling overwhelmed by the prospect of such a responsibility; in fact, he had tried to escape it. Albruna, the Barbeg chief had finally persuaded him. *You cannot hide in the shadows forever. Whether you desire it or not, Asbjorn, you are king.*

King. It still sounded like a foreign word. A king without a throne. His mother, who had instigated the plot to overthrow his father, occupied *that*. Now a puppet of the Mother Church, she helped to enforce the rule of Prester John throughout Prevennis, the very realm that had doggedly defied him for many years. Aided by the Redeemers, the queen had crushed all opposition, all except Bo and his band of rogues and misfits. In his darker moments, Bo felt like a flea threatening a wolf. He tapped the hilt of his sword again, which had once belonged to his father, and to each of the Preven kings going back centuries. It had been wielded in countless famous battles and had been displayed in great halls throughout the land. Although precious to him, Bo did not feel as though he deserved to carry it; he had not earned the right.

Another voice, a deeper voice, broke his thoughts. 'We must be patient, they'll come.'

Bo looked at Black Francis, the *Husker Du*'s captain, who waited next to him, propped up on his elbows for a clearer view of the road.

'The villagers had no reason to lie to us,' said Black Francis.

'You held a knife to their priest's throat,' said Bo.

'Exactly,' he said with a wry grin. 'Men facing death have no reason to lie.'

Men facing death. Bo had seen many of those since he had left the safety of the Gladsheim. As well as Fruma and Black Francis, twelve other men waited on the edge of the wood, all watching the road below from the slope that concealed them. Bo and his followers were wanted men. A host of defaming portraits and pamphlets displayed throughout the realm of Prevennis had declared them *outlaws*, a name the men warmly embraced and one that reflected their ramshackle appearance. They carried an assortment of muskets, pistols, bows and swords. They had neither armour nor uniforms; they wore baggy breeches and doublets made of brown or grey cloth, and cheap caps. Bo had recruited them from the refugees that had fled to the forest of Hlithvid to escape the terror of the Redeemers and the Kingsguard. They had proven good fighters, fierce and courageous, but Bo still felt like a child leading a band of men. Although Bo knew he fought as well as any man, he remained conscious of his slight pale frame and lean boyish muscles. He knew his men named him the ghost, a name born of his white skin and white hair. From how their laughter died when he approached the campfire, he feared that they used less flattering names too.

151

Bo and his followers had fought vicious skirmishes with the enemy for weeks, causing enough mayhem to earn sizable, and ever-increasing, rewards for their capture. Bo wanted to make a bolder stroke but already the men were getting restless. They had waited for two hours already. Bo's cold hands ached and the pieces of stale bread he nibbled did not take away his gnawing hunger. The men mumbled and whispered; he knew they were wondering how much longer they had to wait. Bo wished he knew the answer.

Black Francis hummed quietly to himself and ran a finger along the blade of his sword as though testing its sharpness; despite the many notches, Bo had no doubt it would still bite. When they had left the Gladsheim, Black Francis stated his intention to sail south and pay his debt to the King of the Sea Beggars. Yet he seemed reluctant to do so, always finding a reason, an excuse, to delay the journey. Bo was grateful for his aid but knew it was a dangerous course of action. The Sea Beggars were hunting for Black Francis and they had found him, twice, in the last month. Only through cunning, and no small amount of luck, had the captain escaped them. None of this outwardly troubled Black Francis; he shrugged off the news that the King of the Sea Beggars had put a price on his head.

Bo caught movement in the corner of his eye —Valbrand crawled towards him. Perhaps the fiercest fighter in the band, he had endured great suffering at the hands of the Redeemers and the treacherous Kingsguard. He boiled with a raging lust for vengeance.

Valbrand was not a tall man, and his pale hairless head and wrinkle-ringed eyes made him appear older than he was, but while his strength and courage were never in doubt, neither was his infamous temper. Wrapped around his neck, as always, was a piece of silk ribbon. He gripped a cutlass in one hand and had a crossbow strapped to his back. The crossbow, stolen as Valbrand often boasted, was richly decorated and engraved with stag's horn. Valbrand liked to dip the steel-tipped bolts in poisonous hellebore. It was not enough to kill the enemy; he wanted his victims to suffer. It bothered Bo to have a man such as Valbrand fighting alongside him, a man with no conscience.

When Valbrand got close to Bo he said, 'Perhaps they took another road. I think we should move north. There's still a chance we can catch them.'

'His Majesty did not ask for your opinion,' said Fruma, protective as ever of Bo. Fruma argued with Valbrand on every subject. They glared at each other, the anger and tension between them barely contained.

'I respect Valbrand's opinion,' said Bo to Fruma. He tried to be fair. He did not want his own men fighting among themselves. 'I value his words as I value yours.'

'Of course, and I am sorry if I spoke out of turn,' said Fruma, but he flashed another angry look at Valbrand.

'We must wait,' said Bo to Valbrand. 'They will come, I am sure of it.'

Valbrand huffed but did not argue further. He crawled back into position.

Bo rubbed his forehead. How much longer would they have to wait? His men had followed him through arduous journeys and hard fights and he believed he had earned their trust and loyalty but he took nothing for granted; he

153

remembered how quickly those loyal to his father had turned against him. He often thought about the reward offered for the capture of the outlaws and feared one of the men might, one day, be tempted to betray his companions and claim it.

He heard horses: hooves clopping, neighs. Distant, faint but unmistakable.

'They're coming,' said Black Francis.

Bo wanted to believe that was true but remained cautious. 'Ready yourselves, men. Load your weapons but do not fire until I give the order.'

The sound of horses' hooves grew louder. Wooden wheels squeaked. Bo's heart thumped.

Two Kingsguard horsemen. They rode slowly around the sharp bend in the road. Behind them came a carriage drawn by two horses. There was a single driver, and the carriage's passenger compartment was the shape of a shallow U with a door on each side and a protective roof above. An armed footman sat on the separate hooded seat fixed to the rear. Both doors of the passenger compartment had a small glass window but curtains hid from view anyone travelling inside. A detachment of ten heavily armed musketeers followed the carriage.

'We can take them,' said Black Francis.

'Not yet,' said Bo, feeling a pulse of excitement that simultaneously exhilarated and disgusted him.

The line of horses and men reached the road directly below Bo and his waiting band. Bo knew it was the moment to attack. He pulled himself to his knees and shouted, 'FIRE!'

A volley of musket-fire tore into the soldiers. Three of them fell. A crossbow bolt fired by Valbrand struck one rider in the neck; the other rider was thrown by his horse, which panicked and galloped away. The driver of the carriage slumped forward, holding his shoulder and the horses stopped. The footman leapt from his seat and ran away.

'CHARGE!' said Bo. Brandishing his sword, he sprinted down the slope towards the enemy. The surviving musketeers tried to ready their weapons but Bo's men were on them before they could fire. The air filled with screams, curses and the clashing of steel. The surviving Kingsguard rider scrambled to his feet and grabbed his sword. He lunged towards Bo, who parried but, with his feet poorly positioned, fell backwards. Sensing a kill, the Kingsguard yelled out triumphantly but before he could strike a fatal blow, Fruma appeared between them and drove his blade into the man's flank. The Kingsguard grunted and fell.

Fruma helped Bo to his feet. 'Are you hurt?'

'My pride is a little wounded. You saved my life.'

Fruma wiped his sword clean on the grass. 'It is my duty to serve you, Your Majesty.'

The skirmish was over, the enemy soldiers either slain or fled. To Bo's relief, none of the outlaws had been killed or wounded. A success. His plan had worked.

The outlaws stripped the corpses of weapons, ammunition and other possessions such as coins, water bottles and food. The practice always made Bo blanch.

Valbrand cut in. 'There's one alive here.'

The carriage driver knelt on the ground, his shoulder a gory mess.

'I'll slit his throat,' said Valbrand.

'No, let him live,' said Bo. 'This man is not a soldier.'

'But he helped them, and willingly I warrant,' said Valbrand. 'He's been cursed with the Null, like all these scum.'

'Even so, his death serves no purpose,' said Bo. He pulled the driver upright. 'Go now. Take a horse.'

The driver spat in Bo's face. It surprised Bo so much it felt like a slap or a punch. Fruma and Black Francis stepped forward ready to strike but Bo held up his hand. 'No, he's not worth it, let him go.'

The man cursed under his breath, hobbled to the nearest horse and galloped away.

'This is madness,' said Valbrand. 'He may bring reinforcements.'

'We will be long gone before they get here,' said Black Francis.

'Yes, and we have more important matters to attend to,' said Bo. Followed by the outlaws, he strode over to the carriage. He yanked the windowed door open and a pistol shot rang out; it struck the door frame and showered Bo with splinters.

A reedy voice from inside cried. 'Get away from me, outlaws!'

Bo smiled. It was the voice he had hoped to hear.

A man sat inside the carriage. He wore a green oval cape, a purple tunic and an ankle-length stole. His face was narrow and rodent-like, and the Null stretched the dry skin of his forehead. The pistol in his quivering hands smoked like a pipe. Around his feet lay bulging woollen sacks with openings fastened by drawstring. A folded parchment rested on his lap.

'Greetings, Bishop Neidelhart,' said Bo, staring at the man who had once been his father's counsellor and confessor, and who had betrayed him to his death. 'It is fortunate for me that you are as poor a marksman as you are a priest.'

Neidelhart's jaw dropped and the pistol fell from his limp fingers. 'Prince Asbjorn? You are alive. The rumours are true.'

'Rumours are seldom true, Bishop, but yes, it is me.'

Neidelhart closed his eyes and whispered a prayer.

'You are far beyond God's help now,' said Bo. He had fantasised about this moment many times. What he would say, what he would do, how he would feel. Now faced with Neidelhart, part of him wanted to kill the bishop, but natural caution stayed his hand. He pulled Neidelhart out of the carriage. Gripping the folded parchment in his hand, the bishop slipped and fell down on his stomach. The outlaws laughed heartily.

'By attacking me you have attacked the Mother Church,' said Neidelhart, bringing himself to his knees and scowling at the outlaws.

'As was our intention,' said Bo.

'Then your blasphemies damn you,' said Neidelhart.

'If I am damned, I shall find you in hell also.'

'Let us speed him there now,' said Valbrand.

Bo ignored him. Neidelhart tried to slip the parchment beneath his clothes. Bo said 'Give me that.'

'It does not concern you,' said Neidelhart.

'Let me be the judge of that,' said Bo. He snatched the

157

folded parchment from the bishop's hands. Red and yellow silk cords looped through slits held it together. A golden seal fastened the cords; the seal was impressed on one side with a symbol of a double-headed eagle and the letters 'P' and 'J'. Bo loosened the seal when he again noticed the sacks in the carriage. He folded the parchment smaller, stuffed it into his pocket and pointed at the sacks. 'What do they contain?'

The bishop glowered at Bo but said nothing. Fruma reached inside the carriage and pulled out the three sacks; Bo loosened the drawstring on one of them and silver and gold coins spilled out. The outlaws gasped.

'Now I understand why you had an armed guard, Bishop,' said Black Francis, his eyes wide at the sight of the money.

'These are tithes belonging to the Mother Church,' said Neidelhart.

'Tithes taken from the poor to allow you to live in luxury,' said Valbrand. 'Tithes paid to foreign mercenaries to butcher our people.'

'So Asbjorn, this is what you have become, a thief and a captain of brigands,' said Neidelhart. 'You were the weaker of the two princes. Haakon was always stronger and wiser. Your mother despised you from the day of your birth.'

Anger flared within Bo but he contained it—Neidelhart wanted to rile him. 'Bishop, it saddens me to see you fall so low. But when I remember your treachery, your fate seems just.'

'My *fate*? Am I to die?'

'All men die, Bishop,' said Bo, his words greeted with chuckles by the men, something that pleased him. 'But you will not die this day, at least not by my hand. Indeed, you have a great duty to carry out.'

Neidelhart's eyes narrowed. 'What do you mean?'

'You must carry a message to my mother...the queen and all her acolytes. And to Lord Lucien, if you can stand to be in his presence.'

Neidelhart shuddered. 'And what is this message?'

Bo took a deep breath, drawing cool air deep into his lungs, and recited words he had rehearsed in his mind many times. 'Tell them that I, Prince Asbjorn, live and that I fight. Tell them that I am coming to claim what is mine. Tell them that I am coming to claim the throne of Prevennis.'

Neidelhart laughed. 'The throne of Prevennis? How can a mere boy and a rabble of cutthroats threaten the rule of Prester John? Why, a single Redeemer is enough to send you all wailing back into the forest. I promise to deliver your message but trust me—it will be mocked and then forgotten by all who hear it. And I too shall forget the pitiful name of Prince Asbjorn.'

Bo pulled out the small knife he kept fastened to his belt and grabbed the bishop by the throat. He held the knife to Neidelhart's cheek. 'Bishop, I swear you will never forget me.'

He dug the knife into the skin and dragged it down from the bishop's left ear to the corner of his mouth. Blood gushed out of the wound. Neidelhart moaned in pain and sank to his knees like a penitent sinner.

'From this day forward, every time you look in the mirror, you will remember me,' said Bo, still holding the bloody knife. His whole body tingled; the violence, the sense of

159

revenge, excited him. He slowed his breathing, trying to regain control.

Neidelhart managed to stand although his legs shook. He stared at Bo, his eyes red with tears; blood seeped through the fingers of the hand he held to his wound. He hobbled along the road, like a crippled man weighed down by a great burden.

Bo and the outlaws watched the bishop until he was out of sight.

'You should have slashed his throat, not his cheek,' said Valbrand, to muttered agreement from the other outlaws.

'We have sent a message to our enemies, one that they will not ignore,' said Bo. He tried to deepen his voice, as he often did, unconsciously, when talking to the men. 'We must head back to the *Husker Du*. Somebody please cut those horses free.'

'Aren't we going to take the horses with us?' said Valbrand, flinging out his arms in amazement.

'We can't take them through the forest and besides, what would we do with them once we reached the *Husker Du*?'

Valbrand shrugged. 'If we cannot take them, we should kill them.'

'What the hell for?' said Black Francis.

'If we leave the horses the Kingsguard will find them again. I'll be damned before I see them take anything we've fought for.'

'It cannot be helped,' said Bo. 'We have achieved what we set out to do. Cut the horses free.'

'You don't understand,' said Valbrand, waving his crossbow for emphasis. 'The Kingsguard took everything from me. My wife and child murdered, our home razed to the ground. I don't fight for you or for your dead father, or for this godforsaken land. I fight for vengeance. That's why I want the horses killed. I don't want anything left for the Kingsguard.'

'Killing these horses will not bring you peace,' said Bo.

'Peace? There's no peace in this world,' said Valbrand. 'But I obey your order. The horses go free. But this I say, you're too trusting and merciful—that's a weakness your enemies will exploit.'

Bo wanted to reply but could not think of anything to say to improve the situation. Knowing that he had to prove he was in control, Bo asked Fruma to carry out his command. Fruma unfettered the horses and slapped them on the haunches to make them run away.

Bo said to the outlaws, 'Gather your possessions, we must reach the creek by nightfall.'

They obeyed but the jubilation that had followed the skirmish had evaporated. Black Francis gathered up the money sacks, closely watched by the outlaws. One of them, a nervy man called Scut, hastily drew an 'O' on the carriage door with a piece of chalk: O for outlaws, a sign for others to see, a challenge to their enemies.

Bo led the outlaws through the forest. Slats of dusty sunlight cut through the gaps between the pines. The blood-curdling cry of a capercaillie made the men jump; the forest unnerved them, they were more frightened among the trees than in the heat of battle. There was no talking and the only sounds the outlaws made were the crunching of their footsteps and the jangling and clinking of their equipment.

Despite the successful ambush, Bo's mood remained gloomy. He had hoped to impress and inspire the men, but not for the first time Valbrand's defiance had made him look indecisive and weak. And the truth in Neidelhart's words haunted him. How could a mere boy and a rabble of cutthroats threaten the rule of Prester John?

The gaps between the pine trees widened and the outlaws came to a track flanked by lines of standing stones, each as tall as a man and inscribed with cup and ring marks. The track led to the lip of a cliff, crowned by an abandoned village of crumbling stone cottages and a ruined church. Nature had already begun to hide the work of man. Grass and moss slowly broke and devoured stone, and wood rotted into the soil. All that survived of the church was the fire-blackened west wall of the tower, and that had been split completely down the middle like a jagged tooth. The deserted village had a melancholy atmosphere and Bo heard the outlaws muttering about the Landvaettir, the phantoms that some said haunted such places.

'Many villages have met such a fate since your father's rule was overthrown,' said Fruma. 'This is the work of the followers of Prester John. His rule is a plague upon this land. Those who refuse the Null are murdered or sent to Gorefayne. The servants of Prester John show no mercy. They murder in cold blood and we should not hesitate to kill them.'

Bo sensed Fruma was trying to rebuke him. 'You believe I was wrong to allow Bishop Neidelhart to go free? You think I should have killed him?'

'It is not my place to say that you made a mistake, Your

Majesty,' said Fruma. 'You have a great responsibility to your people. You must demonstrate your right to rule.'

'And that is best achieved through murder?'

'You have killed men in battle.'

'That is different,' said Bo. 'I refuse to kill men in cold blood, whatever their sins against me or this land.'

'You must be prepared to do whatever is required to succeed.'

'I will not become like my enemy in order to defeat him.'

'Then I fear for you, Your Majesty, and I fear for all of us. All our hopes rest in you. If you fail then I can see no hope for Prevennis.'

Bo felt himself getting angry with Fruma. He wanted to end the conversation before he said something he regretted. He ordered, 'Tell the men they can rest here for a short time.'

Fruma hesitated for a second. His face was stiff, expressionless, his lips were tight and he did not make eye contact. He grunted something inaudible and ambled towards the other outlaws. Once Fruma had gone, Bo wandered to the cliff edge. Ahead lay a softer landscape of meadows and ancient oak woods; a river flowed south through the woods. Fast-moving clouds raced across the sky, in too much of a hurry to let the weather settle. When the sun broke through the clouds, its pinkish light drew elegant stretched shadows and the trees glowed in their autumnal colours of red, orange and gold. Yet as soon as the sun disappeared again behind the clouds, the woods ahead grew dark and foreboding.

After a brief rest, Bo and the outlaws found a way down

the cliff and crossed the meadows to enter the oak woods. Feeling the bite of the cool salt-scented wind, they followed a path that sloped downwards and became slippery with trickles of water and moss-coated rocks. The path ended at a tiny, seaweed-streaked shingle beach at the foot of a muddy tidal creek. Gnarled oak trees lined the banks, their larger branches hanging over the water like outstretched fingers. Grey herons lurked on the near bank while shelducks and little egrets foraged in the mud exposed by the low tide. Anchored in the creek, as though it had been washed up by the tide, was the *Husker Du*.

'It's good to see her again,' said Black Francis. 'Always feels like coming home.'

Bo smiled, touched by his friend's affection for the ship. He wished he had somewhere he could call home, he wished there was somewhere he belonged.

Black Francis imitated a bird's call and the crew of the *Husker Du* appeared on deck and lowered the small wooden dinghy. It took two journeys to ferry all the outlaws. Once on board, Shrimp greeted them. Black Francis still called him the coxswain but, popular and respected by the crew, he fulfilled the role of quartermaster and captain's deputy. He helped to maintain order, distribute rations and delegate work. Like the rest of the crew, he wore a linen shirt with plain woollen trousers and he walked barefoot to better grip the slippery deck. He nodded to Bo before turning to embrace Black Francis. The captain let the sacks of coins fall at his feet. The outlaws stared covetously at the gold and silver.

Shrimp smiled. 'So you've returned home safely.'

164

'Have you ever known me not to?' said Black Francis. He shouted to Limpet, the ship's cook, who was leaning idly against one of the masts. 'These men are hungry and they need bread and ale. We eat now, for we must leave before first light.'

Limpet's shoulders visibly sagged at the thought of work but he slipped away to fulfil the captain's command. The rest of the crew and the band of outlaws followed him. Bo noticed Valbrand staring at the money sacks. He only turned away when he realised that Bo was watching him.

*

The outlaws were weary after their long march and most fell asleep soon after eating. Too restless to sleep, Bo volunteered to keep watch on deck. It was a rimy night, the sky cloudless and star-sprinkled; the waxing moon glowed.

Bo listened to the slow lap of water against the ship as the tide crept into the creek. The cries and croaks of nocturnal animals drifted in from the woods beyond.

Deep in thought, Bo jumped when he heard heavy footsteps tramping across the wooden deck. He spun round with his hand reaching for the hilt of his sword, only to smile in embarrassed relief when he saw Black Francis carrying a brass oil lamp.

'It's a chilly night, lad,' said Black Francis, his breath steaming in front of him.

'You forget I am Preven born and bred,' said Bo. 'I am used to the cold.'

Black Francis chuckled and picked out the remnants of

165

his supper from his beard. 'Aye, that's true, and after living with the Barbegs for a while I should be too. The winds that blow around the Gladsheim mountains are as sharp as razors.'

'I often think about Elowen,' said Bo. 'I hope that she reached the sanctuary safely.'

'I'm sure she did,' said Black Francis. 'She's a brave and canny lass.'

'Yes, I think you are right,' said Bo. He missed Elowen and regretted that he had spent so little time with her before their parting. He hoped to see her again one day but knew it was a remote prospect.

Black Francis took a deep breath and looked out over the dark landscape. 'This place is peaceful, I like it. Not a soul comes here. I've often used this creek over the years for free trading.'

Bo winced. 'Free trading? Don't you mean smuggling?'

Black Francis laughed. 'Smuggling is such an *ugly* word. But as safe as this creek is, I fear to linger in one place for too long. We should head north, away from those cursed Ironclads. Your ambush of the bishop will bring enemies down upon us, of that you can be sure.'

'Perhaps,' said Bo, before giving voice to his concerns. 'Neidelhart is right. I am no threat to Prester John. I cannot protect the people of this land. Remember the village we passed earlier, could I have saved them?'

'Your enemies fear you because you're giving hope to those who oppose Prester John, and that's no small feat.'

'It is not enough. I do not think the men trust me. They think I am weak. Even Fruma is losing faith in me, I fear.'

'Leading men is difficult. You reckon I have an easy life with my crew? They're good lads but still they complain, they shirk, they constantly question my judgement, and sometimes I wonder if they aren't right in what they say. When you take charge of men it's natural to feel doubt but you mustn't show it, for they'll sense your weakness and exploit it. You have struck a blow against the enemy, whatever doubts the others may have.'

'And Neidelhart will miss the coins we took from him,' said Bo.

Black Francis picked at his beard again. 'I admit the gold and silver concerns me. Such treasures have a strange effect on the hearts of men. They lose all reason and trouble inevitably follows.'

Bo recalled how Valbrand had stared greedily at the money sacks. 'I'm not sure that all the outlaws are to be trusted.'

'By that you mean Valbrand, of course,' said Black Francis with a raised eyebrow. 'He's a good man in a fight but I wouldn't trust him as far as I could throw him. I'd keep my eye on him if I were you. I'll keep the bishop's coins in my cabin for now but you need to decide what to do with them, and decide quickly. And what of the parchment?'

'The parchment? Of course!' said Bo. He had forgotten about it and pulled it out of his pocket, folded and torn. He slid his finger beneath the seal to open it and unfolded the parchment. The golden seal came loose and Bo held it in his palm for a moment; it was heavy and shone like a large coin. He dropped the seal into his pocket and examined the parchment. He noticed the two-headed eagle insignia of Prester John. There were other diagrams too: a small map, some geometrical shapes, one of which resembled a Sentinel. Most disturbing of all was the image of a face, with flattened features and black cavities for eyes.

Using the flickering light from the oil lamp, Bo tried to read the annotations and elegantly handwritten passages but he could not understand a single word. 'It is written in *Manus*, the ecclesiastical language of the Mother Church.'

'Aye, that's what I expected,' said Black Francis as he squinted at the parchment. Bo glanced at Black Francis with surprise and the captain said, 'I may be an old sea dog but I'm not a simpleton.'

'Can you translate it?' said Bo, passing the parchment to Black Francis.

'A few words perhaps. When I was a lad, a priest lived in my village, mad but a kindly soul. He had an ancient copy of the Holy Book, with beautiful colour engravings made by monks. He showed me the pictures if I agreed to let him teach me *Manus*. I was never the quickest learner but I picked up a little of the language. It has come in useful from time to time. Now, let me see.'

He gave the oil lamp to Bo and ran a finger along the lines of text. He wrinkled his brow and announced, 'These drawings are strange and I don't understand most of what's written here. Just a few words, like monarchs, bishops, God's work. And this map, if I'm reading it properly this shows the city of Gorefayne.'

'Gorefayne, that place keeps being mentioned,' said Bo.

Black Francis tapped the parchment. 'There's something about this. Something in my bones tells me that this is important.'

'Neidelhart tried to keep it hidden from us,' said Bo. 'He worried more about the parchment than the money. But it is of little use if we cannot read it.'

'True, but I know someone who can.'

'Your old priest?'

'Nay,' said Black Francis. 'They buried him many years ago. But there is someone who might help us, one of the Illuminati, although she doesn't dwell in the sanctuary. She's made her home in Farligby, a town on the southern tip of Prevennis, not too far from here. Her name is Sesheta and she's wise in many things. She'd understand what's written in this parchment.'

'And she would help us?'

Black Francis shrugged. 'She might, although she drives a hard bargain. Sesheta is one of the Illuminati but she does not give favours lightly and you cross her at your peril.'

Bo did not like what he was hearing. 'Farligby is not safe. There are bound to be agents of Prester John there, perhaps even Redeemers. Besides, there must be a dozen Ironclads hunting for this ship, we can hardly sail into the harbour and anchor there.'

Black Francis rubbed his hands. 'Nobody knows this coast like I do. There's a cove at Dekning, only five miles from Farligby. We can anchor there safely and out of sight, and make for the town by foot.'

'The name of Black Francis is not unknown,' said Bo. 'The Sea Beggars have placed a bounty on your head, a bounty men will risk their lives to collect. Remember what happened when we anchored at Trangvik? That was close. We might not be so lucky next time.'

'Then we must be very careful.'

'Are you sure that it is wise to keep hiding from the Sea Beggars? You said you wanted to go south, to pay your debt. Perhaps it is time for you to do so.'

'Do you not want my help?' said Black Francis, looking hurt.

'It is not that. I am grateful for everything you have done for me. But you are putting yourself in grave danger. You have the funds to pay your debts, so you should do it. The Sea Beggars will never give up.'

'Let me worry about them,' said Black Francis. The captain hated talking about the Sea Beggars and the danger they posed. Perhaps he found it easier not to think about it; perhaps he hoped the problem would simply go away. 'All you need to worry about is whether or not you wish to go to Farligby. If you do, I will take you and your men there.'

Bo wondered if the parchment was important enough to risk their lives for. He did not know. But his gut feeling told him that it was important and he knew anything that could help them in the struggle against Prester John was valuable.

'Very well, I've made up my mind,' he said, trying to sound decisive. 'We will head south tomorrow.'

CHAPTER NINE

Dangerous Waters

I t was still dark when the *Husker Du* slipped out of the creek and joined the wide river.

The outlaws, refreshed by food and strong ale, slept soundly and snored loudly. Bo preferred to remain on deck, watching the landscape pass from the bow of the ship. He wanted to be alone; being around the other outlaws made him nervous and insecure. He was sure they were judging him, doubting him with every glance and every whispered word. They clearly considered him weak and indecisive, and perhaps they were right to do so. Fear and doubt plagued him. In his mind he went over and over every decision he made. He worried about how he spoke to his men. Was he too harsh, or too soft? He always got it wrong. He was no leader.

And yet, although Bo had never consciously wanted to be king, he often daydreamed about taking the throne of Prevennis and leading his people to glory. Sometimes the fantasies comforted him, encouraged him. But usually the void between his daydreams and the harsh reality of his life simply depressed him further.

Despite the cold, the crew worked silently and without

complaint. The ship creaked and groaned like an old man stretching his aching limbs. As they sailed down the river, Bo saw the ghostly shapes of abandoned buildings, their ragged edges silhouetted by the silvery moonlight. Bo knew that the river had once bustled with boats carrying copper ore, coal and timber, but the inhabitants of the region had paid dearly for their stubborn resistance to Prester John.

They reached the estuary at dawn. The sun rose reluctantly, becoming little more than a hazy golden stain in the sky, unable to blunt the sharp edge of the easterly wind. The estuary was alive with birds. Gulls glided over the wooded banks while noisy groups of oystercatchers argued in loud piping calls; knots and dunlins fed in close flocks, ignored by the scattered turnstones and sandpipers that searched for food among the seaweed and barnacles.

An islet of black rock marked the centre of the estuary and a handful of seals rested upon it. Other seals swam in the water, their heads just above the surface, taking advantage of the high tide to roam the shallows in search of crabs and flatfish. Accompanied by Goby, the ship's second mate, Black Francis came on deck with several nautical maps tucked under his arm and the leather-bound ship's log in his hands. Black Francis spurned the use of astrolabes, handheld quadrants and other navigational devices. He had told Bo many times that he preferred to 'read the sea' and that he deemed magnetic compasses worse than useless. He gauged the *Husker Du*'s speed by watching the sea as it broke along the sides. At night, he steered by the Pole Star and by day took his estimates of latitude from the sun's position. He calculated the ship's position by dead reckoning:

with the aid of a sandglass he estimated how many leagues the ship had covered, noted the direction by the sun and entered his findings in the log, and then calculated the ship's approximate position. To discern if land was close he used clues from the sea—seaweed floating in the water or a bird carrying a fish in its mouth. Bo saw navigation at sea as a mysterious art, one far beyond his understanding.

Black Francis passed the log and charts to Goby and walked over to Bo, all the time taking deep breaths. 'I tell you, lad, there's not a better taste in this world than sea air, or a more heartening sight than the rolling waves.'

Bo smiled. 'I prefer my feet on dry land.'

'Not all of us are made for life on the sea, but there's no other life for me.'

'How long will it take us to get to Farligby?' said Bo.

'No more than two days if we can slip past the Ironclads.'

'And if we can't?'

Black Francis cleared his throat but rather than answer the question, he strode back across the deck, bellowing orders at his young crew. Some were busy swabbing the deck with mops and buckets of seawater. Others examined the ropes for wear and tear, and stitched any rips in the sails. The gunners checked and cleaned the deck-mounted cannons.

Bo's stomach lurched as the *Husker Du* passed into the open sea. One of the crew pointed out the dorsal fin of a basking shark cutting through the low waves. Despite the huge size of the fish, Bo knew that it was harmless, feeding only on the smallest creatures that swam in the sea. He hoped that they would see nothing more dangerous during their journey.

In an effort to avoid patrolling Ironclads, the *Husker Du* sailed out of sight of the shoreline. The sea was calm but that did not prevent Bo from feeling sick and dizzy. He had yet to find his sea legs. The ship's cook had offered him something to eat but Bo had found the prospect of tough salted meat, wormy biscuit and watered-down ale far from tempting, so he decided to risk travelling on an empty stomach.

The promise of sunshine was swiftly broken by banks of thick fog that stole light and silenced the guttural cries of the seagulls. Black Francis posted additional lookouts in the rigging and one of the young sailors used the sounding line, a thin rope with a plummet of lead, to keep checking the depth of the water. Another sailor measured time using the sandglass, which he turned every half an hour.

Valbrand, Fruma and Scut came on deck. Bo's heart sank when he saw them.

'What's going on?' said Valbrand. 'Where are we going?'

'To Farligby,' said Bo. He was feeling sick and his head pounded. He was in no mood for an argument but he knew one was coming.

'Why in God's name are we going there?' said Valbrand. Even Fruma looked alarmed.

Bo tried to explain, 'There is something we have to attend to—'

'Aye, spending the gold and silver that we snatched from the bishop is my guess,' interrupted Valbrand, his face turning red. He pointed at Black Francis. 'He's probably using it to pay off his debts to the Sea Beggars. We're being used, asked to risk our lives to line his pockets.'

174

'That is a lie,' said Bo, trying to keep his anger in check. He told the outlaws about the parchment they had taken from the bishop but it did not seem to impress them.

Valbrand wagged a finger in Bo's face. 'This is all nonsense. We should be fighting the Kingsguard, not skulking around a cesspit like Farligby searching for an Illuminati mystic. If you ask me—'

'Silence on deck.'

The voice belonged to Black Francis and such was its power that all obeyed. The ship's timbers creaked and groaned, the sails flapped in the wind and waves lapped against the hull. Another sound cut in: the clanking of metal striking metal. The air became heavy with coal-smoke. A shape formed in the fog, barely two hundred yards from the starboard side, moving slowly in the opposite direction to the *Husker Du*: an Ironclad.

The sounds of the metal ship grew louder, sounds of wheels and gears turning. Bo failed to control the trembling in his hands and his bowels ached. Flecks of flame spewed from the Ironclad's chimney. It was so close. Surely they would be seen and the Ironclad's deadly cannons would open fire, ripping the wooden *Husker Du* to kindling. But slowly, so slowly it seemed as though time itself was hindered, the Ironclad moved away from the *Husker Du*. The fog had hidden them. The metallic sound faded, becoming little more than a ghostly echo.

'That was close,' said Bo.

'Aye, I didn't expect to see Ironclads this far out to sea,' said Black Francis. 'I need your men to act as lookouts. This fog won't break any time soon.'

'You don't command us, pirate,' said Valbrand.

'When you're on *my* ship you do as I say. I do not argue. I do not discuss. I order and you obey. If you don't like it you're welcome to swim back to shore.'

To Bo's surprise, Valbrand laughed. 'You're a brave one, pirate. Few men have the guts to stand up to me. Very well, I'll keep watch as you command.'

The outlaws reluctantly followed the captain's orders and the rest of the voyage was uneventful. By the following dawn, the *Husker Du* had reached the little cove of Dekning. Tall cliffs cupped the cove like protective hands. The sandy beach, coloured by volcanic ash, resembled a thin strip of black cloth. The sight of land brought all the outlaws on deck, where they stood in a group whispering and smirking. Fruma held their attention. Jealously stung Bo. He knew that the outlaws increasingly looked to Fruma, older, wiser, stricter, as their leader.

Once the ship anchored, Black Francis ordered the crew to lower the dinghy. The captain said to Bo, 'We should make for Farligby as soon as possible. To anchor here any longer than necessary is dangerous. Shrimp and Crab will return the dinghy to the Husker Du as we can't risk leaving it on the beach.'

'I hope you're not thinking of going alone, Your Majesty,' called Valbrand from behind.

Bo said, 'Black Francis will accompany me.'

'I wish to come along too,' said Fruma.

'Yes, of course,' said Bo without hesitation. He was pleased that Fruma still believed in him enough to want to follow him.

'If Fruma goes, I go too,' said Valbrand, cutting into the conversation.

Black Francis started to protest until, to Bo's surprise, Fruma intervened on Valbrand's behalf. 'If there is trouble I would be pleased to have him close. He is good in a fight.'

Valbrand grinned. 'You all know that's true. You'll be safer with me by your side.'

Bo did not want Valbrand to join them, but he saw little to be gained, and much to lose, by arguing. With as much eagerness as he could muster, he said, 'Very well, Valbrand comes too.'

'Wear these to hide that you've not been Nulled,' said Black Francis, as he handed out thick woollen caps to Bo, Fruma and Valbrand. He barked more orders at the crew, instructing them to post lookouts on stern and bow and in the rigging. To Shrimp he said, 'Come back for us at midnight. We won't be late.'

Bo watched as Fruma spoke again to the huddle of outlaws, commanding them, he hoped, to remain alert for danger. Bo knew danger was not far away.

*

After they made their landfall on the beach, Black Francis led the way inland. Bo walked behind him, shadowed, as usual, by the loyal Fruma. Valbrand brought up the rear, his crossbow strapped to his back. The southern edge of Prevennis was less mountainous than the north but Bo knew they were still hard lands.

'Our good cook Limpet told me that our provisions are

177

running low,' said Black Francis as they walked. Without stopping, he dipped into the small leather money bag fastened to his belt and counted the handful of coins there. 'We need oats, cheese and meat, as much as we can carry. These coins should be enough.'

'We have plenty of gold on the ship,' said Valbrand. 'We could buy a fine time with the bishop's money.'

'Don't be a fool,' said Black Francis. 'If we splash those coins around Farligby it'll draw attention, and we don't need attention. However, one of you must seek provisions when we get to Farligby.'

'I'll do it,' said Valbrand.

'No, it should be me,' said Fruma.

Fruma flashed a look at Valbrand before glancing at Bo who divined his meaning: Fruma did not think that Valbrand could be trusted and it was better to keep a close eye on him.

Black Francis gave Fruma the coins. 'Beware. The traders of Farligby drive a hard bargain.'

Fruma nodded, pocketed the coins and gave a quick, furtive glance at Bo.

They pushed on and passed an algae-coated pool fringed by floppy, sickly trees. It reeked of stagnant water. Midges prowled; they landed on Bo's face and neck and pricked him with their needle-like bites. Valbrand and Black Francis cursed loudly with every bite they suffered but Fruma trudged on in silence, deep in thought, either not feeling or not caring about the midges.

They climbed to higher ground, free of the midges, and to a road defined by rows of upright stones. The road never strayed far from the sea and Bo could still hear waves crashing against rocks and the endless yelling of gulls. They walked through a cultivated landscape: flocks of cattle, sheep and goats roamed over rich grazing land punctuated by little copses; orchards of pears and apples sheltered in gentle folds in the land; strip fields of barley, oats and flax waited for harvest; brightly coloured wooden windmills colonised the higher slopes. Bo enjoyed the sounds, sights and smells, savouring their rich textures after interminable hours on board the *Husker Du* surrounded by grey waves.

The road reached the top of a slope. The town of Farligby squeezed into the steep valley below; a rocky promontory with high cliffs shielded the harbour from the sea. Bo and his companions followed the muddy road that led into the town. As they passed the outskirts of Farligby, nervous faces peered out from the darkened doorways of ramshackle timber-framed houses.

'I don't like the look of this place,' said Bo.

'Once this was a prosperous town,' said Black Francis. 'Now there are more vagrants here than merchants.'

'Should we be carrying weapons so openly?' said Bo, conscious of the sword fastened to his belt.

'It is wise to be armed in this town,' said Black Francis. 'If you walk into Farligby with a light heart you might not walk out of it again. We must all be careful. It's not just the Kingsguard or Redeemers. Watch out too for the Sea Beggars. You'll know them if you see them. Their heads are shaven and their faces tattooed. They'll keep a low profile but they have many agents in their pay.'

Valbrand grinned. 'I thought it was only you they wanted.'

'Believe me, friend, if I'm found by the Sea Beggars you'll be in danger too.'

As they came further into the town, the buildings, built of timber and clay, were larger and climbed three, four or five storeys high—they were now shabby with crumbling walls and door posts, and windows with rotten frames.

They passed an alehouse; singing and laughter came from inside. Bo looked through the grimy window and saw groups of men playing shove-ha'penny and draughts. Two soldiers lurked by the door, dressed in red coats, fur-trimmed hats and black boots, and armed with long crescent-shaped axes. They gazed at Bo and the hairs on the back of his neck rose. He hurried along, swerving milk-maids carrying large pottery jugs on their heads, and children who ran among the adults, shrieking like demons, their faces blackened by soot. Dogs and cats picked through the mud and puddles, and rats darted across the street.

'Make way there!' bellowed a porter pushing a wheelbarrow full of nuts and Bo sidestepped to avoid a collision. He hated being in crowds, being deeply conscious of his white hair and pink eyes, though at least his cap hid the former. He lowered his head a little and tried to avoid making eye contact with any passers-by.

After further directions from Black Francis, Fruma slipped away to search for provisions. The captain led Bo and Valbrand on to the harbour, which was lined with whitewashed stone buildings and granite, slate-fronted houses. The promontory loomed over the harbour and the town, its rocky edges and cliffs like the battlements and towers of a fortress.

180

A handful of little fishing boats, merchant galleys and three-masted sailing ships were anchored in the harbour. Bo shuddered as they passed a black, gleaming Sentinel. Black Francis pointed to a white marble statue of a winged woman with a veiled face, which was half-hidden by untidy piles of lobster pots. 'This is where I told Fruma to meet us later.'

'Where is Sesheta?' said Valbrand.

'Do not say that name so loudly,' said Black Francis as they stopped at the entrance to an alleyway. He ran his hands over the wall.

'What are you doing?' said Valbrand.

'Looking for a sign,' said Black Francis, his brow creased with concentration. His fingers touched a small, disc-shaped indent in one of the bricks. 'This is where we'll find her.'

A vagrant lay asleep at the entrance of the alleyway, his coat splattered with dried vomit. Another man crouched against the damp, mossy wall, playing a bone flute. Neither paid Bo and his companions any attention when they stepped over them.

Gangs of pigeons perched on the eaves, cooing incessantly, their droppings staining the mildewed walls. An old woman sat hunched on the muddy ground. An unbleached linen cap hid her face; her ragged dress was torn and filthy with any colour long since faded. A pigeon rested on the old woman's lap, as docile as a cat, and she stroked it with her gloved hands. Black Francis cleared his throat to announce his presence.

'Why are you troubling me?' said the old woman in a dry, smoky voice. 'Can you not leave me in peace?'

181

'I seek knowledge,' said Black Francis.

The old woman paused as though she was thinking, deciding what to do next. She stood and the pigeon flapped away. 'This is a strange place to seek knowledge.'

'It's strange knowledge that I seek.'

'Show me your forehead,' said the old woman.

Black Francis took off his cap and knelt.

'Very well,' she said after running her gloved hands over his forehead. 'Follow me.'

Hobbling, and with one hand on the wall for balance, the old woman led them further down the alleyway. The buildings that flanked them seemed to lean, as though it might take only a gentle push to topple them against each other, crushing whatever stood between.

'We are here,' said the old woman when they reached a dead-end.

'This old crone is mad,' said Valbrand, nudging Bo's arm and pointing at the brick wall in front of them.

'We should trust Black Francis,' said Bo, but the old woman's behaviour puzzled him. She scoured the walls with her gloved hands, rubbing off dust and feeling the edges of each brick. Then she pulled at one of the bricks and at first Bo thought his eyes tricked him. A door opened in front of him, a door made of bricks.

'Go in, swiftly now,' said the old woman. She ushered them inside and closed the door behind them. They stood in total darkness until a candle spluttered into life and revealed a plain square room with another door straight ahead of them.

The old woman whipped away her linen cap. Bo saw that

182

she was not old at all. Although flecked with grey, her hair was a dark cascade that flowed down to her shoulders. Her skin was tanned and smooth, her eyes dark brown. She cast off the rags and gloves of her disguise to reveal a linen tunic that reached below her knees. A knife with a blade of pure gold was fastened to her belt. She had not been Nulled.

'Sesheta, it's good to see you again,' said Black Francis.

The woman looked at Black Francis in a manner that was far from friendly. 'I did not expect to see *you* again. The Sea Beggars placed a high price on your head.'

Black Francis grinned. 'I'm full of surprises.'

'No, you are full of tricks and deceptions,' said Sesheta.

Listening to their conversation, Bo sensed there was a story between them but realised it was not a good time for him to start asking questions.

Black Francis pointed to the ragged clothes Sesheta had worn. 'You're not averse to deceptions yourself.'

'I do not apologise for my disguise. It is easy to hide in such a place. Vagrants are painful to the eyes of the townsfolk and they choose to ignore them. That is fortunate for me because those suspected of heresy and conjuration face serious punishments. The Society has many spies and soldiers here.'

'Those Society scum spread like rats,' said Valbrand.

Sesheta nodded in agreement. 'Once there were just press gangs in Farligby and they were bad enough, but the Society is much more dangerous.'

Bo remembered the two soldiers outside the alehouse and he guessed they worked for the Society.

Sesheta pointed at Bo and Valbrand. 'Who are these?'

Black Francis gave her their names. Sesheta's unblinking eyes boring into Bo, probing, unnerving, exposing. Just at the point when Bo thought he could no longer endure her stare, she turned back to Black Francis. 'So, what brings you all here?'

'We need your help,' said Black Francis.

'Why I am not surprised? Let us go down to my chamber.'

Sesheta opened the other door, which led to the top of a staircase barely wide enough for one person. A dull orange glow from the foot of the stairs allowed enough light to see.

'What is this place?' said Valbrand.

'Somewhere long forgotten by the people of this town,' said Sesheta. 'These passages were made by Thoth during the Long War and the Great Terror that followed. Tunnels stretch under much of this town, but only I remain here now.'

Valbrand whispered to Black Francis, 'Who is Thoth?'

Black Francis said, 'The husband of Sesheta. Say no more of him if you value your skin.'

Once they reached the bottom step, a granite statue of a man with the head of an ibis faced them. The statue was flanked on one side by a door and on the other by a torch that flickered feebly in the musty air. Sesheta kissed the forehead of the statue, pushed the door open and motioned for the men to follow her inside.

They entered a stuffy, windowless room. A handful of tallow candles created a dim, dirty light beneath the plastered, soot-blackened ceiling. Bo had the feeling of walking into a tomb. The walls were painted with mysterious figures standing in profile, with a hint of shimmering movement in

184

their hair and robes. In front of the unlit fireplace stood a wooden chair with a curved back and legs shaped like a lion's paws. Cabinets and chests covered most of the floor, some filled with books, while others stored animal shells marked with exotic symbols, stone tablets carved with figures and shapes, wax tablets, reed pens, and notched sticks. A basalt statue of a scribe, naked from the waist up and with an ink palette around his neck kept watch over the room.

A richly decorated anthropoid wooden coffin stood upright beside the fireplace. Painted on the coffin was the face of a young man with big dark eyes, a slender nose and thin, pursed lips. Beneath the face was a symbol of a winged beetle and below that, on a central panel, more symbols and figures of people and creatures.

Bo loved to explore and study strange objects and Sesheta's room was stuffed full of fascinating treasures. The host of objects, the smell of mouldy paper and the cheap tallow candles reminded Bo of the Vault of Artefacts in the Hammersund palace where he had spent many happy hours of peace and solitude; hours that belonged to another life.

'Welcome to my home,' said Sesheta as she sat in the wooden chair.

'Where is Thoth?' said Valbrand.

Sesheta stiffened. 'He stands before you.'

Black Francis bowed respectfully to the coffin, but Valbrand laughed. 'So that's your husband? I hate to say it but it looks as though he's seen better days.'

Sesheta leapt from the chair and lunged at Valbrand. Such was the surprise and force of the sudden attack that she knocked Valbrand back against the wall. She pulled the golden knife from her belt and held its tip beneath his chin. 'You are not worthy to breathe the air that surrounds his coffin.'

'Enough,' said Black Francis. 'Fighting among ourselves only helps the enemy. Sesheta, let him go. Valbrand is a good man but his mouth sometimes works faster than his brain.'

Sesheta released Valbrand. 'I may be less forgiving next time.'

Valbrand scowled at Sesheta. Bo could only imagine the dark thoughts and intentions passing through his mind.

Sesheta sat back down in the chair and placed the knife on her lap. There were no other chairs so Bo and his companions remained standing. Sounding far from concerned, she said, 'Tell me of your troubles, Black Francis.'

'My friend has come into possession of a parchment,' he said, pointing to Bo. 'It's written in Manus and I need you to translate it.'

She ran her hands through her long hair. 'Any half-witted peasant priest could do that for you, why come to me?'

'Because you have my complete trust, and your wisdom is without compare,' said Black Francis.

'Do not try flattery. It sounds weak on your tongue and I am far too wise and wary to fall for its trap. And you know that I never work for free.'

'I think five crowns is a fair price,' said Black Francis.

Sesheta gave a scornful laugh. 'Five crowns is a fair price for a half-witted peasant priest perhaps, but my services are not so cheap. Ten crowns or you can leave.'

186

'As you wish,' said Black Francis.

Sesheta held out her right hand and Black Francis dropped the coins into it. She counted them first before slipping them into her pocket. 'Let us begin.'

Bo passed the parchment to Sesheta along with the golden seal. She examined the seal and slowly unfolded the parchment. As she read, she silently mouthed the words. When she had finished reading, she gently laid the parchment on her lap.

'Well, what does it say?' said Black Francis. 'Is it important?'

Sesheta looked up at the soot-smeared ceiling as though searching for the right words. She licked her lips. 'Yes, Black Francis, it is important. In fact, I believe it could scarcely be *more* important.'

The Great Undertaking

'This is a Patriarchal Edict,' said Sesheta, holding up the parchment and the golden seal. 'It is signed by Prester John himself and this is his seal. Such seals are used to authenticate a document but are normally made from lead. Gold is only used for Edicts of the very highest importance. This Edict was meant for the Queen of Prevennis. It is my guess that such Edicts have been sent to all the monarchs in Prester John's thrall.'

'No wonder Bishop Neidelhart was so well protected,' said Valbrand.

Sesheta quickly divined the truth. 'As I suspected, you stole the parchment. Well, Black Francis, you have never stolen anything like this before. Did I not always say that one day you would find yourself in trouble too deep for you to cope with? Today might be that day.'

Her words subdued Black Francis and his shoulders hunched.

Sesheta held up the parchment and read aloud:

The one true God has placed me in the watch-tower of mankind with the duty of pastoral care to all.

188

The Sect called the Illuminati is spreading far and wide. Their followers reject the divine gift of the Holy Null and dare to challenge the mission of the Holy Mother Church with every breath. Many are their dishonourable acts and the infection of their heresy is spreading. Much action has been taken to defeat these pernicious foes but it is clear more is required. In especial, we must prevent the hearts of the innocent being perverted and wounded by heresy. To this end, and with authority directly from God, I decree the following.

Desiring above all to protect the young, all infants shall be blessed by the Holy Null on the occasion of reaching five years of age. Furthermore, Sentinels, those conduits of God's eternal love and care, shall be vastly increased in number so that all can find safety in their protection. To achieve these aims, we give the Brotherhood of Redemption and the Society for the Propagation of Pious Labour the free faculty of calling upon the aid and effort of all, and the right to summon them to Gorefayne to labour in this holy mission, this great undertaking. It is my desire and command that monarchs, bishops and other local ordinaries shall aid the Brotherhood to ensure that they pursue and punish, with full severity, those that shun the order to carry out God's work.

This decree is declared by Prester John, God's appointed apostle on earth.

Silence followed Sesheta's reading. It was Black Francis who spoke first. 'They want to force the Null on infants? Why do they want to do that?'

'Is it not obvious?' said Sesheta, her eyes aflame. 'For years the Illuminati relied upon recruiting children before they reach the age of fourteen, the age of the Null. By that age they are hardly children any more and possess keen,

189

questioning minds, minds that can see through the Mother Church's lies. It is those free minds that Prester John fears. He is tightening his grip.'

Black Francis rubbed his beard. 'It seems so. I've also heard rumours of large armies and ships mustering in the south.'

'Yes, those rumours have reached my ears too,' said Sesheta. 'And many talk of the Egregores.'

'What are they?' said Bo.

'Some new contrivance of Prester John,' said Sesheta. She held open the parchment to show the illustration of the disturbing blank face. 'They are said to resemble giant stone heads. They float across the land as though supported by invisible limbs. When they find anyone that has not yet been Nulled they give out a terrible shriek that paralyzes their victim's body and mind.'

'This is a jest surely,' said Valbrand.

Sesheta shook her head. 'Those that claim to have seen an Egregore do not laugh.'

'The Illuminati need to know everything that is contained in the parchment,' said Bo, unsettled by Sesheta's description of the Egregores and keen to move the conversation on. 'We have to get it to the sanctuary.'

'It is too late for that,' said Sesheta.

'What do you mean?' said Black Francis.

'Alarming news has reached me,' said Sesheta. 'The sanctuary has been discovered by the servants of Prester John, discovered and destroyed.'

Bo's blood ran cold. He looked at Black Francis and knew that he shared the same thought: with the Illuminati destroyed, surely all their hopes were extinguished. And Elowen. Was she still alive?

Only Valbrand appeared unmoved by the news. 'How did you come by these tidings?'

'How little you know,' said Sesheta. 'For centuries beyond count Adepts have used birds to carry messages. Master Grunewald believed ravens to be uncommonly intelligent birds and he has been proven right. A raven bearing news of the sanctuary's destruction came to me three days ago, as they will have visited others too. Through Grunewald's far-sightedness, the flames of the Illuminati may be kept alive.'

'Were there any survivors?' said Black Francis.

'I know not, the message was one word only: Omphalos.'

'What does that mean?' said Black Francis.

'It means the sanctuary has been discovered. Discovery has always meant death for the Illuminati, no other words are needed.'

Bo felt hope drain from him. How could Prester John be defeated now?

Even Black Francis shared his despair. 'All is lost.'

'Not yet,' said Sesheta. 'You do not know the full meaning of the word of Omphalos. It is a place sacred to all Eldar, known as the navel of the world, the final rallying place in times of trouble. The message is as much a summoning as it is a signal of the sanctuary's destruction. It is my belief that any surviving Illuminati will now make for Omphalos, as well as many of the Eldar. But it is certainly not my intention to do so. My place is here, with my husband. He cannot leave this place and therefore neither can I. My duty is to remain by his side.'

191

'You're not safe here, not any more,' said Black Francis pointing at the parchment to prove his point.

'I have never been safe here,' said Sesheta. As she spoke, she caressed the coffin, tears welling in her eyes. 'Do not underestimate me. If I choose to stay hidden then hidden I shall stay.'

'But you're powerful, Sesheta, you could do much in the fight against Prester John,' said Black Francis. 'If you stay hidden here you achieve nothing. Surely Thoth did not desire such a fate for you?'

'What do you know?' said Sesheta, her eyes wild, her voice rising with each word. 'You do not know the pain I feel every day, every hour. Without Thoth I am dead inside, I have nothing to live for but such is my destiny, such is my duty. I cannot leave this place. I have no choice.'

'You always have a choice,' said Black Francis. 'Do not let yourself become a slave to grief.'

'I made my decision long ago,' she said. Sesheta stood and walked over to one of the chests. She moved the books that rested on top and creaked the lid open. She pulled out a folded map; she gave it to Black Francis and said, 'Do you recognize these lands and these oceans?'

The captain unfolded the map and held it closer to his eyes. 'Yes, it's an old map but this is all familiar to me.'

'And you see the circle symbol in the east of the map, at the bend in the river Oreg?'

'Yes,' said Black Francis. 'But why show me this?'

'That is Omphalos, the navel of the world. You must go there. The Illuminati need to know about Prester John's plans. I cannot do this journey so you must.'

'There are plenty of Kingsguard to kill here in Prevennis,' said Valbrand. 'We don't need to sail off to foreign lands to look for a fight.'

'And I cannot abandon my people,' said Bo. 'My duty is to fight for Prevennis.'

'Your duty should take you to Omphalos,' said Sesheta. 'Anything you achieve in Prevennis is fruitless while Prester John endures and only those summoned at Omphalos have a chance of defeating him.'

'We can't go to Omphalos,' said Black Francis. 'Sesheta, I value your guidance but what you ask for is not possible.'

Sesheta looked irritated by his refusal. 'But where else can you go? Yes, you are full of cunning, Black Francis, but your luck will run out eventually. What of the Sea Beggars?'

'I've always bested the Sea Beggars,' said Black Francis.

'Only by fleeing from them and there will come a time when you can flee no more,' she said. Without glancing away from Black Francis she threw the parchment at Bo who caught it with both hands. 'You always run from your past, Black Francis, from your mistakes. And you are running now.'

*

'I don't think she likes you, pirate,' said Valbrand to Black Francis as they wound back through the dank alleyway.

The captain remained silent as he walked. At the sound of his heavy footsteps the pigeons resting on the eaves above flew away and a prowling cat scampered for the safety of a dark hole.

193

'Leave him alone,' said Bo, who was tired of Valbrand's sniping and complaining.

They emerged from the alleyway. The harbour was noisy and busy but the fishermen and merchants paid them no attention. The red evening light gave the marble statue of the winged woman a ruddy hue; Fruma stood beside it, holding a small sack. As they approached him, Bo realised that Fruma's face was white with fear and his hands were trembling.

'Are you well, my friend?' said Bo.

'Yes, yes,' said Fruma, his voice at a higher pitch than normal. He cleared his throat. 'We should get moving.'

'Did you find any food?' said Valbrand pointing to the sack that Fruma carried.

'Some oats, that is all,' he said, biting his lip and shifting his weight from one foot to another. 'There is little food to buy in this town and the prices are high.'

Valbrand's face went red and twisted in anger. 'And we have all that gold…'

Black Francis clamped his huge hands on Fruma's shoulders. 'Don't be troubled. You did your best and we won't starve yet. Come, let's get back to the ship.'

They made their way back up the main street. The stallholders and itinerant salesmen were packing up for the day, drawn by the lure of the alehouses. Fishermen trudged towards the harbour, ready for high tide to take them out for another dangerous night on the sea.

The news of the destruction of the sanctuary had shaken Bo. He feared that the Illuminati had been betrayed, but by who? Increasingly he had a sense of being watched. He

194

scanned the high windows and the squalid alleyways but saw no sinister faces. Fruma was edgy too; he jumped at every noise and bit his nails as he walked. Bo found Farligby an unnerving place and was relieved when they left the town behind them.

Once out in the open country, the hedgerows buzzed with the scratchy songs of grasshoppers and crickets, their last flurry before the first frosts of winter silenced their music. A distant stag belched out a challenge. The sinking sun bathed the orchards and fields in soft light; the little copses glowed in vivid oranges, reds and yellows, like daubs of paint on a green canvas.

Black Francis marched in front of them, silent and brooding. Fruma plodded wearily, his head lowered. Only Valbrand acted content, whistling and swinging his cutlass to scythe ears of barley that grew close to the path.

They came to the beach at Dekning after nightfall, their heavy footsteps crunching in the coarse sand. Bo spotted the anchored *Husker Du* silhouetted against the inky sky.

'It's almost midnight,' said Black Francis, the first words he had spoken since they had left Farligby. 'They'll be here soon.'

A few minutes later Bo heard oars splashing and spotted the little dinghy pushing through the waves. To his surprise it was not Shrimp and Crab who worked the oars but two outlaws, Svikefull and Snyteri. They were tall, muscular and blond-haired men from the eastern Ostjord region of Prevennis, and largely kept themselves to themselves. They rarely spoke to the other outlaws, except for Fruma who had recruited them.

As the dinghy beached, Black Francis said, 'What's going on? Where are Shrimp and the other hands?'

'The crew are all asleep so I decided not to wake them,' said Snyteri. 'I can handle a boat, have no fear of that. I was a fisherman for more years than I care to remember.'

'Aye, that is true,' said Fruma. 'He is a good man.'

Black Francis eyed the outlaw. 'I'm astonished Shrimp allowed this to happen, I'll have words with him. The crew might be sleeping now but I'll soon get them up and working. By the gods, you leave them for a few hours and they all go soft.'

They were soon on board the dinghy and making steady progress towards the *Husker Du*. After a barrage of instructions and impatient sighs, Black Francis took over the oars from Svikefull and Snyteri. Upon reaching the *Husker Du*, they climbed the rope ladder only to find an empty, silent deck. The timbers squeaked and the gentle waves gurgled against the ship. A few lanterns offered patches of light.

'What's going on?' said Black Francis. 'Where are the lookouts? Why are these lanterns still alight? The ship could be seen for miles around.'

Laughter greeted him and a tall man emerged from the darkness. His face was painted with a web of tattoos: a Sea Beggar. 'So, Black Francis, we have found you at last.'

'Maybe but you won't live long enough to tell anyone else about it,' said Black Francis, reaching for his sword. Bo and Valbrand did likewise but the Sea Beggar laughed like a carefree child. Fruma stood motionless, seemingly frozen by fear.

Bo heard a click from behind; Svikefull and Snyteri held

196

their pistols, not at the Sea Beggar but at Bo and his companions.

'They call me Alferez, and you see that I am not alone,' said the Sea Beggar. 'There is no escape. Drop your weapons or you will be dead in seconds.'

More Sea Beggars emerged from hiding places on deck. Outnumbered and with no chance of resisting, Bo, Black Francis and Valbrand obeyed; their swords clattered onto the deck. The other outlaws came on deck. They stood, heads bowed, in a close huddle, keeping well away from Bo.

'This is not necessary,' said Black Francis. 'I have the money to pay the *Caudillo*. I intend to sail for Beauteous Isle within the week.'

Alferez licked his lips. 'It is far too late for that, his patience has expired. You have been given many chances to pay. It is not your money the *Caudillo* wants now, but your blood. Only your death will pay the debt.'

'Where are my crew?' said Black Francis.

'They are below deck and alive, at least for now,' said Alferez. 'They will suffer for their misguided loyalty to you. It is fortunate, Prince Asbjorn, that your followers, the so-called *outlaws*, were prepared to follow their conscience, although it took a brave man to bring them to their senses.'

'So we've been sold out,' said Black Francis. He glared at Valbrand. 'I always knew you'd betray us one day.'

Valbrand opened his mouth to protest but Alferez spoke again. 'Nay, it is not him I speak of.'

The truth hit Bo hard. *Fruma*. He only had to look at him to confirm the truth. There was only one word Bo could utter, only one question that held any meaning. 'Why?'

'It is hopeless, can you not see it?' said Fruma, his head lowered. 'We cannot defeat Prester John. It is madness to fight on.'

Bo stared at Fruma in disbelief. Betrayed by his friend, a man he trusted with his life. 'But you wanted…you came to the Barbeg caves at the Gladsheim. *You* summoned *me.*'

Fruma gnawed his nails and gave Bo a darting, edgy look. 'I thought you were a warrior, a leader of men. I tried to believe in you, I *wanted* to believe in you. But you do not have a king's strength of character or the courage. You have failed. The men are unhappy. They lost all faith in your leadership, and in desperation, they came to me. It was my duty to help them.'

'So *that* was why you volunteered to seek provisions in Farligby,' said Black Francis. 'That gave you the chance to find the Sea Beggars, to betray us.'

Fruma stood beside Alferez. 'I am not proud of what I did, but I had no other choice. It was the last chance to save my life and the lives of the others. Alferez has arranged a pardon for all the outlaws, all except Valbrand of course. None of us trusted him to be part of our plans.'

'A pardon is a poor reward,' said Black Francis. 'What else were you promised in return for your treachery?'

Fruma looked away. 'The Queen of Prevennis has offered a generous reward for Asbjorn's capture and I intend to collect it.'

Alferez spat. 'Alas, there has been a change of plan. The prince belongs to us.'

'What of our bargain?' said Fruma.

Alferez laughed. 'It is true that the queen is prepared to

pay well for the return of her wayward and treacherous son, but he belongs to the King of the Sea Beggars.'

'That is not what we agreed,' said Fruma. 'You lied to me, you *tricked* me.'

'I said what was necessary and, in your greed, you believed me,' said Alferez. He gestured to the other Sea Beggars. 'This one has served his purpose. Return him to his home waters.'

Before Fruma could react, four Sea Beggars hurled him overboard. There was a scream cut short by a heavy splash.

Bo's stomach lurched. 'He will die in minutes in that water.'

'What do you care?' said Alferez. 'I thought you would appreciate his drowning.'

'It is murder,' said Bo. For all Fruma's treachery, Bo took no pleasure in his death. He had been a friend once, a good friend. If it had been within his power to do so, Bo would have tried to save him, but it was hopeless. Fruma was lost to the icy black sea.

'Let Fruma's fate be a warning to you all,' said Alferez to the outlaws, ignoring Bo's protests. The outlaws shared fearful looks but remained silent as the Sea Beggars herded them onto the dinghy. Bo wondered what future awaited them. He doubted that the promises of Sea Beggars amounted to much.

Alferez smirked at Black Francis. 'The Caudillo is most anxious to see you. For the next few days, the *Husker Du* will be your prison ship. My brothers and I will sail this vessel south.'

Bo sensed the anger that coursed through Black Francis

but the captain retained his composure. He said, 'And what of my crew?'

'They will come as our prisoners,' said Alferez. 'They will be sold to the Society.'

'I'm surprised the Society deals with scum such as you,' said Black Francis.

His response amused Alferez. 'We have found that, on some occasions at least, our interests cross. The mines of Gorefayne demand many slaves. Your crew are to be blessed with purposeful lives, short and painful too of course, but purposeful and pure, better than being infected by your...abnormality. You have evaded us for too long, Black Francis. The *Caudillo* will enjoy adding the *Husker Du* to his fleet, but most of all, he looks forward to punishing you.'

CHAPTER ELEVEN

The Beautous Isle

The Sea Beggars locked Bo, Black Francis, Valbrand and the crew in the hold. They endured long days of agony and wretchedness. The hold was hot and airless, and soon stank abominably of sweat, urine, faeces and vomit. Bo judged that three days passed before their captors provided any food, food flung down from the door at the top of the stairs: stale bread, mouldy cheese, bones with small pieces of fatty meat sticking to them. The starving prisoners had fought over the scraps, prisoners that, only days before, had been the closest of friends. Hunger strips away dignity, honour and loyalty.

Although painfully hungry, Bo had stayed out of the fights. He knew he had failed his companions. If it came to it, he deserved to starve; the crew did not.

The ship rolled and lurched. There was no talking, only the moans and gasps of the hungry and injured. All those around Bo slept deeply. Black Francis snored, while beside him Shrimp fidgeted and thrashed. Valbrand gabbled in his sleep.

Black Francis groaned and sat upright, awake but dazed. The many beatings he had endured at their captors' hands left his face bloody and bruised. In a weak voice, he asked Bo, 'Have I been asleep for long?'

'Many hours I think, but it is hard to count time down here.'

'Has there been any more fighting among my boys?'

'No, it is calm for now,' said Bo. Talking strained his dry mouth and sore throat. 'The Sea Beggars have given us food. It's not much, but it will keep us from starving.'

'I must remember to thank them for their hospitality,' said Black Francis with a forced smile.

'Where are they taking us?'

'South, to the Beauteous Isle,' said Black Francis after a long, chesty cough. 'It is the one place in the whole world that I'd hoped never to see again, but destiny it seems has other ideas.'

'What is the Beauteous Isle like?' said Bo. He had never left Prevennis or its waters before. He was plunging into a world that was alien to him.

'Before the coming of the Sea Beggars it was said to be a magical place, a jewel of an island rising from tranquil blue waters. The Kojin, a race of seafarers from the distant east, once ruled it. They built Katakani, the city the King of the Sea Beggars now claims as his own. He lurks in the old Kojin fortress he calls the Alcazar. Most Kojin have been forced into the fringes of the island, a shadow of their former glory.'

'Why is the King of the Sea Beggars so powerful?'

'He pays the Mother Church rich tribute, and so buys his freedom from Prester John. You will have noticed his men do not receive the Null. The Mother Church turns a blind eye to his crimes and indeed when it suits their purpose, they help or protect him. The King of the Sea Beggars, the Caudillo, treats his followers well, but he shows no mercy to his enemies.'

'He certainly seems to hate you.'

'Aye, as well he might. Once I served him, a loyal captain in his fleet, feared across many lands. I had a weakness for gambling and that proved my undoing. Fortunes I won in games of chance, but greater fortunes I lost. I stole from my master, the *Caudillo*, to fund my gambling. I sold plunder to other traders and did not pass on the profits. The King of the Sea Beggars has many spies and word of my deceit reached his ears. The *Caudillo* offered me a chance to earn his forgiveness by working as a slave trader. But for all the wicked things I've done in my life, even I could not contemplate doing that. I refused to sell men, women and children like cattle. So, I fled, in fear of my life.'

Bo wanted to say something, anything. He had always supposed that Black Francis had a murky history but the revelation that he had been a Sea Beggar shocked him.

'I've tried to hide the person I was,' continued Black Francis. He pointed to his scarred face. 'An apothecary cured me of my Sea Beggar tattoos. His treatment was cruel but it worked. In exile, my eyes were opened. I witnessed the terror and oppression of Prester John. I turned my back on the life I once lived. I contacted the Illuminati and swore to aid them in whatever way I could. I will never atone for my sins, they're too great, but I won't stop trying to find some small redemption.'

'I think you have done many good deeds,' said Bo.

203

'Perhaps. But my past has always followed me, for the King of the Sea Beggars does not forget a traitor. Sesheta was right. I couldn't hope to run away from the Sea Beggars forever. I should have gone back to pay my debts. It wasn't fear of the Sea Beggars that stopped me. No, I always thought that if I went back I would have to face up to the person I'd been, the terrible things I'd done. But I've been caught anyway and I know I am to die, but the deepest hurt is that my crew will suffer too.'

Black Francis tried to say more but succumbed to another coughing fit.

'You must rest,' said Bo, helping him to lie down again.

Black Francis made a muted protest but sleep took him again. Bo longed for the oblivion of sleep. Hunger and thirst were mere trifles compared to his guilt. Their capture by the Sea Beggars was his fault. He had trusted Fruma, a terrible misjudgement. And deep down he knew that his own weakness had caused Fruma to betray him. Bo realised he should have been a stronger, more decisive leader. He had been a fool. The mockery of his mother, Haakon, Neidelhart and countless others returned to him. They were right; he was a failure, a weakling. All was lost.

The Edict from Prester John they had intercepted would never reach the Illuminati; Bo had watched the Sea Beggars toss the parchment overboard, a meaningless item to those who desired only treasure. It had been different when they found his sword, the sword of the Preven kings. His cheeks had glowed with shame and humiliation as he watched the Sea Beggars paw over the sword, guessing its worth. To them it was a trinket; its history meant nothing.

204

The ship slowed and moments later the anchor dropped. The hold door opened.

'Time to wake up, scum!' came a harsh cry from the top of the stairs. Sea Beggars, among them Alferez, poured into the hold and dragged the prisoners to their feet.

'UP THE STAIRS!' shouted Alferez. They jostled Bo and the other prisoners with punches and kicks, and forced them all up onto the deck. Bo squinted in the blinding sunshine. Even in the height of the Preven summer, he had never experienced such heat. As his eyes adjusted to the bright light, he took in his surroundings. The *Husker Du* had anchored in a harbour with extensive docks and wharfs full of ships and boats of every type and size. From the harbour, the city of Katakani spread inland until it reached the foothills of a table-shaped limestone mountain to the southwest. A large, square fortress with four corner turrets stood between the mountain and the city. It was the Alcazar, the stronghold of the King of the Sea Beggars.

The Sea Beggars disembarked their exhausted, hungry prisoners and lined them up along the dockside. Many of the young crew of the *Husker Du* could barely stand and some had to lean against their comrades to avoid collapsing. Black Francis, his face swollen by bruises and welts, stood between Bo and Shrimp. The captain kept glancing at the *Husker Du*—it was not just a ship to him, it was his home, part of his soul, and now it was lost to him.

The harbour of Katakani throbbed with life. Horse-drawn carts laden with goods rushed to and from ships. Merchants wearing pointed hats and long coats of brocaded velvet argued and forged deals. Sail makers, carpenters, rope makers

205

and blacksmiths hurried about their business. Sailors crawled over the rigging on their ships like spiders repairing a broken web, shouting, cursing and swearing in a myriad of accents. One figure that moved among the crowd captured Bo's attention. He stood taller than any man around him. His skin was shiny and blue-black. Even more striking were his emerald green eyes and webbed hands. Bo guessed it was one of the Kojin. He watched the creature with morbid fascination; it was as though it had stepped out of a book of legend and into the real world.

Alferez stood in front of the prisoners and addressed them. 'Welcome to the Beauteous Isle. Your stay here will be short and it will be unpleasant. Soon you will embark on a journey to the mines of Gorefayne. Until that time, you will be kept in the Pits. If you behave and obey orders, you will be given food and water. If you defy us, expect to be beaten and expect to starve. Pray to whatever god you see fit to but it will not help you. On this island it is only the will of the King of the Sea Beggars that matters. Of course, the captain of the *Husker Du* can expect to receive very special treatment. Long has the Caudillo waited to see you again, Black Francis.'

Two Sea Beggars hauled Black Francis away from the rest of the prisoners. Shrimp tried to lunge at the nearest Sea Beggar but Bo held him back.

'Let go of me,' said Shrimp, angry and weeping, and struggling to free himself from Bo's grip.

'You cannot help him,' said Bo, frightened that Shrimp was going to throw his life away.

Black Francis called out to Shrimp, 'Listen to Bo, don't

give these scum an excuse to kill you. Stay alive to fight another day. They can't part us, not forever.'

His words calmed Shrimp, who dropped his gaze, unable to watch as the Sea Beggars took Black Francis away.

Alferez rubbed his hands together. 'How *touching*. Now, it's time for you dogs to get moving. To the Pits!'

The prisoners were forced into a line and made to stand in pairs, side by side. To his dismay, Bo found himself paired with Valbrand. Each pair was assigned a Sea Beggar to guard them. Bo and Valbrand's guard had a scrawny neck and deep-set eyes. He stared at them with a spiteful grin and tied their hands together with rope.

'Any ideas for escape, *Your Majesty*?' said Valbrand, tugging at the ropes that bound them.

'I think it is too late for that,' said Bo. He wished he could fight back but, being unarmed, he knew it was hopeless. He thought about his lost sword. He wanted to wield it again, to gain a measure of honour, to die courageously, but the chance for heroism had surely passed.

The Sea Beggars marched Bo and the other prisoners to the gate of a vast, many-domed building. The gate was forged from bronze, and decorated with cast figures of sinners and manic demons. One of the Sea Beggars knocked on the gate and it opened with a metallic roar. The building housed a bustling market, dimly lit by the shafts of dusty light that poured through holes in the roof. There were two lines of wooden stalls, each covered by tattered silk canopies.

The stalls offered a bewildering array of goods such as pearls, silks, brassware and textiles with bright patterns.

Joints of bloody meat skewered on hooks attracted swarms of flies. A man wandered through the crowds with a large snake draped around his neck and his shoulders, and there were many other animals for sale: horses, goats, pigs and a startling bird that stood taller than any man, with a long, curved, bare neck and with black feathers except for the ends of its wings and tail, which were white. Kojin walked through the crowds; their clothes were poor and most worked as servants.

The stuffy, smoky heat and the rank odour of sweat and pungent spices made Bo nauseated. Noise bombarded his ears. The haggling and arguing of traders, loud voices competing for mastery in a host of different languages. The screams and groans of trussed livestock. The incessant hum of flute and drums played by a succession of musicians who claimed the few unoccupied patches of ground.

Absorbed in the market's rhythm, few paid any attention to Bo and his fellow prisoners as the Sea Beggars hustled them through the length of the market and out into the quiet streets beyond. Whitewashed, flat-roofed, cubic houses huddled close to one another and all were in poor condition, with rotten wooden doors and peeling walls scrawled with crude graffiti. Bo glimpsed open spaces behind some houses, gardens that must once have glowed with bright flowers and sweetly-scented shrubs and trees; now abandoned and untended, choked by weeds.

Bo saw rats scurry among the rubbish piled up along the side of the sun-baked streets. Scrawny, flea-bitten dogs snuffled for scraps. Bloated flies hovered above splattered horse dung.

'This place is full of vermin,' said Valbrand, shattering Bo's thoughts.

'No talking!' said the Sea Beggar beside them.

Using a crumbling stone bridge, they passed over a shallow river. A decomposing horse partly submerged in the water and a layer of festering scum coated the river's surface. The street on the far side of the bridge climbed with a steady gradient. The heat bullied Bo and he yearned for the cold rain of Prevennis. His mouth was parched, his lips chapped and sore. He tried not to think of water but memories of cool, deep lakes taunted and tantalised him.

The line of fatigued and half-starved prisoners slowed and stretched out. Valbrand was breathing heavily. His footsteps became ponderous and, as he lagged, he pulled on the rope that bound them together, despite the angry shouts and slaps from the Sea Beggar guarding them. They were the last pair in the procession of prisoners and the gap between them and the rest grew.

'Keep moving, you miserable maggots,' said the Sea Beggar, as the rest of the prisoners and guards disappeared behind a bend in the road.

Valbrand gasped in exhaustion and fell to his knees, almost dragging Bo down with him.

The Sea Beggar unsheathed a knife from his belt. 'If you don't move—'

Valbrand leapt to his feet with an explosion of energy and elbowed the Sea Beggar in the throat. With his eyes bulging, he spluttered and staggered backwards, dropping his knife. Valbrand barged the Sea Beggar onto the floor and killed him with a brutal kick to the head.

Shocked by the violence, Bo turned away; none of the other Sea Beggars had come back. They had not heard the fight.

'Quick, help me,' said Valbrand as he picked up the Sea Beggar's knife. Bo squatted down, allowing him enough slack on the rope that tied them together. Valbrand clasped the knife and swiftly cut through the rope.

'I thought you were exhausted,' said Bo, rubbing his sore wrists.

Valbrand laughed. 'So my little ruse tricked you too. Well, there's no point in getting any older if you don't get any wiser. We need to get moving, it won't take long for the other guards to realise we're missing.'

'What about the crew? We have to do something to help them.'

'There's nothing we can do,' said Valbrand. 'I don't like it either but that's how it is.'

As much as it tormented him, Bo acknowledged Valbrand was right. They left the dead Sea Beggar and bolted down a narrow alleyway, which was so shaded from the sun that it was almost dark.

'Where are we going?' said Bo, his lungs aching with the strain of running.

'God only knows,' said Valbrand, red-faced and breathing hard. 'I'm just trying to get as much ground between us and those damn Sea Beggars as I can.'

The alleyway took them into a labyrinth of twisting passages. Tormented by guilt, Bo ran almost blindly, scarcely noticing his surroundings. He was saving his own skin, abandoning the others. It was his fault they had been captured and now he was fleeing, leaving them to slavery or death. His weary limbs ached; thirst and hunger sapped his strength. After several minutes of running, Bo could take no more. He stopped and leant against the wall. 'I have to rest.'

'Do you want to be captured again?' said Valbrand, his fists clenched.

Bo's stomach churned. 'I need a breather.'

'Wait here, I'll scout ahead.'

Valbrand carried on down the passage, soon swallowed by the darkness ahead. Bo tried to suppress a horrible feeling that he had seen the last of him. He waited and waited. Valbrand had abandoned him, he was sure of it. Angry shouts echoed around the passages and stairways. The Sea Beggars had discovered their slain comrade and now the hunt was up. What should he do? He was unarmed and alone. Footsteps pounded down the alleyway, heavy footsteps. Bo pulled himself upright, bracing himself for a fight he could not win, but then Valbrand materialised out of the darkness. He greeted Bo with a grin. 'You didn't think I was coming back, did you?'

'No, no, I trust you,' lied Bo, in a shaky, breathless voice, feeling guilty and a little embarrassed.

Valbrand smirked. 'I'll believe you. The good news is that the way ahead is clear.

'But where are we going?' said Bo.

'We have to get out of the city,' said Valbrand. 'The Sea Beggars will swarm across every street. If we can get out into the wild lands beyond the city, we might stand a chance.'

'We don't know what's out there,' said Bo. 'We might be walking into worse danger.'

'What's worse than being caught by the Sea Beggars again? We've killed one of them and if they find us we'll be dead for sure. We can survive in the wild, just as we did in Prevennis.'

Reluctantly, Bo agreed. They pushed on. The alleyway led onto a winding street, deserted except from an old man sat against the front wall of his ramshackle house, smoking a pipe. He watched Valbrand and Bo with glazed, sleepy eyes.

The street led them to the fringes of the city, which was left in shadow by the flat-topped mountain and marked by a scattering of tiny mud huts topped with thatched roofs. A Kojin drew water from a well, while another worked to repair a roof. Their clothes were poor, robes cut from cheap rags.

'We need to find a way across that mountain,' said Valbrand, looking up.

'And then what?' said Bo. Compared to the soaring peaks of Prevennis the mountain was not high, but traversing it would be far from easy.

'*And then what?*' repeated Valbrand. 'We fall to our knees and thank God we survived that long.'

A shout from behind made Bo and Valbrand jump; two Sea Beggars were sprinting towards them. Valbrand gripped his knife and winked at Bo. 'I'm ready for another tussle.'

Bo had no weapon. He spotted a rock large enough to fill the palm of his hand so picked it up. The Sea Beggars approached and drew their curved, double-edged swords. Bo's heart drummed and his body quivered with fear. The Sea

212

Beggars lifted their swords to strike. With all his strength, Bo threw the rock at one of them. It hit the Sea Beggar on his left shoulder and he stumbled backwards. His comrade swung his sword at Valbrand, who dodged the blow and rammed his dagger into his opponent's stomach; the Sea Beggar groaned and fell. The other Sea Beggar howled with rage and charged at Bo, but he made the mistake of ignoring Valbrand, who threw the dagger and it lodged in the Sea Beggar's throat—he staggered a few yards before collapsing.

Bo retched, repelled by the sight of the two dead men. Valbrand did not share his concerns. He let out a deep breath, stretched his arms and smiled as he picked up one of the swords. 'These pirates are more used to pillaging than fighting.'

His legs still shaky, Bo picked up the other sword. 'You saved my life, thank you.'

It was strange he owed so much to Valbrand, only days earlier he considered him a threat, a traitor in his midst. Now, perhaps, he was his only friend.

Valbrand shrugged. 'It was nothing. Besides, if you get killed I'm on my own.'

Bo and Valbrand climbed into the mountain's jagged foothills. They found themselves sheltered by huddles of straggling, wind-stunted pine trees, around which grew thickly-branched rhododendrons and dwarf junipers. Further on, they found a bilberry bush; they stripped it of berries, eating some and keeping the rest for later. They carried on, and had not been climbing for long when they both spotted a tall figure on the ridge in front of them. At first

213

Bo thought it was a man but as they got closer he realised it was a weather-beaten scarecrow, supported by two wooden beams crossing each other. The scarecrow was smeared with dried blood and had crude symbols of skulls painted onto the tattered rags that formed the body. Sun-bleached bones littered the ground.

'These are a warning against going any further,' said Bo.

'We don't have any choice,' said Valbrand.

They toiled on. An eagle swooped over them, hunting an unseen victim. Close to the summit they came across a small waterfall, little more than a trickle of water squeezing through a scar in the rock, but both Bo and Valbrand cupped their hands and drank greedily. It quenched Bo's thirst and his head cleared a little. Valbrand wiped his mouth and grinned, 'Come on, one last push.'

After one more climb they reached the mountain's flat summit, which stretched at least three miles. The island was tear-shaped, with the city of Katakani filling the narrow northern tip. The rest of the island beyond the mountain was filled with rough, rocky scrubland and small woods, all enclosed by a ring of hills. Divided roughly into two regions by a river that meandered from east to west like a silver ribbon, Bo judged that from tip to tip the island was at least fifteen miles long.

Too tired to attempt the descent down the far side of the mountain, Bo and Valbrand prepared for a cold night on the summit, sheltering in a shallow hollow beneath a rock. They tried to light a fire but the gusting wind defeated their clumsy efforts. The night passed slowly. Bo shivered and his teeth chattered, but the cold did not trouble Valbrand.

He untied the silk ribbon around his neck and stroked it, his fingers moving slowly, sensuously, over its soft surface.

'What are you doing?' said Bo.

Valbrand tied the ribbon back around his neck. Without looking at Bo he said, 'It's all I have left of hers.'

'Who?'

'My wife, you fool.'

'I'm s-sorry.'

Valbrand sucked in air like a swimmer surfacing. 'It's two months you know, two months since they took her and our little one from me. They came at night, the Redeemers and the Kingsguard. I was in the woods, hunting. I should've been there. I should've protected them. They burnt down the village. Killed everyone. I came back too late. I should've been there.'

'You could not have saved them,' said Bo.

'Perhaps not, but by the Gods, I won't rest until I've slain a hundred Redeemers and Kingsguard. And once I've done that, I'll kill a hundred more.'

'That won't bring your wife and child back.'

'Don't you think I know that?' said Valbrand. His tone softened. 'You're right, and you talk sense, but sense won't help me. Sense won't ease my pain.'

'If I am talking sense, it will be for the first time,' said Bo. He kept thinking about Black Francis and the crew of the *Husker Du*. Guilt shadowed him. One thought dominated all others: *I could have gone back. I should have gone back.* Blowing on his aching hands to keep them warm, he added, 'I was wrong about everything.'

Valbrand picked his nose. 'You've made mistakes, lad. No

215

doubting that. Mind you, Fruma took us all in. I'd have never guessed he was a traitor.'

'I thought you were the traitor,' said Bo.

'Aye,' said Valbrand, rubbing his bald head. 'People never seem to trust me. Not sure why. Anyway, enough talk. I need sleep; it'll cure my troubles, if only for a little while.'

Sleep may have helped Valbrand, but it brought Bo no respite. The cries of dying men, grey and bloated corpses, and the ear-splitting sound of steel clashing against steel haunted his dreams. The intensity of his dreams increased until Bo woke with a start, his heart pounding like a drum. It was dawn.

'We ought to get moving,' said Valbrand, who was already wide awake. 'I think it'll be safer down in the middle of the island and we might be able to find something to eat down there.'

The descent was easier than Bo expected and they soon reached the foot of the mountain and headed further inland. It was a scrubby land, covered in evergreen shrubs such as sage, juniper and myrtle. There were few sounds apart from the hum of insects and the distant percussion of waves crashing against the cliffs that caged the island.

They slogged on with no clear direction, no clear plan. The only sign of civilisation was a stone chamber tomb formed by a large convex capstone rested firmly on three slabs. It was ancient, clearly abandoned for centuries. Bo was beginning to think no one lived in this wild place when a guttural cry ripped across the land. Bo and Valbrand stopped in their tracks. It was a cry of anguish and fear and sounded like no animal Bo had ever heard before. It was followed by laughter and whoops of joy: unmistakeably human sounds.

'Let's see what's happening,' said Valbrand.

'We must be careful,' said Bo.

It was too late. Valbrand was already creeping forward, keeping low but moving fast. Bo had no choice but to follow him.

They moved towards a small knot of pine trees. Two men and a child stood under the trees, their backs turned to Bo and Valbrand. One man held a bow, while the other clasped a musket. Their attention remained focused on a Kojin dangling upside down from one of the trees, his arms and legs entangled in ropes, snared by a devious trap.

The men laughed and threw stones at the Kojin, who hissed and shouted at them in response, his fluid voice like water gushing over rocks. The Kojin struggled in vain, desperately kicking his legs.

'We have to do something,' said Bo to Valbrand, angered by the sight of the captured Kojin.

Valbrand looked at him incredulously. 'Why? This has nothing to do with us.'

'We cannot let them torture the Kojin to death.'

'I don't see why we should care,' said Valbrand.

'We should care because it is wrong. Remember what it was like to be imprisoned on the *Husker Du*.'

That struck a chord with Valbrand; he ran his finger along the notched blade of his sword. 'Aye, perhaps we should do something.'

'We have to be careful,' said Bo. 'There is no need to kill them. We don't know how—'

It was too late. Without another word, Valbrand leapt to his feet and charged towards the trees.

CHAPTER TWELVE

The Slave Market

Terror gripped Elowen, body and soul. Led on blindfolded, sounds were her only guide: whispered voices, footsteps splashing in puddles and clanking on wooden planks, wheels grinding along rutted roads, and the distant hum of crowds.

Grigori's hold on her left arm never slackened. Trying to escape was futile, trying to fight was hopeless. Fear fired Elowen's imagination. Were they taking her to Lord Lucien? She dreaded that more than anything.

A door opened. Grigori released her arm. A push on her back propelled her forward. A wave of throat-drying heat struck her. The door slammed shut. Someone, something, breathed deeply, then more footsteps, heavy footsteps, followed by the clanging of metal on metal.

'Take off your blindfold, girl.'

The voice so surprised Elowen that it took her a few seconds to register what the man had said. Warily, she untied the blindfold. She squinted, expecting to see bright light but found herself in a dimly lit blacksmith's forge. She gasped when she realised that she was standing next to a dapple-grey horse, the halter of which a dirty-faced boy held.

219

The blacksmith who had spoken to Elowen was using a hammer to shoe the horse. His sweat-smeared face was like tanned leather. He was huge, bigger than Black Francis, with arms like thick branches and a bull-like neck. A cap came down to his eyebrows and he wore a leather apron over his frayed and scorched jerkin. Elowen scanned the room. Another entrance, wide enough for a horse to pass through, opened out onto the street. Horseshoes, hammers, rasps, files and pincers hung on the wall and an anvil rested on a soot-blackened tree-trunk. The forge fire was positioned against the back wall and a stovepipe connected to the chimney. Another hammer hung on the far wall but it was a weapon, not a tool, with its head shaped to resemble a snarling wolf. There was no sign of Grigori or his accomplices. Elowen's staff lay on the ground close to her feet. She picked it up.

Without looking up from his work, the blacksmith said in a stentorian voice, 'You've wandered very far from your home.'

Not sure what to say, Elowen shrugged and mumbled something even she didn't understand.

'You've no reason to be afraid,' said the blacksmith. 'You're in my safekeeping until my liege returns.'

He finished working on the shoe and pointed for the boy to lead the horse away. When the boy and horse had gone, the blacksmith wiped his hands on his apron before turning to face Elowen. 'You can call me Krukis. I'm not your friend and I'm not your enemy. You'll do as I say. Is that clear to you?'

Still confused and unnerved, Elowen nodded. She had no

idea who Krukis was or what his intentions were. The disappearance of Grigori puzzled her too. Why had he left her with this blacksmith?

'It is important you trust me, so my liege asked me to show you this,' said Krukis. He pulled off the cap; his right ear was missing and he was not Nulled. Krukis pointed to his forehead. 'Like you I've not been given the pustoj. My liege said it was important for you to know this.'

'Is Grigori your liege?' said Elowen, her eyes still drawn to the hole where his ear should be.

Krukis laughed. 'Grigori? No, my liege is Arigh Nasan. He pays well enough to buy any man's loyalty.'

Elowen tingled with relief. She was not going to be sent to Lord Lucien after all.

'Arigh Nasan speaks of you often,' said Krukis.

'He knows me?' said Elowen. 'I'm sure that I've never met anyone called Arigh Nasan.'

'That's his name but it is not one you should repeat too often. He has many enemies and Rynokgorod is a dangerous place.'

Elowen shuddered. 'You don't need to tell me that. But what does he want with me?'

Krukis crunched his knuckles. 'I don't know but you'll discover his purpose soon enough. He'll be here shortly.'

Krukis found her a place to sit in a small alcove at the back of the forge. He gave her some coarse black bread and a bowl of lukewarm, watery broth. He returned to his work and Elowen ate to a percussion of metal striking metal and the whooshing of the bellows as they breathed life into the fire.

221

After she had eaten, the long hard walk to Rynokgorod caught up with her. She became drowsy, her eyes stung with tiredness. She had almost nodded off when she was conscious of someone standing in front of her. It was an Orok, although he was dressed in Rynokgorod garb. He wore a coarse tunic belted at the waist over baggy trousers; his leggings were rags bound with twine above shoes made of bark. A cloth cap covered his forehead and shaded his eyes but it did not hide the deep red scar running against his face. Elowen recognised the face of the Orok, the companion of Grunewald, a face she had feared since she had first seen it.

She scrambled to her feet and cried out.

'So, it is you,' said the Orok, his voice deep and sonorous. 'You survived the attack on the sanctuary. I did not expect to see you again and I am guessing from the look on your face that you did not expect to see me either. Strange that our paths have crossed.'

'What are you doing here? What do you want with me?'

Arigh Nasan held up his hands. 'Be at peace, child, I know you are frightened but for now you are safe.'

'I've been attacked and dragged through the streets blindfolded. I certainly don't feel safe.'

The Orok laughed and removed his cap to expose his head, shaven apart from a short forelock and his braided hair behind. 'I am sorry for the scare. Grigori can be rough but he meant you no harm. Trust me, it was done for your own protection. This town is full of spies, so as soon as I discovered you had arrived in the city I made every effort to bring you to safety.'

'Why should I trust you?'

'A fair question, but perhaps I should begin by asking why I should trust you? You were an ally of Rubens, his spy in the Chapter of Light.'

'I was no such thing,' said Elowen. 'It wasn't my fault. I didn't know what Rubens was planning.'

'Perhaps not, but you showed poor judgement. You allowed Rubens to use you.'

'He tricked me. I didn't want Grunewald to die.'

'I do not doubt that. Grunewald's death was not your fault, I only ask that you show more caution in choosing your friends. You look upon me now as you did back in the sanctuary, with fear and distrust. But I am not your enemy, indeed I may be the only friend you have left.'

'Even if that's true, you still haven't said what you want from me,' said Elowen. Her earlier fear had subsided a little, but she dared not drop her guard.

Arigh Nasan sat on the floor, sighing with the pleasure of taking the weight off his feet. 'I listened many times to Grunewald talk of how special you were. I cannot say that I believed him. I heard tales about your miracles at the battle of the Gladsheim but I was still not convinced. Yet perhaps now I see more clearly. I start to understand why he placed so much faith in you.'

'I always thought he didn't like me,' said Elowen.

'I do not think that was so,' said Arigh Nasan. 'Rather, he saw your potential and so demanded more of you. He did not want you to fail so he pushed you and did not waste time with flattery. He was always unafraid to speak plain truths, however ugly. Compare that to Rubens who spoke with a sweet tongue but the honey of his words masked poison.'

'I got it all wrong,' said Elowen.

'Yes, but at least you will learn from the experience, harsh and tragic though it was. You are a strange one, child, very strange indeed. And strangest of all is finding you here in Rynokgorod. What brings you to this city?'

Elowen saw little point in not telling the truth. 'My friends Diggory and Lárwita were captured by the Society. I believe they're being held in this city and I've come to rescue them.'

Arigh Nasan stared at her and, to Elowen's annoyance, laughed. 'I promise you that if they are being held by the Society you have no chance of rescuing them, especially alone. Bishop Serapion has grown rich on the slave trade and he has not done that by allowing his victims to escape.'

'I have to try,' said Elowen.

Arigh Nasan bowed his head a little. 'And your courage earns you honour in my eyes but it is foolish all the same. Your friends are lost. You cannot help them by sacrificing yourself too.'

'They're my friends. I must save them, or die trying.'

'You have another choice,' said the Orok. 'After Rubens exiled me from the sanctuary, I travelled east, hoping to find shelter in the Orok lands. However, when I received word that the sanctuary had been destroyed, I decided to come to Rynokgorod as I had friends in this city and sought to persuade them to join me in the journey south to Omphalos.'

'Omphalos? What's that?'

Arigh Nasan told Elowen about the navel of the world

and its significance to the Illuminati. He added, 'You must accompany me there.'

'You want me to abandon my friends and travel south with you?' said Elowen. 'I can't do that. I must help Diggory and Lárwita. It's what they'd do for me. Will you let me go?'

'Let you go?' said Arigh Nasan. 'You are not imprisoned. You are free to leave my protection at any moment you so wish, though I believe it to be folly if you decide to do so. I do not desire to hold anyone against his or her will. I know the suffering, the degradation, the pain of imprisonment. I was a prisoner, for a short time mercifully, a slave in the pits of Gorefayne, as has been the fate of many of my people.'

'But you escaped?' said Elowen, her natural curiosity sparked despite her mistrust of the Orok.

'Yes, when I grew strong and wise enough I escaped. I have memories of those days in my mind and on my body. Serapion has been a bane of my people for many years. Once there were many Orok settlements in the borderlands of Gondwana, all within fifty miles of Rynokgorod. Bishop Serapion and his Watchmen destroyed them all.'

'What is Gorefayne like?' said Elowen, eager to learn more about the place she had heard mentioned so many times.

'Like hell itself has found a way into this world. It is a land of fire, ash, smoke and death, a land forged by the darkest dreams and foulest deeds of men. I say nothing more of it. If your friends have been captured by the Society it is likely they were taken to the market square. If they have not been sold already they might still be there. Today is a Saint's day so there is a fair. People will come from all over these lands

225

to barter and trade. Some come for entertainment, others to steal and swindle. Watch your step. And most of all, beware the Watchmen.'

'Who are they?'

'They are the agents of Serapion and all in this city fear them. The Watchmen dress in clothes as black as night and ride horses that are darker still. They search for treason, real or imagined, and the good bishop has a vivid imagination. The Watchmen's emblem is a dog's head and a broom, for it is their appointed task to sniff out and sweep treason from this city. They are so loyal to Serapion that many in Rynokgorod call them the 'Bishop's dogs'. They have orders to torture and kill all his enemies. I have heard tales of their victims being impaled on stakes, cast into vats of boiling water or burnt alive over open fires.'

'I'll try to keep out of their way,' said Elowen, her mouth dry with fear.

'I pray you do so. Will you not reconsider? Will you not change your mind?'

Elowen shook her head. 'Helping my friends is all that matters to me. I cannot abandon them.'

'I admire your loyalty to your friends,' said the Orok. 'But I fear it will cost you your life.'

*

Elowen left the forge's stifling heat and went out into the cold, muddy streets. Keeping a close grip on her staff, she dodged pilgrims, merchants, labourers and the horse-drawn wagons that thundered through the crowds. She had never seen so many people and yet had never felt so alone, so out of place.

Elowen found herself following a line of monks who were stripped to the waist and wearing black cowls; they sang hymns and cried out prayers to God and Prester John. Each monk carried a metal-tipped scourge and they whipped their own backs as they walked, drawing out gouges of flesh. Elowen retched with disgust. She could not imagine what made them punish themselves in such a way. Surely God did not demand such suffering, or take pleasure from their pain? Elowen deliberately slowed her pace and to her relief, the monks turned away towards the cathedral.

The market square filled the space between the cathedral and the citadel. The citadel's golden pyramidal canopy roof glowed. As Arigh Nasan had said, a fair was underway; the sights and sounds overwhelmed Elowen. Drunks lurched around like new-born fowls while skinny, bow-legged children scampered after stray dogs. Clowns, conjurors, jugglers and tumblers walked through the crowd. On a mounted stage, dancers performed spectacular routines involving strenuous knee bends, high leaps and crouching forward-kicks. In little side-booths, mountebanks and merchants jostled to sell their wares and shouted to be heard above the din. A group of men and children formed a circle around a cockfight; the two roosters had gaffs attached to their legs and bloody feathers plastered the ground around them. Another crowd gathered around a small cage, which had bars forged from Cold Iron. A portly keeper perched on a stool beside the cage, charging a coin for anyone who desired a closer look. He dropped each coin into a bag that

227

rested on his knees. Inside the cage sat a sick-looking Eldar. His sleepy, rheumy green eyes peeked out from beneath hairy and heavily protruding eyebrows, and his white beard reached the pod of his stomach. He looked so sad—leered and spat at by the drunk and ignorant. Elowen wished she could help him.

That thought was broken when the crowd parted and through the gap rode several men mounted on huge black horses. They all wore a black uniform. Remembering Arigh Nasan's description, Elowen realised with a chill that their saddlebags carried the emblem of a dog's head and a broom. Watchmen. They scanned the crowd as though they were searching for someone. She lowered her head, turned away and only dared to breathe again once the Watchmen had ridden past.

The cathedral bells tolled for four o'clock and shook the ground beneath Elowen's feet. She spotted a wooden gallows, triangular in plan with three uprights and three crossbeams. Several bodies hung from the gallows, their faces hidden by hoods and placards tied around their necks with messages written on them in a language Elowen did not understand. As she got closer, she realised there were body parts nailed to the gallows: hands, tongues and ears.

Feeling sick, Elowen laboured through the writhing mass of people. A cloud of hot breath steamed above the crowd. With feet and elbows clattering into her, Elowen felt like a tiny boat adrift on a stormy ocean. She nudged, ducked and shoved her way through to a slight clearing in the crowd. In front of her was a roped-off pen filled with dozens of men, women and children, all herded in like cattle. Slaves. Society soldiers brandishing whips prowled outside the pen; Elowen kept her distance, not wanting to attract their attention.

There was no shelter for those inside the pen, just a single dead tree with dried-up branches like skeletal arms. Most of the slaves were huddled together in tight groups, shivering and shaking; others, were tied to posts, their blood-smeared backs exposing the merciless bite of the whip.

A richly dressed couple strolled hand-in-hand along the edge of the pen. They stopped and the woman pointed at one of the prisoners, a tall man who looked as if he had been strong before hunger had gnawed away his muscles. The soldiers called the prisoner over and the couple examined him with pokes and prods. After a brief discussion, the woman shook her head, held a perfumed handkerchief to her nose and the soldiers ordered the prisoner to stand back. It infuriated Elowen to see a human being treated in such a manner but she tried to push it to the back of her mind; despite such horror, she needed to stay focused.

She stood on tiptoe for a clearer view—at first, she thought her eyes tricked her but no, the two boys sat on the ground were Diggory and Lárwita. Their heads were shaven, their faces marked by bruises, dried blood and mud. It was strange to see Diggory without his shock of red hair. Lárwita's spectacles were missing, the first time Elowen had ever seen him not wearing them. He sat with his arms wrapped around his legs, rocking backwards and forwards.

The boys did not notice Elowen and she had to resist an overwhelming temptation to yell out. She needed to work out how she was going to rescue them. She guessed that if she could get them out of the pen they might be able to escape within the swollen crowds, but getting them out was not going to be easy. Elowen knew she could clamber over the rope without too much difficulty but the danger was from the soldiers. She needed to distract them. She peered at the dead tree. She recalled the lessons she had learnt from Baba Yaga. She remembered how it felt to control the Earthsoul and began to form a plan.

Elowen closed her eyes and took a deep breath. She reached out with her mind, feeling the bark of the dead tree, coarse, dry, brittle. The Earthsoul's energy warmed channels and grooves long dry of sap. The bark smouldered and cracked. Elowen opened her eyes. The golden threads curled and twisted around the tree. Smoke poured from the tree, escaping from countless cracks and fissures. The other slaves backed away from the tree, and the soldiers shouted panicky orders. Elowen's skin bristled, warmed by the Earthsoul's power. An explosion ripped the tree apart, and spewed out smoke and charred wood.

Many slaves screamed or fell to the ground in fear. Guilt tore at Elowen as she watched them. It was cruel to worsen their misery, but she could not help them. The commotion attracted onlookers from the fair, all intrigued and a little frightened. The soldiers vaulted over the ropes, shouting and cracking their whips, trying to bring order. While they were distracted, Elowen clambered over too. She rushed over to Lárwita and Diggory. Their eyes widened in surprise when they saw her, and between painful, chesty coughs, Diggory said, 'Elowen? Is it you?'

Lárwita squinted at Elowen. 'How did you find us? Have you been captured too?'

Elowen ignored their questions and urged them to move. 'We haven't got much time.'

The boys managed to get to their feet. Their movements were slow and accompanied by gasps and winces, but somehow they got over the ropes.

Elowen was about to do likewise when a shout from behind stopped her: the soldiers had seen them. Elowen held her staff like a weapon, and tensed the muscles in her arms and legs. One soldier ran ahead of the others and as he reached Elowen, he cracked his whip at her. Elowen deftly sidestepped the attack and swept her staff at his legs, landing a painful blow on his knees. He cried out in pain and dropped to the ground.

The other soldiers closed in so Elowen pulled herself over the ropes and found Diggory and Lárwita waiting on the other side. She pushed them to move forward. 'Keep running. I'll be right behind you.'

Elowen and her friends plunged into the crowd, with the soldiers chasing them. An impulse, though whether it was born of a survival instinct or pure mischief she knew not, made Elowen push bystanders and kick over stalls. Pots, pans and bowls clattered, sparking angry shouts and curses from their owners. Elowen sprinted through the cockfight, disrupted the conjurers, and distracted the merchants and mountebanks. Mud sprayed from her boots as she whisked through the crowd like a malevolent ghost, barely seen but leaving waves of chaos in her wake, waves that slowed the pursuing soldiers.

Elowen saw the Eldar locked in a cage. She stopped and called out to Diggory and Lárwita, 'Keep going!'

231

The cage, made from Cold Iron, chilled the air around it. The scar on Elowen's leg ached. With all her strength, she brought her staff crashing down onto the lock. It cracked under the blow. Her staff broke too, and Elowen dropped the pieces. The Eldar kicked open the cage door. He grinned at Elowen and, before his corpulent keeper could stop him, he sprung out of the cage like a leaping frog and disappeared in the crowd.

The keeper hauled himself up from his stool and screamed abuse at Elowen, spilling all the coins from his bag as he did so. She ran to catch up with Diggory and Lárwita. They were now almost out of the market square—if they got to the maze of the alleyways beyond they might lose their pursuers. They were close, so close...

Hooves thundered. A circle of horsemen surrounded them. The Watchmen.

- CHAPTER THIRTEEN -

The Ordeal of Fire

The Watchmen dismounted, leaping from their horses like birds of prey. They forced Elowen and her friends to kneel and tied their hands behind their backs with cord. One of the Watchmen pulled Elowen's hair back to examine her forehead and jabbered excitedly when he saw she was not Nulled. The Watchman spat and a warm sticky globule dribbled down the back of Elowen's neck.

She glanced at Diggory and Lárwita; they were both crouched down, wide-eyed, sickly white, trembling. The Watchmen dragged them all to their feet and forced them towards the citadel with pushes, shouts and kicks. Elowen's whole body went cold as she remembered the ghastly stories Arigh Nasan had told her about their captors. The words of Baba Yaga echoed in her mind: *you still have much to learn and even if you find your friends you will not be able to help them.* Elowen knew she had failed. Rather than saving her friends, she had dropped them into greater danger.

The citadel exuded power. Ornate features made of white stone crowned the double windows of the upper floors, and interlaced floral patterns and the figures of double-headed eagles filled the broad pilasters. Statues of horses flanked the citadel's arched entrance.

Once inside, they came to the foot of a broad white stone staircase with banisters embellished by intricate carvings. Enormous portraits stared down from the walls. They all portrayed the same person: an elderly, narrow-faced man wearing opulent robes. Elowen guessed it was Bishop Serapion. From the ceiling hung silver chandeliers dressed with rock crystals that glistened as though lit by hundreds of small flames. Elowen had never seen such luxury; she had never imagined such luxury.

They waited as one of the Watchmen ran up the stairs. He returned moments later and clapped once. With their hands still tied, Elowen and her companions were led up the stairs and into a large room, where three stained-glass windows turned the sun's weak rays into pinkish light. A flat ceiling displayed brightly painted scenes from the Holy Book: the nude figures of saints and winged angels, sun-tipped clouds, and garland-crowned prophets. Bas-relief's depicting birds, beasts and flowers decorated the columns supporting the ceiling. Wooden-framed paintings and gilded emblems covered the purple walls. A pyramid of fresh fruit stood untouched on a silver table; beside it lay a Holy Book protected by solid wooden boards embellished with ivories, rich fabric and gold.

An automaton clock lurked in a corner, ticking like an insect. A roaring fire made the room hot and stuffy. A small, plain door stood ajar and a whiff of smoke flowed through the gap. A silver throne loomed at the far end of the room and upon it sat an old man wearing a mitre in the shape of a bulbous crown. He was clothed in a tunic made of rich brocade with wide sleeves that reached below his knees. He had a lean face and his Null bulged from his large forehead. White bushy eyebrows sprouted above his sunken, heavily bagged eyes. Elowen recognised the man from the portraits she had seen earlier. Bishop Serapion. Three guards stood behind him, impassive, unsmiling. They wore open helmets with a flat brim and a crest from front to back. Their uniforms were stripped blue, orange and red.

A smile formed slowly on the bishop's lips and he brought his small hands together as though in prayer. He sported a signet ring on the little finger of his right hand. To Elowen's surprise, he instructed the Watchmen to leave. When they had gone, he said in a voice soft and rhythmic, 'I am a humble man, born a pauper to a drunken wretch of a mother. I am a simple servant of God and Prester John, and I confess now that I am truly confused. Before me stands a pilgrim who comes to Rynokgorod but neglects to visit the sacred bones. A pilgrim without the blessing of the Holy Null. A pilgrim whose hair is streaked as white as snow, usually a sign of witch-craft. A pilgrim who tries to steal slaves that are the property of the Society.'

'I didn't steal anything,' said Elowen. 'They aren't slaves. They're my friends.'

The old man leapt to his feet and his voice turned harsh and rasping. 'How *dare* you speak to me in such a fashion? I am Bishop Serapion. You speak only when I tell you to and you will always refer to me as Your Excellency.'

Elowen did a sort of half-bow, the best apology she could muster.

235

Serapion sat back down in his throne and rubbed his chin. 'You wear the clothes of a pilgrim as a wolf may wear the coat of a sheep. I am old, but by the blessing of God and Prester John I still have my wits. A man in my position is wise to be careful. Many resent that the Almighty selected one as humble as I to carry out His work. Many have tried to fool me, many have tried to conceal their true nature from me but I see through their lies, as I see through yours. I did not rise from poverty by allowing the wiles of females to fool me. Many have stood where you now stand. I know their scent, a scent of corruption, a scent of sin, a *witch* scent.'

'I'm not a witch, Your Excellency,' said Elowen, trying to remain calm. He was trying to intimidate her, to scare her into saying something foolish. She had seen his sort before: self-important, smug, cruel, just like Cornelius Cronack in the Orphanage. Serapion obviously thought she was a weak victim to toy with. She refused to give in so meekly. She thought she could outwit the old man. Trying to sound innocent, she said, 'I'm a pilgrim.'

Serapion gently dabbed his lips. 'Then why do you not wear the Holy Null?'

'I'm not yet old enough,' said Elowen, secure that she was telling the truth in that at least. Less truthfully, she went on to say, 'I look forward to receiving that blessing next summer. I wished to see the bones of the saint before that time.'

Serapion's eyes narrowed. 'I find it strange that one so young should visit this city alone. And your accent tells me that you hail from lands far from here.'

236

'I believe that the hardship of pilgrimage brings one closer to God,' said Elowen, feeling pleased with her quick response. She thought she was getting the better of Serapion.

'And what of the two boys you rescued? How do you explain your behaviour?'

'I acted out of pity,' said Elowen. 'I followed the Saviour's merciful example. And besides, I am certain that their unfortunate detention by the blessed Society was merely a mistake, a misunderstanding.'

The automaton clock struck six o'clock and from a small door the skeletal figure of Death appeared, its skull frozen in a manic grin.

'You speak with skill and cunning,' said Serapion, sitting back in the throne. He rubbed his hands and licked his lips. 'Perhaps you are a witch, perhaps not. But forgive me if I do not take your word for it. Witches have infected this city for many years, I see their filth everywhere, I *feel* it everywhere. By God's grace, it has fallen to me, His most modest servant, to clean away their corruption. I shall leave it to God to judge your innocence. You must undergo the Ordeal of Fire.'

Following the slightest flick of his finger, the three guards moved from behind the throne. One of them grabbed Diggory and Lárwita, while the other two held Elowen, who, for the first time in Serapion's presence, felt truly afraid. She had thought him a fool, a bumptious, puffed-up fool in fine robes. She realised she should have been more careful.

Serapion stood and gestured towards the small plain door. 'Nothing is hidden from the eyes of God, girl. He tests us through pain, tests us to see if we are worthy to serve Him and Prester John. It is time for *you* to be tested. It is time for you to visit the Room of Enlightenment. Down there, God will lead us to the truth.'

The door opened to a narrow staircase. Carrying a candlestick and the Holy Book, Serapion led the way. They descended into a windowless, bottle-shaped room. Painted images of hell covered the sooty ceiling: cackling demons, tormented souls burning in sulphurous pits, a skeletal figure wielding a sickle and many-headed beasts driving sinners into the gaping maw of hell. The grim images made Elowen's skin crawl. Chains hung from the rough walls and the floor sloped sharply. A three-legged cauldron stood in the middle of the room; a fire blazed beneath it and the water inside boiled and bubbled. Steam and smoke escaped through a small vent in the ceiling but a fusty smell lingered.

A table was covered with torture devices: a knee splitter with spikes like jaws; a scold's bridle; thumbscrews; a heretic's fork. There were also two rounded stones on the table—they were not marked or decorated in any way and Elowen wondered what they were for.

The guards forced Lárwita and Diggory to kneel down facing the wall. Serapion stood over the cauldron and peered down at the boiling water. 'We prepared this for you, child. I am sure that in this room we can discover the truth. Many have come here secure within their armour of lies and deceit but against the methods used here, there is no defence and no hiding place.'

The bishop placed the candlestick and the Holy Book down on the table. He examined the torture devices. Elowen trembled from head to foot. Was he just trying to frighten her, or did he intend to torture her?

Serapion inspected the scold's bridle. 'These are blunt instruments, child. Fear not, I have no need of them.'

Elowen experienced a moment of relief but could not dispel the notion that Serapion was toying with her, prolonging her suffering for his pleasure.

The bishop picked up the Holy Book and delicately slid it open at a page marked by a small strip of parchment. He read silently, his mouth forming the shape of the words but making no sounds. When he finished reading, he placed the Holy Book back onto the table and picked up the two rounded stones. He walked over to the cauldron and dropped both stones into the water. 'Child, it is time for you to undergo the trial. The pagan tribes of the north called it the *ketiltak*, the Ordeal of Fire. There were many forms of the Ordeal. In some, the accused were made to walk over red-hot ploughshares, or to carry an iron bar heated to great temperatures in a furnace. I have always felt such practices too crude, too rustic. I prefer to employ a more *refined* version of the Ordeal of Fire. If your injuries heal swiftly, I shall declare you innocent of witchcraft. If they fester, it is God's judgement upon you, and tomorrow you will be hanged by the neck until you are dead.'

Elowen failed to control the trembling of her body. Her head throbbed with tension. 'My…my injuries? What injuries?'

Serapion gave a sickly smile and pointed down at the cauldron. 'I want you to pick the stones out of the water.'

'But the water is boiling. My hands—'

239

'I believe you are beginning to understand,' said the bishop with great satisfaction.

'I won't do it,' said Elowen, her hands clenched into fists. 'Kill me if you want to but I won't be tortured.'

'I *could* kill you, of course,' said Serapion. 'That would be simple enough but in doing so I would not discover the truth about you. Witches are such devious creatures. I fear what mischief and harm you have hatched since you arrived in my city. No, you must undergo the Ordeal, for if you do not I shall instruct my guards to cut the throats of the two slaves you freed. However, if you obey I will allow them to live.'

Elowen knew the bishop was not bluffing. Every instinct told her not to put her hands into the boiling water, but she refused to condemn her friends to death. She sensed Serapion was going to kill her, whatever happened, but she might be able to save Diggory and Lárwita. She looked down at the water. It seethed and hissed as though possessed of a frenzied life of its own. The bubbles and the spiralling tendrils of smoke reached out to her, dragging her hands towards the surface.

She plunged her hands into the water. Her fingers touched the stones and she clasped her hands around them. The pain struck her, burning, searing, agonising. Still holding the stones, she stepped back from the cauldron. She struggled to breathe and her vision blurred. Elowen remained conscious long enough to look at her arms; they were cherry-coloured, like they had been smeared in red paint. The stones dropped to the floor. Elowen heard a scream, a scream that sounded somehow distant but still ripped from

240

her own throat. Her legs buckled beneath her and she fell into darkness.

*

With heavy wing-beats, the woodcock flew straight and fast over the forest. The bird changed direction and zigzagged down between the trees to land at the edge of a clearing. Settling in the thicket, the woodcock probed for earthworms with its long beak. Absorbed in its search, the bird paid no attention to Lord Lucien, who stood as still as a statue, hidden among the slender silver birch trees, nor the four Redeemers who waited with him.

Lord Lucien looked out at the clearing, watching as Baba Yaga repaired the fence that circled her hut. She worked carefully, criss-crossing the bones into intricate patterns, her face a mask of concentration. Behind her, a spindly column of smoke rose from the chimney of her hut. The setting sun bathed the forest in golden light.

The smells, sights and rhythms of autumn sparked memories in Lord Lucien.

Scuffing through piles of crinkly leaves. Red-cheeked and steaming breath. The bonfire crackles. Puffs of grey smoke fill the air. Mother laughs. A happy sound. A reassuring sound...

Lord Lucien bit his lip, using the pain to drag him back to the present. He watched Baba Yaga with disgust. She was a fiend, one he had already decided to destroy. However, he needed patience. The fiend was his best chance of finding the girl. He stepped into the clearing, followed by the Redeemers. He expected Baba Yaga to run or prepare to fight

241

but she did not look up from her work when she said, 'Wherever you are going, it is clear to me that you are lost.'

'I am far from lost,' said Lord Lucien. 'I seek the one they call Baba Yaga and I believe I have found her.'

'Verily, it is so,' she said, looking up at last. She spat into her hands and rubbed them together. 'You are not welcome here.'

'Are you not frightened of me?' he said, surprised by her casual reaction. He was wary of a trap. 'Perhaps you do not know who I am?'

'I know you, Lord Lucien, but I am too old to be afraid.'

'If that is true you are fortunate, for you have reason to fear me. But first I seek knowledge, knowledge that I am sure you hold.'

'I know many things.'

'You recently encountered three children, one of them a girl named Elowen Aubyn. Do you deny this?'

'It is clear you already know the truth of it so you are seeking knowledge that you already possess, an act of a foolish mind.'

'Then the children are still here?' said Lord Lucien. He wanted to kill the witch. Her very existence offended him.

Baba Yaga returned to her work. 'I see no reason to answer your question. I am busy, please be on your way.'

'Do not play games with me,' said Lord Lucien. 'I know you are strong, but believe me when I say your powers are useless against me.'

'Your threats are wasted,' said Baba Yaga. 'You have already decided to kill me. Whatever I say or do not say will not change that.'

Lord Lucien paused, momentarily thrown by her answer. 'Does the manner of your death not concern you?'

'Will I remember it afterwards?'

'I grow tired of this,' he said. The four Redeemers drew their swords. 'Are the children still here, yes or no?'

Baba Yaga closed her eyes. 'All things must end. Winter must come.'

'Answer me,' said Lord Lucien. 'Answer me or die.'

'I choose death,' she said.

The woodcock busied itself with a fat, juicy, wriggling earthworm. A sound, an eldritch scream, filled the bird with blind terror. It dropped the earthworm and zigzagged up and away through the trees.

*

'Elowen?'

The sound of her name echoed. Dripping water became a torrent. The scurrying of mice and rats thumped like the heavy footsteps of giant beasts. Elowen opened her eyes but the world around her was dim and unfocused. The pain struck her, as though fire erupted beneath her skin. She cried out. Her stomach ached and she vomited, splashing a watery discharge over the stone floor. A hand touched her shoulder. She flinched.

'It's only me,' said a voice. Her eyes focused. Diggory sat beside her. Further away, Lárwita lay against the wall. They were in a dungeon with a low, vaulted ceiling, a tiny barred window and an iron gate that was the sole way in or out. On the other side of the gate, a single torch held in a sconce

243

provided the only light; below the sconce sat a guard with a club resting on his knees.

Bandages were wrapped around Elowen's arms. Dirty and torn, they showed the signs of hasty and careless application.

'They put bandages on your wounds after they brought us down here,' said Diggory. 'We tried to protect you but the guards were too strong. They beat up Lárwita. I hope he's all right. He's sleeping now at least.'

'How long have we been here?' said Elowen, dizzy from the pain and struggling to put words together. Even the slightest movement caused her agony.

Diggory shook his head. 'I don't know. I've lost track of time.'

Elowen remembered Serapion's words. *If your injuries heal swiftly, I shall declare you innocent of witchcraft. If they fester, it is God's judgement upon you and tomorrow you will be hanged by the neck until you are dead.*

She held her right arm towards Diggory. 'Peel away the bandages. I need to see.'

He grimaced. 'I don't think that's a good idea.'

'I have to see,' she said.

Diggory nodded. Elowen gritted her teeth as he slowly unwrapped the bandages, exposing her left forearm. It was red raw and covered with festering blisters. She knew what that meant.

'What are we going to do?' said Diggory. He slumped back against the wall. 'Why are they doing this? It must be the Null.'

'You can't blame that alone,' said Elowen, weeping with

244

pain. 'Perhaps all the Null does is bring out the bad side of people, the side that's always waiting for a chance to show itself. The Null doesn't plant the evil there.'

Diggory didn't seem to be listening. 'Once we'd been captured I never thought I'd see you again but you came back to save us.'

'I was wrong to leave you both in the first place,' said Elowen. 'I shouldn't have run away.'

Diggory wiped his dripping nose. 'That wasn't your fault. What else could you've done?'

'You mustn't say that.'

'But it's true. You're only in danger now because of us. You came back, you found us. I think you really are a messenger.'

Elowen closed her eyes. *Messenger.* She had done so little to earn that title. She cursed her arrogance, her misguided belief that she was strong or clever enough to rescue her friends.

Lárwita groaned and stirred but did not wake. Elowen heard doors being unlocked and opened. Bishop Serapion, flanked by two more guards, appeared at the dungeon's iron gate. He smiled at Elowen and beckoned her to come closer. 'It is time for righteous judgement to be called upon you, child.'

Warily, Elowen came to the gate. The bishop took hold of her arms and pulled them through the iron bars. She failed to hold in a scream of pain and Serapion took obvious delight in her suffering. He unpeeled more of her bandages and licked his lips when he saw the blisters and raw skin. He released his grip and said, 'The Almighty has revealed the truth. Just as I thought, you are a witch, the worst of all sinners.'

'She's no witch,' said Diggory. 'Leave her alone.'

'Be silent, boy, unless you wish to join her on the gallows,' said Serapion. 'Guards, take the witch to the condemned cell ahead of her execution at first light; there she is to be stripped and readied by honest women of good reputation. I shall oversee the preparations, of course. Bind her hands tightly. We can take no chances, for witches work with mysterious and infernal powers.'

Elowen backed away from the gate. She knew she had no chance of escaping but she was determined not to give in easily. Diggory stood beside her and said, 'I won't let them take you.'

His words were empty and they both knew it, but his loyalty, his bravery, touched her. It was all she had left. Serapion stepped back and allowed the guards to unlock and open the gate, but as they did so, a loud ringing reverberated around the dungeon.

The bishop looked fearfully at the guards. 'That is the warning bell. The citadel is under attack.'

Three shadowy figures appeared behind Serapion and his men. A sword flashed; two guards fell. The third tried to unsheathe his weapon but he was too slow; a hammer cracked into his chest and he fell with a gurgled grunt. In his eagerness to escape the fighting, Serapion retreated into the dungeon, tripped and landed on his back.

The three shadowy figures stepped forward into the light. Arigh Nasan, Krukis the blacksmith and the Eldar that Elowen had set free in the market square. Krukis carried the wolf-headed hammer Elowen had seen earlier in the forge, while Arigh Nasan held a scimitar. The Eldar lurked behind them, silent, unarmed.

'Who the hell are you?' said Diggory, backing away in alarm. He pointed at Arigh Nasan. 'Wait, I've seen you before—'

'It's all right, Diggory,' said Elowen, wincing in pain. 'He's not an enemy.'

The Orok eyed Elowen gravely. 'So you are still alive. I had feared we were too late.'

'Why are you here?' said Elowen.

'The answer to that question must wait,' said Arigh Nasan. 'First, we have to get out of the citadel.'

Holding his hammer, Krukis stood over the bishop. 'What about this one? Surely we cannot allow him to live?'

'Show mercy,' said Serapion, on his knees and weeping. 'I can give you riches, anything you desire…'

'Spoken like a true man of God,' said Arigh Nasan. He nodded to Krukis, 'Finish him.'

Krukis lifted his hammer above his head. 'With pleasure.'

Elowen hated Serapion; she wanted him to suffer, she wanted him to die. But other images came to her. The corpses at the battle of the Gladsheim. The body of Malengin, the man she killed on the Isle of Ictis. She had seen enough death.

'NO!' shouted Elowen. Krukis froze, his hammer still poised to strike.

'What is wrong?' said Arigh Nasan.

'You can't kill him like this,' said Elowen. 'It's not right.'

'How can it not be right?' said Krukis. He turned his head

247

to show the hole where his right ear should have been. 'I want vengeance.'

'You cannot want him to live, Elowen,' said Arigh Nasan. 'You cannot ignore how he tortured you. For that, and his many other crimes, he deserves to die.'

'Killing him won't undo the past,' said Elowen. 'Being as cruel and heartless as he is won't change anything.'

'Ah, this is foolishness, I'm sending him to hell,' said Krukis. Elowen closed her eyes. She heard a metallic clang and a cry of anguish but realised it came from Krukis, not from Serapion. She opened her eyes and saw what had happened: Arigh Nasan had blocked the hammer blow with his scimitar, saving the bishop's life. The wolf's-head of the hammer hovered inches above Serapion's neck.

'What did you do that for?' said Krukis. He lifted his hammer and took a step back. 'You said yourself that he deserves to die.'

'We came to save the child, Krukis, the fate of the bishop is not our concern,' said Arigh Nasan.

'You are my *liege* and I follow your command,' said the blacksmith.

Arigh Nasan nodded. 'Well, it seems you will live a little longer, Your *Excellency*.'

'You expect me to be grateful to you, *Orok*?' said Serapion, still on his knees. 'You are part of an infernal race, damned in the eyes of God. If it were down to me—'

'If it were down to *me*, Bishop, you would already be dead,' said Arigh Nasan. The Orok punched Serapion hard on the jaw, knocking him out cold. Arigh Nasan turned to Elowen. 'We are in great danger and must go now.'

248

The peal of the alarm bell underlined the urgency of the Orok's words. Fighting nausea and the pain in her arms, Elowen said, 'I won't go without Diggory and Lárwita. They have to come too.'

'They will slow us down, Elowen,' said Arigh Nasan. 'We came to save *you*.'

'If you don't help my friends I'll stay here.'

Arigh Nasan rolled his eyes. 'So be it, but I think it is a mistake. Can you walk?'

'Yes, I can manage,' she said, gritting her teeth against the pain. She gestured towards Lárwita. 'He can't though.'

'Krukis, you must carry the boy,' said Arigh Nasan.

'What am I, a wet nurse?' said the blacksmith.

'Please, he's hurt and he needs help,' said Diggory.

Krukis glared at him. 'So are you giving the orders now, whelp? Perhaps I should show you the back of my hand and then you'll learn some respect for your elders.'

'Krukis, that is enough,' said Arigh Nasan. 'We do not have time for petty squabbles. Take the boy.'

'As you wish,' said the blacksmith with little enthusiasm. He scowled at Diggory and picked up Lárwita.

'Keep close, all of you,' said Arigh Nasan. 'Leave the bishop in this dungeon. It might do him good to enjoy some of his own hospitality.'

'Where are we going?' said Diggory.

'You will find out,' said the Orok. Leading the way, he stepped out of the dungeon, closely followed by the Eldar. Elowen, with Diggory helping her, went next while Krukis, carrying the barely conscious Lárwita, brought up the rear.

From the dungeon, they came to a spiral staircase. The

249

pain and exertion of the steep climb sapped Elowen's already diminishing strength. She longed to rest but knew she had to keep going. Diggory urged her on, whispering words of encouragement between his own laboured breaths.

When they reached the top of the stairs, they stepped into a large kitchen with a floor made of bricks and terracotta tiles, and a fan-vaulted ceiling leading up to a lantern that allowed smoke and fumes to escape. There were two fireplaces with spit-racks, a stone sink basin and baking chambers. Hundreds of copper utensils lined tables, perched on shelves or hung from racks on the wall. Partridges and pheasants dangled from a wooden beam and there were many herbs drying. Brooms, wicker baskets and piles of firewood rested against the blackened, peeling walls.

Three dead guards lay on the floor, crowned by halos of blood.

'They got in our way,' said Krukis, grinning in a manner Elowen found distasteful. Feeling sick, she looked away from the corpses.

A door on the far side of the kitchen led out into a rectangular, gravelled courtyard with an arched gate at its north end. It was a moonless night and the sudden exposure to the raw cold struck Elowen like a slap in the face. Four horses stood in the courtyard, accompanied by two Oroks: one was tall, with dark almond-shaped eyes and a thick moustache; the other was shorter and slighter, bow-legged like Arigh Nasan. Three of the horses were of a small and stocky build, with short, strong legs. The restless fourth horse was much larger, with a long back and shoulders, a fine raven coat and a short silky tail. The Oroks readied the

250

horses to leave. Muted, indistinct words came to Elowen. Without trying, she found she was Linking with the horses, but was too weak to comprehend.

'These are my companions,' said Arigh Nasan, introducing the other two Oroks. He pointed to the tall warrior. 'This is Batu, and beside him stands Vachir.'

The two Oroks bowed. Vachir mounted his horse, swiftly joined in his saddle by the Eldar.

'Elowen, you ride with me,' continued Arigh Nasan. 'Batu will take the injured boy.'

'What about me?' said Diggory.

Arigh Nasan pointed to Krukis, whose shoulders sagged at the suggestion. 'I do not share my horse with anyone. Can the whelp not run behind?'

'Stop calling me a whelp,' said Diggory.

'What are you going to do about it if I don't?' said Krukis.

'Enough bickering,' said Arigh Nasan. 'Krukis, the boy rides with you whether you like it or not.'

'By the gods, I'm not paid enough for this,' said the black-smith, but he obeyed the command.

Shouts echoed across the courtyard. Guards armed with swords and halberds ran towards them.

'They don't want us to leave, do they?' said Krukis, licking his lips. He helped Batu to secure Lárwita on the Orok's horse and then prepared to wield his hammer.

Arigh Nasan turned to the other Oroks. 'Protect the hors-es and the children. Krukis and I can deal with this.'

The guards charged at Arigh Nasan but the Orok moved as though made of smoke; none of the sword cuts and hal-berd thrusts came near him, while each slash of his scimitar

251

slew an opponent. Krukis fought like an angry bear, his hammer swiping enemies away like flies. Faced with such ferocity, the surviving guards fled.

Krukis wiped sweat from his forehead. 'Damn shame. I was starting to enjoy that.'

'Let us hope we meet no further opposition,' said Arigh Nasan.

'You have no sense of fun,' said Krukis as he slapped the haunches of the large, raven-black horse and hauled himself into the saddle. Diggory struggled up to join him, receiving no assistance from the blacksmith.

Meanwhile, Arigh Nasan helped Elowen to mount his horse. Her arms were too painful and too weak to grip onto the high wooden saddle and, once astride the horse, it was all she could do to lean on Arigh Nasan. He said to her, 'Do not fear, I will not let you fall.'

They galloped under the archway, and across the dark, silent market square that, hours before, had thronged with the noise and colour of the fair. Elowen slipped close to unconsciousness. Pain had become part of her skin, part of her body. Her vision steadied a little as they reached the north-gate of the city. The gate was closed and guarded by a line of Watchmen armed with muskets as well as swords.

Arigh Nasan cantered to a halt yards from the line of Watchmen. One shouted, 'Drop your weapons and surrender.'

'If you know what's good for you, you'll let us pass,' said Krukis.

To Elowen's surprise, the Eldar dismounted Vachir's horse. He calmly approached the Watchmen, ignoring their threats. He stopped, knelt on one knee and chanted. The golden threads weaved around him, forming complex patterns. The gate shuddered and then exploded as though punched through by a giant invisible hand. Splinters and broken iron rivets sprayed the Watchmen.

Elowen scarcely believed what she was seeing but she had no time to absorb it, as Arigh Nasan galloped past the dazed Watchmen, followed by the other riders. Vachir grabbed the Eldar as he rode and pulled him up onto the horse. Muskets crackled; red-hot lead shot whizzed close to Elowen but they missed their target.

The riders passed through the broken gate and out of the city.

- CHAPTER FOURTEEN -

Lord of the Trees

T o Elowen, the landscape passed as a green blur. Pain reduced her world to simple sensations: the wind rushing through her hair, the icy nip of cold rain, the smell of damp grass, the horse's heavy breathing. Time meant nothing. Seconds could have been hours and hours could have been seconds. Only her pain mattered.

The horse slowed. Elowen opened her eyes. Her vision was watery, shaky. A single, muddy road led into a village. There was a cluster of shabby log-built houses, some of them ruined and smoke-blackened, a timber-framed granary topped with a cone-shaped roof and beside it a well with a weight beam to raise the water. A watchtower and a small wooden church with a tented roof crowned the slope over-looking the village. A feeling of sadness came over Elowen. Something about the village reminded her of Trecadok graveyard, full of memories, full of loss, as though the ground remembered every single tear that had fallen upon it.

'This is Granica,' said Arigh Nasan, as they cantered to a stop. 'This is as far east as you can travel before reaching the Orok lands of Gondwana.'

'Where are all the people?' said Krukis.

'All dead. They defied Bishop Serapion and refused the Null. Redeemers came—'

'But are we safe here?' said Diggory.

'For a time,' said Arigh Nasan. 'We can shelter here for a few days.'

To Elowen, Arigh Nasan's voice became faint and distant, like a shout swallowed by a noisy storm. She had the sensation of being lifted and carried. Drowning in pain and exhaustion, she tried to keep her eyes open but finally surrendered to sleep.

*

Elowen woke to the sound of singing. The words were strange but she found them calming, reassuring, like a lullaby. She opened her eyes. She was flat on her back. A wave of heat warmed her. She lifted her head; she was on a wooden bench close to a stove. There was a smell of mouldy wood, and water dripped down from the low ceiling. She looked around. Moss filled the gaps in the log walls. Weeds pushed through the sandy floor and wrapped themselves around the pieces of smashed furniture that were scattered across the room. Shelves crammed with the dusty, shattered remnants of icons of saints and angels filled one corner. There was a table topped with a wooden jug, two cups and a wooden bowl filled with blackberries and raspberries. Arigh Nasan was sitting on a stool close to her. He stopped singing when he realised she was awake.

'Where...where am I?' said Elowen, sitting up quickly as

255

she remembered their escape from Rynokgorod. The pain from her arms had eased. They had been bandaged anew with clean, honey scented bindings.

'We are still in Granica, in one of the village houses,' said Arigh Nasan. He stood and passed her the bowl of fruit. Elowen took a handful of berries, savouring their sweet flavour and ignoring how they stained her white bandages.

'What about Diggory and Lárwita?'

'They are both safe and well. Lárwita took a beating from Serapion's guards but he is made of sterner stuff than I expected and is back on his feet. Diggory is well though alas it is clear he and Krukis have formed a mutual antipathy. However, the fault lies not with your friend. Krukis is a brave warrior but not always an easy man to like.'

'Why does he dislike Diggory so much?'

Arigh Nasan gave a rueful smile. 'Who knows with Krukis? He is easily irritated. The smallest detail, a word, an accent, the merest glance can be enough to spark his fury. But don't worry, he'll do as I say. I pay him so I have him under control.'

Elowen realised that Arigh Nasan was dressed completely differently from the last time she had seen him. A long, woollen coat-like garment reached his knees; it was olive-coloured and had five fastenings and an overlap in front, with an orange silk sash tied around his waist. He had on heavy and well-worn boots of red-stained leather, and a tobacco pouch and a clay pipe hung from his sash.

'You look different,' said Elowen.

'It is good to be out of those rags,' said Arigh Nasan as he sat back down on the stool. He had a warm aroma of tobacco and wood smoke. 'I feel like a true Orok again. I can almost taste the air of the steppes but for now, I must rest a little. My legs still ache from hard riding.'

'Thank you for rescuing me and the others,' said Elowen.

Arigh Nasan glanced down at the floor. 'It is Berstuk that you should be thanking.'

'Who is Berstuk?' said Elowen.

'Of course, how foolish of me,' said Arigh Nasan. 'You have not been properly introduced. You saved him in Rynokgorod. You freed him from his cage and certain death.'

'The Eldar?'

'Yes, though he is more than that,' said Arigh Nasan with a wink. 'This village borders the forest of Drevnie, which is Berstuk's domain, and there he has returned, though not before asking me to pass on his gratitude to you.'

'I don't know why I freed him,' said Elowen, the memories of the chase across Rynokgorod flooding back to her. 'I don't like to see anyone, or anything, in a cage. Helping him to escape felt the right thing to do.'

'Indeed it was,' said Arigh Nasan, nodding solemnly. 'After Berstuk escaped his captors he sought me out, for he knew I had taken shelter in that hideous city. He told me you had saved him but that the Watchmen had captured you in turn. He insisted that we try to rescue you. I was unwilling to undertake such an action but I could not refuse. I stand in eternal debt to him for, long ago, Berstuk saved my life, a fact he gladly reminded me. Krukis, Batu and Vachir agreed to aid me, out of loyalty and of course, out of hatred for Bishop Serapion.'

257

'Serapion,' said Elowen, spitting out the word. 'I'd forgotten about him.'

The door burst open, and Diggory and Lárwita nearly fell inside. Lárwita looked very different without his spectacles and squinted as he peered around the room. He moved in a stiff manner, still bruised from his beating by Serapion's thugs.

'I told you not to disturb us,' said Arigh Nasan, trying to sound angry but failing.

'We were wandering past,' said Diggory.

'Do not listen to his gibberish,' said Arigh Nasan to Elowen, a broad smile softening his weather-beaten face. 'They have waited outside your door for many hours, anxious for news.'

Lárwita fidgeted. 'We were worried about you.'

Elowen blushed. 'It's good to see you both well again.'

'Batu found us some food, thank God,' said Diggory, adding a belch as though to prove his point. 'I'd not eaten for days. Mind you, Lárwita and I had to move fast. When that pig Krukis learnt there was food he nearly scoffed the lot.'

With surprise, Elowen spotted that Lárwita clutched his little book. 'You've still got that?'

'I managed to hide it from the Society guards.'

'You know, I think he values that book above his life,' said Diggory.

Lárwita smiled but did not contradict him. 'I was less fortunate with my spectacles though. They took them off me straight after we were caught. One of the guards crushed them with his foot. He thought it was funny.'

'Can you see without them?' said Elowen.

Lárwita shrugged. 'My sight is poor but I can manage.'

'What happened to you outside Old Glum's cave?' said Diggory, bursting with questions. 'How did you get away from the Society?'

'With Baba Yaga's help,' said Elowen, knowing what her friends' reaction would be.

Predictably, both boys were astonished. Lárwita said, 'Did she take you to her forest lair?'

Elowen nodded. 'It's not her *lair* though, it's...her home.'

Lárwita made a strange puffing sound. 'But it's said no one escapes from her clutches.'

'She's not a monster.'

Elowen told them of her time with Baba Yaga and of her journey to Rynokgorod. She talked for more than an hour before the Orok rose to his feet and said to Diggory and Lárwita, 'That's enough for now. We are in danger of tiring Elowen out. We can talk later, for there is much more to discuss. Rest now, we are safe here from the enemy's reach, for the time being at least. This is a respite—you would do well to enjoy it for there will not be many more.'

*

They spent several days in the village, days in which, with Arigh Nasan's patient care, Elowen's wounds began to heal. Dead skin peeled off her arms and they remained tender and sore, but the Orok soothed them with honey and ointments made from herbs that Elowen did not recognize. Nightmares of the boiling cauldron infected her sleep, nightmares that echoed in waking hours.

Still fragile, Elowen limited her exercise to short walks around the village. She spent most of her time with Diggory and Lárwita, exploring the abandoned houses. They discovered fresh clothes to wear such as linen shirts, fur-lined coats and boots made from wood bark. However, Elowen found the houses cold, creepy places and did not linger within them.

She discussed many things with Diggory and Lárwita but they were reluctant to talk about their capture by the Society. Only once did they discuss it, as they strolled around the village on the third evening since their arrival.

'I thought I'd never be free to walk like this again,' said Diggory, changing the subject from their previous conversation about food.

'What do you mean?' said Elowen.

'After we were captured by the Society I thought we were going to die as slaves,' he explained. He nodded at Lárwita before going on to say, 'He was always more optimistic. I lost all hope. It wasn't just the beatings, the cold and the hunger—it was the feeling of helplessness. I saw it in the eyes of the other slaves, like a light that had gone out, never to be kindled again.'

'I thought we'd be Nulled,' said Lárwita, rubbing his eyes. 'I was most frightened of that. Of not being able to control your own thoughts and actions, a puppet. I think that might be worse than death.'

Diggory said, 'Elowen, if you hadn't rescued us, we'd…'

Both boys fell silent for a moment, mulling over that averted, but still terrifying, fate.

'I think there has been some good to come out of this,'

said Lárwita, almost making eye contact. 'I think…I know that I have good friends. Both of you, I mean. This is…important to me, and a *comfort* to me. It makes me…happy.'

Elowen smiled. She knew exactly what he meant.

Diggory gave Lárwita a playful punch on the arm. 'You're not going all *soppy* on me now, are you?'

Lárwita shrugged. 'I think about the prisoners we left behind. They don't have friends to save them. What will happen to them? Diggory, you remember what happened to that old man who couldn't keep up—'

Diggory held up his hands. 'No, I don't want to talk about that. Let's talk about something else, anything else.'

Elowen wanted to ask more questions, her natural inquisitiveness urging her to find out about their journey to Rynokgorod, but she knew the events were still raw, the memories too painful.

During the next day, which was bright, dry and fresh, Elowen wanted to stretch her legs a little. Diggory and Lárwita had joined the Oroks and Krukis in a meal of stewed rabbits. With her stomach still queasy, Elowen preferred to get some fresh air. It was late afternoon and she chose her favourite place in Granica, the grassy slope beside the wooden church. Although the church stood lonely and forlorn, Elowen fancied that if she concentrated, she would hear echoes of the hymns and prayers that once reverberated within its walls.

The sun peeked through the clouds. Elowen closed her eyes as the wind toyed with her hair and caressed her face. She listened to birdsong, and the repetitive scratching of

261

crickets and grasshoppers boomed as loud as beating drums. It was peaceful enough to convince her, fleetingly, that the world was a gentle and safe place, and that the likes of Lord Lucien and Bishop Serapion were only the imaginings of nightmares. But her wounds, physical and mental, told her differently.

Elowen opened her eyes to see Arigh Nasan striding up the slope towards her. With a smile she said, 'I thought you were still eating.'

He laughed. 'I have had my fill, unlike Krukis who eats like a starved giant. And Diggory too—that boy has hollow legs. I'd be happier to see you eat more though.'

Elowen fidgeted. She remembered the smell of burnt flesh too vividly. 'I've lost my appetite a little. Besides, I thought some fresh air would do me more good.'

'Perhaps it will. The sun is a rare visitor to these parts once summer has gone. And you have chosen a fine spot to sit. This is a beautiful church. The people of Granica were loyal to their God.'

'Why did they refuse the Null then?' said Elowen, fiddling with her pendant.

'A man may believe in God, but not trust the Mother Church or Prester John', he said. He sat beside her. 'Once these were happy lands. I visited this village many times after I left Gondwana.'

'Why did you leave Gondwana?'

He winced. 'Some would say because of cowardice. Whatever the truth, I cannot deny that I was a disappointment to my father.'

'Who was your father?'

He looked up at the sky. 'Bagatur Khan, ruler of the Orok tribes.'

'Your father is the khan?' said Elowen, astonished.

'*Was* the khan, he died ten years ago.'

'Why did you not succeed him?'

'My father believed I should, as did many others. I was the rightful heir. I proved myself in the wars against Prester John and *Burilgi Maa*. Yet I decided to forego the right to succession. I had seen what my father had become, what power had done to him. I saw what he did to keep that power, the suffering he inflicted, and I wanted none of that. Many in Gondwana call me coward and mock the very mention of my name.'

'I don't think you are a coward.'

He smiled. 'I wish more people judged me so kindly, child. I am all but an outcast now. I was fortunate indeed to encounter Grunewald, for he recruited me into the Illuminati. He wished to reach out to my people, to forge an alliance against Prester John. Perhaps that was no more than a dream, a glorious dream. I doubt even Grunewald could have foreseen how swiftly events would turn against the Illuminati. So much has been lost, and not just the lives of those at the sanctuary. Irreplaceable books, manuscripts and works of art, all lost, all destroyed. We stand on the edge of a dark age, one from which this world may never recover. And that is why, when you are strong enough to travel, we should head south-west to Omphalos. I fear that to postpone the journey any longer will only increase the danger. After our escape from Rynokgorod, I feel certain Bishop Serapion will be hunting for us.'

Elowen's breathing quickened. 'I'm not going to Omphalos.'

'You cannot stay here, child,' said Arigh Nasan.

'I know and I don't intend to.'

'Then where will you go?'

'To Bai Ulgan. I promised Grunewald that I would.'

'Bai Ulgan? I tried many times to dissuade Grunewald from his plan to go there. Bai Ulgan is within the ancient city of Erdene, the city of my birth, and it is a more dangerous place than Grunewald guessed. Sukhbataar Khan has made his palace there and he rules his people closely and jealously. But he is not the foremost problem. I have heard many tales of the temple of Bai Ulgan and of its labyrinth, and all are tales to chill the heart. And just to reach Erdene you need to journey across the steppes, a dangerous adventure for even the bravest soul.'

'I'm not afraid to try,' said Elowen, not altogether truthfully.

'I did not say you were afraid, Elowen,' said Arigh Nasan. 'However, I do believe you should be somewhere safe. You have already played such a large part in the fight against Prester John and have paid a heavy price.'

'But that is why I must carry on,' said Elowen. She held up her injured arms. 'You've seen what Prester John can do, and those like Lord Lucien and Bishop Serapion who carry out his bidding. If by going to Bai Ulgan I can help in some way to defeat him, that's what I ought to do. If I run or hide, all my suffering and all the suffering of my friends has been for nothing.'

Arigh Nasan shook his head. 'I have discovered that there

264

is little use in trying to persuade you to change your mind once it is set. Moreover, despite the heaviness of my heart, I believe Grunewald would have given his blessing to such a venture. Very well, you travel to Bai Ulgan. And I, Arigh Nasan, shall accompany you, with your leave of course.'

'I didn't ask you to come with me,' said Elowen, surprised and delighted by his offer.

'I know, and that is one of the reasons why I wish to join you. I believe it is what Grunewald would have wanted and I believe it is the right choice. As reluctant as I am to admit it, perhaps the time is right for me to return to Erdene.'

Elowen failed to stop a smile. She regretted her initial mistrust of Arigh Nasan. He could be gruff and grim, but she found his honesty and directness reassuring. 'I'd be glad if you came, and grateful. What about Krukis, Batu and Vachir?'

'They are free to act as they see fit. However, it is my guess that Krukis will travel with us, he is loyal as long as I keep paying him. A fiercer warrior than Krukis I do not know and I shall sleep far easier at night with him in our company. As for Batu and Vachir, one of them must go to Omphalos and pass on what news we have to the surviving Illuminati. Vachir is best suited for the task, for he served for many years as an arrow rider, and there were none swifter.'

'I need to speak to Lárwita and Diggory, to see what they want to do. They said they would go to Bai Ulgan but perhaps it would be safer if they went to Omphalos.'

'Unless I have lost all wisdom, I wager that they will only wish to be by your side,' said Arigh Nasan. 'They are true

265

friends, and you are blessed to have them. True friends are a gift worth more than any treasure.'

The Orok stood and stretched his arms and legs. The sun was sinking fast and the sky had gone from blue to blood red. Arigh Nasan looked east, towards the forest of Drevnie. 'It is getting colder. If we are to journey to Bai Ulgan we cannot delay. Winter approaches fast, I can smell it on the wind. Although Erdene is in the warmer south, first we must cross the steppe and by the time November falls, the soil there freezes rock hard, all the streams, rivers and lakes are frozen, and the snow can reach your knees.'

'I understand and I'll be well enough to travel tomorrow,' said Elowen, trying to appear unconcerned by his frightening description of the steppes. She recalled what Sadko the minstrel had said about the dog-headed men and headless creatures he believed inhabited those lands. Grunewald may have dismissed the tales but the gruesome images lingered in her mind.

*

It was a cold morning, the air crisp, the sky cloudless. Vachir had already left, sent by Arigh Nasan to bring news to the remnants of the Illuminati at Omphalos.

Elowen, Lárwita and Diggory returned from one last stroll around the village.

'Are you sure this is a good idea?'

It was the third time that Diggory had asked Elowen that question since she had told him about the plan to travel with Arigh Nasan. Both Diggory and Lárwita had readily agreed to continue the journey to Bai Ulgan with Elowen, but Diggory had not been shy in expressing his doubts about their new companions. Lárwita shared Diggory's misgivings but had remained, so far, silent on the subject.

'It is a good idea, we could do with Arigh Nasan's help,' Elowen replied, as she had replied on the previous two occasions.

Diggory shrugged but Elowen's plan failed to convince him. 'I don't like that brute Krukis and I'm not sure I trust the Oroks.'

'We have to trust them,' said Elowen. 'They are on our side.'

Diggory frowned and scratched his head. 'Well, if you insist. Just don't come crying to me if you wake up one morning with an Orok knife in your back.'

Arigh Nasan, with the help of Batu, prepared the horses for the journey ahead. They brushed them, removed mud and stones from their hooves, and fastened the saddles. The Oroks had spent much of the previous day hunting and foraging and now the saddlebags on each horse bulged with berries and dried meat. Batu had agreed to travel to Bai Ulgan and now donned an iron helmet with a leather neck-protector and a fur-lined coat over a lamellar-armour cuirass. He carried a composite bow decorated with engravings and eagle feathers. He strapped a quiver full of arrows across the small of his back.

Krukis wandered around, taking swigs from a large, and very full, leather flask. To his delight, the previous evening he had found an unopened barrel of ale and had been downing the contents ever since. To no one in particular he announced, 'Ah, a sip of ale in the morning fortifies you for the day ahead.'

Ignoring him, Arigh Nasan announced, 'It is time to leave. If we ride first east then south, we should circumvent the Balawta Marshes.'

'That's a *long* way round,' said Krukis.

'Perhaps, but it is safer,' said Batu. 'It is said that the mists there swallow horses and men whole. Balawta is also haunted by marsh-gaunts, fearful spirits that hate the living. We cannot go that way.'

'Yes, the Balawta Marshes are all but impassable,' said Arigh Nasan, nodding his agreement. 'Elowen, you ride with me again.'

'We must stay together,' said Batu. 'The lands we are riding through are full of dangers.'

'Batu speaks the truth,' said Arigh Nasan. 'We are a company—we must work together, fight together and protect each other. Only that way can we prevail.'

They mounted their horses and galloped eastward.

Arigh Nasan had told Elowen that his horse was named Suren, the Orok word for majestic, a name she swiftly realised was well chosen. She found the ride exhilarating: the rush of wind, the clumping of hooves on thick cloddy soil, the horse's hard breathing. Arigh Nasan knew and understood Suren's movements and moods. Linking, Elowen felt the horse's excitement, its heart pumping and its hot muscles straining, the instinctive joy of galloping born of countless ancestral memories.

'You are a skilful rider,' said Elowen above the din.

'I should be,' said Arigh Nasan. 'Like most Oroks I learnt

268

to ride as soon as I could walk. I was tied into the saddle during infancy and spent most of my childhood in the company of horses. And I have never had a more faithful steed than Suren.'

'She must be strong.'

'Strong she is. Once we rode six hundred miles in nine days. Few western horses could manage such a feat.'

When they reached the edge of the Drevnie forest, they trotted to a halt. The trees were painted in rich autumnal colours of red, orange and yellow, and glowed in the morning sun.

'We must dismount here,' said Arigh Nasan.

'Why can't we ride through the forest?' said Diggory.

'Afraid to walk are you, boy?' said Krukis.

'I'd be better off walking than sitting on this stinking horse with you,' said Diggory.

Krukis spat. 'You watch your tongue or by God's wounds, I'll cut it out.'

'For pity's sake, cease your quarrelling,' said Arigh Nasan. 'To answer your question, Diggory, the path through the forest is narrow and uneven, so it is wiser to walk and lead the horses through. Do nothing to alarm or frighten the horses, and don't act scared, even if you feel it.'

'Is it safe in the forest?' said Lárwita as everyone dismounted.

Arigh Nasan secured the lead rope. 'If we tread carefully, there is nothing to fear. Follow me at all times and do not wander off. Try not to disturb anything. Do not pick any fruit, whether it is on the branch or windfall.'

With the lead rope in his right hand, Arigh Nasan stepped

269

forward. He clicked his tongue and Suren trotted obediently after him. Elowen walked behind Arigh Nasan and his horse, accompanied by Diggory and Lárwita. Batu and Krukis, and their respective steeds, formed the rear. The forest overloaded Elowen's senses. The earthy, musky smell, the glowing canopy, the busy hum of wasps, the tapping of a woodpecker and the worried calls of bullfinches, blue tits and jays, startled by the trespassers to their realm. Squirrels scampered up and down trees like unruly children playing hide and seek. Elowen felt connected to the forest, attuned to its rhythms, to its sights, sounds and smells.

Autumn was slowly concealing any remaining signs of summer: shortening the days; cooling the air; changing the colour of the leaves; muting birdsong; burying bulbs under leaf mould. Autumn was a benign ruler. Soon winter would return and it was the thought of that chilly tyrant that drove the forest creatures to gobble or store as much food as they could before the frost and snow took hold.

Arigh Nasan led the company along a narrow path crisscrossed with twisted tree roots. The path meandered between huge oaks, many of which soared from the forest floor with beautiful column-like trunks. Tucked in among the oaks were thick mounds of bramble, withered bracken and hazel trees with crinkled leaves and ripe nuts ready to drop. Elowen looked hungrily upon the blackberry bushes loaded with their juicy fruit, but she remembered Arigh Nasan's mysterious warning so resisted the temptation to pick them.

By midday, they reached an open glade, where Arigh Nasan called a halt. Trees tinted in dusty golden light ringed the glade. The company rested by a dead oak, its barrel-shaped trunk completely stripped of bark. Most of the branches had fallen off and were scattered around the base of the trunk. A wood warbler, which had been perched on one of the remaining upper branches and singing a silvery song, flew away once it spied Elowen and her companions.

Leaving the horses to graze, Arigh Nasan and Batu prepared a meal of salted meat. Elowen was weary, her feet ached and her arms were still sore, so she was grateful for the rest and sat on the grass, quickly joined by Diggory and Lárwita who looked equally pleased to have a break from walking. Krukis wandered around the glade, hammer at the ready, humming to himself and drinking from his flask.

'Why is Krukis keeping guard?' said Diggory, his mouth full of food. He eyed the blacksmith suspiciously.

'It is wise to be careful,' said Arigh Nasan.

'Who is going to attack us here?' said Diggory, tearing off another piece of meat with his teeth.

'There are many dangerous beasts in this forest,' said Batu, winking conspiratorially at Arigh Nasan. He pulled a stone out of his pocket and used it to sharpen his arrowheads. 'Wolves, bears and boar roam here.'

Diggory nearly choked. 'You could have told us that before bringing us here.'

'Wild places always have their dangers,' said Arigh Nasan. 'But if we encounter nothing worse than a wolf or an ill-tempered boar on our journey we shall have been fortunate indeed.'

After their brief rest, they picked up the path again and plunged deeper into the forest. The canopy above them

271

became thicker and the spaces between the ivied tree trunks grew dark and knotted with bramble. Thick, sinuous roots latticed the ground, delving, probing, sucking juice from the soil. Around them mounds of fungi feasted on their ooze, growing into shapes redolent of human bodies, with loathsome fleshy torsos, and deformed, greasy limbs.

Elowen was relieved when the path ascended the top of the hill, where the air tasted a little fresher and wholesome. The trees had gnarled, lichen-coated trunks. Large mossy rocks and plumes of brown, dying bracken spread over the ground. Elowen spotted a stag, almost concealed by the trees. Its antlers were like thick branches and it stared back at her with a regal expression, before a twig snapped and it disappeared into the darkness of the forest.

When the company reached the top of the hill, they found an exposed oval-shaped summit. A scattering of silver birch trees swayed rhythmically in the gentle breeze and littered the ground with their fallen yellow leaves and countless winged seeds. Elowen found it refreshing to escape the dark forest's stranglehold and to breathe air not scented by the dank moistness of rotting leaves and wet bark. A standing stone, carved with vertical grooves and spiral shapes, marked the western edge of the summit.

They all stopped. Viewed from higher ground, the forest stretched in every direction, a sea of red, gold and yellow. The sound of red deer howling and elks calling carried from the trees below. To the east, beyond the forest, rose low, grassy hills.

'We must keep moving,' said Arigh Nasan. 'There is barely an hour of daylight remaining.'

'But we've been walking all day,' said Diggory.

'Be silent, whelp,' said Krukis. 'You can stay here for the night if you're too feeble to keep up. I'd be pleased to lose a good-for-nothing wretch like you.'

Diggory swore under his breath and stomped off.

'You shouldn't talk to him like that, Krukis,' said Elowen.

'Ah, I've no time for weaklings.'

'Elowen is right,' said Arigh Nasan. 'You should respect the boy, as you should respect all of your companions.'

Krukis wiped his nose. 'I'll show the whelp some respect, if that is what you command.'

Elowen detected the sarcasm in his voice and, from the way that the Orok scowled at Krukis, concluded that Arigh Nasan did too. She thought that there might be an argument but Arigh Nasan said, 'I know we are all tired but we must keep going and help each other. I promise we shall find rest and shelter by nightfall.'

The horses became restless. Their ears flickered and they swished their tails. They tensed their back and neck muscles. Their nervousness and jittery fear tingled through Elowen.

'Something is worrying the horses,' said Batu.

'We are unwise to linger here any longer,' said Arigh Nasan. 'Elowen, go and bring Diggory back.'

Diggory was kicking at the ground, sending plumes of dust over a blackberry bush that filled the sheltered spot between two birch trees. Elowen hurried over to her friend. 'Come on, we are going.'

He nibbled at a blackberry. 'What's the point? The others think I'm weak and stupid. They don't need me.'

'*I* need you,' said Elowen, waving away a dozy wasp. 'I couldn't have got this far without you.'

'It's all right for you, you're a *messenger*,' he said. The words tumbled out, as though he was performing a rehearsed speech. 'You're *important*. Me? I'm not a warrior. I'm not clever like Lárwita. Perhaps that brute Krukis is right, perhaps I really am a good-for-nothing.'

'That's absurd. Think about what you've done since you escaped from Trecadok, think about what you've endured and survived, and then tell me you're not strong and brave. Courage isn't just about fighting. You saved my life, not only when Draug attacked me, but countless other times too. You kept me going when I thought I was too weary or in too much pain to carry on.'

A flicker of pride showed on his face. 'I don't suppose you would've got very far without me. I always said you were trouble.'

Elowen laughed. 'After all we have been through, I admit you were right. Come, the others are waiting and—'

She stopped talking. Something caught her eye: a face within the bush. Elowen blinked, thinking that her eyes played tricks on her. But no, the face was still there. A whole body pushed out from the bush, a wizened, stooped creature covered from neck to ankles in long, tangled green hair, and with pale green protruding eyes.

The creature emitted a high-pitched shriek that made Elowen's ears ache. More creatures dropped down from the trees or sprang out of the bushes. Arigh Nasan shouted, 'LESHY!'

A Leshy leapt at Diggory and knocked him onto his back.

274

Diggory fought with the creature, kicking and throwing punches but the Leshy was quick and strong. Elowen went to help her friend but she had not moved three steps when something tugged forcefully on her leg and pulled her down. Another hissing and spitting Leshy clasped both her legs. She tried to kick him off but he clung on fiercely with his sharp nails. Swift, heavy footsteps approached; a blade glinted. The Leshy cried out in pain and slumped beside her, dead. Someone pulled her up. It was Arigh Nasan. 'Are you hurt, child?'

'Don't worry about me,' she said. She pointed at Diggory, who was still fighting. 'Help him.'

Arigh Nasan pushed past her and thrust his scimitar into the Leshy's flank. The creature groaned, shuddered once and slid onto the ground like a gutted fish.

The Leshy were everywhere. Some threw stones; others used long springy branches like whips. Batu's bow twanged as he and Krukis fought a dozen of the creatures, trying to protect Lárwita and the horses. More Leshy came over the brow of the hill. Cackling and shrieking, they formed a wide circle around Elowen, Diggory and Arigh Nasan, leaving them hopelessly outnumbered.

A roar like thunder boomed across the summit; the ground trembled, the trees shook. The Leshy squealed in terror and fled for the safety of the dark forest below. Following Arigh Nasan's lead, Elowen and Diggory ran back to their other companions and the horses. All were safe and unharmed. Nine Leshy lay dead.

Krukis wiped his sweaty brow. 'Filthy little beasts. That's the toughest fight I've had for many a day.'

275

'The danger may not have passed yet,' said Batu as he pulled out arrows from the Leshy corpses.

'What happened?' said Diggory. 'What the hell made that noise? And where did all those savages go?'

'Troublesome are the children of the trees, angry and reckless.'

All the company spun round to face the source of the sudden, unexpected voice. To Elowen's amazement, Berstuk stood only four feet away from them. No one had seen or heard him approach.

'Lord of the trees,' said Arigh Nasan, bowing.

Berstuk looked down at the corpses. 'Your arrival here did not go unnoticed. It is always sad to see such death and waste.'

'We beg your forgiveness for those Leshy we slew,' said Arigh Nasan.

'There is no blame. The Leshy's attack was unprovoked. Hatred of mankind festers in their hearts. I think no ill of you and your companions, Arigh Nasan. You are all favoured in my eyes, especially the girl. I did not properly thank her for saving me, a mistake I now amend, for deep is my gratitude.'

Elowen blushed. 'It was nothing.'

'You showed compassion, and courage too. As a reward, I offer you all safe passage through the forest. None shall hinder you in my presence.'

'You are generous, and we humbly accept your offer,' said Arigh Nasan.

'That is well. Keep close to me and do not wander off. As evening draws in, the forest becomes more perilous still.'

'What about the Leshy?' said Batu, pointing at the corpses.

'Leave them. Their kin shall claim the bodies when we have gone.'

Berstuk led them down the hill and back into the forest's embrace. Elowen sensed a change in the forest, as though the presence of Berstuk brought calm to the trees, animals and birds.

They reached the Drevnie forest's eastern border as the last embers of sunlight faded. Ahead of them, a meadow stretched down to a sandy-banked river. Elowen was surprised to see the ruins of a building close to the river. The roof had fallen in and only three walls remained upright; beside it grew a sprawling crab apple tree with branches wrapped over the nearest wall. The air was thick with the sickly-sweet smell of mouldering, worm-nibbled apples.

'I can go no further,' said Berstuk. 'I will watch over you all tonight, but once you are beyond the river, you will be outside of my protection.'

They made camp in the ruined building. Broken bricks and rotten pieces of wood covered the ground, but Arigh Nasan and Krukis managed to clear enough space to lay out some blankets, while Batu lit a fire.

Night fell. A still night, the wind but a murmur. Despite her tiredness, Elowen's mind refused to settle, running over troubling thoughts and memories. Lárwita sat with his legs crossed, writing and drawing in his book, lost in a world of his own. The others slept soundly, especially Krukis whose snores sounded loud enough to bring down the walls.

'You do not sleep, child?'

The sudden question startled Elowen. Berstuk, who sat opposite her on the other side of the fire, was wide awake.

She sat upright. 'No, as usual.'

'Your mind is troubled, that is clear. Much has happened to you, much for you to consider. You are fearful of what the days to come may bring.'

'Yes, I am.'

'Your fear is understandable, for the peril is indeed great. But if I judge correctly, courage enough to endure you have.'

'I don't *feel* courageous,' said Elowen.

The wavering, eerie call of a tawny owl carried across the meadow. The Eldar gently stepped over Elowen's sleeping companions to sit down beside her. 'Through your actions is courage revealed. It is wrong that you should have to endure so many hardships, but it is the way of the world.'

'It does seem that way,' said Elowen. 'Everywhere there is cruelty and misery.'

'Wickedness grows in the hearts of many men,' said Berstuk, a bitter edge to his voice. He stared at the fire and added, 'They have broken their bond with the Earthsoul. They seek to push back nature, to tame it, to control it. Not all the blame lies with Prester John. Think of the men that tortured you. Was it the Pustoj that drove them to their terrible acts? If free of the Pustoj would they have acted with kindness and mercy?'

Elowen picked at the flaky dead skin on her arm. 'No, I suppose not.'

He turned his eyes slowly to her. 'Only through the weakness of mankind does Prester John thrive. Elowen, do not forget that. Trust in the trees, trust in the earth beneath your feet, trust in the sky above, but in Men, trust not.'

With that he gently patted her hand. 'Now sleep, child. You are safe here tonight. To the songs of the wind, listen. To the chattering of the flames, listen. Let them take you to sleep.'

Elowen snuggled back down under the blankets, closed her eyes and soon drifted into a dreamless slumber.

*

Lord Lucien settled down in the silver throne belonging to Bishop Serapion. The stained-glass windows coloured his white robes in a rainbow of hues. He glanced up at the ceiling. He hated the paintings of sun-kissed saints, angels and prophets. Empty, garish images for empty, garish minds. The automaton clock's insect-like tick-tock irritated him.

Bishop Serapion knelt in supplication in front of the throne, fear twisting his gaunt face and a fat purple bruise on his jaw. He clasped his hands together and said, 'Never before has such an incident occurred in this city. Under my pious stewardship, Rynokgorod has become a place of pilgrimage and faith. Though I was blameless in the failures that led to the prisoners' escape, I humbly beg your forgiveness, Lord Lucien.'

'Only God and Prester John can forgive you,' said Lord Lucien. 'By allowing the girl to escape you may have unleashed a great danger upon the Mother Church.'

'My guards failed me,' said the bishop. 'Those cowards will not go unpunished, I swear it.'

'Such matters can wait,' said Lucien, with a dismissive wave of his hand. 'You are certain it was the girl that I described?'

'I have no doubt,' said Serapion, a little calmer. 'She was a wicked, scheming child. A witch if I ever saw one.'

Anger swelled within Lord Lucien. 'And you are certain *Oroks* aided her escape?'

Serapion rubbed his bruised jaw. 'I am *quite* sure. One struck me. He was a brute, with a scarred face and eyes like a demon.'

'It is strange that Oroks dwelt in Rynokgorod, undetected by your much-vaunted Watchmen, and stranger still that they came to the girl's rescue,' said Lord Lucien as he leant back in the throne. The unexplained, unexpected involvement of those pagans perplexed and troubled him. 'Did she ever mention Bai Ulgan?'

Serapion looked puzzled. 'Not that I recall.'

'I hope you are speaking the truth for it is clear to me that some dangerous heretics have been skulking within this city, heretics you should have discovered long ago. I can only wonder at your claim that this is a city of piety and pilgrimage. Perhaps Rynokgorod would be better served by a new bishop.'

Serapion's hands trembled. 'Lord Lucien, I am a humble servant of God and Prester John. I have devoted my life to the Mother Church. Please, I beg of you, allow me the chance to right this wrong. I shall root out every heretic and dissenter within the city, and every heretic and dissenter within a week's march of its walls.'

'It seems as though you are, at last, beginning to under-

280

stand the gravity of the situation,' said Lucien. He knew that Serapion's greatest fear was losing his power; he would prefer the oblivion of death to the humiliation of losing his high office. Lucien saw beyond the bishop's fine clothes and jewels. He saw an empty man, a weakling, a pig snuffling in mud. But such wretches had their uses: slaves to their base desires, they could be easily manipulated. Lord Lucien stood and said, 'What is done cannot be undone. Begin your purges, Serapion, and do not fail me again, for I shall be less forgiving next time. Leave me now.'

As soon as Serapion had scuttled out the room, Lord Lucien wandered over to the stained-glass windows. He removed his mask, enjoying the warmth that the light provided as it touched his skin. He closed his eyes, seeing not darkness but golden shapes that took forms at will. If there is a heaven, he thought, perhaps it is like this. He opened his eyes again and peered down through a clear patch of glass. Beneath him, the city lived and breathed and ate and drank and died. He stared at the rows of decaying wooden buildings; they looked like rotten driftwood that had been dragged in and abandoned by a gigantic wave. The people scurried around like ants, living lives that had no meaning, no significance. No, this was not heaven.

Lord Lucien put his mask back on and sat down at the silver table. He pushed away a pyramid of rotting fruit, picked up the blank parchment and quill beside it, and began to write. He wrote for almost an hour and then folded and sealed the parchment. He called out and a Redeemer stepped into the room. Lord Lucien handed him the parchment and said, 'See that this is taken to Sukhbataar

281

Khan. Choose your fastest rider and command them to go by the swiftest road. Seldom will they carry a document of greater importance.'

'It will be done,' said the Redeemer.

Lord Lucien sat in the silver throne. The girl had proven both resourceful and elusive. Intrigue and mystery swirled around her, fate aiding her with uncanny good fortune. But now she was within his grasp. She would not evade him for long.

CHAPTER FIFTEEN

A Hard Land

Rough hands shook Elowen awake. Diggory whispered, 'We're leaving.'

She sat upright. The rest of the company already stood outside the ruined building, preparing the horses. It was a misty morning, the air biting. The trees dripped. The wet bricks sparkled. The fire had reduced to a pile of smouldering embers.

'What time is it?' said Elowen after a long yawn.

'Not long after dawn,' said Diggory. 'Arigh Nasan wants to leave as early as possible.'

'What about Berstuk?'

'He's gone,' said Diggory, scratching his head. 'He left without saying a word.'

'Why did he leave like that?' said Elowen.

'Because his task was done,' said Arigh Nasan, walking back into the building.

'I know but I wished…I'd like to have said goodbye.'

Arigh Nasan smiled. 'That is not his way. Remember, you stand in his favour and for that, Elowen, you should be pleased. Do not think too long and hard about the ways and manners of the Eldar, they are a mystery to us.'

Elowen quickly gathered her belongings and followed Arigh Nasan and Diggory outside. The rising sun sparkled in the thousands of spider webs draped across the long dewy grass. Wasps buzzed around the crab apple tree. Batu and Lárwita were already mounted on their horse. Krukis tore into an apple he had picked from the tree only to spit it out. He wiped his mouth and complained, 'Ah, this tastes foul. What sort of apple is this?'

'A crab apple,' said Diggory, for a moment returning to his head boy mannerisms. 'They're too bitter to eat raw, everybody knows that.'

'By the devil, don't be smart with me, boy, not unless you want a black eye,' said Krukis. He threw the remains of the apple at Diggory, who ducked just in time.

'That's enough bickering,' said Arigh Nasan.

The Oroks had smeared bloody handprints on the horses' necks. Horrified, Elowen pointed to the horses. 'Why have you done that?'

'The blood wards off the demon-spirits that lurk within the steppes,' said Batu. 'They are cunning and can lure unwary travellers from the path by the power of their voices or by whipping up terrible sandstorms.'

Elowen gulped and shared a worried glance with Diggory.

'Fear no demons in my presence,' said Arigh Nasan, trying to reassure them. 'It is time to leave, we ride east and we must ride swiftly for many miles lay ahead of us. Batu, Krukis, keep close to me at all times.'

They crossed the shallow stream and as Suren stepped onto the far bank, Arigh Nasan said to Elowen, 'You are now passing into Gondwana, the Orok Lands as you call them.'

Once over the river, Arigh Nasan urged Suren onto greater speed. The rushing wind in Elowen's face took her breath away. She clung onto Arigh Nasan's midriff but was never frightened that she would fall, such was the Orok's skill as a rider. A couple of times she risked a glance backwards and saw the other two horses galloping behind them.

The lands beyond the forest were dreary, filled with lonely gatherings of mournful twisted trees and wind-battered hills. Little streams wound around the hills, shining like silver snakes. They passed remains of settlements long forgotten: the ghostly outlines of walls and embankments; faint paths that stretched through the hills like scars; faceless stone figures bigger than any man, their features eroded by wind and rain.

'Were these Orok settlements?' said Elowen, shouting above the wind and the thud of hooves.

'Yes, once there were many fine towns in these lands,' said Arigh Nasan without turning his head.

'What happened?'

'Like all Oroks they refused the Null. In the name of God, Redeemers and armies of the Mother Church came here, bringing fire and death. Those who attacked the Orok lands were promised absolution from their sins and eternal salvation; such was their reward for murder and destruction.'

Elowen's muscles tightened. 'Do you think we'll encounter any Redeemers out here?'

'No, we are far from Lord Lucien and his creatures. They committed their foul deeds in these borderlands long ago.'

They rode for three days. During daylight hours, Arigh Nasan urged them on, allowing only brief stops for hastily

285

eaten meals. Before the company went to sleep each night, Batu set up markers using available rocks and pebbles to point in the direction they had to travel. Elowen realised that it was sensible precaution in such a featureless, disorientating land.

The weather was dry but with each passing day the wind became stronger and colder. And the further east they rode the more the landscape changed. There were fewer hills, and trees became sparse and then vanished all together. Seemingly endless flat grasslands stretched out in all directions, broken only by scattered rocks and low-growing shrubs. The wind boomed and howled. To the north loomed white-tipped peaks of mountains; huge glaciers ran between them like curled ribbons.

'Behold the steppes,' said Arigh Nasan. 'Too many years have passed since I last breathed its air.'

Elowen smiled but did not share his enthusiasm. She found the steppes an unwelcoming place, one she imagined rolled on to the very ends of the world. It was not a landscape for mortals, for mortals were too small here, lost in the vastness of the plains. Elowen thought she discerned sinister voices on the wind and uncomfortably recalled Batu's talk of demon-spirits. She tightened her grip around Arigh Nasan's waist.

On the fourth day since leaving the forest, just as dusk fell, Arigh Nasan slowed his horse and pointed ahead. Elowen could see something less than a mile in front of them, squat and cylindrical in shape. As they approached, she perceived that it was a felt-covered tent. There was a wooden cart beside the tent but no sign of life.

286

Arigh Nasan signalled for the company to halt. Batu dismounted and, with an arrow notched in his bow, he crept towards the tent. Elowen's heart quivered as she watched. The Orok circled the tent like a prowling cat. He stopped and examined something on the ground, and slipped inside the tent. When he re-emerged seconds later, he took the arrow from his bow and gestured to Arigh Nasan.

'All is clear, the tent is empty,' said Arigh Nasan. 'We can shelter here tonight.'

Even the horses, once they had been tethered outside the tent, appeared grateful for the rest and nibbled greedily on the tough wiry grass. The wooden cart was full of woollen goods and animal skins, all damp and mouldy. Krukis picked through them but grumbled in disgust and frustration when he found nothing of value.

The sight of sun-bleached bones scattered around the outside of the tent disconcerted Elowen and she said aloud, 'Are those human bones?'

Batu scratched his moustache. 'Yes, they are. More than one person died here. This kind of tent is commonly used by nomads, I have seen many over the years.'

'How do you think they died?' said Diggory.

'I know not,' said Batu. 'Once there might have been tracks clear enough to tell me the story of what happened here but if so, the wind has long since erased them. Bandits have been known to attack nomads. Or perhaps it was wild animals. Steppe lions roam this land and they are dangerous, especially when hungry.'

Elowen remembered seeing drawings of lions during zoology lessons in the sanctuary, savage creatures with mouths full of sharp teeth and huge claws. She shivered at the thought of being close to such monsters.

'Bandits and lions,' said Diggory. 'What a charming land this is.'

They went inside the tent. It was bare inside and constructed from a framework of thin wooden struts and a central pole. There was a hole at the apex of the domed roof designed to allow smoke from the stove to escape. Once all six of the company were inside the tent it was a little crowded but with enough room for them all to sit or lie down.

'Whatever misfortune the person that put up this tent suffered, it's damn good luck for us,' said Krukis, chuckling.

The blacksmith's laughter soon faded though when, despite the pile of wood and kindling, he failed to light the stove. Even Arigh Nasan and Batu had no luck with it.

'This is a stupid device,' said Arigh Nasan.

'Let me try,' said Lárwita, squinting as he examined the stove. He cleared the firebox of ash and opened the air vents at the bottom of the stove. He lit the kindling in several places and closed the firebox door. Once the kindling was burning well, Lárwita reopened the firebox door and shoved in some of the wood. Soon, the fire was glowing.

Arigh Nasan patted Lárwita on the back. 'You may be quiet, friend, but you are wise.'

Lárwita blushed and smiled nervously.

The relief of escaping the wind, and the welcome warmth of the stove, lifted everyone's spirits. After a meal of berries and strips of salted meat, Batu told stories of the Great Sky Mother and frightening tales about the ogre witch, *Burilgi*

Maa, who rode into battle upon a black unicorn and was the ally of Prester John and the bane of the Oroks. Hearing about the cruel, pitiless *Burilgi Maa* sent a shiver down Elowen's spine. Even Arigh Nasan looked uncomfortable. He gave Batu a hard stare. 'This is not the right time for *that* story. Perhaps a song is better suited to the occasion.'

So the two Oroks sang. The words may have been completely alien to Elowen but she was happy to lie down, close her eyes and listen to the songs. Diggory had already fallen into a deep sleep. When the Oroks finished singing, Krukis and Lárwita played a game of knucklebones. In turn, they tossed up the bones and tried to catch them on the back of their hand.

Between each turn, the blacksmith quaffed from his leather flask, cursing when he finally emptied it. 'Not a drop of ale to drink from here to Erdene, that's torture for a man.'

The game did not improve his mood. He swore loudly whenever he dropped one of the bones, and when Lárwita was more successful, the blacksmith complained bitterly that the boy was somehow cheating. Eventually Krukis tired of the game and ended it by collecting all the bones in one hand and throwing them at Diggory, who woke with a startled cry.

Krukis laughed when he saw Diggory's shocked expression. 'Look at the whelp! I thought he was going to wet himself.'

Diggory stood and swore at the blacksmith. Krukis sprang to his feet, hands made into fists. 'Do you want to fight me, boy?'

Arigh Nasan moved between them, his hand rested on the

hilt of his scimitar. 'Ale has addled your brain, Krukis, and not for the first time. We should all sleep now; our voices may attract unwelcome visitors otherwise.'

Krukis spat on the floor and said to Diggory, 'One day, boy, you'll be sorry you crossed me.'

He sat, his face stained by anger. Arigh Nasan watched him and only released his grip on his scimitar when Krukis settled down to sleep.

*

A cold draught sneaked through the flap of the tent and roused Elowen from her sleep. She opened her eyes. The tent was dark. The embers in the stove glowed softly. Her companions were asleep and snoring. The skin of the tent rustled in the wind. With his back to Elowen, Arigh Nasan sat cross-legged, looking out through the flap. His scimitar rested on his lap. He had left the flap open, which puzzled Elowen until she realised that he was keeping watch over the horses tethered outside. She felt sorry for the horses. They were tough, hardy animals and no doubt used to such conditions but Elowen wondered if they ever dreamt of warm stables and rich, fresh straw.

'Go back to sleep, child,' said Arigh Nasan. Elowen jumped, as the Orok had made no sign that he knew she was awake. She smelt tobacco and, as her eyes adjusted to the dark, saw Arigh Nasan was smoking his pipe.

'Is it nearly dawn?' said Elowen.

'No, dawn is many hours away yet,' he said between puffs of his pipe. 'The nights are long in—'

Arigh Nasan fell silent. He leant forward, taking the pipe from his mouth.

'What is it?' said Elowen.

He slowly rose to his feet but did not answer. The wind battered the tent. The horses grunted and neighed in alarm.

'What is it?' she repeated.

The Orok signalled for her to be silent and took half a step back. A feline head burst through the flap, much bigger than any cat Elowen had ever seen. It had long teeth, yellow eyes and brown fur. Elowen screamed. Arigh Nasan struck the creature on the jaw with the hilt of his scimitar and it reeled backwards out of the tent, hissing and spluttering. The rest of the company awoke and filled the tent with shouts and cries.

'We must protect the horses!' said Arigh Nasan. 'Batu, follow me. Krukis, stay here and guard the others.'

The two Oroks dashed out of the tent. Still groggy, Krukis reached for his hammer. 'What the hell is going on?'

'We're being attacked,' said Elowen. 'A lion I think.'

The colour drained from Diggory's face. 'A *lion*!'

Shouts came from outside, accompanied by the sharp ringing sound of Batu's bow. Something thumped against the tent but this time it was not the wind. The felt ripped and a lion burst through the jagged hole. Growling, it leapt at Krukis. He swung his hammer but, still drunk, he was off balance and missed. The weight of the lion pushed him down on his back. Lárwita opened the stove door; he scooped up a handful of ash and embers and threw it in the lion's face. The beast howled and swiped its right front claw at Lárwita, missing by only an inch. But before the lion

291

could attack again, a bow twanged and an arrow stuck into the creature's throat. It moaned, tottered and fell on its side, gurgling and expelling a heavy breath before it died. Elowen spun round to see Batu standing behind her, holding his bow. 'The other lions have fled. Are you hurt, Elowen?'

'No, I'm fine, but I think Krukis might—'

'Don't worry about me,' said the blacksmith as he scrambled upright. 'A few scratches and bruises—they'll heal in a day or two. I lost my footing, that's all. The beast got lucky.'

He gave the lion a hard kick.

'Stop that,' said Batu. 'This was a proud and noble animal, one worthy of our respect.'

'A proud and noble animal that tried to rip my throat out,' said Krukis.

'And it did so out of hunger, not out of malice,' said Batu. 'We are intruders to its domain. I mourn the slaying of the beast as much as I accept the necessity of the deed.'

'Are the horses injured?' said Lárwita.

Batu shook his head. 'They are frightened but unharmed. Not for the first time in my life, I give thanks to Arigh Nasan's skill and instinct. We frightened away the lions by standing tall, shouting and firing off warning arrows. Yet we failed to spot the beast that attacked you.'

'The lion would've killed Krukis had Lárwita not acted so quickly,' said Diggory. He took delight in saying that and Krukis threw him a filthy look before grudgingly thanking Lárwita, the wound to his pride worse than any physical injury.

*

292

Shaken by the attack, they left the tent at first light. The moon was still visible; pale, almost translucent, in the pink-tinged morning sky. The wind shrieked and wailed across the grassy plains like a wild animal unleashed, glorying in its freedom.

By midday, they reached a slight rise and stopped for a rest. Arigh Nasan stood in his stirrups to survey the lands ahead.

Batu shouted above the wind. 'Is the way clear?'

'It seems so…wait, look north,' said Arigh Nasan.

When Elowen did so she could hardly believe her eyes: she beheld a line of huge, hairy, four-legged creatures walking slowly southwards. The adult creatures had a high-peaked head and broad shoulders, and stood at the height of three men. Each had an enormous trunk and pair of spiral tusks.

'What are they?' said Lárwita, his eyes wide.

'Mammoths, a rare sight these days, for few remain now,' said Arigh Nasan.

'Are they dangerous?' said Diggory.

'Not unless you are made from grass,' said Arigh Nasan. 'Or fall asleep in their path.'

Elowen watched open-mouthed and entranced by the creatures' slow, deliberate walk, the gentle swinging of their trunks and the busier movements of the young mammoths, who lacked tusks and were dwarfed by the adults.

'They are leaving their summer pasture lands early this year,' said Arigh Nasan. He sniffed the air. 'I fear something has disturbed them. I have heard rumours of unnatural weather. Of snow in the summer, of strange clouds bringing filthy, burning rain. I was sceptical but perhaps there is truth in the rumours.'

They rode on and encountered other animals too, all following migration routes south. Bands of wild horses, each with dark grey coats, black legs and thick necks; giant deer with huge antlers; stocky cow-like creatures with horns on their heads, wiry fur, small ears and short thick legs.

'I've looked at drawings and woodcuttings of such creatures, but I never thought I'd see them with my own eyes,' Elowen said to Arigh Nasan as they rode on.

'This is a hard land but not without beauty,' said Arigh Nasan. 'You are privileged to witness such sights.'

'I'd always believed the Orok lands to be a desert inhabited by monsters,' said Elowen. She told him about Sadko the minstrel's stories of the steppes.

Arigh Nasan laughed. 'Dog-headed men! Creatures with faces in their chests! Still those old tales are told. Yet, it is said that before we Oroks had contact with the lands beyond Gondwana, we spoke of similar creatures dwelling in the west. It is remarkable how we fill the empty spaces of maps with monsters born of our own imaginings and fears.'

After having travelled east for almost a week, the following day they veered southward. The flat, plain grasslands surrendered to dry, sandy stretches interspersed by low rocky hills and small birch woods. The sun was stronger; the wind's biting edge softened. Far ahead loomed mountains, their peaks lost in cloud. The horses never tired, on and on they pounded. Elowen marvelled at their strength and stamina.

For two days they followed the course of a winding river, the turbid waters of which had a milky, greenish hue. The river fed into a crescent-shaped lake fringed with reed groves, willows and alder. Herds of moose and deer roamed the shoreline. A flock of migrating cranes passed overhead, flying south in a 'V' formation.

The company camped by the lake for the night in a hollow circled by willow trees. Arigh Nasan and Batu kindled a fire in a pit, which they had lined with flat rocks from the shore of the lake.

Batu then went hunting; he returned an hour later with a clutch of green branches in his hand and a dead deer over his shoulder. He gutted and skinned the deer, and cut away thick joints of meat. Using a sharpened branch, Arigh Nasan opened the pit, unleashing a wave of heat and plumes of smoke. Batu dropped the joints into the pit on top of, and surrounded by, the white-hot flat rocks. He placed the green branches across the pit and covered them first with moss and then with a layer of sand. Two hours later, Arigh Nasan carefully rolled back the sand and moss, releasing a warm, appetising smell. Using a knife, he cut the venison into small slices and handed them out. A brief, flashing memory of the stink of burning flesh made Elowen's stomach twinge, but hunger overrode the sensation and her mouth watered. She closed her eyes as she ate.

'By God's guts, it's good to have proper food again,' said Krukis as he finished eating. He had grabbed the largest share of the venison. He wiped grease from his mouth and licked his fingers. 'I feel ready to sleep now.'

'We must take turns in keeping watch,' said Arigh Nasan.

'Bears dwell close to the lake and may be drawn to the smell of cooking meat.'

'If it isn't lions, then it's bears,' said Diggory. 'Is nowhere in this land safe?'

'No,' said Arigh Nasan. 'Nowhere is safe.'

Bears did not trouble them during the night and as dawn broke they set off again. They rode on for two more days. The hot sun was relentless. Dust got into Elowen's hair, eyes and throat; she choked and coughed, her eyes constantly watered. She perspired heavily and the occasional swigs from Arigh Nasan's water bottle failed to quench her thirst. Hordes of flies pestered them. The featureless, unchanging landscape itself was enough to lower her spirits. Other than a few hardy trees and shrubs, there was little vegetation. Arigh Nasan pointed to the hills and mountains ahead, little more than bumps on the horizon. 'The city of Erdene lies beyond those peaks.'

Nevertheless, the vast arid plains devoured them and the peaks did not appear to be getting any closer. As hot as the days were, the nights were bitterly cold and Elowen shivered even when close to the fire.

Yet, at last, they reached the rocky foothills of the mountains. A welcome fresh breeze flowed down from the mistshrouded peaks and cloud shadows glided across the plain. The company progressed along a crooked route through the hills, which were covered by stacks of oddly-shaped rocks, carved into precarious and fantastical shapes by the wind. Cypress and ash trees clung to the stony ground and Elowen spotted eagles and vultures circling in the sky above.

Sheep and goats wandered over the hillside, nibbling on

tufts of grass and low shrubs. A shepherd strolled among them. He was an Orok and dressed in a woollen cloak with openings for his bare, muscular arms. He used a crooked branch as a staff. He stopped and watched the company ride along, his face inscrutable.

'We are close to the city,' said Arigh Nasan.

'Will it be safe for us?' said Elowen. 'I mean, for those of us who aren't Oroks?'

'*Gadadihans*, outsiders, are permitted to live in the city, though they have to pay a special tax to do so,' explained the Orok. 'But not all welcome *Gadadihans*. Bitter memories still linger and there is always the fear of further attacks from the west, fears I do not dismiss as unfounded. One day the armies of Prester John will march back into Gondwana, of that I am sure.'

They rode to the top of the hill. Elowen gasped at the view. Ahead stretched a luscious green valley divided by a river and flanked by hills and mountains. The valley was full of olive groves and rich pastureland dotted with cattle. A city filled the far end of the valley. Elowen had always been taught that the Oroks were a primitive, uncivilised race, and lived in mud huts and caves, but the city she beheld proved that such lessons were just lies.

Arigh Nasan pointed to the city. 'That is Erdene.'

A steep-edged hill rose from the heart of Erdene. A building with thick encircling walls, box-shaped towers and tipped buttresses crowned the summit, half-hidden by mist. It was the temple of Bai Ulgan.

PART THREE

- CHAPTER SIXTEEN -

Court of the Kojin Queen

Valbrand ran as though possessed by demons. He yelled and waved his sword around his head. Not knowing what else to do, Bo ran after him.

The two men and the child, who up to that point had been enjoying tormenting the Kojin they had trapped, turned heels and scampered for their lives, disappearing from view among the shrubs and bushes. Bo feared that Valbrand was going to charge after them but his yelling reached an ear-splitting climax and he stopped running when he reached the trees.

'That's a scare they won't forget for many a day,' said Valbrand, straining for breath and hoarse from shouting. 'They won't be coming back, that's for sure.'

Bo laughed from sheer relief. He was pleased Valbrand had stopped before the battle frenzy had possessed him. The laughter died on his lips when he looked again at the Kojin who was struggling to free himself from the ropes. The Kojin's smooth blue-black skin glistened with sweat and his webbed hands worked in vain at the rope, trying to break it by pulling at the frayed strands. On the ground beside the tree lay a longbow and a quiver full of arrows. The

Kojin stopped pulling at the rope and stared at Bo and Valbrand, his green eyes full of hate. He made a hissing sound like an angry cat. He was tall and powerfully built, but Bo realised the Kojin was not old, perhaps only an adolescent, though it was hard to judge.

'What the hell do we do now?' said Valbrand, still red-faced and breathing hard from his exertions.

Bo hesitated. Although he was afraid the creature might attack them, he wanted to cut the Kojin down. He was clearly in great pain, the rope digging into his flesh, the blood rushing to his head. He could not survive for long in such a state. Bo took a couple of steps closer to the Kojin. 'We are going to free you.'

'Then be swift, white-skin,' he said, surprising Bo with his sudden reply.

'It can talk,' said Valbrand.

'My forefathers were building cities while yours skulked in caves,' said the Kojin.

Valbrand swore at the Kojin but Bo gestured to him to be quiet. Bo edged a little closer. He carefully cut the ropes with his sword. The Kojin dropped to the ground. Bo stepped back smartly, wary of an attack. However, the Kojin simply wiped the dust, leaves and twigs from his clothes and stretched his arms and legs before standing upright. He wore a white silky robe secured by a wide belt, which also tied a black ankle-length garment, and sandals made from straw rope. He scowled at Bo and Valbrand, an expression of disdain and arrogance.

'I owe you my life,' he said, the words reluctant, his mouth screwed up as though he found them distasteful.

'Who are you and why are you here?' said Valbrand.

The Kojin spat onto the ground. He reached down and picked up his bow and quiver. 'It is I who should be asking you those questions, for you are both intruders in the realm of my people. All white-skins are trespassers here. Tell me who you are, and why you are here.'

Bo was sparing with the details of their story. He gave their names but told the Kojin only that they had been captured by the Sea Beggars and the tale of their escape.

The Kojin's lip curled at the mention of the Sea Beggars. 'Well, Asbjorn and Valbrand, whatever the truth of your story, it cannot be denied you saved my life, so I am in your debt. I would betray the customs of my people if I failed to offer you the courtesy you have earned by your actions. My name is Jeimuzu, son of Hiroto. I decree that you can pass through the land between the Teburu-Yama and the River Kawa unhindered by the Kojin. By this action, I consider my debt to you both is paid.'

Bo sensed Jeimuzu's offer stemmed more from his respect of an ancient custom than by a genuine desire to help them.

'If it hadn't been for us you'd already be dead,' said Valbrand. 'Who are you to tell us where we can or can't go? I'm not taking orders from you—'

'That's enough, Valbrand,' interrupted Bo, holding up his hands to his companion. 'We have no quarrel here.'

Jeimuzu snarled at Valbrand and crouched in a fighting stance that reminded Bo of a cat about to pounce on its prey. 'If you wish to argue, white-skin, we can fight,'

Valbrand rose to the challenge, holding his sword ready to

strike. 'We ought to have left this demon to hang. I don't care what—'

There was a loud crack. One of the men that Valbrand had chased now stood yards away, smoke spewing from the barrel of his musket. The Kojin moved swiftly. He attached the nock of an arrow to the string of his bow, and in one fluid motion drew, aimed and fired. The man gave a gurgled cry and fell with the arrow lodged in his neck. The Kojin whispered something to himself and swung the longbow over his shoulder.

Valbrand slumped to his knees. Blood gushed from a wound in his left forearm and he let out a long moan of pain. A musket ball had struck him.

'Hold still,' said Bo as he improvised a bandage around Valbrand's arm with some material torn from his shirt.

To Bo's surprise, the Kojin walked away. Bo called after him, 'You're leaving us?'

With his back still turned, the Kojin stopped. 'Moments ago your companion wanted to kill me, now you want me to help you?'

'We saved your life,' said Bo. 'Show some pity.'

Jeimuzu whirled round, his green eyes ablaze with outrage. '*Pity?* For white-skins? Where was pity when our homes were taken from us? Where was the pity when the *Shikome* butchered our elders? You ask for too much.'

'I cannot change the past,' said Bo. 'I only ask for you to do what is right, here and now.'

The Kojin shook his head and mumbled something. After a deep sigh and an exaggerated, petulant shrug of his shoulders, he said to Bo, 'Very well, follow me.'

'Where to?' said Bo.

Jeimuzu strode away. Realising that the Kojin was not going to answer, nor wait for them, Bo pulled Valbrand to his feet. 'We have to get going.'

'I can walk on my own, damn you,' said Valbrand but he made no further protest and allowed Bo to support him as they followed the Kojin.

They stumbled along beneath a blue sky. It was hot, and the dry, dusty wind swirled. There was little shelter, only a few isolated trees, mainly olive, fig and stunted oaks. Shrubs such as mint, laurel and myrtle scented the air. Weak from hunger, Bo found it hard to support Valbrand, who was bulky and clung stubbornly to his sword, reluctant, as ever, to go anywhere without a weapon. Only after a protracted argument did he allow Bo to carry the sword for him.

Jeimuzu marched so far ahead of them he was almost out of sight. He did not attempt to talk but every now and then he stopped and allowed them to catch up, sighing impatiently as he waited.

After they had been walking for about an hour, they came to a road paved with cracked, weed-choked slabs. Valbrand was still bleeding heavily; his bandage was already damp through. Colour drained from his face and he winced with every breath.

'Where are we going?' said Bo when they were within earshot of the Kojin.

'Somewhere safe,' said Jeimuzu.

'I don't think Valbrand can walk much further.'

'It is not far now,' said Jeimuzu. 'We will get there much quicker if you hurry.'

'We can't *hurry*,' said Bo. 'Valbrand is getting weaker all the time.'

'That is out of my control.'

So they struggled on. Bo judged that it was midday and such was the sun's merciless pounding that he savoured every brief moment of shade offered by the few trees that abutted the road. Smoke-stained shells of stone buildings, roofless and empty, and ornately carved stone columns littered the gentle slopes of the land around them. They passed a tall statue of a Kojin, portrayed with one hand resting on a sword, the other holding a vine stick. Time had worn the statue's nose down to a nub and small pieces of stone had broken away from the forehead, leaving the figure with a mournful, hopeless expression.

They arrived at the river that Bo had first seen from the summit of the mountain. The river was neither deep nor wide, but it clearly divided the island, as beyond it the landscape was different from the dry scrubland they had just traversed, with cultivated fields and pasture enclosed by ditches, and in the distance, a settlement of mud huts and tents.

'We do not have much further to go,' said Jeimuzu before he led them across the river. The swift-flowing water came up to Bo's waist, so he waded across slowly, gripping onto the ailing Valbrand. Jeimuzu had no such problems, sweeping through the water, as graceful as a swan.

Five other Kojin were waiting for them on the far bank. They were warriors, all with identical armour: a cuirass consisting of small iron plates laced together by leather cord, an armoured skirt to protect the upper part of the legs and shin guards. They were armed with asymmetric composite bows and one had a slender, two-handed sword strapped to his back. They bowed to Jeimuzu and huddled around him as he spoke in the Kojin language. The warriors stared at Bo and Valbrand, and it was clear to Bo that they were the main subject of the conversation. Valbrand's wound still leaked blood and his eyes had glazed over. Bo knew that his companion was fading fast and a sudden anger, fuelled by frustration, possessed him. He yelled at Jeimuzu, 'Are you going to stand there and let him bleed to death?'

Jeimuzu said something to the warriors and, to Bo's amazement, the biggest of them lifted Valbrand off the ground and carried him in the direction of the settlement. The other warriors followed him. Jeimuzu said to Bo, 'They are taking the white-skin to the monks. It is best that you leave him in their care, for they are skilled in healing.'

'Thank you,' said Bo, grateful and relieved.

'Give me your swords,' said Jeimuzu, pointing to the two blades that Bo had fastened to his belt.

'Why?' said Bo.

Jeimuzu sighed with visible irritation and, as though communicating the most obvious thing in the world, said, 'We are almost in Hinanjo, the settlement, and only Kojin carry arms there.'

Bo was reluctant to hand over their weapons but knew that he was in for trouble if he refused. He gave the swords to Jeimuzu who studied them briefly, sneering as though amused and unimpressed by the workmanship. He marched on and urged Bo to follow him to Hinanjo.

Small ploughed fields, orchards and olive groves edged

the sandy path. On the higher slopes, herds of bony sheep nibbled on tufts of wiry grass. Kojin farmers worked in the fields; they wore cotton trousers and a smock that covered their upper bodies. A scratch plough drawn by four oxen yoked in pairs cut through the dusty soil.

Hinanjo had no encircling wall, no paved roads and there were no brick or stone buildings. There were a number of mud huts but most dwellings were rectangular-shaped tents, all brightly coloured with vertical stripes of alternating shades. A handful of Kojin weaved their way through the tents carrying buckets of water and sacks of grain. Warriors prowled, armed and ready to fight. Bo sensed fear and watchfulness, an uneasy quiet.

Jeimuzu led Bo to a much smaller tent on the edge of the settlement. He pulled back the opening and motioned for him to go inside. 'You should find food and drink in there. Someone will attend to you later.'

Bo went in and expected Jeimuzu to do likewise, but the Kojin fastened the opening and left Bo alone. The tent was furnished with a straw mat, several circular cushions, a six-legged wooden chest decorated with black lacquer and a low circular table. Wooden boards formed the flooring and a single lamp, no more than a cotton wick floating in a shallow clay bowl filled with oil, flickered feebly. The smell of sweet herbs filled the tent. A wooden bowl was positioned in the far corner of the tent; it was full of water and carved with images of ships and rolling waves.

A pile of neatly folded clothes lay upon the straw mat. A long robe-like shirt, a belt and wide black trousers. Their clean smell made Bo more conscious of the dirty rags he was wearing and for a second he thought about changing, but thirst and hunger were the more pressing needs.

A glazed stoneware dish, a decorated porcelain jug full of water and a plain clay cup stood on the table. The dish bulged with food: a red apple, a small round loaf of bread and a sprinkling of olives. Bo sat on the floor and drank three cups of water before tearing into the food. He ate the bread first, wanting to fill his stomach as quickly as possible. He devoured the apple and was about to start on the olives when he noticed the silhouette of someone pacing around the outside of the tent—a guard, armed with a spear. He wondered if he was now a prisoner. Jeimuzu had helped them, albeit reluctantly, but Bo knew they were not welcome in Hinanjo. He had to be careful.

Bo finished the olives and was about to lie down to sleep when someone pulled back the opening to the tent. Bo looked up, expecting to see Jeimuzu but the visitor was an old man, not a Kojin. He walked with a stick and his long-sleeved, hoodless black cassock came down to his ankles. He had a long face with a neat white beard; thick tufts of white hair sprung wildly from the sides and back of his head. His blue eyes sparkled and above them arched untidy black and grey eyebrows. There was no Null in the man's forehead.

'I apologise if I have interrupted you, my son,' the man said in a mellifluous voice that caressed each and every word.

'Who are you?' said Bo, the tone of his reply harsher than he had intended; the man's sudden and unexpected appearance had startled him.

The man sat cross-legged on a cushion and rested his stick across his legs. With a lopsided smile that exposed his crooked, yellowing teeth, he said, 'I am Father Ladislaus.'

'You are a priest!'

'Your skills of observation are impressive.'

'But what are *you* doing here?' said Bo.

'By that of course, you mean why does a priest live with the Kojin?' said Ladislaus. 'I can understand why that seems strange to you, indeed it still seems strange to me. The truth of it is I am their guest. Many years ago the Kojin saved me from slavery and I have dwelt here in Hinanjo ever since, with the leave of the Kojin, a privilege I understand Prince Jeimuzu has extended to you.'

'*Prince* Jeimuzu?' said Bo.

The priest frowned. 'Yes, he must have told you that he is the son of Queen Okaasan, and heir to the throne?'

Bo shook his head.

Father Ladislaus rubbed his beard. 'Extraordinary. I am surprised he did not mention it but then, the prince is not much of a talker.'

'I had noticed that.'

'Jeimuzu is brave and strong beyond his tender years. He has seen but fifteen summers and, for all his undoubted courage, his youth is sometimes illustrated by his more impetuous actions. And he has little love for *white-skins*, as he calls us. However, although it may be ungodly to say it his unwillingness to forgive what happened to his people is understandable.'

'I have heard that the King of the Sea Beggars seized control of this island from the Kojin.'

'My son, if that is all that you have heard then there is much you do not know. The suffering inflicted by the Sea Beggars, the *Shikome*, on the Kojin was unspeakable.'

'I saw several Kojin in the city,' said Bo. He moved over to sit on the straw mat.

'Indeed, and more settle in Katakani each year.'

'And that is allowed?'

'The King of the Sea Beggars permits them to live there if they are willing to work for him. They become little more than his slaves, and they are forsaken by the Kojin that remain here in Hinanjo. They are named outcasts, *Etah* in the Kojin tongue.'

'So why do they go there?'

'They go because they have lost hope living here. Hinanjo, as you have doubtless discerned, is not a happy place. The Kojin are permitted to dwell south of the River Kawa as long as they pay tribute to the King of the Sea Beggars, or the *Kegare*, as they name him: the beast. There is a truce of sorts but raids from the Sea Beggars are not uncommon. Worst of all, the Sea Beggars deny Kojin access to their lifeblood—the sea. In such circumstances it is easy to see why despair has polluted their hearts.'

'But why do they not fight back?' said Bo. 'They have warriors here.'

'Yes, and perhaps if they rose in force they might be a foe to challenge the King of the Sea Beggars but their losses have made them fearful and indecisive. Perhaps the Kojin do not know their own strength; perhaps they simply do not have the will to fight any more.'

'Why are you still here?'

Ladislaus laughed. 'I sometimes ponder that myself but the answer is quite simple. I feel I belong here. As you can see from my garb, I have chosen to serve God and I deem I can best fulfil that role here. I do not believe coincidence led me to this island.'

'You are a missionary?'

Father Ladislaus shuddered. 'Heavens, no. I have no wish to convert the Kojin. Their religion is their own. In truth, I find little contradiction between their beliefs and my own. I find a peace here that eluded me before. The Kojin are noble people and I have been privileged to learn their language and customs.'

'And you are not Nulled?' said Bo, still not believing what his eyes were showing him.

'I am a servant of God, not of the Mother Church, and especially not of Prester John,' he said emphatically. 'He has poisoned the Church and used it for his own ends. He uses the Holy Book as a weapon, and a cloak to hide evil deeds behind. It seems to me that any manner of wickedness can be justified if one declares it God's will.'

Bo was shocked to hear a priest speak in such a manner. 'I marvel that you have survived this long.'

Ladislaus nodded. 'For years I fled from the Redeemers' persecution, a recusant running from priest-hole to priest-hole, serving and being protected by the brave few that still oppose Prester John. But one day my good fortune failed me. I was betrayed to the Sea Beggars and taken to this island to be sold into slavery. As grim as that was, it was incomparably better than being captured by the Redeemers. Death is better than being forced to wear the Null.'

312

'And Jeimuzu saved you?' said Bo, starting to feel comfortable with the genial priest.

'Yes, but that is a tale for another day. I have been waylaid by our discussion, fascinating as it is, and I am forgetting the real purpose of my visit. First of all I bring you news of your friend.'

'Valbrand?' said Bo, feeling a little guilty that he had not asked before. 'Is he all right?'

'Rest assured he is in safe hands. The wound is clean and the Kojin monks who tend him are certain of his full recovery. You need not worry. It is clear to me that both you and your friend have endured many adventures. Your accent intrigues me and it is my guess that you hail from the cold lands of the north. And as you have not been Nulled either, I believe you are Preven.'

Bo nodded warily, disarmed by the accuracy of the priest's guess.

'I must warn you to see beyond any formal courtesy shown to you by the Kojin, your welcome is doubtful here,' said Ladislaus. He leant forward. 'For all the latent strength of the Kojin and the integrity of their queen, the court is ridden with fear, doubt and cowardice. And into the serpent's nest you must walk, for Queen Okaasan has requested to see you.'

Bo was a little startled. 'I had hoped to see Valbrand first.'

Ladislaus smiled but his tone was firm. 'I am afraid that you can hardly refuse the queen's request.'

Bo was not sure he liked the sound of that. 'Why does she want to see *me*?'

'I do not claim to know the queen's mind. But you should

consider this a test, as well as an honour. I advise you to wash and change your clothes. I will wait for you outside.'

Bo took off his dirty clothes and washed with the water left in the bowl. He dressed in the fresh clothes left on the bed; they felt clean and light on his skin. Bo stepped outside. It was a clear, chilly night, with the moon luminous and swollen and the stars bright punctures on the dark canopy. The guard posted outside the tent gave Bo a hard stare.

Father Ladislaus led Bo through a haphazard maze of tents and huts until they came to the very heart of Hinanjo and to a tent much larger and more ornately decorated than any that surrounded it. A warrior in full battledress guarded the entrance. He wore a horned steel helmet, a mask in the shape of a scowling face, body armour made from lacquered-iron scales, an iron collar, broad shoulder-guards, thigh-pieces, gauntlets and leg-guards. He was a terrifying sight, more like a demon than a mortal being. Ladislaus spoke to the warrior, who nodded for the two of them to go inside. As they did so, Ladislaus briefly took hold of Bo's arm and said, 'Do not forget what I told you earlier. Take care with every word you speak. Not all courtiers are to be trusted. I wish you luck.'

Bo took a deep breath and stepped inside, and into another world. Strange sounds. Strange aromas. Dizzying. Bewildering. Unnerving. Bronze and wooden sculptures, figured silks, ink-paintings and embroidered banners furnished the tent. The same motifs were used repeatedly: ships, curling waves, mountains wreathed in misty clouds. Charcoal braziers provided warmth. Yet for all the richness, the colour, the vibrancy, Bo detected an impression of faded grandeur.

314

The sculptures were old, chipped and worn. The silks, banners and paintings were faded and dirty. Echoes of a lost, barely remembered glory.

Bearded courtiers sat on the floor, dressed in long robes and black lacquered wooden shoes. They played a board game with pebble-like counters. Their wives wore straight-lined, ankle-length robes with broad collars and wide, full-length sleeves; they stood in huddles, whispering and gossiping. Entertainers in loose gowns and wooden masks chanted verse, danced and played flutes, drums and a three-stringed musical instrument.

At the far end of the tent, Queen Okaasan sat upon a low throne, almost swallowed by a costume of twelve unlined and overlapping robes. Her face was deeply wrinkled but her eyes were bright and clear. Jeimuzu sat beside her.

As Bo and Ladislaus approached the throne, all conversations and music stopped. The masked performers slipped out of a side opening. The courtiers sneered at Bo.

The priest touched Bo's arm. 'Bow to Her Grace.'

Bo did as Ladislaus instructed.

'Ah, Ladislaus, so you have come,' said the queen in a dry, scratchy voice. She had been eating a peach. She dropped the stone onto a plate and wiped her hands.

The priest bowed. 'Your Grace, may I present Asbjorn?'

'So, you rescued my son,' said the queen, her green eyes boring into him. Jeimuzu grimaced with resentment when reminded of the story. 'For that act, you have my gratitude.'

Remembering his years of courtly training, Bo said, 'You honour me, Your Grace. I also must give thanks to Prince Jeimuzu, for my companion and I owe him our lives.'

315

Okaasan made a sound that could have been laughter or a derisory snort. 'You have a gracious tongue, Asbjorn. But the truth is plain. My son acted rashly, as he is apt to do. He wandered far from Hinanjo, alone and without a guard, vulnerable to the bandits that wander this land. He displayed a lack of sense and wisdom unbecoming my heir. Do you not agree, Asbjorn?'

The queen did not look at her son as she spoke. Jeimuzu sat stony faced but Bo detected the anger boiling within him. Bo picked his words carefully. 'It is not my place to judge Prince Jeimuzu. All I observed was your son's bravery.'

The queen's eyes narrowed. 'These are strange days. Many portents and signs have been witnessed since the last moon. Swirling lights in the sky. Visions of demons adorned in the shining bones of their victims. Even the divine dark bird has been seen. It is yet to be decided how these signs are to be read. Yes, these are strange days indeed, and it is a strange fate that brings you, an outsider from lands distant, here. My son told me your tale of how you escaped from the clutches of the *Shikome*, though it seems most of your companions were not so fortunate. So, I am curious. What is your intention now?'

Bo's throat was dry. He swallowed hard. 'I have had little time to consider, but, if it remains possible, I seek to rescue my friends.'

'The same friends you abandoned in Katakani?' said Okaasan. 'The same friends that now languish in the Pits?'

Momentarily thrown by the queen's response, Bo paused before answering, wary of being tricked. 'It pained me to leave them behind, but at that time they were beyond my help.'

'And I fail to see what you could do to help them now. Your friends are in the Pits, how do you plan to rescue them from such a place?'

A thought that had been growing in Bo's mind came into flower; he said it aloud and as he spoke, he could scarcely believe that he was doing so. 'I respectfully ask the Kojin to help me.'

Bo's words caused an icy silence, followed by an explosion of gasps and angry words.

'How dare you make such a request, white-skin?' said Jeimuzu, leaping to his feet. The courtiers all muttered agreement. 'For your insolence you should be whipped and driven from—'

'That is enough, Jeimuzu,' said Okaasan, simultaneously silencing both her son and the courtiers. 'Do not address our guest in such a manner, especially as you owe him your life.'

Unwilling to defy the queen, Jeimuzu sat, still simmering.

'Please forgive my son,' said the queen to Bo. 'Youth sometimes gives voice to feelings that age and experience tame. The injustices we Kojin have endured burn fiercely within him.'

'There is nothing to forgive, Your Grace,' said Bo, not wishing to enflame the situation further. 'Indeed, I ask for your forgiveness, for I spoke plainly, perhaps too plainly.'

'I never condemn plain speech,' said the queen. 'As to aid, we can give you food and clothing, weapons if you desire them, but nothing more. Anything further risks war. Great has been the suffering of my people since the coming of the Shikome. I cannot ask them to make any more sacrifices.'

'Besides, there is the truce that King Hiroto, your late, beloved husband, forged,' said one of the courtiers, his silky voice eliciting nods and mutterings of support.

'A truce the Sea Beggars regularly break,' said Bo, remembering what Ladislaus had told him.

'That is so,' said the queen. 'But there have been isolated incidents only. The truce says that the *Shikome* may not cross the River Kama, and for all their many crimes, that promise they have yet to break.'

'But this is *your* island,' said Bo. 'Take it back. The Kojin are strong, I have seen this.'

She lowered her eyes. 'You do not know the full terms of the truce. The *Kegare* holds a special prisoner in the Alcazar, my daughter Princess Moriko, the twin sister of Jeimuzu. As long as we Kojin uphold the truce, Moriko lives. If the truce is broken, it is certain that she will die.'

'How do you know she is still alive?' said Bo.

'I sense her life with every part of my being,' said the queen. 'And the *Kegare* has given his word that she is safe and being well-treated.'

Thinking on his feet, Bo said, 'But if the princess were rescued, what then?'

There was a ripple of incredulous laughter from the courtiers. Okaasan said, 'We do not have the strength to assault the Alcazar. The *Kegare* is wary. Rarely does he venture outside its walls and with good reason. The Alcazar is impregnable.'

'No fortress is impregnable,' said Bo, remembering how

318

his father had believed the Hammersund safe from any enemy, a misjudgement that cost him his kingdom and his life. 'There will be a weakness, I promise you that.'

The courtiers exchanged worried glances and whispers.

Bo guessed the truth. 'You already *know* of a weakness.'

Jeimuzu said something to the queen but she brushed him away and pointed to Ladislaus. 'Priest, you know of this. Enlighten our guest.'

Ladislaus blushed and stuttered a protest that swiftly faded under the queen's hard stare. The priest cleared his throat and said, 'The Alcazar is not as old as it appears. The Kojin constructed it during the reign of King Ashikaga the Cunning, grandfather to King Hiroto. It was built in stone but designed to echo the mighty wooden palaces of Bokoku, the Kojin ancestral homelands. Ashikaga built the fortress upon an ancient stronghold of the *Kodai-no*, the Dawn Men, the primitive stone-hewers who lived on the Beauteous Isle ere the arrival of the Kojin. Beneath the Alcazar are deep catacombs, believed to be the tombs of the Dawn Men.'

Bo perceived how uncomfortable the mere mention of the Dawn Men made all the Kojin. He wondered why but did not want to interrupt the flow of the priest's words.

'There was a scryer by the name of Kaimyo, many will remember him,' continued Ladislaus. 'He told numerous tales about King Ashikaga the Cunning. Kaimyo said that Ashikaga built a secret passage from his private chapel in the bowels of the fortress that led down into the catacombs of the *Kodai-no*, catacombs built into the roots of the Teburu-Yama mountain. Kaimyo claimed that Ashikaga

319

visited the catacombs many times and was aged by the experience, worn down by some great terror.'

'Kaimyo claimed many things,' said one of the courtiers. 'He was a drunken fool.'

'He possessed many eccentricities but he was no fool,' said Ladislaus. 'If he said that there is a secret passage into the Alcazar then I believe him.'

'I am not convinced,' said another courtier. 'Many legends have grown around King Ashikaga, they are all lies and fantasies.'

'Not so,' said the queen. 'My husband, who was a great favourite of his grandfather, believed Kaimyo's tales of King Ashikaga were true, though wisely he never ventured into the catacombs himself, for they are the realm of the *Kodai-no*, not of the Kojin. Even if the passages there do still lead into the fortress, there is little hope. To we Kojin, the way is blocked.'

'But I am not a Kojin,' said Bo. A plan grew in his mind. He needed the Kojin's help to save his friends and he knew they would only march against the Sea Beggars if he could rescue the princess. The thought of entering the catacombs terrified him but he saw no other way. The crew of the *Husker Du* were suffering because of his mistakes. He had to try to save them. He heard himself say, 'I will enter the catacombs. I will find a way to rescue Princess Moriko.'

Queen Okaasan rose to her feet. 'Asbjorn, do you really wish to undertake such a quest?'

Bo nodded and with his throat tinder dry, croaked, 'Yes.'

Okaasan looked him straight in the eyes. 'There is little hope of success, but if you choose to take this darkest of paths... you travel with my blessing and my gratitude. You risk much, perhaps everything, for your friends. That is proof of your integrity. If you succeed, if you return Moriko safely to me, I shall deem the ancestors have spoken and that the signs are clear. We must then go to war and march on the Alcazar.'

The courtiers gasped and many shook their heads in despair.

'I promise not to fail you,' said Bo, hoping that the tremor in his voice did not betray his doubts.

The queen adjusted her ropes. 'You must not go alone. Jeimuzu shall accompany you.'

Bo wondered if he had heard the queen correctly. The shocked gasps from the courtiers confirmed that he had. Jeimuzu fidgeted and looked at his mother in amazement.

'My son has urged me countless times to launch a raid to rescue his sister,' continued Okaasan. 'Strong in body he is, but his temperament has yet to mature. This is a chance for him to prove himself. For generations beyond count it has been Kojin tradition for the heir to the throne to undergo a test to prove that they are worthy to lead their people. Our ancestors fought terrible monsters, or ventured across perilous lands to seek treasure. This, I believe, is Jeimuzu's test. My son, do you accept this challenge?'

'Yes, Your Grace,' said Jeimuzu without hesitation. Bo realised the prince had no choice but to accept the test, for he would lose all credibility and honour if he refused.

'I am pleased,' said the queen to her son. 'This condition I place on you: follow Asbjorn's command at all times. Follow his orders as strictly as though they were mine. Wiser he is than you, Jeimuzu, and less likely to let anger dictate his actions. Do you have any objections to this condition?'

This time Jeimuzu did hesitate before answering. After a swift, sharp, stabbing glare at Bo, he shook his head and said, 'I have no objections, Your Grace.'

Bo shifted his weight as he stood. He did not like the idea of having the Kojin prince as a companion; he feared that Jeimuzu was as likely to stick a blade in him as the Sea Beggars were.

'The entrance of the catacombs is through the Tomb of the Eagle, which is found on the peak of Teburu-Yama, the mountain that stands above Katakani,' said Okaasan. 'A guide shall lead you both there. Ladislaus, do you accept this duty?'

The priest made a poor attempt at hiding his surprise and alarm. 'I…I…of course, I am honoured to help, Your Grace.'

'Then it is settled,' said the queen, clapping her hands together. 'You leave at dawn tomorrow, and the hopes and blessings of our people go with you.'

Bo bowed and followed Ladislaus out of the tent.

'Well, you certainly made an impact,' said the priest.

'I am sorry if I embarrassed you or let you down,' said Bo, his breath steaming in the cool air.

'Nonsense. You spoke skilfully and honestly, and in that much you won the queen's admiration I think. Though I fear the courtiers are less enamoured with you.'

'Do you believe I was foolish to promise to rescue the princess?'

'It was bravely done.'

322

'And you are happy to guide me to the catacombs?'

'Yes, truly I am. However, I admit that I fear for you.'

Bo shrugged in an unconvincing effort to show that he was not afraid. 'I hope that if we succeed in rescuing the princess, the queen will remember her promise and attack the Sea Beggars.'

'You ask much of her,' said the priest. 'Do not think that she lacks courage. She is, however, bound by her duty to her people, many of whom are tired of fighting and wish now to have a quiet life, even if such a life is far from their past glories. Queen Okaasan wishes to enforce her people's will, not to enforce her own upon them.'

'A leader should be strong.'

'Yes, but it is more important that a leader be just and wise. I believe that the queen is both of those.'

'But if she does not act the Kojin will be destroyed. One day the King of the Sea Beggars will finish what he has started.'

'I fear you are right but the Kojin place great emphasis on honour. The King of the Sea Beggars may consider the truce worthless but the queen, I assure you, does not. And she fears for her daughter, her beloved Moriko. If the princess were returned… much would change.'

'I was surprised the queen wanted Jeimuzu to go with me.'

'As, I believe, was the whole court. Yet, it is as Her Grace says. Jeimuzu is of the age to test himself, though he could hardly have been given a more daunting challenge.'

'I don't think he likes me very much.'

The priest chuckled. 'I'm sure you will learn to cope. But come, you need sleep.'

'I would like to see Valbrand first.'

Ladislaus looked a little reluctant but his kind, wonky smile broke out again. 'As you wish, my son.'

It was a short walk to Valbrand's tent and Ladislaus did not dawdle. A Kojin warrior kept guard outside the tent. He was wrapped in a thick coat and stamped his feet to keep warm. He greeted Ladislaus with a friendly smile, but when he saw Bo he frowned and tightened his grip on the spear he held. Ladislaus spoke to the Kojin again in his calm, fluid voice and the warrior stepped aside.

'Your friend is inside, Asbjorn,' said the priest. 'Be swift—the guard is not a patient fellow, and while I shall wait outside for you, I am cold and should be in bed.'

Ladislaus winked as he spoke but Bo knew that he was not joking. The warrior pulled back the opening of the tent and Bo ducked inside.

Valbrand was stretched out on a straw mat bed and partially covered by a thin blanket. His eyes were closed and he was breathing slowly. His left arm was heavily bandaged. He still had his silk ribbon tied around his neck.

A charcoal brazier warmed the tent. A wooden cup and a plain clay jug stood next to Valbrand, close to his head. A Kojin knelt beside him. He was bald but had a grey-flecked beard that reached his chest. His saffron robes were made of patched pieces of cloth. He stood as Bo entered, bowed once and slipped out of the tent.

'I wondered when you would come to see me,' said Valbrand. He opened his eyes and grinned.

Smiling, Bo sat beside Valbrand. 'I thought I had better check you were still alive.'

'I'll see a few more dawns, I think,' he said. He pointed to the cup beside him. 'And they have this drink, fine stuff it is too. You should try some.'

Bo picked up the cup. It was half-full of a cloudy liquid. Bo took a sip, it tasted like wine, only much stronger and he choked a little as it reached his throat.

Valbrand spluttered with laughter as Bo wiped his mouth and put the cup down. 'It's potent stuff, eh? Warms the bones on a cold night and it's taken away most of my pain.'

'You are feeling better?' said Bo, his eyes still watering from the drink's strong aftertaste.

'Aye, much better,' said Valbrand. 'These Kojin are odd folk but they seem decent enough. Their monks know their medicine. My arm is as stiff as a rock but they've staunched the bleeding and I'll be on my feet in a couple of days, I'm sure of it.'

'You should be careful.'

'I've had worse injuries and lived,' said Valbrand. As though to prove a point he sat up and pulled away the blanket, exposing his naked torso that was latticed with numerous scars. 'What have you been up to? You look like one of the Kojin with those clothes on.'

Bo told Valbrand about the priest Ladislaus, and of Queen Okaasan and her court. And he told him about the quest to rescue the princess.

Valbrand listened intently and when Bo finished he said, 'You've got some guts, I'll admit that. Do you think the Kojin will attack the Sea Beggars if you free this princess?'

'I hope so, for without the Kojin there is no chance of rescuing the others.'

325

'Aye, I reckon those Kojin are good fighters. Even I might think twice about getting into a tussle with them.'

Bo laughed. 'I find that hard to believe.'

'Maybe you're right,' said Valbrand after emptying the cup with one swig. 'It's a raw deal I tell you. I ain't always seen face to face with Black Francis, that's no secret, but I take no pleasure from thinking of him and his crew in the hands of those Sea Beggars. Those scum stole my crossbow as well. Damn them all, filthy thieves.'

Bo judged it was not the correct moment to remind Valbrand that he had actually stolen the crossbow in the first place, so settled on saying, 'I have to leave tomorrow. Will you be all right here?'

'Aye, and I'd come with you if I could, you know that don't you?' said Valbrand. He filled the cup from the jug. 'At least there's always drinking to fortify us in times of trouble and hardship.'

Ladislaus stepped into the tent. 'It is time for you to leave, Asbjorn.'

Bo nodded and got up.

'So he really is a priest,' said Valbrand, burping after a long gulp of drink. 'You're a long way from God here, my friend.'

'I am never too far from God, I hope,' said the priest. 'Yet now is not the time for a theological debate, my eyes burn with the need for sleep. Late nights and an old man are not a happy mix.'

Ladislaus hobbled out of the tent and as Bo turned to follow him, Valbrand cleared his throat and said, 'I ain't always been good to you, Asbjorn. I've said some harsh things.

Well, I ain't one for apologising. The past is the past. What's said is said and what's done is done. But you're a decent man and that ain't the drink talking. Good luck. I hope we meet again soon.'

With that, he belched loudly and settled down to go to sleep.

Life takes many unexpected turns, Bo thought. A man he had distrusted, hated, had become a loyal companion. He knew that his earlier view of Valbrand as a mindless thug was wrong, coloured by his own fear and weakness. Yes, Valbrand could be fiery, argumentative and ruthless, but the boiling rage within him came from real suffering, from a sense of loss that Bo could scarcely imagine. There was no deceit about Valbrand; he was blunt and forthright, but he told no lies, weaved no webs of intrigue. Bo knew he had misjudged him. He had been too blind to see the truth. He hoped to learn from his mistake. He hoped he would be wiser, less swift to judge, in future.

As he left the tent, Bo said, 'Good night, my friend.'

CHAPTER SEVENTEEN

The Great Khan

Wind screamed down from the mountains, whipping up clouds of dust from the long, wide road that flowed into the city of Erdene. The road ran alongside the river that neatly divided the valley. Elowen looked down at the rippling water, unsettled by the sight of her contorted, writhing reflection.

They rode slowly and in silence, keeping a wary eye on the fields and olive groves that flanked the road. Elowen sensed the tension within Arigh Nasan as he kept looking around, reacting to every sound whether it was the cry of a bird or the restless rustle of a wind-thrashed tree.

As they drew closer to the city, they passed a tall circular pillar. At first, Elowen thought it was another stone monument, a relic from antiquity, then she realised with horror that human skulls were mortared and plastered into the pillar.

'What's that?' she said, breaking the silence of the company and looking away from the pillar in horror.

'A warning to enemies,' said Arigh Nasan, who avoided looking at the pillar. 'The khan does not forgive those who dare to oppose him.'

A curtain wall of stone surrounded the city. As they approached the main gate, Elowen spotted sentries marching along the high battlements, their spear tips sparking tiny flashes as they reflected the sunlight. The gate was open but Orok guards armed with swords, bows and javelins loitered outside.

Arigh Nasan brought Suren to a halt and gave the guards a friendly greeting, which they returned less warmly. The guards pointed at Elowen, Diggory, Lárwita and Krukis, clearly uncomfortable with their presence. Arigh Nasan dismounted and began an animated conversation with the guards.

'Do you think they'll let us in?' said Diggory.

Batu patted the neck of his horse. 'Arigh Nasan can be very persuasive.'

'What do you know of the khan?' said Elowen.

'Sukhbataar Khan is powerful, a leader to be respected,' said Batu. 'A proud khan, a fearsome khan.'

Elowen didn't like the sound of that. 'Does he rule all the Oroks?'

'He strives to but there are many tribes. Some still follow the old ways, living as nomads. Others have built towns and cities, though none as large as Erdene. All the tribes vie for supremacy. Sometimes it spills over into war. For now, there is peace among the Orok tribes but little unity. For all our strength, we still shiver in the cold shadow of Prester John.'

Arigh Nasan returned and remounted his horse.

'Is everything all right?' said Elowen.

'Yes, for now at least.'

329

'Are we going to Bai Ulgan?' said Elowen, remembering her first glimpse of the mist-haunted towers.

'Not yet,' said Arigh Nasan. 'Bai Ulgan is a sacred place and it is forbidden to go there without permission. Therefore, we must go to the khan's palace and present our case. Only with his leave can we enter Bai Ulgan.'

'And will he give us permission?'

'Perhaps,' said Arigh Nasan. 'I know the khan. Many years ago we fought together, side-by-side.'

'Well, it must help that he's a friend,' said Elowen.

He winced. 'I do not think of Sukhbataar Khan as a *friend*. I have not seen him in over five years but he might help us. He holds no love for Prester John, and these lands have suffered more than most at the hands of the Mother Church.'

'Do you trust him?' said Elowen.

Arigh Nasan looked away and offered no answer.

They rode into the city. Dingy shops and inns choked the streets. Oroks sat at rickety tables supping black coffee from small cups, or smoking tobacco from long pipes. Some Oroks pointed at Arigh Nasan and there were looks of surprise and alarm. Elowen wanted to ask him about it but guessed it was not a good time to do so.

They reached a square lined with tents, booths and stalls, and bordered by dilapidated two-storey brick buildings. The shops and stalls sold a bewildering range of goods: furs, jewellery, silks, satins, trunks and boxes, locks and keys, and spinning wheels. Poorer traders simply spread their fruit and vegetables on the ground and squatted among their goods. There were horses, mules, pigs and sheep for sale,

330

although a hairy, four-legged creature with a long neck and a hump rising from its back, drew Elowen's attention. It gazed at her with a sad but comical expression.

The noise of the market was like a relentless barrage. The shrill cries of traders clashed with the hundreds of conversations taking place. Friends greeted each other by bowing and placing their right hand across their chests. Fortune-tellers and singers filled any spare spaces on the street. Music played on copper trumpets and drums poured down from the upper floors of the surrounding buildings.

The square was far too crowded to ride horses through safely, so Elowen and her companions dismounted. Even though she took care to stay close to Arigh Nasan, Elowen felt vulnerable and the scornful stares and sneers she received from many Oroks unnerved her. She felt panicky, as though the crowds were all pushing towards her, crushing her, smothering her. She struggled to breathe. Her panic was only relieved when Arigh Nasan led them into a quieter side street. Elowen felt as though she had surfaced from deep water, swallowing air to relieve her aching lungs.

They did not stop again until they came to the khan's palace. Beyond a whitewashed brick wall, Elowen glimpsed the roof of the palace, coloured with many hues and shining like a crystal, and topped with a nine-tailed standard. They approached the palace's southern wall and in front of them loomed the Great Gate, firmly closed because, as Arigh Nasan explained, it was only opened when the khan went forth. Beside the Great Gate was a smaller open gate through which a steady stream of people flowed back and forth.

'It is time to enter the palace,' said Arigh Nasan. 'Su-khbataar Khan is not to be trifled with. Say nothing of our quest. Indeed, leave all the talking to me for any unwary words from your lips will only serve to antagonise him and we don't want that.'

'I'm my own man,' said Krukis. 'I don't hold my tongue to avoid offending others.'

'If you do not hold your tongue in the court of the khan, you may lose it,' said Batu.

Arigh Nasan gave Krukis a hard stare. 'Batu speaks the truth. In the court of the khan, show respect and deference.'

Guards ordered them to leave their horses in stables just within the palace walls. The palace sat amidst lush lawns crisscrossed with gravel paths and dotted with cherry plum, apple and peach trees, and aromatic shrubs. Wooden statues of Orok warriors stood among the trees, their moustached faces stern and grim. Elowen and her companions crossed a marble bridge, which spanned a pond fed by a tiny stream. On the edge of the pond, mallards squabbled and scoured the ground for food, while swans glided across the water, their white feathers gleaming.

Although it had a lofty roof, the palace was only one storey high, standing on a paved platform several feet tall, from which extended a wide marble terrace surrounded by a handsome balustrade. There was a single entrance, an ivory door. It was guarded by a dozen warriors, all bristling with swords and spears. They wore narrow, cap-like helmets and coats of chain mail, decorated with gold bands, that reached down to the knee.

'The warriors belong to the Kushiku, the khan's Life Guard,' said Arigh Nasan to Elowen.

The Kushiku frightened Elowen. Her mouth became dry and her heart hammered. The ivory door opened. An Orok emerged, his leathery face wrinkled and tanned. He had a flat nose, a thin, pointed beard and a long moustache that drooped around his small mouth. His ankle-length robes were of white silk, and a wide waistband, tied at the side with ribbons, was stretched by his protruding stomach. A hat decorated with white fur perched on his head. He walked with confidence, arrogance even, his penetrating eyes glued hawk-like on the visitors. It was Sukhbataar Khan.

The khan approached Arigh Nasan and embraced him, much to Elowen's relief. Arigh Nasan took half a step back and said, 'May I request, Great Khan, that you honour me by speaking in the Common Tongue, for the benefit of my companions?'

Sukhbataar Khan looked at Elowen, Diggory, Lárwita, Batu and Krukis in turn. Elowen wondered if she imagined it but his gaze rested on her for longer than it did on anyone else. In a deep, smoky voice he said, 'You are companions of Arigh Nasan, and therefore welcome guests here.'

Elowen thought the khan seemed friendly enough, certainly not as frightening as she had imagined.

'We are humbled by your gracious welcome, Sukhbataar Khan,' said Arigh Nasan.

The khan laughed. 'You have a silver tongue, my old friend. When we fought together at Boghumta against the hordes of *Burilgi Maa* you spoke in coarser tones.'

333

'That was a long time ago,' said Arigh Nasan. 'Much has changed.'

'But you are still as serious as ever,' said the khan, wagging his finger in a jovial manner. 'Your father always said you were too grave to become khan and I suppose he was right. You look as though you carry the world's woes on your shoulders.'

'I am sure that my cares are insignificant compared to those of the khan.'

'My subjects turn to me for protection and guidance, that is true,' he said, patting his large belly. 'But whatever hardships and trials I endure, I find solace in food and drink. And I feel the need for both now. Come, in the Hall of Great Brightness I have a feast prepared. Please, honour me by sharing it.'

Before entering, the Kushiku warriors instructed the company to take off their shoes and put on white leather slippers. Elowen gasped when they stepped into the Hall of Great Brightness. A fountain loomed over the entrance: a trumpeting angel topped a silver tree, entwined by a gilded serpent and guarded by golden lions. Mares' milk bubbled forth from the maws of the lions, while from the branches flowed liquors made from rice, milk and honey.

As Elowen walked further into the hall, she discovered other spectacles and curiosities too. Rich silks and sculptured representations of horses, birds, gods and warriors adorned the walls. Dragons were carved into the pillars, their outstretched limbs supporting the roof. Golden light poured through the narrow windows, illuminating parts of the hall, while leaving others veiled in shadow.

The khan led them through the Hall, passing through waves of fawning courtiers and servants. Cocooned by opulence, Elowen felt self-conscious in her weather-beaten clothes. The khan stopped at a pedestal at the far end of the hall and sat at a table laden with cheese, butter, olives, figs, cooked mutton and a pot full of vegetable stew. Behind the khan stood an Orok much taller than any Elowen had seen, a warrior in scale armour made from leather and iron, and an iron helmet. He was taller than Krukis, his skin weathered with a reddish hue, and with small, unblinking eyes. Elowen guessed he was the khan's bodyguard, as fierce a deterrent to any would-be assassin as she could imagine.

'Come, eat as much as you can manage,' said the khan, tearing off pieces of mutton and cheese with his fingers.

Servants brought pillows for Elowen and her companions to sit on, as well as giving them each an earthenware plate and a bowl. Achingly hungry, Elowen put her nervousness at her surroundings to one side and eagerly filled her plate. The cheese tasted a little bland but the olives and figs were succulent and the stew warmed her stomach. Krukis gorged as though he had not eaten for days, ripping off huge chunks of mutton and filling his bowl with stew.

Sukhbataar Khan sank cup after cup of wine and fermented mares' milk. He belched loudly and announced, 'It takes me back to see you again, Arigh Nasan. I had feared you were dead.'

'I have been lucky so far,' said Arigh Nasan.

'Of that I am glad, old friend,' the khan said, his speech slurred. 'I hold many good memories of the time we spent campaigning together.'

335

Arigh Nasan's expression darkened. 'I too hold many memories of that time, but in truth few of them are happy. I chiefly remember death, hunger and suffering.'

The khan emptied another cup of wine and threw his head back in laughter. 'You have not changed, Arigh Nasan. You are still as gloomy as ever. Tell me, what brings you to my palace, and with such…interesting friends?'

'We wish to visit Bai Ulgan,' said Arigh Nasan.

His reply silenced the khan, his laughter a memory. He frowned and rubbed his beard. His voice rose to an incredulous high pitch. 'You have travelled for countless miles just to visit Bai Ulgan? I am intrigued.'

'There is no intrigue,' said Arigh Nasan, with a casual shrug of his shoulders. 'My friends have a scholarly interest in the temple and in the labyrinth. And they pay well.'

Sukhbataar Khan nodded but Elowen could tell he was not convinced by the story. 'Bai Ulgan is a temple, sacred and holy, and it is my duty to protect it. You know this well, Arigh Nasan. The temple threshold is not to be crossed lightly by those seeking mere learning. These three young-blood *Gadadihans* are your scholars?'

'Yes, but do not let their age blind you to their learning.'

'I see,' said the khan. He gestured to Krukis. 'You do not look like a scholar.'

'He is my bodyguard,' said Arigh Nasan before Krukis said anything. 'We have journeyed through many dangerous lands.'

'I am shocked to learn that the great Arigh Nasan needs a *bodyguard*,' said the khan. 'With Batu by your side, you surely have little to fear?'

'Batu is my trusted companion but as you can see I have others to guide and protect. It is wise to be cautious in days such as these.'

'Perhaps that is so,' said Sukhbataar Khan, his voice now carrying a colder tone. He tore off another piece of mutton and with his mouth still full said, 'So you wish to see Bai Ulgan. It is my duty to protect my people, a sacred duty that I hold above all other considerations. Such a duty weighs heavily on me and makes me suspicious. I have a talent, a gift you might say, for knowing when my subjects are lying to me, when they are planning to betray me. My gift is warning me now. I demand to know the truth your fine words mask.'

Elowen shivered. A chill danced on the back of her neck. Without trying to be too obvious, she looked up at Arigh Nasan, wondering what his response would be.

'Sukhbataar Khan, I have no desire to deceive you, let alone betray you,' he said, his voice lowered in humility. 'I have come here for your aid, in the spirit of friendship, in the memory of the comradeship we shared through the heat of battle.'

'A memory you declared unhappy,' said the khan, using Arigh Nasan's own words against him.

'The memories I have of battle are cruel, but I think fondly of our friendship and treasure it far too much to want to deceive you.'

The khan slumped back in his chair and rubbed his beard. 'Forgive my suspicions, for they are born of a mind plagued by many burdens. The ogre witch *Burilgi Maa* has vanished but countless threats still face my people. I do not object to

337

your request but neither can I grant it without first seeking the shamans' guidance. I shall consult them and vouch for your integrity and, of course, your honourable family history. The answer may not be quick, for the shamans do not make hasty decisions, and are often deep in their prayers and meditations and may not be disturbed. Until a decision is made, you are my guests here. Is this agreeable to you?'

'Of course,' said Arigh Nasan, his face inscrutable. 'I am in debt to you.'

'We shall see,' said the khan. He clicked his fingers at a servant, and said to Arigh Nasan, 'An apartment room will be prepared for you and your companions. Tolui will take you there. I wish you all a good night.'

As the servant named Tolui led them away, courtiers surrounded the khan—they huddled in deep conversation.

*

The apartment room was comfortable, even luxurious, and the Orok hosts provided food and drink aplenty. However, to Elowen it was like being a prisoner, a prisoner in a gilded cage perhaps, but still a prisoner. Three days passed, long and dull days. A quiet, listless gloom spread over the company. Krukis proved most disturbed by the boredom. He grumbled incessantly and picked arguments over the most trivial of subjects. He resorted to long silences. He slipped in and out of the room, seeking, Elowen guessed, yet more food and drink.

Only Lárwita seemed content, humming to himself and scribbling down ideas and observations in his book, squinting and rubbing his eyes as he wrote. He often discussed his writings with Arigh Nasan, and Elowen heard them discussing flying machines, boats that sailed beneath the waves and carts that moved without being pulled by animals. Diggory occasionally joined in the conversations to add an incredulous laugh or a disbelieving groan, all taken by Lárwita with his customary patience.

On the fourth night since their arrival in the city, Elowen stood on the marble terrace, leaning against the balustrade. Dozens of lamps flickered throughout the city, mirroring the sparkling stars in the sky. The air was cool, the wind persistent and biting. It was well past midnight but Elowen had given up trying to sleep.

The apartment room had a door opening out onto the terrace so Elowen had decided to seek some fresh air. Framed by wispy clouds, the moon loomed like a giant lidless eye, all seeing, all knowing. Elowen stared at the silhouette of Bai Ulgan. The turrets resembled talons clawing at the sky, as though the temple was not a building but a creature with a life and mind of its own, with a purpose hidden and deadly. Elowen's stomach rolled over when she thought about the temple and the labyrinth within; she feared what secrets and dangers lurked there. As she looked up at Bai Ulgan part of her wanted to run away, a thought that left her ashamed.

The sound of footsteps made her jump. It was Arigh Nasan.

'I am sorry, did I startle you?' he said.

'No, not at all,' lied Elowen, her heart still pounding from the surprise.

'Are you are having difficulty sleeping again?'

She nodded. 'Something about this place unsettles me.'

'You are not alone in feeling that way,' he said. 'Sukhbataar Khan has brought many changes to Erdene and as I see it, few are for the better. This palace, the elaborate gardens, the fountains, this is not how we Oroks should live.'

'Do you trust the khan?'

Arigh Nasan looked up at the sky. 'It depends on what you mean by trust. Sukhbataar has a cunning mind and he is not easily fooled. It is not in his nature to grant favours lightly and he does nothing without a purpose that is to his advantage. I suppose we should be grateful that he is at least *considering* our request to enter Bai Ulgan.'

'If he does grant us permission, what do you think awaits us there?' said Elowen. An upturned beetle struggled on the balustrade, its legs flailing as it tried in vain to move. She nudged it gently upright and it scurried away.

'Many legends have been told about the temple,' said Arigh Nasan. 'Legends about piles of gold, silver and jewels. Nonsense, I am sure. All I know is that the shamans of Bai Ulgan guard the temple and have done so for years beyond count. It is my belief some ancient holy relic dwells in the labyrinth's depths, though what that relic is I cannot begin to guess. Perhaps we shall discover some of Bai Ulgan's secrets, but for now you must return to bed, child. Rest while you still have the chance.'

Elowen tiptoed back into the room so as not to wake the others, though they were so deeply asleep she wondered if anything short of thunder could stir them. Krukis was missing again and Elowen dreaded to think how drunk he would be when he finally stumbled back in.

Arigh Nasan remained on the balcony, looking out over the darkened city.

*

At dawn, Tolui came to the apartment room and told the company to assemble outside the palace. It was cold and the sun only peeked over the eastern horizon.

Diggory wiped his dripping nose and stamped his feet. 'Why do we have to wait out here?'

'Because that was the khan's order, you idiot,' said Krukis, scowling at Diggory. Elowen guessed he was suffering from yet another hangover.

'I wasn't talking to you,' said Diggory.

'Be silent, both of you,' said Arigh Nasan.

Batu and Lárwita wisely kept out of the argument. Batu inspected his bow, running his hands over the string, testing its strength, while Lárwita wound a ball of twine in his hand before stuffing it into his pocket.

'What have you got that for?' said Elowen.

'I was going to give it to you later,' said Lárwita. He pulled the ball of twine out of his pocket and shoved it in her hands. 'I thought it might be useful. In the labyrinth you can tie it around something and unwind it as you walk, so you should be able to find your way back to where you started.'

Before Elowen could thank him, the ivory door of the palace opened and Sukhbataar Khan emerged, followed by

341

a retinue of courtiers and Kushiku guards. The khan looked tired and drained. In a low voice barely above a whisper, he said to Arigh Nasan, 'The shamans of Bai Ulgan have granted you and your companions permission to visit the temple.'

'We are deeply honoured and grateful,' said Arigh Nasan, failing to conceal a grin. Elowen drew a deep breath. They were going to Bai Ulgan.

Sukhbataar Khan pulled something out from his robes and passed it to Arigh Nasan, though the khan avoided making eye contact as he did so. It was a round gold medallion marked with a symbol of a labyrinth. 'When you get to Bai Ulgan, give this to the gatekeeper. He will not let you pass without it.'

'Thank you,' said Arigh Nasan. 'I shall not forget your kindness.'

'Say nothing more of it,' said the khan, sounding irritated, flustered. 'Now be gone, I have much to do this day and can waste no further time with you.'

Sukhbataar Khan marched back into the palace; the trail of Kushiku and courtiers followed, trying to keep up.

Arigh Nasan slipped the medallion into his pocket. He turned to Elowen and the others. 'We make for Bai Ulgan.'

From the palace, he led them through a network of alleyways and passages. The temple perched on top of a limestone hill that rose from the heart of the city. A ring of bare, dusty ground surrounded the foot of the hill, as though no one dared to build close to such a sacred place. Wind, rain and sun had left the hill's steep slopes fissured and pock-marked. Arigh Nasan pointed out a narrow stair-

342

way carved into the stony slopes. Elowen's stomach rolled over when she looked up at the steps: they rose at what appeared to be an impossibly steep angle before disappearing into the clouds of mist that coiled around the summit.

'Surely there is an easier way?' said Diggory.

'The shamans of Bai Ulgan do not welcome visitors,' said Arigh Nasan.

'And their vows dictate that they never leave the temple,' said Batu. 'From the day they are admitted as novices they are forbidden to step off this hill. Even when they die they are buried in the temple cemetery.'

A standing stone painted with four strange symbols denoted the foot of the stairway; an elderly, skinny Orok waited beside it. He was filthy, with a tangled beard, greasy, uncombed hair and encrusted phlegm on the sleeves of his brown robes. His skin was pale for an Orok, a sickly green hue. When he noticed Elowen and her companions approaching, he took a step forward, blocking their route to the stairway. He wagged his finger in Arigh Nasan's face and the two Oroks had a short but animated conversation. Arigh Nasan sighed and shook his head. 'We must leave our weapons with the gatekeeper.'

Krukis crunched his knuckles. 'Over my dead body.'

'These are ancient customs and we must obey them,' said Batu, placing himself between Krukis and the gatekeeper. To prove his intent, Batu gave his bow and sword to the gatekeeper, an act mirrored by Arigh Nasan as he surrendered his weapons. The gatekeeper placed them in a pile around the standing stone.

Still grumbling and complaining, Krukis grudgingly placed

his hammer on the pile and said to the gatekeeper, 'Only God can protect you if you damage this.'

The gatekeeper responded with a wry toothless smile. Arigh Nasan gave him the gold medallion. He peered at it with his rheumy eyes and traced his fingers over the labyrinth symbol. He finally stepped aside and signalled for them to pass.

Arigh Nasan looked up the stairway. 'I shall go first. Elowen, follow me and stay close.'

She watched as the Orok climbed. Batu nudged her in the back. 'It is your turn now, child.'

The stairway was as steep as a ladder. Elowen's legs trembled. The cracked, uneven steps were barely wide enough for her feet. Her fingers struggled to find grip and pieces of limestone broke off in her hands. Sweat dribbled down from her forehead, stinging her eyes, and her knees ached with the strain.

Several yards above her, Arigh Nasan stopped and shouted down, 'Are you still with me, Elowen?'

'Just about,' she gasped, barely able to speak. Below her, Diggory and Krukis argued furiously as they climbed. She guessed they did so to mask their fear.

'Keep going, Elowen,' said Arigh Nasan. 'It is not much further.'

Elowen doubted that. The ascent turned into a torment seemingly without end: the agony in her knees; her pounding, dizzy head; a vertiginous sickness in her stomach; her hands sore and bleeding. The higher she climbed, the more the clammy mist wrapped itself around her, muffling sounds and distorting her vision. She stopped for a moment

344

to catch her breath. She could no longer hear Diggory and Krukis arguing; in fact, she could not see or hear any of her companions. Arigh Nasan was now little more than a blur, swallowed by the writhing mist. Not wanting to fall too far behind him, she pushed on.

At last, Elowen came to a stretch where the steps were shallow and wider. Voices, raised voices, one belonging to Arigh Nasan, swirled but the mist was too thick to see anything further away than the length of her arms. She stopped for a rest when the heads of two snarling hounds burst out of the mist with an explosion of slavering jaws, barking and bloodshot eyes. Elowen screamed and almost fell backwards. She thought the heads belonged to the same creature, some terrible demonic monstrosity, but as she scrambled away, she realised they were actually two large dogs, both shackled by metal chains. A soothing voice calmed the dogs and they stopped barking.

A tall figure appeared in front of Elowen, an Orok, alarming in a headdress decorated with deer antlers and eagle feathers. He wore a white silk cloak over which he had tied an apron of tapered strips of many colours. With numerous metal objects attached to his cloak such as arrowheads, bells and tiny mirrors, he clinked and jangled musically as he moved. He carried a staff, the final of which had been carved into the shape of a horse's head. He spoke in a rich, lilting accent, his tongue struggling with unfamiliar words. 'I am Qutugh, Chief Shaman of Bai Ulgan.'

Elowen smiled awkwardly, feeling more than a little intimidated by the shaman's frightening appearance. Keeping her distance from the dogs, she climbed two more steps and came at last to level ground. The temple loomed in front of her, the pointed towers and thick, tapered mud-brick wall visible through the watery mist. Figures reduced to ghostly silhouettes approached Elowen but she could not see Arigh Nasan and was annoyed he had gone on ahead without waiting for her.

The dogs barked again and Elowen heard angry swearing and shouting. Qutugh became agitated and stepped away from her, his hands waving and shaking. He spoke, his voice tremulous. 'I did not want this. Believe me. We had no choice—'

Another voice cut in, a voice Elowen had heard before. A voice that haunted her nightmares.

'At last I have found you again, child.'

Lord Lucien emerged from the mist, flanked by Redeemers. Elowen retreated and stumbled, landing heavily on her backside. She scrambled to her feet but bundled straight into Krukis. 'We have to get away.'

Rather than retreating, Krukis grabbed both her arms. 'You're going nowhere, child.'

'What are you—'

Krukis slapped her hard across the face. 'Be silent. By God's blood, I'd be happy to kill you and those other swine you call friends.'

Her cheeks still smarting from the blow, Elowen looked past Krukis. Kushiku guards dragged Batu, Diggory and Lárwita up the stairway, and behind them came the khan himself, red-faced and puffing.

'Your luck has run out, child,' said Krukis. He picked her up, put her over his shoulder and carried her back to Lord

Lucien. Arigh Nasan knelt in front of the Redeemers, his hands tied together by rope.

Krukis dropped Elowen at Lord Lucien's feet. She looked up at the blacksmith. 'Why are you doing this?'

'Because he is a traitor,' said Arigh Nasan. 'I'm sorry, Elowen. They got me before I could warn you. Krukis has sold us out to the enemy.'

'Your enemy, not mine,' said Krukis. 'Ah, a pox on you, Arigh Nasan, and those foolish enough to follow you. You've failed me too many times. I've heard enough of your empty promises. I've got a new master now.'

'Yes, and he is the biggest traitor of all,' said Arigh Nasan, pointing to the khan, who now stood close by, with his Kushiku guards surrounding Batu, Diggory and Lárwita.

The khan's face twitched. 'A herald of Lord Lucien reached the city several days ago and brought warning that a child was expected to journey to the temple, a child that presented terrible danger. The command was clear. Lord Lucien was to be summoned if the child arrived, and if I refused then Prester John's armies would attack Erdene.'

'And since when has a khan bent his knee to Prester John's will?' said Arigh Nasan.

'Times have changed since you fled into the wild, abandoning your people. We no longer have the strength to withstand Prester John. It is my duty to protect my people. I had my suspicions that the girl was the one Lord Lucien sought, suspicions confirmed by Krukis when he approached me on the night of your arrival to offer his service to me. It appears he was dissatisfied with you and wished to offer his loyalty to one more worthy of his talents.'

'Loyalty?' said Arigh Nasan. 'Krukis is loyal only to the pursuit of gold.'

'Yes, you're a filthy traitor, Krukis,' said Diggory.

'And you're close to death, boy,' said Krukis.

'That is enough,' said Lord Lucien. He towered over Elowen. She wanted to do something, to strike against him but she was weak and powerless in his presence. He reached down and pulled her to her feet. She heard his breathing, muted behind his mask. 'I know that you are here to seek a great treasure. Well, it is time for you to fulfil your quest, child. It is time for you to enter the labyrinth.'

'I'm not taking orders from you,' said Elowen.

'That is exactly what you will do. For if you choose not to cooperate I will execute your friends. Obey and they will live.'

'Don't help him,' said Diggory. 'It doesn't matter what happens to us.'

'He is right, Elowen,' said Arigh Nasan. 'By saving us, you may condemn countless others to death and enslavement.'

Elowen hesitated. She knew that if the quest failed their last hope to defeat Prester John was lost. But if she sacrificed her friends what would she have left to fight for? Whatever the price of saving them, it had to be worth paying. Elowen was almost too shaken to speak but managed to find her voice. 'Even if I do as you ask, how do I know you'll keep your word?'

'If you bring me the treasure from the labyrinth, then you and your friends are no longer of any importance to me,' said Lord Lucien. He leant forward. 'I know of the Four Mysteries and I know what it is you seek.'

Elowen was shocked and failed to conceal it. Lord Lucien laughed. 'You have no secrets from me, child. Rubens told me much. It is strange that the Illuminati placed so much faith in one so weak and treacherous.'

Elowen felt exposed and broken. Lord Lucien knew everything. The cause was lost. The only choice left open to her was to try to save her friends. 'I'll enter the labyrinth, if you promise to keep your word.'

'I am pleased to see that you have come to your senses,' said Lord Lucien. He addressed the Redeemer closest to him. 'Brother Malchus, take the other prisoners to the Inner Chamber of the temple. The girl stays with me.'

'Let Elowen go, Lucien,' said Arigh Nasan. 'For pity's sake she is only a child.'

'She is much more than that, as well you know.'

'If you hurt her, I'll kill you,' said Diggory struggling with his captors, defiant despite the overwhelming danger. Lárwita too resisted; he kicked at the Kushiku guard holding him, only to receive a hard cuff to the back of his neck.

'Charming, the importance that your companions place on your friendship,' said Lucien. 'Charming, but also foolish and misguided.'

'They're worth a thousand of you,' said Elowen.

'You may hate me, child, but your hatred comes from ignorance. When you know more, you may think differently of me.'

'I doubt that,' said Elowen.

'Time may erase your doubts. Shaman, take us to the labyrinth.'

Qutugh took Elowen by the hand, his grip surprisingly

tender, and led her towards the temple. Lord Lucien followed two paces behind them. She glanced back at her friends; they were still surrounded by the khan, his Kushiku guards and the Redeemers. Arigh Nasan looked at her despairingly and mouthed, 'I am sorry.'

As they walked, Qutugh whispered, 'You must show great caution in the labyrinth. There are traps and deceptions down there. Take only the treasure.'

'What is the treasure?'

'You will know it when you see it,' said the shaman. 'Take it but touch nothing else. And most of all beware the Malign Sleeper.'

'Who is the Malign Sleeper?' said Elowen as quietly as she could. She wondered if it was the earth Elemental Grunewald had mentioned.

'He is deadly. Do not wake him. Seek only the treasure. Go down deep, where the underground river runs, there you will find the cave. Others you may find down there. Ignore them! Help them not! Do as I say and you may live. Forget my words and you will die.'

Elowen followed Qutugh up the steps that rose to the temple gate. The body of a dead shaman lay in front of them, the steps sticky with his blood. Qutugh gave a moan of despair and whispered a prayer, but he did not stop. They edged past the corpse, through the arched gate of Bai Ulgan and into the temple courtyard. Lord Lucien walked silently behind them.

The tall, thick walls of Bai Ulgan encircled a motley collection of ramshackle brick buildings. A cat poked around a weed-choked fountain that had long run dry; a magpie flapped around and a line of shamans, their hooded heads bowed, filed silently into one of the brick buildings, shepherded by three Redeemers. A tree stood in the courtyard. The branches were bare of leaves but the contorted corpses of several shamans were wrapped around them, legs and arms stiff. Elowen retched and cried.

Qutugh shook his head. He steered Elowen away from the grisly tree and towards two stone statues of a strange creature encased within a shell, like a snail but with a lizard-like head. A horizontal wooden hatch lay between the statues. Qutugh knelt and, with the long key he produced from his belt, unlocked the hatch, which opened with a complaining wooden groan and a rush of stale, tangy air.

Qutugh pointed at the open hatch. 'Down there is the labyrinth. A torch has already been lit, you must take it. May the ancestors guide and protect you, child.'

Elowen took a step closer and peered down at a narrow spiral staircase. Although a torch in a sconce illuminated the top steps, the rest descended into complete darkness.

'I shall be waiting for you, child,' said Lord Lucien. 'Do not forget your friends, as their lives are now in your hands.'

- CHAPTER EIGHTEEN -

The Catacombs

A ccompanied by Ladislaus and Jeimuzu, Bo left the Kojin settlement at dawn and set off for the Tomb of the Eagle. Heading north-east, they hiked through the dry scrubby land. Salty sea breezes softened the sun's growing heat, but the bright morning light stung Bo's weak, juddering eyes. The surge of courage that had emboldened him to undertake the quest shrivelled away to leave only a writhing knot of fear and anxiety in his stomach. Nervousness sparked a barrage of questions that he fired at the ever-patient Ladislaus.

'Are you sure we are going the right way?'

'Quite sure,' said Ladislaus. He pointed to the south-facing side of the table-top mountain. 'A path ascends those slopes.'

Bo licked his dry lips. 'And how long will it take us to get there?'

'Several hours, it is a hard march. Alas that I am not twenty years younger!'

Jeimuzu traipsed behind them, silent, sullen, his sword gripped firmly in his right hand. Bo had expected the prince to don full Kojin armour, but he had on the same simple clothes he had worn when they first met. When Bo mentioned this to Ladislaus, the priest had said, 'Kojin armour is the preserve of the warrior; he is yet to come of age.'

Bo carried a curved, single-edged sword, a weapon loaned reluctantly from the Kojin armourer, who had assured him of its sharpness, balance and cutting ability. Bo admired the blade's workmanship, but it was no replacement for the sword he had lost, his father's sword, the sword of the Preven kings. He was unworthy of its lineage.

They pushed on beneath the cloudless sky. The hot sun made Bo's face glow and even in the light, loose garments he wore, he was soaked with sweat. He thought wistfully of his Preven homeland, of autumn rains soaking the land.

Ladislaus hummed and whistled hymns, accompanied by the crunch-crunch of their feet on the sandy soil. The priest moved sprightly enough despite his stick and the heavy bag he carried, and did not seem to tire. Bo's legs ached and blisters on his feet nagged with needle-sharp pain. Birds chattered ceaselessly among the trees and bushes; normally Bo found birdsong a comfort, but now it screeched in his ears, harsh and oppressive. Flies and gnats swarmed around the sweet-smelling shrubs and irritated Bo by landing in his hair and getting into his mouth.

'This is a wretched land,' said Bo to himself, as he pulled yet another fly from his lips.

'I disagree,' said Ladislaus, breaking from his whistling. Bo realised that there was nothing wrong with the priest's hearing. 'The Beauteous Isle is very different from Prevennis, I imagine. But I think if you spent long enough here you would begin to appreciate its beauty.'

353

Bo was not persuaded. 'Every moment on this island is a moment too long.'

'You do not need to stay here, white-skin,' said Jeimuzu, breaking his silence. 'I would not grieve to see you leave.'

'You were happy enough to see me when I saved your life.'

Jeimuzu's anger flared. Eyes wide, teeth clenched, he squared-up to Bo, ready to fight. With surprising speed, Ladislaus stepped between them. 'Do not waste your energy on petty arguments. You both have a duty to fulfil.'

Jeimuzu and Bo glared at each other, violence in their eyes. The Kojin Prince looked unwilling to back down but, seeing the obvious sense in the priest's words, did so.

'That is better,' said Ladislaus, playing the peacemaker, the role, Bo guessed, the queen had picked him for. He spoke to them like a kindly but stern schoolmaster admonishing naughty pupils. 'I see little hope for your quest if you cannot help but fight each other. Now, let us put this childish squabble behind us and get moving—there is precious little time to waste.'

By mid-afternoon, they had got as far as the slopes that sheltered beneath Teburu-Yama. A welcome cool wind embraced them as the sinking sun's heat faded. Ladislaus had described the last stretch of the journey as a path but Bo soon found that it was little more than a goat track, rocky, narrow and winding. Tall standing stones, all carved with representations of human faces and swords, flanked the path at various points.

Flagging and footsore, Bo begged for a rest. The priest acceded and sat with him. Bo gulped down some water and massaged his aching feet. Jeimuzu wandered ahead, scowling and muttering to himself.

'Are these Kojin monuments?' said Bo, pointing at the stones.

'No, they were made by the Dawn Men,' said Ladislaus as he rubbed his legs.

Bo stared at the stones, feeling that he was stepping backwards in time, treading on ground untouched for centuries. 'Who were the Dawn Men?'

The priest cleared his throat and wiped his sweaty brow. 'Little is known about the Dawn Men, the *Kodai-no*, for they were a primitive race and left no written records. All that we know of them is handed down in Kojin tales and songs.'

'What happened to them?'

Ladislaus looked at Jeimuzu, who was now standing some distance away, gazing out to sea. The priest checked that the Kojin prince was not listening and said, 'The same as always happens when a stronger tribe discovers a desirable land inhabited by a weaker, more primitive one.'

'The Kojin attacked the Dawn Men?' said Bo, horrified at the idea.

'Destroyed them in fact,' said Ladislaus. 'However, I know that the Kojin are repulsed by the acts of the first settlers here. Indeed, they carry a great burden of guilt regarding the fate of the *Kodai-no*. Some Kojin claim their suffering at the hands of the Sea Beggars is divine punishment for their treatment of the Dawn Men. All Kojin fear the ruins and tombs of the *Kodai-no* and believe such places to be haunted and dangerous.'

'And we are going to just such a place,' said Bo.

355

'Yes indeed,' said the priest with an ironic laugh. 'Life leads us down many unexpected paths, does it not?'

Bo surveyed the glistening turquoise expanse of the ocean; it stretched to infinity, to countless lands and wonders that lay far out of sight. He looked up. A sea eagle swept over them; its short gleaming white tail flashed.

Ladislaus placed a hand on Bo's shoulder. 'We need to keep moving, I do not want to get to the Tomb of the Eagle after dark.'

They caught up with Jeimuzu. The three travellers did not speak as they walked, the effort required to do so being too great. Even the surly Kojin found the going hard; he walked at a slower pace and took deep heavy breaths. When they reached the summit of Teburu-Yama, Bo looked down at the city of Katakani and the Alcazar fortress. The Alcazar rested on a plinth more than twenty feet high. There were four corner turrets, each crowned with a battlemented top. The land around the fortress was dusty and flat apart from an oval-shaped amphitheatre dug into the ground with an arena surrounded by rising stone rows. A wide slope had been carved out of one side of the amphitheatre: a procession route down to the arena. Bo had heard stories of the ancients holding games in such places, games that involved men fighting to the death, either against other men or fierce beasts, roared on by huge, drunken crowds.

Something far closer drew Bo's attention. Ladislaus pointed to three stone slabs silhouetted by the setting sun. They were arranged side by side, buried on end in the ground. Rounded on top and much taller than the others, the central slab had a doorway cut into it that faced east.

'This is the Tomb of the Eagle,' said the priest.

A raven pecked on the ground in front of the doorway and flapped away as they approached. Lewd symbols and words disfigured the stones. Ladislaus ran his fingers over the markings and said, 'This is the work of the Sea Beggars. It sickens me to witness their desecration. They have broken many tombs and monuments, taking the stones for their own use or simply destroying them for some sick pleasure.'

A sea eagle carcass lay in front of the dark tomb entrance along with a scattering of other bones. Bo started to get a headache, like a band tightening around his skull. Jeimuzu stood proud, trying, Bo thought, a little too hard to appear unafraid.

'This is as far as I can take you,' said Ladislaus. He pulled a terracotta lamp from his bag along with a small clay flask full of olive oil. Once he had filled the lamp with oil, he managed, after some fumbling, to light it with a flint and striker. The lamp had a small handle wide enough for one finger. Ladislaus held it up and said, 'This you will need in the dark of the catacombs. One of you must take it.'

'Give it to the white-skin,' said Jeimuzu, throwing a contemptuous look at Bo. 'He is the one giving orders. And the eyes of white-skins are too weak to see in the dark.'

With a knowing wink, Ladislaus gave the lamp to Bo. 'I wish I could do more, Asbjorn. I should go with you but I am too much of a coward.'

Bo placed his hands on the priest's shoulders. 'You are not a coward. I thank you for all your kindness. You are a good man.'

'May God bless you, my son,' said Ladislaus. 'I shall pray for you and your safe return.'

Bo nodded but he did not share the priest's confidence. 'I don't feel strong enough for this.'

'Yes, you are. You are a fine warrior, I am sure, but being strong is not just about fighting. You have the strength to make the brave choices. That is why you shall prevail.'

'Come on, you go in first, white-skin,' said Jeimuzu, gesturing impatiently towards the tomb. Bo knew that the Kojin prince was testing him, trying to see if he was scared. Bo was afraid but he refused to show it, so with the lamp balanced in his left hand, he stepped through the doorway. He emerged into a rectangular drystone chamber. The ceiling hung only an inch above Bo's head, and thick slabs reinforced the walls, all finely chipped with spirals, radiating and concentric circles, zigzags, diamond shapes and cup marks. Animal and bird bones littered the ground.

'This is a foreboding place,' said Jeimuzu as he entered the tomb. 'The stench of the *Kodai-no* is all around.'

'Perhaps we ought to be more respectful to the Dawn Men, considering we are within one of their tombs.'

Jeimuzu curled his lips and mumbled in the Kojin language.

The only way forward was through a low passage at the far end of the chamber. Bo crawled on all fours—his head only just cleared the ceiling. As he crawled, he managed to keep the terracotta lamp upright in his left hand; had he failed to do so the dark would have swallowed him whole. Jeimuzu followed close behind him and hissed, 'Hurry up, white-skin. You are too slow.'

The passage was straight and flat, but while Bo was relieved to encounter no sharp climbs or drops, the effort of crawling through was considerable and scraped the skin off his knees. The passage was stiflingly hot. Just as Bo thought he could not endure any more, the passage widened and cooler air caressed him. They found themselves at the top of a spiral staircase with misshapen steps and walls hacked out with rough tools. Bo held the lamp out to throw more light down onto the staircase. Water dripped down from the ceiling onto the steps, making them slippery and shiny. A sickening charnel-house stench blew up from the hidden depths of the staircase as though exhaled from some hideous, unseen mouth.

'What are you waiting for?' said Jeimuzu. 'If you're afraid, it is not too late for you to turn back.'

Bo did not answer. Jeimuzu's jibes riled him, all the more so because he did want to go back. He had no courage left, guilt alone forced him on; guilt fuelled by the suffering of Black Francis and the others, suffering that he had caused by his weakness and indecision.

Bo went down the stairs. He retched and gagged as he breathed in wafts of putrid air. Jeimuzu followed, spitting and cursing. The tiny, shifting light of the terracotta lamp illuminated only a little space around them. Bo counted each step, a mechanical action to keep his mind from lingering on more frightening thoughts. His score reached two hundred before tiredness and tension made the effort of counting too much.

It came as a shock when they reached the bottom step of the stairway, which ended in a circular chamber. In front of them was a plinth topped by a carving of two heads facing in opposite directions. At the far end of the chamber two skeletons in rusty Kojin armour hung on the wall, one each side of a framed opening.

Skulls and bones built into the floor formed geometric shapes. A rat scuttled across the floor. Jeimuzu acted instinctively, or out of fear. He swung his sword at the rat, his blow missed and the blade struck the stone floor with an explosion of tiny sparks. The rat scampered down a hole.

'The rat is a cunning foe.'

The shock of hearing another voice made Bo feel as though his heart had burst from his chest. Jeimuzu yelped in surprise. A figure stood in front of the opening at the opposite end of the chamber. The stranger took a few shuffling steps forward into the feeble light offered by the lamp. He was lame and used a huge hammer as a walking stick. He had a beak-like nose, pointed ears and a patch over his left eye. He wore a heavy cloak, and a sleeved and belted tunic that must have once been colourful but was now faded and dull. Although he had the appearance of a mortal man, something about the stranger prompted Bo to think that he was perhaps an Eldar, although unlike any Eldar Bo had seen before.

'The Kojin demon I can see clearly enough,' continued the stranger. He pointed at Bo. 'My eye tells me that you are not one of the blue-skinned usurpers and yet I smell their ghastly scent on you and you are dressed in their garb.'

'It is you that is the demon here,' said Jeimuzu. 'For your insolence, I should cleave you—'

Bo held up a hand. 'I think it is best you let me talk.'

Jeimuzu scowled but, to Bo's surprise, he backed down, perhaps remembering his promise to the queen, his promise to obey Bo's orders.

'So, who are you and what is your purpose in coming here?' said the stranger.

'My name is Asbjorn and I seek passage through the catacombs, along with my companion.'

'Then, Asbjorn, you are either brave or foolish,' said the stranger with an evil smile. He pointed to the opening behind him. 'You do not know what lurks within the darkness. Turn and run, boy. Turn and run while you still can.'

'I have a duty to fulfil, so for good or ill, I must enter the catacombs,' said Bo, trying to sound courageous and defiant and not even convincing himself.

'I am Grenchos, protector of the catacombs and this is my domain. None may cross this threshold unless I allow it.'

Bo detected a threat within the protector's words. He sensed Grenchos was trying to provoke them, trying to make them angry. Bo said, 'I do not wish to fight you.'

'Fight *me*?' said the protector. He nodded towards the two Kojin skeletons. 'No mortal can defeat me, not here. If you choose to fight me, you choose death.'

Jeimuzu held his sword, ready to attack. 'I have heard enough. This *Kodai-no* demon needs a lesson.'

No, Jeimuzu,' said Bo, holding the Kojin back. 'I command you to withdraw.'

With great reluctance, the Kojin took a step back and lowered his sword.

'At last you show some wisdom,' said Grenchos. 'However, I still do not grant favours, especially not to usurpers.'

'It is of great importance that you do,' said Bo.

'Of great importance to usurpers, perhaps. Their woes do not concern me.'

'It is not just the Kojin who are threatened,' said Bo. 'Their foes are now your foes. The tombs and monuments of your people are being defiled and destroyed.'

Grenchos looked at Bo, his eyes narrowed. 'It is true I have sensed others on our island. Perhaps now the usurpers understand what it is to suffer. Perhaps now they understand the trials of my people and the misery inflicted upon them.'

'They do,' said Bo. 'By aiding our quest you are helping to defeat those who threaten you, a defeat that would protect your sacred stones.'

'Fine words you speak,' said Grenchos. 'But you are not one of the blue-skinned ones. What assurances can they give?'

With a reluctance that reminded Bo of someone drawing poison painfully from a wound, Jeimuzu said to Grenchos, 'By the royal blood that flows in my veins, I swear your holy stones shall be protected by the Kojin, from this day forward.'

Grenchos gripped his hammer a little tighter. '*Royal* blood? Are you a descendant of Ashikaga?'

Warily, Jeimuzu said, 'Yes, he was my father's grandfather.'

Grenchos smiled. 'Much weakened is the bloodline, I see. Yet, I am gladdened by this knowledge. Many times did Ashikaga visit the catacombs, seeking knowledge, solace, perhaps forgiveness, for he sincerely repented for the great

362

wounds inflicted upon my people. You may enter the catacombs if you choose, but know this: others have come before you, their heads full of ideas of gold and glory. None returned. Those that dwell within the catacombs have no love of flesh and blood, and hate the usurpers most of all. They will test you. If you succeed, you shall pass unharmed through the catacombs. If you fail, you will never see sunlight again.'

The protector thumped the end of his hammer on the ground and light filled the opening behind him, revealing a long tunnel lit by the orange glow of flaming torches. Bo left his little lamp beside the statue; he hoped he would have reason to come back and use it.

Grenchos stepped to one side. Shadowed by Jeimuzu, Bo walked round the statue, through the opening flanked by the skeletons and into the tunnel. A gloomy, ominous atmosphere swallowed them. The air inside was musty, ancient. Niches pock-marked the tunnel walls, all filled with cobweb-smothered skeletons. Small alcoves contained dusty bronze statues of fighting men, animals and ships: votive offerings to the gods of the Dawn Men.

Bo heard hollow whispered voices, and weeping. As he peered down the many passages branching off from the tunnel he saw, or thought he saw, people lurking there, not corporeal but phantasms, apparitions. He rubbed his eyes. Perhaps tiredness and fear were making him see things. Then, Jeimuzu cried out in horror.

A man was standing in front of them, barely two yards away. He had a beard but no moustache. He was dressed in a tunic that extended halfway down his legs. A cape was thrown over his shoulder. He had a pallid complexion, his skin almost translucent.

'It is a wraith of the *Kodai-no*,' said Jeimuzu, his swagger, his bravado, withered away.

The wraith gazed at Bo and, moving as though he was a marionette controlled by a puppet-master, brought his hands together. Bo felt as though he tumbled into a dream.

Mist clears to reveal a village of beehive-shaped mud huts surrounded by a rickety reed fence. A woman draws water from the stone well in the north-east corner of the village. A line of pelts dries in the sun; beside them stands a dozen red-and-white striped clay pots. Staff in hand, a shepherd boy drives his flock of goats into the fields surrounding the village. Children run among the huts, playfully chasing after a scruffy mongrel dog. There are screams. From the crest of the nearby hill, Kojin warriors sweep down upon the village. Revelling in their battle-lust, they spare no one. They hack down men, women and children. The village is alight. Furious flames consume homes, grain stores and temples alike. Dead bodies hang over the fence like grisly dolls; lines of blood slowly mix with the sandy soil; a Kojin warrior laughs at a wounded, dying dog.

The visions attacked Bo, relentless and brutal. They pummelled his head; his skull ached so much he feared it would crack. His stomach groaned and lurched. Tears stung his eyes, blinding him for a time. Jeimuzu wept and howled like a child injured and abandoned. Bo cried out, 'Enough! Leave me alone!'

The visions ceased. Bo stood still for a moment, jolted awake from a nightmare, confused and blinking, the silence unsettling, disorientating. Still trembling, Jeimuzu wiped away tears, and blubbered words in the Kojin language.

The wraith drew his sword, the blade like a shimmering strip of silvery light. In a voice that reminded Bo of wind moaning through icy winter thickets, the wraith said, 'The way is blocked. Only the strong of heart and mind may pass.'

The challenge revived Jeimuzu. The Kojin gripped the hilt of his sword with both hands. The shame and embarrassment of crying made him angry and vengeful. 'So, this is the test we must face. You may not be of flesh and blood, demon, but my blade will still bite.'

Jeimuzu crouched in a fighting position, ready to attack. The wraith smiled a cruel smile. Bo thought that the wraith wanted Jeimuzu to fight him, and if that was so, he must be certain of success. The wraith's challenge echoed in his mind. *Only the strong of heart and mind may pass.* Then, like unexpected but welcome guests, the earlier words of Ladislaus came to Bo. *Being strong is not just about fighting. You have the strength to make the brave choices.* Bo understood what he had to do. He ordered Jeimuzu to lower his sword.

'Are you mad?' said the Kojin in disbelief. 'This is the test of which Grenchos spoke. I have to defeat this creature.'

'If we fight we die,' said Bo. He knew the wraith wanted to see humility, deference. 'We are trespassers here. This is the realm of the Dawn Men. Only with their consent can we pass. We must be strong enough, brave enough, not to resort to violence. Put down your sword, that is my command.'

To reinforce his words, Bo knelt before the wraith, laid his sword on the ground in front of him and lowered his head in respect. Jeimuzu grunted in frustration and threw his blade down onto the ground. He knelt, and as he did so, said to Bo, 'You are a coward and a weakling, white-skin.'

Bo bristled at the insult. In his heart, he feared that Jeimuzu was right. He tried to compose himself and in a wavering voice, he said to the wraith, 'This is your realm. We lower our weapons before you. We submit to your will.'

Bo's heart pounded, conscious that they were now unarmed. He had made another mistake. He had failed again. They were doomed…

The wraith sheathed his sword. 'Outsiders, you have passed the test. The way is now open to you.'

With that, the wraith faded into the darkness. Bo and Jeimuzu stared at each other for a moment, both struggling to absorb what had happened. After a long silence between them, Jeimuzu said, 'It appears you were right, white-skin. Or perhaps fortunate.'

Bo smiled. Relief at passing the test left his limbs light and his head a little giddy. 'Come, I don't want to spend a moment longer down here than we have to.'

'We agree on that at least,' said Jeimuzu.

They picked up their swords. The line of torches that had lit the way ran out, so they advanced in utter darkness. Bo used his sword to test the ground around him in the same way he had once seen an old blind beggar use a stick.

The walls either side of them were wet and when Bo touched them an oozy slime dripped over his fingers. A choking smell filled the tunnel. Bo's eyes streamed and he stopped twice to vomit, eliciting more scorn from Jeimuzu. Bo had the sense of descending deeper and deeper into the depths of the earth.

He plodded on until the tip of his sword clunked against something that was not stone, but wood. Bo took a couple of cautious steps forward and reached out with his right hand. He touched wooden panels and as he traced his fingers they ran over rusty hinges and a ring handle.

'What is it?' said Jeimuzu. 'Why have we stopped?'

'I think this is the door into the Alcazar,' said Bo. He gripped the ring handle and pulled. The door refused to open more than a couple of inches. 'It will not budge.'

'Let me try,' said Jeimuzu. After several hard pulls, the Kojin managed to force it open wide enough for them to squeeze through. He rubbed his hands and grinned smugly at Bo. 'You are not as strong as I am, white-skin.'

Bo smiled wanly. He decided to let Jeimuzu enjoy his small triumph.

They stepped into a damp room full of dust-smothered barrels, piles of mouldy linen and rat-gnawed clothes. Thick cobwebs dangled from every corner and wooden steps led up to a trapdoor in the ceiling. Mounds of phosphorescent fungi grew through cracks in the floor; the ghastly blue light they emitted revealed faint images on the walls, images of monsters and haloed Kojin warriors. Religious images. Bo remembered the story that King Ashikaga used to enter the catacombs via his private chapel. He guessed this had to be the same place although it was now a basement storeroom. It was the kind of place that he had always cherished: empty of people, quiet, full of secrets waiting to be discovered but he had no time for such things now.

Bo and Jeimuzu looked at each other and smiled. They had done it; they were in the Alcazar.

'I suppose we have to go up,' said Bo. So with the Kojin following closely behind, Bo ascended the steps. He was relieved to find that the trapdoor was unlocked and lifted it enough to peek out. The trapdoor opened into a high-ceilinged kitchen. There was a circular hearth, vents for letting out smoke, a stone sink-basin and a floor drain. An array of pans and glazed pots hung on the walls, and a pile of chopped firewood filled a corner. There was no sign of any people. Bo turned to Jeimuzu. 'It seems quiet.'

They both climbed up into the kitchen. There was a door left ajar on the far side. Bo heard whistling and a young man strolled in. By his worn, frayed apron and cheap clothes, Bo guessed that he was a servant. He had been rolling up his shirtsleeves as he entered the kitchen but the sight of the two intruders halted him and he stood frozen still with his left sleeve up and his right sleeve down.

Bo grabbed the man by the throat. His first instinct, an instinct that shamed him, was to kill but reason and logic calmed him. 'Where is the Kojin princess?'

The young man gawped at Bo, too dumbstruck to reply. Bo realised how frightening he must look with his white skin and his Kojin clothes filthy and stinking from the catacombs.

Without warning, Jeimuzu pulled Bo away. He held his sword against the man's throat. 'Tell me where she is or die.'

Shaking, the man pointed behind him. 'The oubliette. There are two stairways outside, one of them leads down to the oubliette.'

Oubliette. Bo shuddered. There had been an oubliette in

the Hammersund palace, a place of punishment for the very worst criminals. A dungeon within a dungeon, where the prisoner suffered in complete darkness, until they either went mad or died.

'And what about the crew of the *Husker Du*?' said Bo.

'They're being held in the Pits until Katsu Eve, which is tomorrow. They are to be sent to the amphitheatre. The *Caudillo* has got something planned for them, something secret, and he'll be there to see it in person, or so the rumours tell.'

Bo closed his eyes for a moment. His friends were surely beyond his help now. He had failed them. He wanted to curl up, hide away, try to block out his guilt and anger, but he knew that was cowardly. He had to face up to reality. And at least the King of the Sea Beggars was leaving the fortress, if only for a short time. It was a chance for the Kojin, the faintest of chances, but still a chance.

'We have heard what we need to know,' said Jeimuzu. 'Let us slay this one to silence his tongue.'

'We cannot kill him in cold blood. He is not a Sea Beggar, just a servant.'

'There's no choice. We cannot take him prisoner and if we release him then he is bound to alert the *Shikome*.'

Bo knew that the safest choice *was* to kill the servant but he could not bring himself to do that. Doubt nagged at him, doubt that told him he was being weak and cowardly, but he tried to dismiss it. 'Let him go, Jeimuzu.'

Jeimuzu swore and took his hands off the servant, who, stunned by his unexpected release, scampered out of the kitchen.

Jeimuzu watched him leave, his body tense with anger. Without looking at Bo he said, 'What next, white-skin?'

A straight passage ran from the kitchen door. Distant conversations echoed. Bo wondered if the servant was raising the alarm; he regretted letting him go but it was too late to do anything about it now.

A graceful flight of stairs curved upwards on the left-hand side of the passage. On the opposite side, a far narrower stairway plunged downwards as described by the servant.

'The oubliette must be down there,' said Bo.

'You go first then,' said Jeimuzu.

Bo did so, wincing at the noise of his footsteps. The stairway ended in a small chamber lit by tallow candles. There was a trapdoor in the floor with a loop of rope beside it and a single chair. A man sat in the chair with his back to Bo and Jeimuzu. From his shaven head and tattoos it was clear that he was a Sea Beggar. The Sea Beggar had pulled his tunic up to his chest and was picking at his navel, singing in a low voice as he did so. A ring of keys dangled from his belt.

The Sea Beggar was a large man. Bo knew their best chance was to surprise him. But before he could act, Jeimuzu lunged at the Sea Beggar, who only had time to look around with a stunned, horrified expression. Showing no mercy, Jeimuzu drove his sword into the man's stomach; the Sea Beggar groaned and thrashed, blood spilling out of his body like water from a punctured bucket. Jeimuzu stabbed the man again. The salty stench of blood filled the chamber.

Jeimuzu smiled at Bo, an ugly, gleeful smile. He had enjoyed the kill. Feeling sick, Bo reached down and took the ring of keys from the slain Sea Beggar, and after two failed attempts, found the correct one to open the trapdoor. He peered down into a tiny, unlit cell. As the feeble light of the tallow candles crept in, he could make out someone standing at the bottom of the oubliette. As his eyes adjusted, he saw that it was a Kojin woman.

Jeimuzu pushed Bo out of the way. 'MORIKO!'

A voice replied, a voice that reminded Bo of the Kojin queen.

'It is her,' said Jeimuzu. 'She is alive.'

Using the rope, they helped the princess to climb out of the oubliette. She resembled Jeimuzu: the same intelligent green eyes, the same noble features and demanding, questioning gaze. Dirt and soot smothered her face; simple, tatty robes clung to her emaciated body. Nevertheless, she possessed a vigour and strength that surprised Bo considering the terrible conditions of her imprisonment. There was no defeat in Moriko's eyes.

She warmly embraced her brother, laughing and chattering in the Kojin language. Then, her eyes fell upon Bo, her gaze so intense that it made him uncomfortable. 'So, you are commanding my brother. You do not look much like a warrior.'

'I do not claim to be one,' said Bo, suspecting that she was mocking him. 'Can you walk?'

'Do not worry about me, white-skin,' she said. 'I am strong. I will not fall behind.'

'Curse the *Kegare*,' said Jeimuzu. 'He swore you were being well-treated. He must be punished for his treachery.'

371

'I hope so,' said Moriko. 'But first we must escape from this place.'

With Bo leading, they sped up the stairway. They found the passage still empty, as was the kitchen. Bo knelt and was about to lift the trapdoor when the sound of running feet stopped him. Four Sea Beggars, all armed with swords, burst into the room.

'There they are!' shouted one of them, a huge man, his face dark with tattoos.

Before Bo stood, Jeimuzu and Moriko attacked the Sea Beggars, jumping like cats springing on their prey. Bo knew that Jeimuzu was a fearsome fighter but Moriko was no less formidable. The two Kojin kicked and punched, their movements as graceful as dancers but with savage consequences for their victims: broken bones, blood and bruises. Jeimuzu did not draw his sword. Three of the Sea Beggars were on the floor before they knew what hit them. The other ran, screaming, 'Alarum! Alarum!'

Panting from exertion but exhilarated by the fight, Jeimuzu said, 'The *Shikome* cannot match the Kojin in combat.'

'That may be so, but they will be back and with reinforcements,' said Bo. He pulled the trapdoor open and they climbed down into the basement.

'Is this the way you came in?' Moriko said.

Bo nodded.

Moriko threw a sideways glance at her brother. 'Where does it lead to?'

Jeimuzu answered in the Kojin language. She shrugged haughtily but Bo thought he detected fear in her expression.

As Jeimuzu pushed the door to the catacombs open, the chamber echoed with angry shouting. A Sea Beggar glared down from the trapdoor, a Sea Beggar holding a musket. Lead shot cracked into the door, missing Jeimuzu by inches. The Kojin prince drew his sword. 'It is time to fight again.'

Bo knew it was hopeless. For all the Kojin's bravery, they had little chance against foes armed with muskets and pistols. Bo knew exactly what he had to do. He said to Jeimuzu, 'Go now. Take Moriko into the catacombs. I will hold the Sea Beggars off for as long as I can.'

'We can fight them,' said Jeimuzu, to Moriko's agreement.

'Not this time, you must get back to Hinanjo,' said Bo. 'Tell the queen that the Kegare leaves the fortress tomorrow. This is the chance she has been waiting for. Remind her of her promise to me. That is more important.'

'But—'

The Sea Beggars climbed down the steps.

'I command you to go,' said Bo. And at last, after one final look, not of scorn or hate, but pity, Jeimuzu obeyed, disappearing with Moriko into the darkness of the catacombs.

Bo pulled the door shut behind them. A pistol shot rang out. Bo felt a sting in his leg. The shot had grazed his skin.

A Sea Beggar jumped from the steps and landed only a few feet away from Bo. He turned his pistol around, holding it by the barrel, ready to use the butt as a club. He had wild, bloodshot eyes and a toothless mouth. He swung the pistol; Bo swerved but not enough to avoid a glancing blow on his shoulder. The Sea Beggar swung again but this time Bo met the pistol with his sword and the blade deflected off the barrel and sliced deeply into the man's arm. The Sea Beggar howled in pain and anger. Bo struck him with the hilt of his sword, knocking him down.

A voice said, 'Surrender or die.'

More Sea Beggars bundled down the steps. Bo gripped his sword, ready to fight, but saw that it was hopeless. The Sea Beggars carried pistols and carbines. He had a fleeting thought to fight a suicidal fight, to bring the oblivion of a heroic death. Foolish. Pointless. Wasteful. The thought passed. Bo dropped his sword and held up his hands. A voice within him said, 'Coward.'

He knew that he had failed. He had been captured again. The Sea Beggars forced him down onto his knees and one of them said, 'It is time for you to meet the king.'

CHAPTER NINETEEN

King of the Sea Beggars

The Sea Beggars dragged Bo along corridors, and up and down long, winding stairways. They kicked and punched him, but with each and every kick and punch, Bo had only one thought: I hope Jeimuzu and Moriko got away. If they had escaped, if they had got through the catacombs and back to Hinanjo, then their plan was a success. If…

After more kicks, they pushed him through an open door and into a fusty, windowless passage. Faded and ripped tapestries of velvet, brocade and silk hung on the walls. At first glance, through watery, tired eyes, Bo thought that the passage was full of people but a second glance revealed life-sized bronze and marble sculptures of young muscular men and full-bodied females. Bo glanced at a marble sculpture of a dying man, naked apart from a torc around his neck. Blood leaked from a gash in his side, a mortal wound. The man seemed almost real, breathing, sweat glistening on his face.

Many sculptures showed signs of damage, with noses worn to stubs and heads missing; pieces of arms and legs lay broken and scattered on the floor like the grisly debris

of battle. Dozens of paintings were wedged behind and between the sculptures, all with chipped and broken wooden
frames. Discarded like rubbish, dust slowly buried them.

The passage ended in front of ceiling-high doors, which
one of the Sea Beggars shoulder-barged open. Still shadowed by his four captors, Bo came into a hall, the sheer
scale of which made him feel tiny. Dusty beams of light
drove through the high windows. Chandeliers hung down
from the ceiling. Paintings covered all the walls, paintings of
different sizes and shapes, from many different lands and
ages. Coated in thick dust, there was no plan or order as to
their arrangement; it was as if an infant had hung them,
prizing colour and vibrancy above design, before growing
bored and abandoning his work. Kings, queens, priests,
gods, angels and devils looked down from the paintings; all
frozen in time, all forgotten by time. Bo felt as though hundreds of pairs of eyes followed him.

A stringed instrument played, the eerie sound grew louder
as Bo's captors led him along a straight path, delineated by
two lines of sculptures, towards a dais at the far end of the
hall. The dais climbed to a marble throne and as soon as Bo
saw the man who sat upon it, everything else in the room
faded into the background. He wore a crown made of gold,
silver and red velvet; hundreds of diamonds were set within
three rows of natural white pearls, and a large emerald dominated the crown's apex. He was dressed in purple, fur-lined
robes and his fingers sparkled with bejewelled rings. His
small, pebble-like eyes held Bo in a firm stare. The King of
the Sea Beggars.

Despite the self-proclaimed king's fearsome expression

and trappings of power, Bo found something absurd about him. He was eating from a silver plate held by a servant, gorging on buttered crabs, prawns and lobster. Bo's stomach growled at the sight of food.

On the wall behind the throne hung an enormous portrait of the King of the Sea Beggars; it portrayed him in modest, sombre clothes, his hands crossed in front of his chest, his head tilted, his eyes large and sympathetic: a picture of humility. In front of the throne was an animal with buff-coloured fur and a thick brownish mane. The animal raised its head as Bo approached; a feline face, with smouldering golden-hued eyes. There was a collar around its neck connected to thick chains. Other chains gripped its legs, and a rope muzzle clamped its jaws together. Bo had seen such a creature once before, in a travelling circus that had visited Hammersund. A lion. Bo watched it with pity; it was painful to see a creature shackled, reduced to a pet, a plaything. The lion licked his lips, exposing his terrifying teeth, and settled down again to sleep.

A young boy sat at the foot of the dais. He wore a drooping hat that was too big for him and he played a viola. As Bo came closer, the King of the Sea Beggars clicked his fingers and the boy stopped playing and retreated backwards into the shadows on the far side of the hall.

Bo was made to kneel. One of the Sea Beggars said, 'This is the intruder we captured, *Caudillo*.'

'You have done well,' said the king, his voice rough but measured, as though he was attempting to adopt a courtly manner of speaking. He wiped his greasy hands on a towel and pushed away the servant holding the silver plate. The king looked down at Bo. 'So, Prince Asbjorn of Prevennis, at last we meet. I was disturbed to learn you had escaped, for as soon as word had reached me that you were one of the prisoners captured on the *Husker Du*, I was very much looking forward to making your acquaintance. It was fortunate you were foolish enough to try to rescue the Kojin princess.'

'Foolish, but successful,' said Bo.

The king gave him a supercilious look. 'She will not get far and the Kojin will pay for their treachery.'

'Perhaps one day they will make *you* pay.'

'The Kojin? Those web-footed cowards? I'll let them skulk in their stinking camp until the day I see fit to destroy them. Maybe that day is close.'

'What do you want with me?' said Bo, trying to sound undaunted by the king.

One of the Sea Beggars gave him a hard slap on the back of his head. 'Address the king as *Your Majesty*.'

'That is enough,' said the king. 'We need no violence here, this is a royal court.'

The Sea Beggar apologised profusely. The lion woke up and slowly lifted his head as far as the chains allowed, his eyes tired and baleful. Bo sensed the animal's power but it was distant, an echo.

Like a pig squeezing out of a sty, the king rose out of his chair. His finger and wrist joints were red and swollen, and he huffed and winced as he moved. He hobbled round the lion and down the steps of the dais to stand over Bo. 'It is wondrous, is it not, that you, born to royalty and privilege, should kneel before I, born fatherless and into poverty?

378

The difference is my power and wealth comes from hard work, not from fortunate birth.'

'Your power and wealth comes from murder and thievery,' said Bo.

The king laughed. 'Maybe so, but how am I different from any other man of power? Do you believe divine providence bequeathed the throne of Prevennis to your ancestors? Was your father's throne not founded in the blood and suffering of others? Yes, I have taken power. Consider what I have in my possession. Behold my riches, my works of art. Do I look like a man who ever takes no for an answer? If I desire something, I take it. If you live any other way then you are worthless and weak, condemned to be trodden on by stronger men. I am a king, a man of power.'

'Perhaps if you say that enough you might begin to believe it,' said Bo. He knew it was risky to speak in such a manner, but everything about the king offended and sickened him.

The King of the Sea Beggars laughed again and returned to his throne, grunting and gasping. 'You have some spirit, boy, I cannot deny it. In truth, it pains me to see you here as a common prisoner. It is an unnecessary waste. I could find a use for one as strong-willed as you.'

'You want *me* to work for *you*?' said Bo.

The king frowned, his offer clearly a serious one. 'Is that such a terrible prospect? Anything you desire you could have, if you serve me.'

Deep down within Bo, a voice flickered. *Take his offer. Take it.* No. Bo knew it was the voice of weakness. It was not the voice of his true heart. 'There is nothing you could offer that would persuade me to join you.'

Bo's refusal surprised the king, surprise that swiftly flared into anger. 'Perhaps you think that as you are royalty, you are afforded some protection here, but you are gravely mistaken. Your punishment for spurning my generosity is to suffer as those scum from the *Husker Du* suffer, more so if possible. And do not think that your friend Black Francis is in any position to help you.'

The king leant forward and pointed to his left. Bo's eyes followed the direction of the king's hand —among the paintings on the wall was Black Francis, hanging limp and lifeless from chains tied around his wrists. He was naked from the waist up, his body bruised and swollen.

Bo wanted to shout, he wanted to scream, he wanted to attack and kill the king, but he found himself paralysed, unable to speak, fury and grief freezing his body.

'Of all my art collection,' said the king, 'I find Black Francis the most pleasing to my eyes.'

'You are a murderer.'

'A murderer? The traitor is not dead. His suffering has scarcely begun.'

Bo looked again at Black Francis and to his relief and astonishment, the captain moved his head. He was alive.

'Tomorrow is Katsu Eve,' continued the king, stroking the chained lion's back. 'I will entertain my loyal subjects with a spectacle worthy of such an auspicious day. Black Francis will receive his deserved punishment for his treachery: to be hanged, drawn and quartered. And you and the rest of the *Husker Du* scum will enjoy a very special treat.'

*

Bo sat in complete darkness. He waved his hands an inch away from his face and could not see them. The Sea Beggars had forced him into a tiny square gaol with a narrow, barred window. Bo had always found comfort in the dark. He had often retreated to the murky, forgotten depths of the Hammersund palace, seeking solace from the crushing boredom of court life or escape from hostile, mocking eyes. Now darkness encouraged greater horrors to seep in; his defences had crumbled, with nothing left to block out grim thoughts and troubling images. A feeling of utter helplessness infected him like a foul, gibbering demon that brought all his failings, all his doubts and fears, bubbling to the surface. He remembered Black Francis, chained, hanging, close to death. The knowledge that he could neither save his friend nor punish those responsible for his suffering filled Bo with impotent anger.

Before the cell door had slammed shut, the gaoler had lobbed a piece of bread onto Bo's lap. It was as hard as stone, with sharp edges that nicked his tongue and gums. He sucked on the bread to moisten it, but with his mouth already parched, it made little difference. In frustration, he threw the bread down.

He thought of Jeimuzu and Moriko. Had they escaped the Sea Beggars? Even if they had, would Queen Okaasan fulfil her promise and lead the Kojin to war? As he sat alone in the dark, it seemed less and less likely.

He stood and thumped his fists against the wall. He wanted to cry out, to scream with despair and frustration, but his throat and mouth were too dry. Tears tumbled down his cheek, tears that brought him more shame. *Weakling. Fool. Coward.* He slid to the ground and hunched himself up, trying to shield himself from the world around him.

Long hours elapsed before a little light crept through the window, announcing dawn. Bo listened to the activity from outside: carts creaking as they rolled past; the hum of conversation and laughter; the ringing of hammers. Something was happening. He recalled what the King of the Sea Beggars had said about a *special treat*. No doubt it was going to be something particularly unpleasant.

The cell door opened and Bo looked up to see two Sea Beggars, both reeking of alcohol, standing in the doorway.

'It's time for you to get ready, little prince,' said one of the Sea Beggars, his speech slurred. 'The revels begin soon and the *Caudillo* does not want you to miss them.'

The Sea Beggars hauled Bo to his feet and marched him out of the cell. Bo was cautious because he knew drunken men were unpredictable and quick to anger. The Sea Beggars took him along a succession of corkscrewing passages. Weakened by thirst and hunger, Bo stumbled more than once and bumped into his guards, who reacted with angry curses and punches.

After ascending a winding stairway, they passed through a triangular-headed archway and Bo found himself outside. The harsh light blinded him for a moment and he recoiled like a nocturnal creature forced out into the sun's brilliant glare. He rubbed his eyes and blinked. He was standing close to the Alcazar's main gate. Thick vertical cracks disfigured the walls, some filled with weeds; many of the bricks were crumbling.

The heavy wooden gate was open, with numerous horse-drawn carts trundling through. The Sea Beggars jostled Bo towards the amphitheatre, joining the long lines of people that had walked from Katakani. The rows of stone seats were filling with excited spectators. Colourful flags, limp and lifeless in the absence of any wind, lined the rim of the amphitheatre and the sound of drums, pipes and trumpets filled the air. Stalls had been set up, selling fruit, roasted nuts and bread. Bands of Sea Beggars wandered around, heavily armed with swords or muskets.

Bo was forced down a flight of steps all the way to the amphitheatre's sandy- floored arena, where upon a scaffold rose a stark and skeletal gallows. On the far side of the arena stood two sturdy wooden posts, both at least twice the height of a man; Bo wondered what purpose they served.

Looking up at the rows of spectators, Bo felt exposed but he was not the only prisoner in the arena. The crew of the *Husker Du* were crammed inside a cage of crisscrossed iron bars. They were grimy, their ragged clothes covered in sand and blood, their hair lank and greasy. Bo glimpsed Whelk, Limpet, the red-haired foremastman Crab and the coxswain Shrimp. All stood disconsolate, their heads bowed. Sea Beggars circled the cage, tormenting their prisoners by poking sharpened sticks and spears through the gaps between the bars, which earned laughter and applause from the crowd. The spectators had come to see death, to see blood spilled—a swarm of faces, drunk or frenzied by collective hate, scowling, leering and mocking.

The Sea Beggars shoved Bo into the cage, with the door slammed and locked behind him. Inside, there was little room. Elbows battered against his back. Curses sounded. Weeping. Praying. Wedged in, Bo came face to face with Shrimp. Tears smudged the dirt on the coxswain's cheeks. In a broken, husky voice, Shrimp said, 'So they caught you again. I feared you were already dead.'

'I think I soon will be.'

'Have you see Black Francis? The King of the Sea Beggars imprisoned him in the Alcazar.'

'No,' said Bo. Haunted by the memory of the captain, he thought it best to lie.

The coxswain rubbed his eyes. 'What of Valbrand?'

'He lived when last I saw him,' said Bo, who explained what had happened since they had escaped from the city. 'I hope he lives still.'

'I have forgotten what it is to hope.'

'Hope might be all we have left,' said Bo.

Shrimp shook his head. 'They're going to kill Black Francis, aren't they? This is what this is all about. Punishment. Vengeance. I thought the Pits were hell. The darkness, the smell and the rats, but this place is worse, far worse. I'm going to have to watch him die and there's nothing I can do.'

Bo tried to say something but the words died in his mouth. Words were meaningless.

Trumpets sounded in unison and a wave of excitement rippled through the amphitheatre. A procession made its way down the slope into the arena, and at its head limped the King of the Sea Beggars, accompanied by the muzzled lion, which the king walked like a dog on a chain. A young boy followed a step behind, holding a huge shade over the

384

king to protect him from the brutal sun. The crowd chanted, '*Caudillo! Caudillo!*'

An honour guard of Sea Beggars marched behind the king, and at the rear of the procession, a horse dragged a rectangular wooden hurdle behind it. Black Francis was strapped to the hurdle by thick rope.

The crowd cheered as the procession reached the arena. Two servants placed a mahogany chair close to the gallows. The Sea Beggars untied Black Francis from the hurdle and hauled him towards the gallows. Meanwhile, the king waddled into the centre of the arena, gestured for silence and spoke aloud. 'Friends, I welcome you all on this wondrous day, Katsu Eve, the feast of victory. On this day, the traitor Black Francis receives his long overdue punishment. I am a benevolent and merciful ruler, kind to my subjects. But I never forgive treachery. And once Black Francis has been dealt with, there will be more sport, for I have devised a most diverting entertainment for you all, a spectacle not seen for long ages.'

A commotion from the procession slope caused most of the crowd to stand; many pointed, shouted, laughed. Bo stood on tiptoe to see, peering over the heads of the other prisoners. Two huge beasts lumbered down the slope. They reminded Bo of wild boar but were easily twice the size of shire-horses. Their bodies were hairless and mottled emerald green. Cracks showed across their ill-fitting skin, apart from around the neck where thick, fatty folds bulged. They wheezed and slobbered as they walked, long strings of drool dripped down from between their oddly angled, protruding teeth. Their tiny eyes peeked out from behind a long snout spiky with stiff bristles. Bo's bowels ached with fear. So this was the King of the Sea Beggar's *special treat*.

Balebeasts. Monsters that lurked within countless old stories and legends. Bo had believed they were just an invention of storytellers to frighten children. But in the stark sunlight, they were real, painfully real.

The crowd cheered as the balebeasts entered the arena, dragged down the slope by keepers who had tied chains around the necks of both creatures. Sea Beggars swarmed around the balebeasts, pushing them forward with prods and whips. When the keepers brought the creatures to a halt, they tied them to the thick wooden posts. The balebeasts snorted and more than once snapped their fearsome jaws at the keepers, who jumped away in time to avoid losing an arm or worse.

The King of the Sea Beggars held up his hands and addressed the crowd again. 'Behold the balebeasts. Terrors of ancient times. These specimens are but dwarfs compared to their ancestors, but I promise you they are every bit as fierce. For nigh on three days they have been starved. Soon, they shall feast on the crew of the *Husker Du*. Of course, the prisoners will try to run, maybe if foolish enough, try to fight. Against the balebeasts, there is no hope. Their deaths will provide you all with a spectacle worthy of the emperors of antiquity. But first, it is time for Black Francis, the lowest of all traitors, to die. This I shall watch at close hand, though when the balebeasts are unleashed, I plan to move to a higher seat.'

The crowd roared with laughter at his last comment. Smiling smugly, the king settled in the chair and forced the lion

386

to lie down at his feet. The crowd cheered again as the Sea Beggars heaved Black Francis onto the gallows. Three drummers stood in front of the scaffold.

The King of the Sea Beggars rubbed his swollen wrists. 'Wake the prisoner.'

A bucket of water was thrown over Black Francis. It revived him and his eyes opened.

'So, the time for your execution has come, Black Francis,' said the King of the Sea Beggars.

'Then why don't you get it over and done with?' said Black Francis, his voice still powerful despite his suffering.

'Oh, it shall not be long delayed, I promise you that. But I am noble and so must offer you the chance to beg for mercy.'

Black Francis snorted. 'I'll not beg. If you want to kill me, then kill me. But be a man and do it yourself, instead of ordering one of your lackeys to carry it out for you.'

Despite the desperate situation, Bo smiled at the sailor's defiance, all the more so when he saw the flicker of anger and embarrassment on the face of the King of the Sea Beggars, whose attempt to humiliate Black Francis had backfired.

'I weary of talk,' said the king, with a dismissive flick of his hands. 'Begin the execution.'

Black Francis did not flinch as the Sea Beggars tied the noose around his neck. The sailor was so weak he could barely stand and one of the Sea Beggars had to prop him upright. Bo watched in despair. This is my fault, he thought. Shrimp closed his eyes and covered his ears with his hands.

An expectant hush fell over the crowd. Bo thought about

the Kojin. They would not come now. Perhaps Jeimuzu and Moriko had been captured, or had not survived the journey through the catacombs. Or perhaps they had both escaped, but the queen still refused to risk war. Whatever the truth, he and the others were alone. His mind racing, Bo considered trying to break out of the cage, rushing the guards, anything to help his friend, but he knew it was futile; he could not help Black Francis now.

A guard said, 'He is ready, *Caudillo*.'

The king sat back in his seat. 'Then begin, but do not allow him to choke to death. I want to prolong his agony.'

The Sea Beggar bowed and opened his mouth to say something but the words never came—he jolted violently and held his hands to his throat. Blood gurgled from his mouth and he fell from the scaffold, an arrow lodged in his throat. An unearthly cry reverberated around the amphitheatre, a cry that ended all conversation. Dozens of figures appeared around the eastern edge of the amphitheatre, all silhouetted by the sun. Bo shielded his eyes. His heart skipped with amazement and joy when he recognised the horned helmets, thick armour and sinister masks. The Kojin had come.

Kojin warriors charged down the rows of stone seats, scattering the crowd as they did so. Sea Beggars ran to confront the attackers but the Kojin cut them down, their sunreflected swords gleaming as though coated with fire. To Bo's surprise, Valbrand was among the warriors. His injured arm was bandaged but in his right hand he brandished a sword and his face was alight with the joy of battle.

The king leapt to his feet and screamed orders at his honour guard, who formed a protective circle around him. The Sea Beggars that guarded Bo and the other prisoners looked shocked. One of them, his back to the cage, slowly retreated, afraid of the approaching Kojin. A ring of keys dangled from the Sea Beggar's belt. They were only inches away. Bo knelt and put his hands through the bars. The Sea Beggar, transfixed by the growing battle, failed to notice as Bo nimbly slipped the ring from his belt. Feeling a surge of triumph, Bo found the right key before slowly, quietly, unlocking the cage door. He whispered to Shrimp, 'This is our only chance.'

Shrimp nodded, understanding his meaning.

Bo turned to the crew. He took a deep breath. He needed to take command. He needed to show leadership. 'Come on, we have to fight. I know you are tired and hungry but it is the only way out of here. It is the only way we can survive.'

Bo kicked the door open, and the crew followed his lead, pouring out of the cage. The sudden onslaught took the Sea Beggars guarding them by surprise. A Sea Beggar faced Bo, brandishing a sword. He was young, a teenager only, and his eyes were wild with fear. Drained from lack of sleep, water and food, Bo had felt sluggish, but the excitement of the escape reinvigorated him. He charged at the Sea Beggar, knocking him over and falling on top of him. Before the Sea Beggar could react, Bo punched him firmly on the chin and knocked him out cold. He picked up the Sea Beggar's sword and scrambled to his feet. He watched the rest of the prisoners charge into the guards, washing over them in a wave of punches and kicks. Weak and tired the prisoners

389

may have been, but anger possessed them and they fought like wild animals.

Shrimp pointed to the gallows. 'We have to cut Black Francis free.'

Bo clambered up the scaffold. A Sea Beggar stood in front of the gallows, a huge brute with thick, muscled arms. He lunged a spear but Bo moved swiftly; he cut the spear in half with his sword and plunged the blade into the Sea Beggar's gut: a killing blow. Bo stood for a second, barely able to comprehend what he had done, the blood dripping guiltily from his sword. An image of his dead brother, Haakon, flashed in front of his eyes: grey skin, blank eyes, the vivid lines of blood. Bo rubbed his eyes. The vision evaporated.

Shrimp had already ascended the scaffold and was untying Black Francis, who was barely conscious. Bo helped Shrimp to put the captain down on his back. His eyes flickered open. He looked at Shrimp and held a hand up to his cheek. In a weak voice he said, 'Is it you? Am I dreaming?'

'No, this is not a dream,' said Shrimp.

Black Francis closed his eyes. 'I'm so tired.'

'He's badly hurt,' said Shrimp to Bo. 'We need to get him somewhere safe.'

Bo knew that was no easy task. The battle raged around them. Some Sea Beggars had muskets and they fired at the advancing Kojin, killing some. The foul gun smoke polluted the air. More Sea Beggars flooded out of the Alcazar. Some wheeled out light cannons such as a falconets and culverins, which vomited iron shot and splinters of sizzling shrapnel that hissed and fizzed like angry wasps, eagerly searching for flesh to tear and rip. There were hundreds of Sea Beggars, maybe a thousand, far outnumbering the Kojin who now gathered on the arena floor.

Yet the armoury of the Sea Beggars was no match for the fighting skills of the Kojin, whose bowmen fired with unerring accuracy. The slow-loading, inaccurate muskets and light cannons of the Sea Beggars proved of little value. As soon as the Kojin warriors got close enough to their foes, they cut them down with their swords, daggers and spears.

With the battle turning against him, the King of the Sea Beggars yelled, 'UNLEASH THE BALEBEASTS!'

The keepers unchained the creatures and whipped them towards the Kojin warriors. The balebeasts snarled and roared, waddling with surprising speed. The first Kojin warriors they met bravely stood their ground but to no avail, the balebeasts trampled over them. Mad with hunger, the creatures stopped to gore and devour their victims. It gave the Kojin a chance. Bo watched as their bowmen fired volley after volley into the balebeasts. One of the creatures, pierced by countless arrows, gave a mournful groan and slumped to the ground. The other balebeast ran wildly in the opposite direction, towards Bo, Shrimp and Black Francis. Bo froze in terror. The scaffold they stood upon was no defence against the balebeast; it would tear right through it, killing them all. The creature gathered pace, hurtling towards them. There was no time to jump from the scaffold, no time to run, no time to hide.

Something, someone, appeared in front of the scaffold, standing between it and the advancing balebeast, a blur in Bo's eyes—a masked Kojin warrior. The warrior knelt on one knee and drew his bow. The balebeast came closer and closer. Still the warrior did not fire. Bo could smell the creature now, a putrid, vomit reek. Just at the last, the warrior loosened his arrow. With terrible force and speed, it struck the balebeast between the eyes. It grunted and skidded to a halt, barely three yards from the scaffold, throwing up plumes of sand. It took one last deep shuddering breath and died.

The warrior removed his mask and looked up at Bo. It was Jeimuzu. His face was impassive, inscrutable and somehow older, more mature. He gave the faintest of nods to Bo and re-joined the battle.

With the balebeasts slain, the fighting soon descended into a rout. The Sea Beggars' courage broke and the survivors ran for the safety of the Alcazar, abandoning muskets, cannons and swords. The King of the Sea Beggars screamed at his fleeing men. 'STAND AND FIGHT, DAMN YOU!'

His words had no effect. Even his honour guard chose to run rather than face the Kojin. The king stood alone apart from the chained lion. The Kojin warriors swiftly surrounded him.

The king unsheathed his sword and waved it weakly towards the Kojin. 'I am still the ruler of this island.'

'That is no longer true,' said Jeimuzu, pushing through the ring of Kojin warriors to stand face to face with the king. 'You should have stayed in the Alcazar.'

The king gripped his sword but he did not attack Jeimuzu; he used it to strike the muzzle and chains of the lion.

'Taste the jaws of death, demons!' he said, urging the lion to attack the Kojin. The beast roared, shaking his head and thick mane. Freedom gave long-lost strength to his muscles and limbs. Jeimuzu and the Kojin retreated several paces but the lion ignored them. Instead, it pounced upon the king, driving him down onto the ground. Fighting for his life, the king stabbed his sword into the lion's flank. The beast bellowed in pain before clasping his jaws around the king's neck. The king's legs jerked once and then he lay still. With the sword impaled into its side, the lion exhaled deeply and died, its body crushing the King of the Sea Beggars.

There was a terrible silence, the quietness as intense as the clamour and din of battle. The rows of stone seats were empty of living beings, only corpses populated them now; the crowd had fled. Still standing on the scaffold, Bo watched as Jeimuzu knelt and placed a hand on the lion. 'This is a noble creature and it is a crime that it should have been enslaved and tortured in such a way. Bury it with honour. As for the king, make a pyre, burn his body. He deserves no tomb.'

As the warriors carried out Jeimuzu's command, and others secured the perimeter of the amphitheatre, Bo looked down from the scaffold and saw Valbrand. With a broad grin, he said, 'You are not an easy man to kill.'

'It's the best quality a man can have,' said Valbrand. Bo helped him up onto the scaffold. When Valbrand saw Black Francis, he said, 'So the old rogue is still alive. He has more lives than a cat.'

Jeimuzu cut into the conversation. Bo had not heard him climb onto the scaffold. 'I had feared that we would come too late.'

'I think you came just in time,' said Bo.

Jeimuzu almost managed a smile. 'Humbly I ask for your

393

forgiveness. I was wrong before. You are not a coward. In fact, I have met no one braver.'

'There is nothing to forgive. I am glad you and your sister escaped safely.'

Jeimuzu's face darkened. 'The journey back through the catacombs was very cruel.'

Great was the queen's joy when my sister returned. And greater still was her fury at Moriko's treatment at the hands of the Kegare. She resolved at once to attack the Sea Beggars. The court advised against it of course, cowards and flatterers all, but Her Grace is strong. She knew it was time to act. For too long we have waited in the shadows, slumbering, afraid, indecisive. Now we have awoken, we have found our strength and our courage. And you pointed the way, Asbjorn. It took the plain speaking of an outsider to show us the way forward. I regret all of my harsh words to you. You saved my life and the life of my sister. You have proved your worth.'

Jeimuzu's words left Bo too stunned to respond. He was about to try to say something back when Shrimp said, 'Black Francis needs water, and his wounds cry out for dressing.'

'We have many injured, and with the Alcazar still held by the Sea Beggars I fear that the fighting is not yet over,' said Jeimuzu. 'But I will make sure the monks tend to your friend. They are not far away, they are travelling with the queen. She is coming to reclaim our city.'

*

394

When they heard tidings that the king was dead, the remaining Sea Beggars lost all will to fight. Once Jeimuzu had promised them safe passage to the mainland, they surrendered and the Alcazar fell without a shot being fired.

Queen Okaasan arrived close to midday, leading her people in procession; Hinanjo had been emptied. Weary from the journey across the mountain, the Kojin made a temporary camp beside the amphitheatre; tents sprang up like mushrooms, all contained within a curtain wall made of strips of cloth sewn together horizontally and decorated with crests and emblems. The Kojin monks tended to the wounded. Shrimp had insisted on staying with Black Francis and despite their initial misgivings, the monks relented when they saw that, short of force, nothing could keep him away.

Bo stood beside Valbrand and watched as the long line of Sea Beggars drifted out of the Alcazar, casting their weapons onto an ever increasing pile of swords, spears, axes and muskets.

'Do you trust that they will keep the peace?' said Bo, taking another bite into the juicy apple he had purloined from an abandoned food stall.

'I reckon so, at least for now,' said Valbrand. 'Would you want to fight the Kojin?'

'No, I suppose not but I wonder where the Sea Beggars will go now?'

'If it is mischief they seek they'll find it somewhere.'

'Yes, I imagine you are right. But whatever happens, I have to leave here, and soon.'

'Good. This Beauteous Isle is a fine place and all, but we

395

need to get back to Prevennis. I want to crack some Kings-guard heads again.'

'We can't go back to Prevennis, at least not yet.'

Valbrand gawped at him. 'By the gods, why not?'

'You have forgotten about the parchment we took from Bishop Neidelhart, the Patriarchal Edict. We have to tell surviving Illuminati what it said. We have to go to Omphalos.'

Valbrand sighed irritably and scratched his bald dome. 'You weren't taken in by that mad Sesheta were you?'

'She wasn't mad,' said Bo. 'She was telling the truth.'

'Even if you're right, how are we going to get to that place, that navel of the world?'

'The *Husker Du*. We'll sail there.'

'Only if Black Francis agrees. After all he's been through, he might just want to sail to some lonely, sun-soaked island and spend the rest of his days drinking rum.'

'I hope he will agree,' said Bo, knowing that it was a lot to ask of Black Francis.

Ladislaus hobbled towards them. 'I am glad to find you alive and well, Asbjorn. I prayed for you many times since I left you at the Tomb of the Eagle.'

'Thank you,' said Bo, pleased to see the priest, someone who had shown him much kindness. 'You travelled here with the queen?'

'Yes, a hard journey for an old man, but I was spared the battle at least. That would have been too much for my frail heart. God willing, the Beauteous Isle is free from the scourge of the Sea Beggars. And that is in no small part down to your bravery.'

Bo blushed. 'I am not sure that is true.'

'It most certainly is. But forgive me. My tongue runs away with me and I have neglected my true purpose. Her Grace very much wishes to speak with you both. She sent me to find you.'

Bo and Valbrand followed Ladislaus into the Kojin camp, which was centred on a rectangular, wooden-framed pavilion; the roof fabric was brightly coloured with horizontal stripes of yellow, black, white and red cloth. Queen Okaasan sat within the pavilion, cross-legged, her arms hidden by the sleeves of her gown. Jeimuzu stood beside her, still in his full battle-armour with his helmet and mask tucked beneath his arm. On the other side of the queen stood Princess Moriko, regal in T-shaped, straight-lined, long-sleeved silk robes. Courtiers sat in front of the queen, all dressed in angular black ceremonial robes but with their heads lowered. When Okaasan saw Bo, Valbrand and Ladislaus she gestured for them to come closer and dismissed the courtiers, who stood and departed swiftly, pausing only to hurl angry looks at the three men.

'Sit here in front of me,' said the queen, leaning forward and smiling. 'You have all helped my people to reclaim our land and end our long years of exile. And, Asbjorn, for your rescue of my daughter you have my undying gratitude.'

Bo looked at Moriko. She smiled but he saw the horror of the catacombs in her eyes. Words were not needed.

'Yet for all your courage,' continued Okaasan, 'I have more to ask of you.'

An uncomfortable knot twisted in Bo's stomach. He feared yet more fighting and killing.

'A battle has been won but dangers fill every corner of this world and I believe those dangers will soon reach the shores of this island. Despite our victory, we Kojin are not strong. We can muster scarcely five hundred warriors. Against the *Kegare*, that proved enough. Against greater foes, stronger foes, we would be swept aside like dust. When Prester John discovers what has happened to the foul *Kegare*, will he not assail us with all strength available to him?'

'I fear it will be so, Your Grace,' said Ladislaus.

'As do I, good priest,' said the queen. 'My courtiers, their courage fortified by our victory, now espouse punishment for those who profited from the exile of the Kojin. They wish to drive all non-Kojin from the island and for the *Etah* to be executed. They tell me power is within my grasp and I should take it.'

'If I may be so bold,' said Ladislaus, 'I believe your courtiers are trying to conceal their own weakness, a weakness illustrated by their counselling against war in the first place. I do not belittle the suffering of the Kojin, but it is folly to allow your people to be guided by vengeance for acts that cannot be undone. Such a response only sows the seeds of further conflict. With every ounce of my soul, I beseech you not to heed their advice. Do not seek vengeance.'

Okaasan gave a smile of satisfaction. 'And that, Ladislaus, is why I wish for *you* to be my chief counsellor. I trust you to speak plainly and honestly. Do you accept?'

Flustered by her offer, Ladislaus took a moment to compose himself. 'Your Grace, I am flattered beyond words. But it is impossible. I am not Kojin.'

'It is your wisdom that is important, not your race,' said the queen with a casual wave of her hand.

The priest took a deep breath. 'Therefore, I shall serve you in whatever way I can.'

'You gladden my heart, Ladislaus. This island no longer belongs just to the Kojin, others live here too. I refuse to treat them as outcasts. If they wish it, they can remain here, to be treated as equals.'

'How do you know they won't betray you?' said Valbrand.

'Nothing is certain but to me it seems the best way to achieve peace here. That makes the risk worth taking. We should learn from the mistakes of our ancestors, who wantonly ravaged the *Kodai-no*. We *must* act in a more enlightened fashion.'

'I concur,' said Ladislaus. 'Although I confess I am bothered by those who have been Nulled, they are under the control of Prester John.'

'Kill them all,' said Valbrand.

'No, they must not be harmed,' said the queen. 'Yet I share your fears, Ladislaus. Tell the Nulled to leave the island. Good ships and sufficient provisions will be provided. They are free to go to any port that will take them.'

'A just and wise decision,' said Ladislaus.

The queen glanced at Jeimuzu before saying, 'I also pronounce that all ancient sites of the Kodai-no are sacred and may not be disturbed by anyone, Kojin or otherwise. Small recompense maybe, but I vow to protect their tombs and the spirits of their ancestors.'

'I will strive to ensure your will is enforced,' said Ladislaus.

'And what of you, Asbjorn?' said the queen.

Bo cleared his throat. 'I have a message of great importance that I must deliver to opponents of Prester John on the mainland. I need to depart at the earliest opportunity.'

The queen frowned and adjusted her seating position. 'I am saddened to hear this. I had hoped you would remain here. You could be of great value to my people.'

'I am humbled and grateful that you think so, but I have a duty that I cannot ignore.'

The queen turned to Valbrand. 'Is it your intention to travel with Asbjorn?'

'Aye, I'll be going with him.'

Bo looked at Valbrand and smiled, receiving only a grimace in reply.

'If I may speak, Your Grace?' said Jeimuzu.

The queen nodded.

'Prester John is our enemy. He supported the *Kegare*, and as Your Grace says, one day he will seek to destroy us. I believe we should aid Asbjorn in his quest. I propose that a detachment of our warriors should accompany him, and furthermore, I propose that I should go with them, with your leave. It is time that we Kojin reached out to the wider world.'

Bo was shocked. Jeimuzu had said nothing to him about his idea and he was dumbfounded as to why the Kojin prince desired such a thing.

'You are asking to leave?' said the queen. 'You are my heir. Your place is here, to defend this island and your people.'

'If we stand alone, then what defence can succeed against Prester John?'

The queen glared at her son for a moment before moving her gaze to Ladislaus. 'What is your counsel?'

'Your Grace, there are no easy choices here—'

'You are my counsellor, tell me what your counsel is,' interrupted the queen.

The priest took a sharp intake of breath. 'I believe the prince speaks wisely. He should go with Asbjorn.'

Okaasan brought her hands together and rested her chin on the tips of her fingers, deep in thought. 'These are tempestuous days and the old certainties vanish with the wind. Perhaps events move faster than my mind. Prince Jeimuzu, you have proven worthy of your bloodline. You passed a test more dreadful than any of your ancestors faced. You have the strength and wisdom to meet the challenges ahead. So be it. My son, you *shall* travel with Asbjorn and his companions, and take with you a detachment of twelve warriors. You may select those you feel most suited to your purpose. Asbjorn, I trust you have no objection to my son's presence on your journey?'

'The prince honours us, Your Grace,' said Bo. As surprised as he was by Jeimuzu's offer, Bo knew the Kojin prince was a good ally to stand beside in a fight.

'I shall not fail you, Your Grace,' said Jeimuzu.

'No, my son, you will not.'

Moriko broke her silence. 'If you allow it, I too should like to travel with Prince Asbjorn.'

The queen gaped at Moriko, as though searching for the right words to express her shock and outrage. At last, she found them. 'That is impossible. A foolish, irresponsible thought. It wounds me to think of Jeimuzu going forth across the sea, but I cannot contemplate the thought of you accompanying him.'

'That is not fair,' said Moriko, her voice growing louder. 'I can fight as well as any warrior, you know that. I endured the catacombs, just like Jeimuzu. I have spent long months in a hideous dungeon—are you to imprison me too?'

'Enough, I have given my decision, you must accept it,' said the queen.

Moriko and Jeimuzu shared a glance before the princess nodded and said meekly, 'I obey.'

*

Bo stood on the harbour, watching as the crew of the *Husker Du* prepared the vessel for the journey ahead. They carried provisions onto the ship: barrels of water and ale, loaves of bread, hunks of cheese, and joints of meat. Bo did not savour the thought of another voyage at sea and, despite the importance of their mission, he was in no hurry to go on board. Three days had passed since the battle, days of rest, days of healing. To give up such comforts for a journey across the waves was not an enticing prospect.

'Are you going to stand there all day, lad?'

The familiar booming voice of Black Francis dragged Bo from his musing. A warm smile lit up his face but the signs of his ordeal at the hands of the Sea Beggars were not erased. His beard had become patchy, with scabby skin visible beneath the thin curly black hair, and his eyes, which had always sparkled with life and mischief, were now dull, like a fire burned down to embers.

'How are you feeling now?' said Bo, a question he had put to Black Francis repeatedly since the battle.

As usual, the captain shrugged it off. 'Ready for salty air and the rolling waves, that's how I am. If I stay on dry land for much longer I'll become a lubber.'

Bo laughed. 'I doubt that.'

'Well, whatever the truth of it, the journey ahead will be a hard one.'

'I am in your debt for agreeing to this voyage. After all that you have been through, I would have understood had you declined.'

Black Francis blinked and his face twitched. He glanced at the Alcazar. 'That I am standing here, alive, on my ship is down to you.'

'Well, not *just* me. The Kojin defeated the Sea Beggars.'

'Aye, but they wouldn't have done so without your bravery. You showed a path for others to follow. And I think it's a path for me to follow too. I once told you I can never atone for my sins, and I stand by that. But I can try and I will try. If getting this message to the Illuminati helps the struggle against Prester John, that's what I have to do. I'm not running away again. I'm with you, Bo, to the end.'

Black Francis placed his hands on Bo's shoulders and smiled. A tear trickled down his left cheek. He wiped his cheek, gulped in a deep breath, released his grip on Bo's shoulders and said, 'Any sign of Valbrand yet? He should have been here an hour ago. We can hardly wait for him. He's probably in a heap somewhere, drunk.'

'He'll be here,' said Bo. 'I *hope.*'

A metallic clatter and the sound of marching feet announced the arrival of Prince Jeimuzu and his warriors. Servants carried their iron and leather armour on board, although one of the warriors was still wearing his helmet and fierce mask. Jeimuzu approached Bo and Black Francis, and as the warriors filed on board the *Husker Du* he said, 'We are ready to embark.'

'Are you sure your boys are up to this journey?' said Black Francis. 'We'll be heading into some rough seas.'

'My forefathers were navigating the oceans while your descendants were paddling in rivers and streams,' said Jeimuzu. 'There are no finer sailors than the Kojin. Salt water is in our blood and in our soul.'

Black Francis looked a little taken aback. 'If I offended you, my friend, I'm sorry. It's in my nature to speak plainly and my tongue can be a little coarse.'

The Kojin accepted the captain's apology with a stiff bow and made his way on board the ship.

Black Francis raised his eyebrows at Bo. 'This could be an interesting journey.'

'It is always an interesting journey when I sail with you,' said Bo, grinning. He heard the sound of running— Valbrand hurried towards them. He was carrying a rolled-up pile of rags.

'There you are, *at last,*' said Black Francis.

Red-faced and gasping for breath, Valbrand said, 'I hope you weren't thinking of leaving without me?'

Bo laughed. 'If you had returned any later we might have done. Where have you been?'

'The Kojin have been dividing the spoils of the King of the Sea Beggars and I didn't want to miss that. There were piles of stuff in the Alcazar. Gold, jewels, weapons, you name it they had it. Of course, the Kojin took most, which is fair enough, but they let me have a little share too. Black Francis, you should have been there.'

The captain's expression changed. 'I never want to return to *that* place.'

'Ah, I suppose you have your reasons,' said Valbrand.

'Did you find much?' said Bo.

'Aye, quite a bit,' said Valbrand. He turned around—he had his old crossbow strapped to his back. 'It's like finding an old friend.'

'I'm surprised you managed to keep your hands off the gold and jewels,' said Bo.

Valbrand winked and patted his pockets, which clinked with the sound of coins. 'I thought I was due a little compensation for my suffering. But it's not all for me. I've something for you too.'

'Oh?' said Bo, trying to sound indifferent but he was eager to discover what Valbrand had brought.

'This will put a smile on your face,' said Valbrand. He knelt and unravelled the bundle of rags he was carrying. As he peeled away the last layer, something glinted in his hands and it took Bo a moment to realise that Valbrand was carrying the Preven sword of kings. 'I found this on the pile of weapons and thought you might like it back.'

Trembling, Bo took it in his hands. 'I thought I had lost this forever. I don't know how to thank you, not just for this sword but...for everything.'

Valbrand stood. 'I suppose these last few days have changed me a bit. I'm not a complicated man. Since they murdered my wife and child, only fighting Redeemers and Kingsguard has made me feel alive, feel as though I have some worth. But it felt good helping the Kojin. It reminded me that there are decent folk around. And you've changed a bit too. You showed real courage. Whether you're a king or a prince makes no odds to me, couldn't care less. What does matter to me is what sort of man you are and you've shown that. I reckon you've earned the right to carry that sword. You should hold it with pride.'

Tears watered Bo's eyes and he quickly held up his hand to his face as though shielding it from the sun's glare. For the first time he could remember, Bo did feel proud. He had endured hardships and survived, survived to take the fight to Prester John. He knew he faced great challenges, not the least being the daunting struggle to free the subjugated people of Prevennis. Yet now he faced those challenges with a greater resolve, a greater confidence. Bo knew he was only one man, a boy really, but he would do everything in his power to fight Prester John, whatever the risk, whatever the cost to himself.

'Come on, lubbers, we set sail soon,' said Black Francis. Singing a shanty, he strode on board the *Husker Du* and, a little more reluctantly, Valbrand and Bo followed him.

- CHAPTER TWENTY -

The Labyrinth

Elowen grabbed the torch and took step after tentative step, slowly descending the stairway. Her arms scratched painfully against the rough walls. The dry and dusty air trapped inside made Elowen sneeze, a sound that boomed around the walls and low ceiling like an explosion. The torch shook in her trembling right hand, and its light juddered and danced. She was almost too frightened to move forward. She paused, her heart banging so hard her chest ached. She remembered the words of Lord Lucien: *do not forget your friends, as their lives are now in your hands*. She touched her pendant, took a deep breath, and continued down the stairway.

When she reached the bottom step, she stopped for a moment, catching her breath and stretching her aching legs. She held her torch aloft and looked around; she was standing in a room, a vestibule. The jerky light exposed a statue of a woman draped in flowing robes. Her face was beautiful and proud, and in one hand she held a staff and in the other a tuft of grain. Faded wall paintings depicting flowers, fruit and grain decorated the room.

There was an unlit torch attached to the wall by a sconce;

Elowen stood on tiptoes and lit it with her torch. If she had to return the same way, she did not want to come back to darkness. She uncoiled a little of the ball of twine that Lárwita had given to her and tied the end firmly around the statue's left arm. There was an opening in the far wall, roughly isosceles in shape and fringed by wall paintings of thick foliage. Elowen surmised that it was the entrance to the labyrinth. She approached it slowly, her footsteps clicking on the tessellated floor. She pulled at the twine to test the strength of her knot and, when satisfied, entered the labyrinth.

It began with an arrow-straight passage, which ended at a junction with passages leading off from each side. She reached the end of the straight passage and looked left and right, trying to decide which way to turn. Still clutching the twine, she took the left passage but soon came to another dead-end, so she retreated and tried the other, which was longer and twisted and turned. She forked right and came face-to-face with another blank wall, another dead-end. She double-backed and tried other passages but always with the same outcome, always a dead-end. Her chest tightened with frustration and she wanted to scream. There was no way through. She was trapped. The words of Baba Yaga came to her: *settle your body. Feel the weight of your feet on the ground, take a deep breath and feel the air flow into your body.*

Elowen did so. She stood perfectly still, with her eyes closed. After a few moments of silence, she heard the musical tinkling of fast-running water splashing over rocks. She remembered Qutugh had spoken of an underground river—if she followed the sound of water it had to lead her to

408

the cave she sought. She took slow, deliberate steps, holding the torch in one hand and using the other to unwind the twine.

She allowed herself to be guided by sound. She turned into a wider passage and the roar of running water echoed like thunder. Cool, damp air kissed her face. The torch hissed and spat. Elowen approached a flight of steps that rose to three doorways. She climbed the steps slowly, trying to decide which doorway to use. They were all different in appearance. The middle doorway was rectangular and framed by an ornamental architrave; the right-hand side doorway was narrower and capped with a lancet arch; the circular left-hand doorway was roughly hewn and unadorned, like the entrance to a cave. Elowen scrutinized each in turn. Faint lines of dusty footprints led into the middle and the right-hand side doorways but not into the opening on the left.

Elowen moved to the middle doorway but intuition stopped her. Without being conscious of making a decision, she took the rough left-hand opening. Once she was through, Elowen was startled to discover she stood upon a narrow rocky ledge that looked down into a vast cavern—both the other doorways led to sheer drops, plunging down into the fast-flowing river that curved through the cavern. Had she chosen either of those doorways she would have surely fallen to her death. She muttered a prayer of thanks, although she doubted any god could hear her in such a place.

A waterfall tumbled noisily down the far end of the cavern, gushing through a crevice carved out by centuries of watery erosion. Enormous stalactites hung menacingly above Elowen's head. On either side of the river rose tall pillars of stone, shaped by the slow-dripping deposits from tiny fissures in the cavern roof. The wet, mineral-rich rocks sparkled in the light of Elowen's torch and revealed hundreds of white-bodied insects and arachnids scuttling around on the ground. Elowen flinched and yelped; her skin prickled in disgust.

Trying to ignore the little creatures, she looked ahead. A narrow stone bridge spanned the river. To reach it, Elowen saw that she needed to climb down from the ledge. She held the torch to search for a safe way down the cavern wall. The fluttering light showed that the wall was not quite sheer; fissures misshaped the rock-face, forming a path of sorts down to the bridge, steep but climbable. Elowen's stomach corkscrewed at the thought of the descent, but with no other way, she tied the rest of the twine around a sharp outcrop of rock close to the doorway and crawled down. Insects wriggled over her hands, weaving between her fingers; their sticky legs tickling her skin. She shuddered and struggled to hold onto the torch, which was all that kept her from total darkness. She wanted to stop. She wanted to go back; only the thought of her friends and the danger they were in pushed her on.

After the slow, painful descent, Elowen's feet landed on the surface of the bridge. Light glowed on the far side. The roaring of the river, and the waterfall that fed it, blocked out all other sounds. She edged across the bridge, one hand clutching the torch, the other stretched out for balance. Several dips, holes and cracks riddled the bridge. Elowen

410

knew that if she slipped or tripped, she would plunge down into the inky, relentless flow of water below. She tried not to look down and focused on the orange glow of light at the far end of the bridge.

Once across, Elowen found herself at the entrance of a tunnel that looked as though it was the warren of some huge burrowing animal. The glow came from an unseen source of light deep within the tunnel. Water dripped down from the ceiling and Elowen's footsteps squelched as she inched her way through. A loamy whiff filled her nostrils. She was terrified of coughing or sneezing in case it alerted some horror to her approach. She kept thinking about the Malign Sleeper. What was it? Why was Qutugh so frightened of it? She wished he had told her more.

A fire crackled. The orange glow of light turned into something more defined: a room lit by a central pit-fire, round with a domed ceiling and with walls covered by simple, stark images that reminded Elowen of the Barbeg cave paintings. Bones were strewn across the floor: rib cages, cracked skulls, limb bones and vertebrae.

On the far side of the room hunched a large figure, man-like in shape but in no other way human. The Malign Sleeper. At least three times the size of any man, he sat with his legs crossed and hairless head bowed, asleep and breathing heavily, his shoulders lifting and falling with each inhale and exhale. His thick arms and legs bulged with muscles. His body was not made of flesh or bone but clay. Elowen glimpsed a golden glint between his fingers and guessed it must be a ring. To her relief, the creature's face was hidden; she barely dared to imagine how terrifying it must be.

411

On the ground lay a long two-handed sword, and there stood three plinths, each supporting a different object. On the left plinth, an emerald glowed with a green light of its own. A gleaming gold cup in the shape of two female faces, their foreheads studded with precious jewels stood on the middle plinth. A small clay tablet inscribed with strange writing and symbols topped the last plinth.

'He sleeps deeply, does he not? But it is unwise to wake him.'

The unexpected voice made Elowen jump. A woman sat on the floor against the wall, half-hidden by shadow. Her hair tumbled down to her hips, and her face was heart-shaped with a broad forehead and a small, narrow chin. Her robes shimmered though there was no draught. The woman's slender arms were manacled at the wrist, with the manacles chained to the wall. Elowen could not guess her age as she appeared at once both young and old.

Elowen kept thinking about Qutugh's advice. *Others you may find down there. Ignore them! Help them not! Do as I say and you may live. Forget my words and you will die.*

'You are young—what brings you to such an accursed place?' said the woman in husky tones.

Elowen kept her mouth shut. She had no idea of who the woman was or if she could trust her.

'You have come for the treasure,' said the woman. Her eyes glowed as they captured the light of the fire. She held up her chained arms. 'Well, go ahead, child, I shall not thwart you. But do not wake the sleeper. He guards his treasure most jealously.'

Deciding it was safer to keep quiet, Elowen tried to ignore

412

the woman. She tiptoed towards the plinths. *Take only the treasure; you will know it when you see it. Take it but touch nothing else.* The words went round and round in her mind. Which one was the treasure? She had to choose but had no idea what she was looking for. But the emerald drew her eye; she wanted to touch it, to savour its smooth cool surface. She desired it, she could not imagine ever tiring of looking at it. Her hands reached out to it, her fingertips inches from its edge.

You will know it when you see it.

Was this how she was meant to feel? Filled with lust for a jewel? She saw herself as a greedy grasping thing, bulging eyes and dribbling mouth. She took a step back and cleared her head, shaking off the covetous thoughts like the lingering remnants of a bad dream. The emerald diminished, grew dull, its light fading. She looked at the cup. Bejewelled and shiny, it was gaudy, ostentatious, no, that was not it. Elowen studied the little clay tablet. It made sense. Clay. The earth element. She recognised the markings and symbols on the tablet: they matched the markings and symbols on the Map of the Known World. It too was a map, a map carved into clay rather than drawn onto paper, surely the Mystery, the next step to finding the Tree of Life. Elowen picked it up, barely able to breathe as she did so. She glanced again at the Malign Sleeper. His head was still bowed, his breathing remained even and deep.

'You have chosen wisely,' said the woman, reminding Elowen of her presence. 'Had you taken one of the other treasures, things would have turned out less well.'

Now that she had the Mystery, Elowen wanted to get out.

413

She wanted to escape the Malign Sleeper's presence. She wanted to get back to her friends, she knew every second she wasted increased the danger they were in. She made sure the clay tablet was safely inside her pocket and went to leave.

'You can't abandon me here,' said the woman. 'Don't leave me at his mercy.'

Others you may find down there. Ignore them! Help them not! Do as I say and you may live. Forget my words and you will die.

Elowen hesitated. Qutugh's warning nagged at her, pulling her away. But it was resisted by pity. The woman was helpless. Surely the Malign Sleeper had to wake soon and then what chance would the woman have? Elowen remembered how she had suffered at the hands of Bishop Serapion; she knew what it was like to be imprisoned and tortured. She remembered the pain, the suffering, the despair. She refused to stand idle and let another endure such a fate. She had to help her.

She knelt by the woman, examining the iron manacles around her wrist.

'Good child, wise child,' said the woman. 'But these irons are strong, too strong for you to break. You must unlock them.'

'How?'

'With the key,' she said, nodding towards the Malign Sleeper. Something glinted between the creature's fingers and Elowen realised it was not a ring but a key.

'You don't expect me to—'

'The sword,' said the woman eagerly. 'Use the sword. You can slay him before he wakes up.'

414

Elowen glanced down at the two-handed sword that lay on the ground in front of the creature. It looked heavy and she wondered if she was strong enough to lift it. She reached for the hilt of the sword and stopped. It was not the weight of the blade that made her hesitate. She looked again at the Malign Sleeper. What right did she have to slay him? It would be murder, cold-blooded and cowardly. She stepped back from the sword. 'I cannot do this.'

'There is no other way. You must hurry. He will not sleep forever. You must kill him. It is the only way.'

Elowen ignored her. She would get the key but not by killing him. Trembling, she approached the creature. His earthy odour of clay thickened the air. His heavy, metronomic breathing thumped in her ears.

'He will wake, child,' said the woman. 'Take the sword, kill him before it is too late.'

Elowen shook her head. She stepped over the sword. She saw the key clearly, wedged between the creature's middle and index fingers of his left hand. Holding her breath, Elowen stretched forward. Her fingertips touched metal. She gripped the bow of the key and slowly began to pull it from between the Malign Sleeper's fingers.

The creature snored. Elowen froze, her heart palpitating. But the Malign Sleeper did not stir. Shaking, Elowen plucked the key free from his fingers. She retreated, walking backwards.

'Hurry, child,' said the woman. Elowen unlocked the manacles and they opened with a metallic click.

The Malign Sleeper jerked. He lifted his head from his chest and sat upright. He opened his eyes. They were amber

415

and glowed like small fires. A toothless mouth opened, a dark gaping hole. As he noticed Elowen, his face tightened and his eyes narrowed. He bellowed. The whole room shuddered. Dust exploded from cracks in the walls and ceiling.

'Now we run,' said the woman, pushing Elowen out of the room. They ran down the passage, splashing, slipping and sliding through puddles. Her ears still ringing, Elowen felt dazed and dizzy. She struggled to keep hold of the torch and the flames singed her cheek as she ran. The light behind them was abruptly extinguished. Elowen risked a glance over her shoulder. The Malign Sleeper was following them; his lumbering steps clomped like colossal drumbeats.

They sprinted to the bridge. The woman went first, scampering across with assurance and perfect balance. Elowen followed her, conscious of the drop either side of the bridge, but the Malign Sleeper gave her no time to hesitate so she ran as fast as she could.

By the time Elowen reached the far side of the bridge the woman was already scrambling up to the high ledge. She stopped, looked down at Elowen and said, 'Faster, child. He is gaining on us.'

Elowen wheeled round to see the Malign Sleeper crawling across the bridge, his bulky body and thick limbs surprisingly nimble. She climbed, straining every muscle and sinew to move as fast as possible, her earlier fear of falling conquered by a greater terror. She scratched her hands on sharp outcrops of rocks and bruised her knees and elbows, but with the woman's help reached the ledge and hauled herself up. Just as Elowen stood, the woman screamed.

Elowen ducked. A rush of air howled over her. The creature had swung a fist at her and missed. The torch slipped from Elowen's fingers and it dropped down the rock face; the creature watched it fall before returning his focus on Elowen.

The woman pulled Elowen away and back into the labyrinth. 'Which way, child?'

Elowen remembered the twine. It was their only chance. She reached out and grabbed the line. 'Follow me.'

The woman took Elowen's free hand and allowed herself to be led. They stumbled forward in utter darkness, the twine their only guide. The Malign Sleeper thumped around behind them, getting closer and closer.

They pushed on. Elowen spotted light ahead. They were almost out. They emerged into the vestibule where the torch she had lit earlier was still burning.

They had escaped the labyrinth. Tired beyond words, Elowen stood with her hands on her knees, trying to catch her breath. Her head was spinning and she was afraid that she was going to pass out. The woman put a hand on her back and said, 'You did well, child, but we are not safe yet.'

The Malign Sleeper burst through the doorway, shattering bricks and mortar. He towered above Elowen and the woman. They could not escape this time. Elowen tensed her body, ready for the hammer blow of his enormous fists but the woman stepped forward, right in front of the creature. She held up her arms and the Earthsoul's golden threads spun and curled around her. The Malign Sleeper crumbled to a pile of dust and clay, a pile that quickly sank through the cracks in the floor.

417

'You have passed the test, child,' said the woman, turning to Elowen and wiping her hands.

'What test?' said Elowen.

'The test that all others before you failed. Wise was your choice of Mystery. As well as courage, you showed pity by rescuing me, and by not using the sword against the creature. Many resort to violence and murder when taken by fear.'

'But the creature, the Malign Sleeper…what happened?'

'He is my creature, my summoning. He obeys my will and follows my command.'

'So you weren't his prisoner?' said Elowen, confused, angry and relieved all at once.

The woman chuckled. 'No more than the sea is the prisoner of a fish that swims in it.'

'But I thought he was the earth Elemental and the guardian of the Mystery?'

The woman laughed again and shook her head.

Elowen understood. 'It's you. You are the earth Elemental.'

'You perceive the truth at last,' she said, as she gently laid her hands upon the statue. Elowen thought she saw a resemblance between the statue and the Elemental. 'The name Itugen was given to me when the world was young, though it is a name few remember now. I have waited innumerable days for this moment. Is it the Tree of Life you seek?'

Elowen nodded but said nothing of Lord Lucien, ashamed that she was doing his bidding.

'I sensed that the day was close when one would come to

418

discover the secrets of the Four Mysteries. For many years I have suffered changes in the earth: the withering of growing things, the poisoning of roots, soil and rocks. There is no division between my being and the earth. I am here and everywhere else at the same time. A great change is approaching—an end or a beginning. Your presence here is proof. Please, let me see the Mystery for one last time.'

Elowen pulled the tablet out of her pocket and passed it to Itugen, who cradled it gently in her hands. The Elemental said, 'Long has the Mystery been in my keeping but now I must let it go. You have earth, now you must seek fire, air and water. I believe you are beginning to understand the importance of your quest.'

'But there is so much more she does not yet understand.'

The voice of Lord Lucien filled every space in the vestibule. He strode down the stairway towards them.

'You are not welcome here,' said Itugen. She stood in front of Elowen and held up her arms. The golden threads spiralled around her, but Lord Lucien attacked first; he leapt forward and stabbed the Elemental in the chest with his sword. Itugen screamed and staggered backwards but rather than fall she crumbled, as the Malign Sleeper had crumbled, to dust. A gust of wind came from nowhere and swept the dust away. The clay tablet dropped to the ground.

Elowen looked on in horror, it had all happened so fast, too fast for her to do anything to help Itugen. Lord Lucien reached down and snatched the Mystery. He sheathed his sword and held up the clay tablet like the trophy of a great victory. 'These Elementals have no power left, their time is over.'

419

'You're a murderer,' said Elowen. One thought, one instinct, came into her mind: run. She plunged back into the
labyrinth, ignoring the shouts of Lord Lucien. Consumed
by darkness, she ran blindly, with her hands out in front of
her, but some other buried sense guided her. Elowen knew
she was being followed; Lord Lucien's footsteps pounded.
On and on she ran. The sound of running water grew louder. Elowen stretched out her arms to touch the walls but
could not find them again. She was lost. There was no point
in running any further. She waited.

She did not have to wait for long. Lord Lucien appeared
with the flaming torch in his hand. As the light from his
torch embraced her, Elowen realised that she had once
again reached the end of the labyrinth and faced the cavern's three openings.

'It is pointless to flee, Elowen,' said Lord Lucien. 'You
cannot escape me.'

'I have done so before.'

'By good fortune perhaps, but this time your luck has run
out. You must understand that I mean you no harm, I am
offering to *help* you, to give you the life no one else can.'

'I want nothing from you. Don't think that I'm weak.'

'I am not making that mistake. I know you are strong.
And everything Baba Yaga taught you makes you stronger
still.'

Elowen failed to suppress a gasp of surprise. How did he
know about Baba Yaga?

'Yes, I was most interested in the time you spent with
her,' said Lord Lucien. 'I wished she had told me more but
she refused to co-operate.'

Elowen's legs buckled as she realised what he meant. 'You…killed her?'

'It was the will of Prester John and God,' said Lord Lucien.

Elowen trembled. A host of emotions assaulted her, pitiless in their barrage. Guilt. Anger. Despair. She pictured Baba Yaga alone, at the mercy of Lord Lucien. 'You are a murderer—you can dress it up if want to and pretend it is the will of God, but it doesn't change what you are.'

'You are too sentimental,' said Lord Lucien, and he held the Mystery up for Elowen to see. 'Baba Yaga was not important. What I hold in my hands is important.'

'You're wasting your time,' said Elowen. 'Only the child of an Adept can use the Mystery.'

'That is so, which makes it fortunate indeed that it has come into my possession, for I too am born of an Adept.'

Elowen jolted with surprise.

Lord Lucien said, 'You know less than you think, Elowen. We were born for a purpose, you and I, as was the Saviour, as were all the messengers. We were born to guide this world, to rule the hearts of Men. Your true destiny has been denied. The Masters of the sanctuary failed you. They tried to use you for their own ends. I am different. I want to help you.'

'*Help* me?' said Elowen. 'I've already said that I want nothing from you.'

'That is because you do not understand.'

'I understand all right. I understand that you killed Baba Yaga. You'll probably kill my friends. And you tortured and killed my mother.'

421

'Your mother's death was unfortunate,' he said. 'But it was not of my doing. You have been deceived about that, and about a great many other things.'

'I'm supposed to believe *you*?'

'You would be wise to do so. Your mother was no enemy of mine, and she was no enemy of Prester John. Indeed, she served my master loyally.'

'THAT'S A LIE,' shouted Elowen. 'She'd never have helped you. She was an Adept.'

'Yes, an Adept as formidable as any I have ever seen. The difficulty is, Elowen, you have swallowed a black and white version of history. A wiser mind sees only shades of grey. You believe all Adepts opposed Prester John. A neat story, a convenient story, but one that is not true. For decades before Prester John came to save us, the Mother Church persecuted Adepts, as it persecuted anyone it perceived to be an enemy.'

'Just as it does now.'

'No, now there is order and only the guilty are punished. Then, it was a time of chaos, Elowen, only if you had lived through such times would you now appreciate the beauty, the purity, of what my master is trying to achieve. Within the chaos of those times, unspeakable savagery and suffering abounded. Your mother suffered as did many other Adepts, tortured by the officials of a corrupt church and sold as a slave to the degenerate Oroks. So when, like the sun breaking through a stormy sky, Prester John came to us, your mother supported his efforts to return the Mother Church to its previous grandeur, and to seek righteous vengeance on those who had despoiled its values.'

422

'Even if that was true, which I don't believe, then you must've tricked her, deceived her in some way.'

'Not at all. She swiftly became a trusted ally, and a good friend. We fought countless campaigns together, all of them victorious. Your mother in her prime was a sight to behold. She rode into battle on a black unicorn. How her enemies broke and fled before her! The Oroks called her *Burilgi Maa*, the destroyer mother in the Common Tongue. They feared her, and with good reason.'

Elowen flinched. She recalled the tales told by Arigh Nasan and Batu. The black unicorn. The scourge of the Oroks. Her heart fluttered, her chest ached. She had a cold, tingling, prickling sensation in her arms and legs. She shook her head. 'No, that can't be true. You're lying.'

'You are like her, Elowen. Strong. Clever. Cunning. She is a part of you.'

Elowen kept shaking her head. 'But you killed her.'

'No, a thousand times no. It was Lord Hereward, the one you called Tom Hickathrift who has her blood on his hands.'

'That's ridiculous. Tom Hickathrift was her friend.'

'Ah, he *pretended* to be her friend. I never trusted him and I tried to warn her about him. I suspected he was an Illuminati agent. Your mother dismissed my doubts and it resulted in her death. Lord Hereward deliberately led her into a murderous ambush. And you, a baby, were stolen from her, stolen from her hands as she lay dying from her wounds. Stolen by Lord Hereward.'

Elowen's whole world, everything she had trusted and believed in, was breaking up around her. She tried to fight it, tried to find holes and weaknesses in Lord Lucien's story. 'If this is all true, why didn't Tom Hickathrift take me to the sanctuary when I was a baby?'

'I do not know for certain, but it is my belief that he tried to hide you from me. Your mother would have wished for me to have been your guardian and protector, of that I am certain. But, even now it is not too late. Take your mother's place by my side; it is what she would have wanted. Help bring order and peace. It is the only way. Mankind is cruel, capricious and venal. Any attempt, however well intentioned, to lead them to redemption is futile and dangerous. The feeble, the corrupt, the degenerate must be winnowed. Only through control can there be peace. Your mother understood this. She shunned human contact, knowing only too well what they are capable of. Alas that the devious lies of Lord Hereward exploited a chink in her armour. She dropped her guard and was murdered. Do not let the same happen to you. You may think you have friends, they may feign kindness, consideration, comradeship, but I assure you they are using you for their own purposes, their own schemes.'

'We have risked our lives for each other time after time,' said Elowen.

'That is why your friends are your greatest weakness. You think of them and their petty needs, and ignore your true purpose, the destiny for which you were born. Your friends are nothing; you have no need of them.'

'You don't know as much about people as you think.'

He took a step closer to her. 'You know the story of the Saviour. The bringer of peace. The creator of miracles. My

424

story is very different. I was barely five years old when the Mother Church discovered the secret of my birth. You would think that one such as I could be of great worth to the Church. The truth was very different. All the cardinals and bishops, those self-proclaimed envoys of God on earth, condemned me as a threat to their dominion. For what use are cardinals, bishops or priests when there is a direct link to the divine? They imprisoned me for more than ten years in a dark, cold cell. And I endured torture the like of which can be barely described.'

Elowen opened her mouth to say something but before she made a sound, Lord Lucien removed his mask. His face was a ruin. Deep red scars crisscrossed his flattened nose, cheeks and forehead, and what skin remained was pasty white. 'Oh, I know plenty about people, child. I have seen them as they truly are: demons in flesh and blood, slaves to impulses incomprehensible to their pathetic minds.'

'It's wrong you were tortured,' said Elowen, shaken by the sight of his face. She felt a morsel of pity and hated herself for doing so. 'But not all people are like that.'

'Are you certain?' he said as, to Elowen's relief, he put his mask back on. 'Think of your torture at the hands of Bishop Serapion. And remember how Rubens betrayed you, a betrayal repeated by your companion Krukis, and do not forget your torture at the hands of Bishop Serapion. Even if through some miracle you and your allies overthrew my master, what would be your reward? Would men herald you as their saviour? Or would suspicion, jealously and hatred grip their hearts? What evil there is in this world comes only from mankind. They are bringers of chaos and misery.'

Elowen had no answer and tried to resist a nagging sense that part of her, a part deeply buried, agreed with Lord Lucien.

His voice became softer, persuasive. He sounded so reasonable, so convincing. 'You need not throw your life away, Elowen. You have suffered so much already. I can offer you safety, security and a life free of risk. We need not be enemies. We are kin, you and I. We are messengers. We shall always be feared, always mistrusted, but there is much we could achieve together. I desire order and justice, to build a world where men are controlled for their own good, and the wildness of nature is tamed, and freed from the Eldar's hostile influence. That is a worthy aim, a noble aim. If you take your place by my side, you shall be worshipped, and your thoughts shall guide the actions of men for generations to come.'

Visions of power quickened Elowen's heart: commanding armies, the rampaging black unicorn. And revenge upon those who had wronged her, like Bishop Serapion. She would be wise, just and vengeful.

Lord Lucien placed his hands on her shoulders. 'Join with me, child. Finish the task that your mother started.'

The mention of her mother broke the spell. Everything Elowen had aspired to be was undone, overturned. She had wanted, more than anything, to be like her mother, but now she knew her mother personified everything she hated, everything she had struggled against. She did not want to be the same. She glanced behind and saw the three doorways. She knew what lay on the other side of them. 'I'd die before joining with you.'

426

Elowen stepped back so that she stood beneath the elaborate rectangular frame of the middle doorway. Cold air played along the back of her neck. The roar of rushing water pounded in her ears. She was not afraid. Here, at last, she was in control. She was not doing the bidding of Lord Lucien, nor of Rubens, nor of anyone else. It was her decision. She took another step back. Too late, Lord Lucien realised what she was doing. He shouted, 'NO!'

*

She is gone.

Lord Lucien looked down at the dark angry river. Tears stung the tender skin of his cheeks.

She is gone.

He was alone, isolated, lost. There had been within him a flicker of something warm, but now it had died, leaving an empty, dark and cold place. Elowen had slipped through his fingers again; he had reached out and lost her. She had been strong. Lucien knew they could have achieved so much together. Had he said too much? Had he tried too hard to persuade her?

He tried to block out such weak thoughts. The girl had made her choice. Yes, she was strong, but also immature and sentimental. Her misguided, childish attachment to her friends had led to her death. Without such distractions, she would have seen, would have *understood*, where her true destiny lay. She would not have thrown her life away so needlessly, so foolishly.

Lord Lucien looked down at the clay tablet. His path was

clear now. He needed to return to the Ulsacro, both to prepare his armies for the battles to come and to unlock the secrets of the Mystery. He decided to leave a small detachment of Redeemers in Erdene, under the command of Brother Malchus, enough to cleanse the temple of heretics, as well as ensuring that the vain, ignorant, greedy Sukhbataar Khan remembered his bargain. He knew the Oroks could not be trusted. Under the rule of Sukhbataar Khan they were weak. They had a latent strength of course, but with such a timorous leader, their power and ferocity ebbed away. Lord Lucien hoped to keep the Oroks under control until finally, one day, eliminating them forever. That day of reckoning, of cleansing, would surely come. He looked forward to seeing Erdene as a smoking ruin.

As for Elowen's friends, he would leave them to the khan, who was sure to carry out their execution with sadistic pleasure. They deserved such a fate. Yes, they would howl, they would curse and threaten, but all their words and actions were in vain. Only at the very end, as the shadow of death loomed over them, impenetrable, all-consuming, would they learn the price for opposing the Holy rule of Prester John.

He pocketed the clay tablet. The pain of Elowen's loss still jabbed at him but, with a patience and self-control perfected over many years, he pushed it aside. His Master needed him. He would set off for the Ulsacro. He sensed momentous days were ahead, and that he faced great challenges. He would not fail.

*

Elowen fell backwards. Air rushed around her, too quickly for her to breathe. She hit the water; an icy explosion co-cooned her whole body. She sank fast, the currents dragging her down. This was the end. Her brain played its last actions: she heard Black Francis laugh and saw Bo's shy smile. And she saw Lárwita and Diggory, frightened, abandoned, at the enemy's mercy. The vision of her friends sparked energy within her. She could not abandon them; she had to fight to save them. She struggled, battling the currents with every sinew, with every breath.

She broke the surface, the stale air sweeter than any spring breeze. She cried out; not a cry of fear or anger, but a primal cry, a new-born cry to announce the arrival of life into the world. Straining with all her strength, she clambered back onto the bank, close to the bridge that crossed over the underground river. Wet and shivering with cold, she looked up at the ledge. There was no sign of Lord Lucien. He had gone.

Burilgi Maa. The name stabbed her. Her mother was *Burilgi Maa.* She tried to convince herself that Lord Lucien lied, but the effort failed. His words had sounded like the truth. She touched the pendant, feeling a fresh pang of pain. She had measured every decision, every action, against what she expected her mother would have done or thought. Now Elowen realised that following her mother's example would only lead to becoming everything she wanted to avoid, everything she hated. *She is a part of you.*

No. She is part of me but I don't need to be like her.

Elowen remembered her friends. Their lives were still in

jeopardy. She wiped the tears from her eyes, stretched her aching, bruised limbs and climbed.

She soon reached the ledge and, still shivering, picked her way back through the labyrinth. Water dripped in a pit-patter from her sodden clothes. Her damp boots squelched. She walked almost in a trance. The golden threads surrounded her, faint wisps that created enough light for her to see where she was going. They energised her body, gave her fresh strength. Her skin prickled and tingled. Her every sense was razor-sharp. Insects and spiders scurried and scratched. She detected different smells on the currents of air that drifted through the labyrinth. Elowen had no plan, no purpose other than finding her friends.

She found her way back to the vestibule and raced up the stairs. To her relief the hatch was still open. The fog had cleared to leave a bright day and Elowen blinked in the sunlight. A crude wooden gallows loomed in front of her. Arigh Nasan, Batu, Lárwita and Diggory stood on stools, nooses around their necks. They were about to be executed. Sukhbataar Khan, the Kushiku guards and several Redeemers stood around the gallows, as did Qutugh who waited with his head lowered, wiping tears from his eyes. Elowen spotted Krukis lurking in the shadows. There was no sign of Lord Lucien.

Something alerted the khan to her presence. He gasped in surprise and said, 'Lord Lucien said he saw you die!'

'Then I must be a ghost,' said Elowen. 'Let them all go.'

'You are in no position to threaten me, *child*,' said Sukhbataar Khan. 'How do you expect to rescue your friends?'

The earth trembled and cracks streaked around Elowen's feet. A large patch of ground lifted as though pushed up from underneath. The twisting, churning soil took shape, moving to form arms, legs, a torso and a head. It was the Malign Sleeper. He stood fully-grown and roared, shaking the temple walls. The heaving, grinding ground toppled the gallows and Elowen's friends fell with it, winded, bruised but still alive. The sight of the creature was too much for the khan. He fled, closely followed by the Kushiku, who tossed aside their weapons to hasten their escape.

However, the Redeemers were not so easily daunted. Two of them charged the creature. The Malign Sleeper smashed his massive fists down onto them, leaving their bodies broken and twisted like squashed insects.

Elowen ran to her friends. Arigh Nasan and Batu picked up swords abandoned by the Kushiku. Lárwita and Diggory floundered under chunks of broken wood and rope. With Qutugh's help, Elowen managed to free them but both were dazed and shaken. A deep cut across Diggory's forehead leaked blood into his eyes.

While some of the Redeemers fought against the Malign Sleeper, the others rallied to attack Elowen and her friends. Arigh Nasan and Batu faced them with their swords drawn. The Oroks fought savagely, thrusting and parrying; the metallic clashing of metal blades echoed around the courtyard. One Redeemer slipped between Arigh Nasan and Batu and ran at Elowen, swinging his sword above his head, ready to strike. Elowen sidestepped his blow, feeling the blade's draught as it slashed close to her face. She caught a glimpse of a Kushiku sword half buried in the dust. She ducked down and grabbed the hilt. Elowen parried the Redeemer's next blow with the sword and he stepped backwards in surprise at the unexpected resistance. He snarled something unintelligible and attacked again but, with her body and instincts sharpened and tempered by Baba Yaga, Elowen was a match for his every move. The Redeemer was stronger but impatience got the better of him. He overstretched and stumbled. It was enough. Elowen drove her sword into his throat. The blade snapped in two, the tip-end impaled. Elowen froze, left aghast by the grisly slaying.

A sudden wind sucked up dust and stones into a twisting tube, which divided Elowen and her friends from the Redeemers. The dust created a shape and, to Elowen's astonishment, Itugen stood in front of her, alive and unharmed. She raised her arms, around which golden threads formed pulsating rings. The ground ripped open again and most of the Redeemers that had been fighting Arigh Nasan and Batu tumbled down into the fissure, grasping vainly at the breaking soil before they disappeared. The few Redeemers that survived retreated, only to run into the Malign Sleeper. Their blades of Cold Iron were useless against him. Using his fists like mighty hammers, he crushed each one in turn.

Once the clouds of dust settled, Arigh Nasan, helped by Batu and Itugen, searched the courtyard, poking the corpses of the Redeemers with swords to check they were truly dead. The Malign Sleeper stood motionless, arms by his side, his hands still curled into fists.

Elowen and Qutugh stayed with the two boys. Diggory looked whey-faced; his wound was shallow but bled freely. Lárwita and the shaman helped him to sit upright.

'Where am I?' said Diggory. 'Elowen? The Redeemers…they…told us you were dead. I never believed them. I knew you'd pull through.'

'It's all right, you'll be safe now,' said Elowen to reassure him. She became aware of movement in the shadows behind them. It was Krukis. He brandished a knife and his eyes smouldered with malice.

Bravely, Qutugh stood up to him. 'Your treachery has caused enough damage. Go from this place and never return.'

Krukis laughed and felled the shaman with a punch to the jaw. He pointed to Diggory and his lips formed a maniacal smile. 'It's you I want, boy, not this shaman. I warned you that one day you'd be sorry you crossed me. Well, that day has arrived, or the devil fetch me.'

Elowen screamed. Krukis lunged at Diggory, aiming his knife at the boy's heart. Lárwita threw himself in front of Krukis, taking the blade intended for Diggory. Krukis stood still, a dumb expression of anger, confusion and surprise on his face. Lárwita dropped like a felled tree and lay face first on the ground, a growing pool of blood emerging from underneath his body.

Elowen gently rolled Lárwita over. The knife had pierced his chest causing a terrible injury. His skin became cold, mottled and clammy, and his breathing was rapid and shallow. Elowen cradled him. 'What have you done, Krukis?'

'This is all your fault,' said Krukis, pointing at Elowen accusingly. 'The khan is sure to reward me if I kill you next.'

'You have done enough killing,' said another voice. Arigh Nasan appeared behind Krukis. The Orok was breathing

433

heavily and an angry gash ran the length of his right arm but his sword was ready. 'You'll die for your treachery.'

Krukis lifted his arms to protect himself but he was too slow and Arigh Nasan hacked him down. Arigh Nasan dropped his sword and knelt to examine the boy's wound. He shook his head. 'He is beyond my aid. I heard your scream and came as fast as I could. I wish I had been swifter.'

Lárwita spoke, choking out his words. 'I'm so cold. Don't leave me, Elowen, I'm afraid.'

'I won't leave you, I promise,' she said, blinded by tears. Then, his breathing stopped and he lay still in Elowen's arms. Lárwita was dead. It did not seem real. She expected his eyes to open any moment, for that slight, shy smile to warm up his face but it did not happen.

Diggory crawled next to her. 'Lárwita saved my life. Krukis wanted to kill me. It's my fault.'

'No, you are not to blame,' said Arigh Nasan. 'Lárwita gave his life to save you. He was a true friend and a loyal, brave companion.'

Batu returned, his face red with exertion. When he noticed Lárwita, he closed his eyes and exhaled, shock and grief written on his face. He helped Qutugh to get up. The shaman looked woozy, and he rubbed his red, swollen jaw.

Diggory wiped away tears. 'What do we do now?'

Before anyone answered, Itugen approached, trailed by the hulking, silent Malign Sleeper. The Elemental said, 'Misery and grief hangs over you all. Painful is your loss.'

'I thought…I thought you were dead,' said Elowen, wiping her eyes.

434

'A sword forged from Cold Iron is a fearsome weapon, even to Elementals,' said Itugen. 'Yet, I am not as easy to slay as Lord Lucien supposed.'

'Are we sure that the enemy has gone?' said Arigh Nasan, eyeing Itugen and the Malign Sleeper suspiciously.

'Yes, but much of the temple is ruined and many shamans have been murdered,' said Qutugh, still rubbing his jaw.

'What about Lord Lucien?' said Elowen, chilled by the very sound of his name on her tongue.

'He took flight as soon as he emerged from the labyrinth,' said Batu. 'He only tarried long enough to order our execution, a task Sukhbataar Khan was all too eager to carry out.'

'Lord Lucien has the Mystery,' said Elowen.

'Then I guess that is why he left,' said Arigh Nasan, as he bandaged his own wound. 'There was nothing more you could have done.'

'And at least he believes you are dead, Elowen,' said Batu. 'That may prove fortunate.'

'Yes, that may be so,' said Arigh Nasan. 'Lord Lucien is a blight upon this earth. He has brought evil, murder and terror to a place of peace.'

'Sukhbataar Khan is also to blame,' said Qutugh. 'It is the sacred duty of any khan to protect Bai Ulgan. Instead, he betrayed his own people to Lord Lucien. For that crime alone, he is unworthy to be the khan. He must be challenged for the right to rule our people. The khan must undergo the ancient trial of the Halz Tulaan.'

'Who would dare to challenge him?' said Batu.

Qutugh pointed at Arigh Nasan. 'He must do this, as he should have done many years ago.'

435

'I do not wish to be khan,' said Arigh Nasan without looking up. 'I have no desire to be a tyrant.'

'Then do not become one,' said Qutugh. 'Tyrants are not born to follow such a path; they choose it out of weakness and expediency.'

'That is the path my father took.'

'But you are not your father, Arigh Nasan,' said Qutugh. 'Sukhbataar is not worthy to rule. If you do not accept the Halz Tulaan then you condemn your people to more suffering.'

Arigh Nasan took a deep breath and stood, cradling his wounded arm. 'I shall think on this, but let Sukhbataar stew in his palace tonight. I will decide tomorrow how best to deal with him. First, we must attend to the dead.'

*

Half-buried by brick fragments and smouldering wood, and surrounded by the corpses of his fellow Redeemers, Brother Malchus lay flat on his stomach, with his head lifted enough to spy on the child. He was in great pain; the wounds inflicted by the ungodly abomination summoned by the Elemental were deep. Yet he did not die. The Cold Iron embedded in his flesh sustained him, and he was strong.

Defeat was a fresh taste on his lips, and a bitter one. The abomination had been too strong. Malchus knew he had failed Lord Lucien. He did not expect forgiveness. He did not deserve forgiveness.

It pained Malchus to play dead, an act he considered, un-

436

der any other circumstances, too cowardly to contemplate. But he did not hide out of fear of death, for he possessed no such fear. To die in the service of Prester John would be an honour, a blessing. His decision to hide was motivated not by weakness but by a greater need—if he threw his life away then Lord Lucien may never learn that the girl had survived, and the Redeemer was certain his master needed to know that above all else. Malchus did not know why the girl was so important. He did not need to know. If he delivered the message of the girl's survival to Lord Lucien he could accept his death as a just punishment for his failure. He praised God for giving him such an opportunity. How wondrous, he thought, to witness His mighty providence in action!

Malchus watched the girl as she followed the Oroks out of the courtyard. She was an instrument of the devil, along with her Orok and heretic accomplices. When all was quiet, the Redeemer muttered a prayer, rose to his feet and crept away. He knew that going down the stairway back into the city risked leaving him far too exposed to the enemy so he decided to climb down the other side of the hill. He dismissed the idea of asking Sukhbataar Khan for help. He could not be trusted. He had fled at the first sign of danger, a show of cowardice that deserved a brutal punishment.

Malchus was alone, but it did not matter. He gained strength from the glory of the Almighty. Lord Lucien was far away now, riding hard towards the Ulsacro. Malchus knew the Ulsacro lay hundreds of miles to the west. To reach it, he would have to cross barren moors, windblown wastes, deep forests and raging rivers. Yet he swore by the saints to endure any hardship and pain. He could not fail. He would not fail. He swore to fulfil the duty God had given him.

CHAPTER TWENTY-ONE

The Halz Tulaan

In a land made dark by night, the flames from the funeral pyre shone like beacons. The graveyard of Bai Ulgan lay outside the temple walls on the northern edge of the hill. The murdered shamans had all been covered from head to toe with shrouds of white silk and placed, with their heads pointing north, on a pyre of logs and branches doused in oil. Qutugh and the surviving shamans had performed many rites and blessings before lighting the pyre. They sang songs and recited prayers, their words making no literal sense to Elowen but they evoked feelings of great loss within her. The fire spread rapidly, swallowing the shrouded corpses.

Elowen and her companions watched the ceremony in silence. Itugen stood behind them, her head bowed. The Malign Sleeper had returned to the earth; he had completed the task for which Itugen had summoned him.

'The fire is pure and cleansing,' said Arigh Nasan as the ceremony unfolded. 'It allows the spirits of the dead to rise to heaven without desecration.'

Elowen could not take her eyes off the shrouded body of Lárwita. He had not been placed on the pyre but left beside

439

a rectangular grave dug by Arigh Nasan and Batu. Unlike the shamans he was to be buried not cremated, a funeral in keeping with the customs of his native Volkgard. Elowen was no stranger to death, but the loss of Lárwita defied her understanding, she could find no way to absorb the knowledge of his death, no way to make sense of it. It was as though she stood within a dream, watching ghosts of people she knew act out a macabre performance. She thought back to moments she had shared with Lárwita; light words and laughter, all empty now, hollow and meaningless, like beautiful dreams shattered by the harsh light of waking.

When Qutugh finished the blessing for the shamans, he said to Elowen and her friends, 'The time has come to bury your friend.'

Elowen nodded, her eyes watery with tears. She held Lárwita's book, finding a strange comfort in doing so. Arigh Nasan and Batu carried Lárwita, and slowly lowered him into the grave. Qutugh said, 'Go now into eternal rest, to dwell forever within the arms of the earth.'

Elowen could watch no more. Diggory sniffed and without hesitating, she embraced him; he held her tightly, sobbing as she sobbed. They did not speak, words were nothing, meant nothing. Elowen took comfort from the embrace, a confirmation she was not alone in her suffering.

When the ceremony was over Elowen felt a hand on her shoulder. It was Itugen. 'Will you walk with me for a little while, Elowen? I promise not to keep you from your friends for long.'

They walked without sharing a word. The night air was

440

frosty, the sky pinpricked with stars. Elowen's teeth chattered. Itugen strolled as though enjoying a walk on a summer's day. The Elemental stopped by a weathered marble statue of a woman holding a goblet to her chest. Itugen ran her fingers over the statue and smiled sadly at Elowen. 'In great distress you are, child.'

Elowen wiped her eyes. 'Everything has gone wrong. The sanctuary is destroyed. Lord Lucien murdered Baba Yaga, and now Lárwita is dead too.'

'All true, but you cannot spend your life standing by your friend's grave. You must carry on.'

'How can I just carry on? I've never asked for any of this. Why is it my duty to find this damn tree? I've done enough. I don't care any more. Lárwita is dead. All the things he could have done, all his hopes, all his ideas, all his plans, they're gone forever.'

'And that is why you have to carry on,' said Itugen. 'To surrender to grief and despair helps neither you nor your friend. Honour your friend's sacrifice by living your life to the fullest. Remember him in all you do, take strength from his memory. Be thankful for the time you had with him, however brief. Be thankful for the friendship you shared, it is a gift beyond price. That way he lives on.'

'It hurts so much. And I feel guilty because I survived. Lárwita and Baba Yaga were killed because of me, if I hadn't known them they'd still be alive.'

Itugen's eyes narrowed. 'You are not to blame for their deaths.'

'Perhaps Lord Lucien is right. He said that all evil comes from people. Why should I fight to save them?'

'With great sadness have I watched many of the deeds of men. Yet to lose all hope is a mistake. There is goodness in the hearts of many of your kind. Hope endures, even when all seems lost.'

'How can you talk of *hope*? The Mystery was the last hope, the very last hope. Lord Lucien has won. Prester John has won.'

Itugen laughed. 'If Lord Lucien believes he has won victory for his master then he has much to learn. It will take him no short time to discover the secret of the second Mystery.'

'But he will find it, eventually.'

'Ah, yes, but you will discover it first, child.'

'How? Without the first Mystery it's impossible.'

Itugen shook her head. 'By passing the test of the labyrinth you earned the reward of the first Mystery, and Lord Lucien cannot deprive you of that.'

'I don't understand.'

'I would be surprised if you did, child,' said Itugen. She placed her hands on Elowen's head. 'Close your eyes, feel the Earthsoul flow through you. Let me guide you and do not be afraid. Let me show you the knowledge Lord Lucien seeks.'

The features of the world around Elowen disappeared. She stood in a blank space, surrounded by grey mist. A shape formed in the mist. A spider the size of a large dog. It scuttled towards her and stopped. Hundreds of eyes. Long hairy legs. A thick, bumpy, bulbous body. Elowen trembled in fear but she could not run away. Something, some invisible force, held her still.

The spider spoke to her in a voice that sounded like

Itugen's, although each word echoed. 'A journey is before you. My steed you shall be.'

With Elowen unable to move, the spider bound her in the soft, clinging bonds of its web. Then, it wrapped its warm, sticky legs around her, the stiff hairs like a brush on Elowen's skin.

They lifted from the ground. Elowen had the sensation of floating, drifting like a feather toyed with by a warm breeze. Strange shades and colours revolved around her. Slowly they took shape.

The mist cleared. Land passed far beneath them. Rivers, lush green plains and craggy hills. On and on they flew, west, always west. A vast forest, like a sea of emerald green, stretched to the horizon. They lowered, plunging down into the forest. The spider unwrapped its grip on Elowen. The sticky web broke away. Elowen stood at the foot of a hill with steep sides and a flat top. Crows cried mournfully. The cool wind caressed her cheeks. A light flickered at the top of the hill, a glow of red and orange. Metal tinkered on metal.

'You have been shown the way,' said the spider.

The mist returned. The forest vanished. The spider vanished. Elowen realised she was still on Bai Ulgan; Itugen was still standing in front of her.

Her mind spinning, Elowen said, 'What happened to me?'

'There are many gateways to wisdom, strange though they may seem to you.'

'The spider, was it…real, or was it a dream?'

'Is there a difference?'

'Well, whatever it was, I thought that it…the spider, was

443

trying to show me something,' said Elowen, shuddering at the memory of its warm, sticky grip.

'It was, for you have seen the Ogonberg, the resting place of the second Mystery, the element of fire,' said Itugen. 'That is your reward. I have shown you the way. You must now journey west to Varna, the ancient country of the Brisings, and search for the Ogonberg. What you have seen will, I hope, take Lord Lucien many long days to discover. But I do not prophesise. The future is uncertain, not even we Elementals, who have lived since the earth was born, know what the days to come will bring. A great burden is placed upon you. I fear you face hardships and many difficult choices, but you are stronger than you know.'

'I don't feel strong. I'm more frightened than I've ever been. Everything Lord Lucien said scares me. He said that my mother was his ally, his friend, and that she was the *Burilgi Maa.*'

Itugen pondered that for a moment. 'Even if what Lord Lucien says is true, you do not have to follow the same path as your mother, you are not compelled to make the same choices. She does not guide your destiny—that is for you to make. Now, I have served my purpose. I cannot tarry with mortals. I leave you now and return to the earth. I wish you good fortune and the blessings of the ancestors. Farewell, brave Elowen, so much depends on you.'

The Elemental bowed and walked away, slowly dissolving in the darkness.

Elowen stood, motionless, locked in thought. The moon and lively stars gave the darkened landscape a frosty sheen. The world seemed so large—she was an insignificant speck

444

on its endless canvas. How could she complete the quest before her? She wanted to run away to a place where she was not being hunted, where she did not fear for her life every moment of every day. But she knew there was no such place. She had believed the sanctuary was safe, a place hidden and protected from danger and fear. But hiding from danger had not made it go away.

The words of Lord Lucien haunted her. *Would men herald you as their saviour? Or would suspicion, jealously and hatred grip their hearts?* The answers to those questions terrified her. And what would Arigh Nasan think if he learnt that she was the daughter of *Burilgi Maa*, the scourge of the Oroks? She had never felt so alone.

*

Qutugh allowed Elowen and the remainder of the company to sleep in a small antechamber of the temple. There was no fire and a sneaky draught blew underneath the ill-fitting door. Frightening papier-mâché masks hung on the wall. Brass statues were mounted in each corner of the room: two male and two female figures, all decorated with crowns, earrings and curvilinear scroll patterns. Elowen found them eerily lifelike and disturbing.

Arigh Nasan remained awake all night. He sat in a chair, smoking his pipe and staring out of the window. He had recovered his scimitar and it lay across his lap. Elowen finally drifted into a hateful, fitful doze haunted by memories of Lord Lucien, the Malign Sleeper and of Lárwita's pale, lifeless face. Dreams came to her. She rode across a corpse-

445

strewn battlefield. A thousand fires smouldered. Torn flags fluttered and flapped like birds tied to the ground. She looked down. Her steed was not a horse but a unicorn, with a black coat and a horn sharpened to a deadly point. Hordes of warriors chanted as she rode past, their faces shadowy, indistinct. Chants of *Burilgi Maa, Burilgi Maa…*

Elowen sat bolt upright in bed, sweat-soaked, the chanting still reverberating in her head. She looked at Arigh Nasan. He smiled at her kindly, reassuringly, despite his tired, haggard eyes. She settled back down to sleep.

As the first light of day crept through the window and the cracks in the doorframe, Arigh Nasan, who looked drawn and pensive, roused the company. 'Time to go outside, my friends.'

Qutugh was waiting for them in the courtyard. He approached Arigh Nasan and said, 'Have you made your decision?'

'I have decided to go to the palace. I say no more.'

Qutugh winced and bit his lip. 'Then I shall accompany you. A shaman has not stepped off this hill for generations beyond count. Yet I feel certain that the ancestors will forgive me. The circumstances demand it.'

'I believe they do,' said Arigh Nasan. 'Elowen, it is safer for you and Diggory to remain here.'

'No, we're coming with you,' said Elowen. 'We're part of this too. Isn't that right, Diggory?'

Diggory scratched his head. 'Aye, I guess so.'

Arigh Nasan bowed. 'You both honour me, although stay close, Sukhbataar Khan's pride will have been wounded and a wounded beast is always dangerous.'

Led by Qutugh, Elowen and her companions picked their way down the dizzying plunge of the stairway and back into the bustling city. The sight of the chief shaman astonished all onlookers. Crowds parted to allow the company to pass. Even the throaty cries of traders were silenced. Some of the Oroks fell to their knees and prayed while others reached out to touch Qutugh's robes.

Elowen walked at Arigh Nasan's shoulder, fearful of the pressing crowd. 'Why are they acting this way?'

'For Qutugh to leave the temple and walk among the people is unprecedented,' said Arigh Nasan.

'I see. Are we really going back to the khan's palace?'

'Yes, that is my intention.'

'And you will fight Sukhbataar Khan?'

'Such things are not yet decided.'

'But you can beat him, can't you? Even with your arm hurt, you can still beat him?'

He squinted at the bright sun. 'Nothing is certain, child.'

*

Within the Hall of Great Brightness, Sukhbataar Khan waited. He stood at the far end of the hall, flanked by Kushiku guards. Among them, Elowen realised, was the enormous Orok she had seen when they first visited the hall, the Orok with the unblinking eyes. He was armed and armoured—ready for battle. Courtiers huddled half-hidden in shadowy corners, whispering nervously.

Diggory tugged on Elowen's sleeve. 'Do you think that Arigh Nasan is going to fight the khan?'

447

'I don't know,' said Elowen.

'I hope he does. He's as much to blame for Lárwita's murder as Krukis was. I hope Arigh Nasan kills him.'

'But Arigh Nasan is injured.'

'He'll beat the khan one-handed if he has to,' said Diggory.

As they drew closer to Sukhbataar Khan, Elowen thought Diggory's confidence well placed. The khan appeared diminished in size, his face grey and drawn. If it came to a fight, surely he was no match for Arigh Nasan?

They stopped in front of the dais. The khan gazed at them blankly. Elowen thought she detected the very faintest of smiles but dismissed it; it must have been a twitch, a sign of fear.

Qutugh placed his right hand on his chest and bowed. 'I speak now in the Common Tongue so that all present can understand. To be khan is to have the fate of the people in your hands. There can be no greater bond of trust and it is a bond that you, Sukhbataar Khan, broke when you sided with Lord Lucien, the chief servant of our greatest foe, Prester John. In accordance with our ancient laws, we declare that your right to hold the title of khan must be disputed. You must face the challenge of the Halz Tulaan. Is there anyone in this hall who accepts the challenge?'

The hall was silent. Nobody moved. Arigh Nasan remained still and Elowen feared he was going to say nothing, do nothing. After an agonising delay, he stepped forward. 'I accept the challenge.'

Qutugh gave a deep sigh of relief.

'So the traitor is unmasked,' said Sukhbataar Khan. 'As

448

soon as you returned to this city I divined your true purpose, Arigh Nasan. You wish to usurp me, to make amends for the cowardice of your past. But do not think that I shall step aside lightly. Tell me, shaman, is it not true that the ancient laws you speak of allow one that is challenged to the Halz Tulaan to appoint a champion to fight on their behalf?'

Qutugh shuffled and cleared his throat. 'Yes, that is so.'

Slowly, deliberately, savouring the moment, the khan pointed to the huge Orok. 'Then I appoint Chinua to fight on my behalf.'

Elowen cried out. She looked at Diggory; his mouth was open in shock.

Qutugh toyed with his staff. 'Arigh Nasan, do you accept this contest?'

'Yes, I accept,' he said.

'Then we must commence,' said Qutugh, more than a little reluctantly. 'The Halz Tulaan is a fight until one of you yields, or is slain. The victor shall be declared khan, and shall also decide the fate of the vanquished, if he survives the contest. The law states that punishment must be either exile or death. Are these terms understood?'

Arigh Nasan nodded.

'I understand,' said Sukhbataar Khan. He grinned at Arigh Nasan. 'I look forward to adding your skull to the tower outside my city.'

'Let me take your place,' Elowen heard Batu whisper to Arigh Nasan, 'You are injured—'

'No,' said Arigh Nasan. 'This challenge is mine alone.'

Qutugh instructed everyone to back away and clear a

space in the middle of the hall. With his scimitar drawn, Arigh Nasan waited. Chinua approached, looming over him as an adult looms over a child. He carried a huge sword. Without warning, he launched an attack. He held the sword vertical and brought a cutting blow down towards Arigh Nasan, who just managed to lift his scimitar above his head in time to parry. Chinua swung a horizontal cut. Arigh Nasan moved his scimitar to the left side of his body and deflected the blow. The sounds of clashing steel reverberated around the hall.

The two Oroks circled each other warily. Elowen barely dared to breathe as she watched them. Arigh Nasan looked slow and pained by his wounded arm. Chinua, his eyes still unblinking, licked his lips like a predator tracking an injured, weakened prey. The huge Orok attacked again, a downward cut to his opponent's right leg. Arigh Nasan countered the blow but in doing so lost his grip on his scimitar; it skittered across the floor and out of reach. Elowen tried to cry out but no sound came from her dry mouth. Arigh Nasan stood still. Unarmed, he was now at the mercy of Chinua.

'KILL HIM!' said the khan, his eyes wide with triumph.

Arigh Nasan lowered his head, ready for the killing blow but Chinua bowed and retreated several paces. Arigh Nasan stared at him, disbelieving, wary of a trick. Then he walked over to his scimitar and picked it up.

'What madness is this?' said Sukhbataar. 'Have you lost your wits, Chinua? Attack him, you fool.'

Chinua spoke in the Orok tongue, his voice slow and heavy.

'What did he say?' Elowen asked Batu.

450

'That there's no honour in killing an unarmed opponent.'

Arigh Nasan bowed to Chinua and the duel recommenced. Despite his chivalry, Chinua attacked more fiercely than ever. Blows rained in from right and left, which Arigh Nasan struggled to contain. Angry sparks flew as the two blades met. Arigh Nasan lurched back drunkenly, as though every ounce of his strength had been spent. Elowen wanted to help him, to fight alongside him but she knew it was impossible. He fought alone. He would die alone.

'You are beaten, Arigh Nasan!' said Sukhbataar Khan. 'Death awaits you, traitor.'

The khan's words further emboldened Chinua and he made a thrust at the centre of Arigh Nasan's torso, his whole body lunging forward. He was unbalanced; Arigh Nasan reacted instantly. He deflected Chinua's attack with a tight downward cut and shoulder-barged him. Chinua fell onto his back and Arigh Nasan brought the tip of the blade to his throat. 'Do you yield?'

Elowen perceived no fear in Chinua's eyes, only a look of resignation, of defeat. The giant Orok nodded once; he was beaten. Arigh Nasan withdrew his sword and helped Chinua to his feet. He had won.

Elowen's heart soared with relief and joy. Flinging aside formality and reserve, she ran over to Arigh Nasan and embraced him. He grunted with pain as she excitedly squeezed his injured arm but laughed nonetheless.

'I was so worried,' said Elowen. 'I thought he was too strong for you.'

Arigh Nasan laughed again. 'He was too strong. I was fortunate. Perhaps fate does intervene from time to time.'

451

Elowen looked up at the dais. Sukhbataar Khan stood as still as stone, his mouth agape in shock, his face pasty white.

Qutugh stepped forward, shaking with excitement. 'I declare Arigh Nasan the victor of the Halz Tulaan and the new khan. It is his first duty to pass sentence on the vanquished.'

Arigh Nasan looked weary beyond words and blood seeped from several small cuts and grazes. 'Chinua fought with honour in the best traditions of our people. He is free to choose his own path, but I offer him a place in the Kushiku.'

Chinua bowed, signalling his acceptance.

'And what of Sukhbataar?' said Qutugh. 'His life is in your hands.'

Arigh Nasan took a deep breath. 'I do not wish to take that life. Exile is his punishment. Sukhbataar shall be denied food, water, fire and shelter within forty miles of Erdene. Such is my decree.'

'This is cruelty dressed up as mercy,' said Sukhbataar. 'You shall rule as a tyrant, just as your father ruled. One day it will be your turn to be vanquished in the Halz Tulaan.'

Arigh Nasan ignored the insult. 'If I become a tyrant then I pray my people are wise enough to overthrow me.'

'The khan's judgement has been given,' said Qutugh. 'The sentence is passed. You must go now.'

Sukhbataar turned to the courtiers and the Kushiku guards. 'Who will accompany me?'

Silence greeted his question.

Sukhbataar looked around in astonishment. 'Have I not been a generous khan? A giver of gifts? The builder of this splendid palace? You owe everything to me. Without me you would be nomads like those primitive tribes to the east. Where is your loyalty now?'

'You taste the fruit of your weakness and treachery,' said Qutugh.

Sukhbataar threw the shaman a hateful look before descending the dais and striding down the hall. He passed within two feet of Arigh Nasan. Elowen saw the shape of his hand beneath his robes. By instinct, she blocked out all other sounds. Fingernails gently tapped on steel, steel being drawn from leather. As though time slowed around her, she watched as Sukhbataar pulled a dagger from his robes and stabbed at Arigh Nasan. She did not have time to think. She grabbed Sukhbataar's wrist. She felt a stinging pain in her hand, but, surprised by Elowen's sudden move, Sukhbataar lost his grip on the knife and it dropped to the floor. Chinua rushed at Sukhbataar, thrust his scimitar into the defeated khan's chest. Sukhbataar made no sound. He did not cry out. He did not scream. He staggered forward, one, two, three steps and dropped down dead. A terrible silence, a silence of shock, filled the hall.

'I wish this had not happened,' said Arigh Nasan. 'Sukhbataar brought this doom upon himself but I did not wish to see the spilling of Orok blood.'

His words sounded distant to Elowen. She inspected her hand and blanched: a deep cut scythed across her palm. Her vision became blurred. All strength left her legs. She heard her name being cried out, faint, distant…

*

The cooing of pigeons. Ducks quacking. The chatter of starlings. Elowen opened her eyes, unlocking another sense. She looked up at a plain ceiling and walls covered in paintings of soft peaks, watery clouds and shadowy figures, all framed with silk brocades. Behind her, an open window allowed sweet, fresh morning air to flow in.

Elowen realised she was in a low bed and that Arigh Nasan was sitting on a chair beside it. His arms were bandaged, his face puffy and bruised. 'Do not exert yourself. The wound to your hand is deep and may take some time to heal.'

'My wound?' said Elowen, still feeling groggy. She looked at her right hand; it was heavily bandaged.

'Have you forgotten already? You saved my life. If you had not moved so swiftly, Sukhbataar's blade would have dealt me a mortal blow. Your hand deflected his dagger and in so doing you were injured. You swooned, through shock and loss of blood. You will be left with a scar, I fear.'

Memories of the Halz Tulaan poured back to Elowen. She fidgeted uncomfortably in her bed.

'Slight in stature you may be, child, but you displayed speed and dexterity worthy of any Orok warrior's boasts,' continued Arigh Nasan. 'Much that Grunewald said about you now makes sense. Indeed you are special.'

Elowen blushed. 'I was lucky, that's all.'

'Luck is not the word I choose to use,' said Arigh Nasan, leaning back in his chair.

'What of the others? Diggory? Batu?' she said, almost adding Lárwita's name before bitter memory stopped the word in her mouth. His little leather-bound book lay on the table beside her bed.

'All are safe for the present,' he said. 'They are resting too, but have been greatly anxious about you, since the events of yesterday.'

'*Yesterday*?' said Elowen, rubbing sleep from her eyes.

'You have slumbered for many hours.'

Elowen took a few moments to absorb that. She pointed at Arigh Nasan's bandages. 'You were injured too.'

'My wounds pain me but they are not mortal,' he said with a wink. 'We Oroks have good physicians, much better than those in the west.'

Elowen sat up. 'So you are the khan now?'

'Yes, though only by dint of an ancient custom, and by my skill with a blade. I have been given the title of khan, but I have not yet earned it.'

'You don't seem particularly pleased to be khan.'

'All my life I wished to escape my father's shadow, now it seems as though it has caught up with me.'

His words caused Elowen to shiver. She thought of her mother, the *Burilgi Maa*, who now cast such a shadow over her. 'Is it true what Sukhbataar said about your father being a tyrant?'

'Yes, I cannot deny it,' said Arigh Nasan, sounding as though he wanted to do just that.

'Was your father hated?'

'*Hated?* There have been few khans loved more. Great honour he bestowed on those loyal to him, though little pity he showed to all others, be they Orok or otherwise. He died peacefully in his bed, drunk I doubt not, having reached a

455

great age. There was no assassin's blade for my father, no defeat at the Halz Tulaan. With reverence he was sent to his ancestors and with much fondness he is remembered by my people, or at least by those that survived his rule; the dead speak not.'

'I find it hard to imagine anyone loving a tyrant.'

'The people loved him because he made them feel strong. For this, they overlooked his brutality. We ask too little of our leaders, it seems. I suppose I should admire him and bless his memory, but I cannot. For good or ill, I am not like him. But power does strange things to the mind; it can make the most unpalatable act seem like the sweetest kindness. It is an intoxicant, a drug, a bewitchment, and few are strong enough to resist it.'

'You are strong enough,' said Elowen.

'Only time will prove if you are right or wrong. Perhaps the very idea of there being a khan is a fundamental mistake. Perhaps it is too much power in the hands of one soul. Perhaps one day we might see a different kind of ruler in Gondwana, one chosen by the people, chosen for their wisdom and not for their war-skill. But forgive me; I talk of myself when I should be asking after your wellbeing.'

'I'm fine, it's just that… so much has happened, so much to take in.'

'Indeed it has. I can only imagine what you went through in the labyrinth. To have confronted Lord Lucien and survived, well, you are a marvel to me.'

Elowen felt words welling up inside her, a pressure that had to be relieved. 'Lord Lucien he…said things. Horrible things.'

456

'Do not trust the tongue of Lord Lucien.'

'But…I don't think he was lying to me.'

Arigh Nasan frowned. 'What did he say?'

Elowen took a deep breath. 'He said…he said that my mother was the *Burilgi Maa*.'

The Orok did not react. He stared out of the window. 'So, he told you. I feared he might.'

Elowen looked at him, open-mouthed. 'What do you mean? You knew who she was?'

He faced her again. 'Yes, I knew. Grunewald told me.'

'And about me being a messenger—'

'Yes, that too.'

'But what does it mean—'

'To me it means nothing,' he said. 'Your mother's sins were hers alone. You are not to blame for them, no more than I am to blame for my father's crimes. Yes, Burilgi Maa was terrible, a scourge of my people. But you are not her. I have seen this. In truth, I did not wholly trust you at first. I looked at you with prejudiced eyes. I saw you as tainted by the treachery of Rubens, and yes, perhaps tainted by your mother too. That was wrong of me. You are brave, you think of others before yourself, you have risked your life to save your friends, you risked your life to save *me*.'

Elowen cried. 'I thought…I thought—'

'You thought if I knew the truth I would break our friendship, punish you for your mother's evil. It is not so. I am honoured to be your friend. You are safe with me, although, caution dictates that you should not share the truth about your mother with anyone else here in Erdene. Batu knows, and I trust him completely, but tell no one else.'

457

Elowen wiped her eyes. 'I feel as though a burden has been lifted.'

'Then I am glad.'

'What…what was she like?' said Elowen, both desiring and dreading the answer.

'I saw her only once, in the field of battle. She was tall, her hair raven. I suppose some would call her beautiful, but if so, it was beauty mixed with terror and something else…'

'What else?'

'You must understand I saw her just once and from a distance. Perhaps my memory is faulty, but when I recall her, I always see sadness and suffering in her eyes. But above all, she was terrifying, none could withstand her in battle. We cursed her as a fiend, the devil made flesh, for through her control of the Earthsoul she could move rocks as though they were pebbles, rip trees from their roots and tear holes in the ground. Grunewald once said that she had been the strongest Adept of all, possessing a strength he had scarcely considered possible. Grunewald believed that your mother's suffering at the Church's hands caused her to reject all human comfort and friendship. She lived only for revenge and drifted away from the person she could have been, the person she should have been. Prester John snared her, by poisoning her with lies and corrupting her with power.'

'Grunewald told me I was nothing like my mother. I thought he was insulting me, now I realise he meant something else.'

'Yes he did. He knew your mother's history well. He saw the pain and terror she unleashed. Grunewald wanted to ensure you did not follow her path. He believed you would make wiser choices than your mother did. His last words to you were a compliment.'

There was a knock at the door. It opened and Batu entered. He smiled at Elowen. 'I heard voices. I thought you must be awake.'

The Orok was pushed through the door by someone bundling in behind him. It was Diggory. He beamed and dived onto the bed to hug her.

Arigh Nasan laughed. 'Be careful. You will crush her injured hand.'

'I can't hurt *her*, she's a messenger,' said Diggory. 'With all that she's survived I'm beginning to think she's indestructible.'

'If only,' said Elowen.

Arigh Nasan stood, grunting with pain as he did so. 'I am glad we are all together for there is something I wish to say. Elowen, I believe that soon you must leave here and continue your quest for the Tree of Life.'

Elowen nodded. She told them all about her vision and of her trance-like journey with the spider. 'Itugen showed me the way. Lord Lucien is hunting for the second Mystery; I have to find it before he does.'

Arigh Nasan said, 'I do not seek to dissuade you from this quest, for as dangerous as it is, I know it is of profound importance. Yet, I do desire to aid you in any way I can. Diggory, am I right in guessing you will continue to accompany Elowen?'

Diggory shifted his weight from one leg to the other. 'Yes, I've come this far, I'll see it through to the end.'

'That is good, but as brave as you both undoubtedly are, I

cannot let you go off alone. Varna is a land old by the reckoning of the Oroks. Once the civilisation of the Brisings thrived there, though what happened to them is lost to time. Now the southern reaches of the Altheart forest cover much of Varna, and is in places so dense that no sunlight pierces its canopy. Many are the songs and tales of Varna, and all chill the blood. Therefore, I have asked Batu to go with you.'

'And I shall go gladly,' Batu added.

Elowen smiled. She liked and trusted Batu. He was quiet, kind and dependable. She felt safer with him close. After digesting Arigh Nasan's description of Varna, she recognised that they needed all the help and protection they could get.

'What is more,' said Arigh Nasan, 'I have also asked Chinua to join you. A fiercer warrior I can scarcely imagine.'

That thought made Elowen nervous. She remembered the frightening Orok who had fought Arigh Nasan during the Halz Tulaan and she exchanged a worried look with Diggory.

'I failed you by misjudging Krukis, but Chinua is trustworthy and loyal,' said Arigh Nasan. 'Of course, I would go with you but I have to leave for Xural, the ancient capital of the Orok tribes, and I must go this very day, so this is also a farewell.'

'You're going away?' said Elowen.

'Yes, I have called a Kiyot, a gathering of the tribal leaders. It is my hope that many will come. I wish to unite the Orok tribes, for only then can we face the peril of Prester John with any chance of success. And that peril is real. You remember Vachir? After he aided our escape from Rynok-gorod he rode to Omphalos and then east here to Erdene. Worrying tidings he has brought with him, rumours of war and of Prester John mustering huge armies. The Eldar and remaining Illuminati are gathering but they are not great in number. A storm is brewing and soon it will break. If my wish is carried, the Oroks shall march west to Omphalos and then to war against Prester John. There are dark and momentous times ahead.'

'Every day seems to bring more hardship,' said Elowen.

'In such times, all are tested,' said Arigh Nasan. 'But, Elowen, I believe you are strong enough to meet the challenges before you. It has been an honour to journey at your side.'

'Thank you. I owe you my life. I was so wrong about the Oroks. The old stories, they were all nonsense.'

'Yes, there is good and bad in all people,' said Arigh Nasan. He stood, placed his right hand across his chest and bowed. 'Let us hope that in the days to come, it is good that prevails, however unlikely that seems at present. And I hope that whatever fates rule this world, they bring us together again, Elowen, one day.'

*

She is alive.

Lord Lucien stood in the Ulsacro's highest tower, pounded by the dusty winds sucked up from the Salvinian plains. *She is alive.* It was two hours since Brother Malchus had arrived at the palace and given him the news. The Redeemer

461

was half-dead, deranged, but Lord Lucien did not doubt his word. *She is alive.* A storm of emotions struck him: fury at his mistake, bewilderment at the manner of her escape, and, strangest of all, relief.

Lucien yelled, a primordial scream devoured by the howling wind. The effort ripped at his throat but it calmed him. All was not lost. He had the Mystery and believed he would soon discover its secrets. The Grand Army was ready. Hundreds of ships waited in the southern ports. Legions of troops waited at the border, ready to march. Prester John's plan was brave, arguably reckless, but Lord Lucien trusted his master. The plan would succeed.

He did not forget Elowen. Having her slip through his fingers again only increased his determination to find her. She was strong. She could be a threat. Lucien knew that he had to find her. He still hoped she would see sense. He still hoped she would join him in serving the glory of Prester John. But if she refused him again then she had to die. It was simple and that understanding brought him a little peace.

He looked out over the grim, granite mass of the Ulsacro. Lord Lucien knew that despite the elimination of the sanctuary, there were still enemies beyond the palace walls, enemies he needed to draw out from their hiding places. They plotted against Prester John and the Mother Church, but they would not prevail. The day of final reckoning was close.

*

Elowen stood over Lárwita's grave. Diggory was by her side, silent, his head bowed. The disturbed soil of the grave

462

was still fresh, damp and dark. Sunset drew close. The wind heralded the coming of winter, carrying whispered promises of snow and ice, even to the warmer lands of the south.

They were leaving the next day. Elowen's wound had not fully healed but they could delay no longer. They could not risk Lord Lucien finding the second Mystery. But Elowen had wanted to return to Lárwita's grave before they left Erdene, a desire so strong she had been willing once again to endure the vertiginous climb up the winding stairway to the summit of Bai Ulgan. Diggory had insisted on going with her. He helped her up the stairway, supporting her, encouraging her, never once complaining. Her wounded hand stung abominably, a pain that made her grind her teeth with discomfort, but that failed to stop her. She had to say goodbye.

Elowen knelt and gently pressed her fingertips into the moist soil. She felt guilty at the thought of leaving Lárwita behind. She knew he was gone forever, but the grave was so lonely, a forgotten patch of ground on a windswept hill in a foreign land. To walk away was to abandon him, to forget him. Then the words of Itugen returned to her: *you cannot spend your life standing by your friend's grave.* Elowen knew she had no choice but to carry on, to move forward. Without Lárwita, the journey would be harder but she would find a way to cope, a way to endure.

'I feel bad, you know,' said Diggory.

'What do you mean?'

'I mean about all the times I teased him. I did like him; he was my friend, a good friend. I couldn't have got through our imprisonment by the Society without him, and he saved

463

my life, twice. I never told him he was a good friend, and I should have.'

'You didn't need to, he knew,' said Elowen. She placed Lárwita's book down onto his grave.

Diggory cleared his throat. 'Are you sure you want to leave that here?'

'He always kept it with him. It belongs to him.'

'I know, but…perhaps others should read what he had discovered. He had so many good ideas. If we leave the book here it will rot away, and be lost and forgotten.'

Elowen knew he was right. Others should share his ideas. She reached forward and picked up the book, brushing the small clumps of soil from the cover and spine. She opened it and the sight of his scribbled writing and distinctive drawings brought tears to her eyes. Within those pages, he lived still.

Elowen closed the book, stood and looked to the west. She knew great struggles lay ahead. She touched her mother's pendant. It meant something different to her now. Once it had been a source of strength, of comfort. Now as her fingers stroked the curves of the pendant it reminded her of the dark path her mother had chosen. Elowen wanted to be different. She refused to submit meekly to a world shaped by Lord Lucien and Prester John. To defeat them required sacrifice. She knew that to fight for what she believed to be right risked pain, suffering and death. She understood and accepted that now. She would seek the remaining Mysteries, whatever the peril.

Without a word, Diggory placed an arm around her shoulders. Elowen looked at him through watery eyes, and

464

saw that he too was weeping. Elowen took heart from Diggory, and from all her friends. She needed them. They had protected her, risked their lives for her and asked for nothing in return. She took strength from her memories of Lárwita, memories of his wisdom, kindness and friendship. She remembered others too: Grunewald, Hyllebaer and Baba Yaga. In their different ways, they had all tried to help her, tried to guide her, tried to protect her. They were a part of her, a strong part. Lord Lucien was wrong. Her friends were not her greatest weakness; they were her greatest strength.

Here ends the second volume of the TREE OF LIFE saga.

The third volume, THE LAST DAYS, tells of the final struggle against Prester John.

Printed by Amazon Italia Logistica S.r.l.
Torrazza Piemonte (TO), Italy